ADVENTURES

Full of Stories a Lifetime Shouldn't Miss

ADVENTURES

PEOPLE AND STORIES THAT SHOULD NOT BE FORGOTTEN

Summer 2025

ISBN: (PAPERBACK) 978-1-950464-80-7
ISBN: (EBOOK) 978-1-950464-82-1

ReadAdventures.com

ADVENTURES

FULL OF STORIES A LIFETIME SHOULDN'T MISS

SUMMER 2025 **ISSUE #16**

WHAT

WHERE

Editor's Note

"SUMMER READING" MEANS A LOT OF DIFFERENT THINGS, DEPENDING ON THE type of reader you are. But to us at "Adventures," it means having an easily portable book with a variety of tales inside the covers. With that in mind, we filled up this issue with some fun reads that are sure to keep your interest this summer, whether you're reading on the porch with a cold lemonade, or reading in a cozy chair at the air-conditioned library.

First, we have two new original stories that touch on the bizarre and macabre. There's "The Leopard" by Nick Badot, who writes on "all things speculative, mythological, macabre and fantastical." Then we have "Strange Kindness" by E.W.H. Thornton, which, well, is almost beyond description - just know it's really good!

We also have included an overlooked classic called "Calumet K" by Samuel Merwin and Henry Kitchell Webster that is about a man who rises above the odds to build a grain elevator. Sounds about as exciting as watching paint dry, right? Well, it's much more than its description, we assure you. We think you'll love it. And you know who else loved it? Ayn Rand. She's on record as saying this is her favorite novel!

If you're looking for something different, we also have included a long poem about a boxer that anyone will love, not just boxing fans. It's called "The Set-Up" by Joseph Moncure March. We have used the version in which March took out a character after receiving feedback that he was deemed anti-semetic. Also please note there is some strong language in this poem, including the N-word. Bear in mind that the poem was written in 1928, so like "Huckleberry Finn" or "To Kill A Mockingbird," context is important.

We hope you take "Adventures" with you on your summer adventures this year, and if you happen to snap a photo of the book in the mountains or on the beach, please share it with us!

Michael Brian

Michael Brian

THE LEOPARD

AN ORIGINAL STORY:

BY NICK BADOT

"Beauty is a luster which love bestows to guile the eye."
—*Jack Vance, The Dying Earth*

The demon, Hephastaeles, ducked. The spear flew a half-inch over this head and shattered a tree behind him.

No mortal could throw with such force. *The Leopard stalks me.* He let his hand trail to the hilt of his sword and took a step in the direction the projectile had come from. There was no sign of her. No flash of a bestial form amidst the brush, no rustle detectable beneath the cacophony of birds and frogs. This was her way - a quick strike from beyond the trees and then she would not appear again for days. Sometimes he would sense her leaping away branch to branch above, but most of the time she simply vanished.

Feeble rays of crimson light filtered through the canopy to illuminate the beads of moisture that clung like babes to the leaves and flowers around him. Hephastaeles hated the jungle: the way the air was thick with sweet-rot and heavy enough to feel that he was wading through a sea of molasses; the insects that would swarm on him, whose stingers could not pierce his skin, so they assailed the soft tissue of his eyes and ears instead; how the very ground here was fickle, solid one step, treacherous mud or stagnant swamp-water the next.

Mostly, he hated that the jungle was *hers*.

He might have thought of the Leopard as an equal, had she not constantly struck from the shadows. Hephastaeles preferred a direct approach. He did not have any illusions about it being more honourable to kill someone this way, he merely believed that defeating someone face-to-face was a clear and undeniable display of superiority. He had rehearsed how he would explain this to the Leopard once he'd skewered the bitch.

The Leopard had pursued him since the desert broke into scrublands, first in the skin of the jungle cat and later taking on new forms. Sometimes she flew, and sometimes she crawled, and sometimes she looked nearly human, but she always had the distinct spotting of the leopard somewhere on her, tattooed on skin or scale or fur. Her hunt had been relentless, only becoming more vicious when scrubland gave way to forest, and forest contorted itself into the unforgiving maze of jungle. How many weeks had she pursued him? It was all blurring together.

Hephastaeles scowled. There was a cluster of plants ahead of him with foul-smelling petals the size of elephant's ears, and bulging thorns that looked ready to spring from the stem. He swung his great sword through the greenery. Dismembered fragments fell and the surviving flowers shrieked in agony. The sound was so shrill it felt like his eardrums would burst. He could not stay here.

He charged forward, hacking flowers out of his path and adding to the crescendo of death-cries. A figure sprung out from the thicket. Hephastaeles struck with his great sword. The creature's head rolled past him and into the wailing flowers. Its vaguely apelike body teetered for a moment, as if deciding what it would do next, before falling forward to reveal a patchwork of orange fur and grey scales weaving along its spine.

Checking that there were no more creatures around, he turned and inspected the head. It was insectile, with wide compound eyes and feelers distending from the forehead - entirely unsuited to the body from which it was severed.

"Beauty of nature my infernal red arse," he said to the screaming plants before kicking the head away.

In the underbrush ahead, a warren of vines writhed like snakes. They fled from his presence as he approached, exposing bare earth. Hephastaeles smiled.

The jungle had finally learned to fear him.

THERE IS NOTHING SO BEAUTIFUL AS SEEING A TOOL ACHIEVE THE PURPOSE OF ITS creation. Where did those words come from? Had they come to him during his quest, or some time before? Memory was becoming more and more unreliable.

In any case, beauty had compelled this journey.

In another life, Hephastaeles had died defending the walls of a dying city. Destruction had been his only purpose then, a creature weaned on wrath and bred for war. A soldier that towered above his mortal brethren, whose crimson skin and bestial horns filled his foes with horror. A living weapon, they called him, a thing that exists for the battlefield.

Why he found himself alive once more was a mystery - perhaps it was because he was never really alive to begin with, as insensate as an axe or spear until it was enlivened by the kiss of blood. His only memories were of battles and the sick exhilaration of the fray.

When he awoke in the desert there was nobody around to fight. He had to find something to do. A purpose other than warfare to guide him.

At first, he entertained the notion of establishing his own kingdom in the desert, though he'd never much cared for kings. He started building his grandiose castle from the blocks scattered around the dunes, hauling and stacking them over decades until he could finally erect a throne in the great hall and declare himself as supreme tyrant over an empty court. The futility of the concept appealed to him, at least until the fifth brick was placed, at which point he abandoned it.

Hephastaeles recalled the clamouring voices of poets and philosophers in the city square, arguing on blackened podiums, each one of them believing they knew what gave life purpose. Perhaps they knew better than him.

He tried to remember some of their arguments.

There was Duty, that one came up a lot. It was familiar, almost comforting. But now he dismissed it as sterile and unworthy. Religion was abandoned for the same reason. Love was another that arose frequently, but he deemed it too sentimental to choose as a *raison d'être*. Others were considered and set aside: Community, Knowledge, Transcendence… From the few ideals that remained, he picked the one that was least distasteful to him. The one most unlike the destruction he had been built for.

That is how the quest for beauty began.

More abominations crossed his path.

Never the same form twice. Each was brutish, bipedal, and uniquely deformed: babbling hairy creatures with stubby tusks sprouting from shoulders; slithering fish-folk boasting shark's eyes with iridescent purple irises in the palms of their hands; shrieking minotaurs with oozing pustules along their forelimbs. A handful of these creatures proved dangerous. Most were just pathetic. Hephastaeles slew them all with a single, perfunctory blow.

Well, nearly all of them.

One of the creatures had the face of a leopard. He had been careful with that one. The skull pleased him once he detached it from its twitching body. He struggled to identify the nature of this pleasure. 'Is this beauty?'

he asked himself. After looking into its dead eyes for a few minutes, he decided that it probably wasn't. Nevertheless, he drove metal pins through the soft bone above the nape to pin the skull to his belt, where it soon became a familiar weight.

Of the Leopard herself, there had been no sign since she had flung the spear at him. Yet Hephastaeles felt her presence everywhere; the wounds of many previous encounters ached. But he had wounded her too. He was sure of it. Next time he would do more than wound.

He passed through another thicket of vines before reaching an outcrop of weathered limestone. Finding handholds in the craggy rock face, he began to climb. As he ascended, he could see that this was not a natural formation - he noted the rectangular outlines of carved stone blocks, partially obscured by scree and arrayed in a rough circle. There had been a tower here once.

Reaching the top of this structure, he had his first view of the jungle from above the canopy. The red sun loomed over the eastern horizon like a docile god, bleeding an ethereal blanket of claret and gold on the tree-line, creating a discordant tapestry of life in its myriad forms. The birdsongs faded to a low hum and a breeze brushed his face. For a moment, Hephastaeles felt something that he could not describe. A warmth just under his skin, but not the uncomfortable heat of fever - it was like his entire body was being embraced in silk.

Before he could examine this feeling further, a keening pierced the air. Winged figures emerged from the nearest trees, flying directly towards him. Hephastaeles drew his greatsword and struck at the first, cleaving through a leathery wing and sending the beast spiralling into the jungle below. A swift sideways strike sent the next one plummeting too, its twisted grey beak split in the centre. More came; the sword became a blur, and purple blood sprayed his torso.

Only the largest of the creatures remained. It rose, then swooped. Hephastaeles extended his blade forward. They collided in a sickening crunch.

The creature was dead, impaled on the sword, but the momentum of its dive was enough to send Hephastaeles off the ledge, landing on one of the stone blocks of the foundation. The winged beast thudded down beside him.

Before he lost consciousness, he noticed that the skull on his belt had partly broken his fall and had been crushed in the process. *There is nothing so beautiful as seeing a tool achieve the purpose of its creation.*

WHILE HE SLEPT, THE LEOPARD VISITED HIS DREAMS.

She took the form of a woman, sinuous and catlike, dark skin contrasting with the furious yellow of her eyes. Hephastaeles attacked. His blow passed through her. The Leopard smiled.

"Curse you," Hephastaeles said. "Why must you taunt me?"

"Why do you do the things that you do?"

It was his first time hearing her voice. There was something both seductive and menacing in its notes, just like the sweet scent of rot that permeated this verdant hell.

"Plague not my dreams, She-Beast, " he said. "Come to me in the waking world with a weapon in hand and we shall settle this at once."

The Leopard let out an inhuman cackle. "Tell me what drives you, and I may grant your wish."

"I seek what lies at the end of this jungle," he said at last.

"And what is it you think you will find at the end of all this?"

"Beauty."

The Leopard's laughter echoed through his skull as the dream faded.

HEPHASTAELES COULD BARELY REMEMBER HOW HE CAME TO BELIEVE HE WOULD discover beauty on the opposite end of this jungle - there were vague memories of a lavish tent in the desert, and a sage draped in blue veils that spoke in portents and prophecies.

Follow the sun beyond the trees.

Had she truly spoken these words? He had come to her half-mad with thirst and hunger. Was this sage the fabrication of a strained mind? There had been an oasis, clear water and glistening green melons, lizard meat charred on a spit over coals. This much he was certain of. But once he had feasted and became lucid, the tent was gone.

There is nothing so beautiful as seeing a tool achieve the purpose of its creation.

Could it be that he had conjured these instructions to give himself purpose? That his memories were constructed to keep him sane?

It does not matter. I must keep moving.

Reaching the pinnacle of the outcrop once more, this time in the crisp light of the morning, he surveyed the path eastwards. The thick carpet of green stretched on for miles, sloping downwards into a ravine.

He could not see into it, but he knew this was where he must go.

MORE DAYS PASSED AND STILL THE LEOPARD DID NOT APPEAR.

The only sign he saw of her was in a tunnel of thick branches. A dozen bodies had been strung up from the boughs with crude ropes made of vines, and their flesh bore the unmistakable wounds of tooth and claw. These bodies were in various stages of decomposition. Some still had some tautness to their skin where on others bone poked through as their bodies rotted on the vine.

Was this her idea of beauty?

THE JUNGLE THINNED TO REVEAL THE PASSAGE INTO THE GORGE, ONLY TO thicken again when he descended. Ancient trees gathered around the bed of a dead river, where their branches battled for the faint sunlight. This entire ravine had been carved over the aeons by the ceaseless motions of water. Now the river was gone, but not the wounds of its passage. Those trees, Hephastaeles decided, were the last living witness to this tragedy, and thus were worthy of reverence. When he had no choice but to push past their criss-crossed branches, he did so gently, and he muttered apologies when wood inevitably splintered in his wake.

He was approaching his goal; he was certain of this without knowing why. Perhaps it was the rising sense of dread that burdened him. The feeling that he was approaching an anticlimax, that it would all come to nothing. That he would have to find something else to do once this was done. The notion terrified him. At least if he could kill the Leopard, he would feel that something had been achieved.

He longed for her to return.

The trees began to thin out again. A curtain of moss spread out before him, behind which he could see vine-encrusted spires thrusting into the sky. But underneath the greenery there were sheets of basalt and the faint glimmer of bronze engravings. An old city, devoured by the jungle, its inhabitants long perished. He followed the wall until he reached a gate and entered the city.

Waterlogged boulevards sprawled in front of him in three directions, following the walls in a diamond pattern. Blocks of fallen masonry were scattered haphazardly around the thoroughfares. Some had bushes with ochre flowers sprouting from them; others were perches for the eyeless newts that occasionally snapped up the fluorescent orange dragonflies that hovered about the surface. There was not a single piece of stone or metal not heavily marred by time. In the windows of the few surviving buildings, ferns and flowers poked through to lap the meagre light.

Hephastaeles followed the central boulevard. He could see a domineering structure in the centre, a temple of bone-white marble to contrast with the dark stone around it. Steps led to an entrance. Hephastaeles heard voices inside. Chanting.

He kicked the door open.

A man in violet robes stood in the centre of a ritual circle and recited incantations in a language Hephastaeles could not understand. Human and animal bodies surrounded him, the circle drenched in their blood. As the mage chanted, magic weaved into their flesh, fusing blood and bone.

This was where the abominations came from.

Hephastaeles charged. Some of the misshapen creatures rose from the ground to grab at him, but quick strikes from his weapon hacked off encroaching hands and claws. The wizard stumbled backwards. Frantically, he yelled a new set of incantations. Coruscating waves of sorcery struck Hephastaeles.

And folded against him like paper. *I am the living weapon.*

A single blow from the great sword cut the wizard in half. The miserable creatures still twitching on the ground ceased moving.

Hephastaeles inspected the bodies. The humans had been slain recently. Probably slaves or members of a nearby tribe captured by the wizard. There were youths amongst them. He dropped his sword.

Despair seized him like a vice. "Is this it?" he roared to the bodies of the dead. "I search for beauty, but at every turn find its opposite. Is this my answer? My purpose? Am I to know a thing only through its absence? How can a man who knows only darkness be asked to conceive light?"

Something creaked above him.

The Leopard struck.

Blood trickled into his eye as her claws tore into the flesh of his cheek and forehead. Hephastaeles tried to step away but the Leopard pulled A claw wedged behind his cheekbone. He stumbled forward, falling to one knee. With one hand, he grabbed at the claw that grappled his face, and with the other he flailed wildly, attempting in vain to parry the next blow. The Leopard struck him beneath the rib, claws tearing through the leather of his armour and raking bloody furrows beneath. He abandoned his attempts to defend his side and clasped both hands around the Leopard's other paw. He squeezed until he felt bones break, and the claw retracted from his cheek.

The Leopard screeched and leapt away. Skin shifted on her broken hand, tissues melded together and claws were subsumed into flesh. What had been feline became human before his eyes.

Hephastaeles rose to his feet and picked up his great sword.

Now in human form, the Leopard drew her own weapon: a spear, not like the crude ones she had thrown at him before - this one had a haft of lacquered hardwood and a curved bronze blade that reflected torchlight.

They charged at each other. Hephastaeles swung straight for her legs. He struck only air. She leapt over him, the tip of her spear catching him beneath the clavicle. He felt muscle tearing as she landed behind him and twisted the blade. A twirl and lunge with his left foot were the only thing that stopped him from falling prone. The next blow came from his right. He barely managed to parry it.

The pair fought unevenly. As the duel progressed, they alternated between animalistic fury and cold, methodical strikes. What one combatant brought, the other had an answer for. They fought until they both glistened with sweat and bled from countless wounds. Both on the verge of collapse, they geared up for a final strike.

Metal met flesh. Blood slickened the ground.

Hephastaeles staggered to the centre of the room, half-disbelieving, the spear impaling him through the abdomen. Beside him, the Leopard clutched the bleeding stump of an arm. The world spun.

A stentorian voice rang through the room, as if through a fog. *Blood of my creation.*

The floor beneath them opened.

Hephastaeles awoke on a cold slab of stone.

A goblin-like creature was applying a coat of a citrus-scented gel to the hole in his abdomen. Hephastaeles bolted upright and the goblin ran. He was in a square, windowless room. The only discerning feature, save for the slab he lay on and the door the goblin fled through, was a rack displaying an array of rusted scalpels, callipers, and other tools whose purpose he could not guess.

Hephastaeles clutched his gut. Sitting up was painful, but he could not rest - what if the Leopard still lived? He rose, grabbed a scalpel from the rack, and headed through the door, arriving in a corridor with other cells like the one he had woken in. Dim green light came from a series of torches.

He followed the corridor until he arrived in a long, spacious room. Here, all manner of grotesque curio was collected. Organs and limbs - most unrecognisable - floated in jars. Vats of unknowable liquid and shelves replete with contorted vials and measuring jugs were crammed together along the edges of the room. In the centre stood a pillar of glass, and within he saw the twin of the creature who had tended his wounds, but this one was suspended in gel and his midsection was sliced open to reveal innards. A homunculus, doubtless an assistant to the alchemist who had built this laboratory.

Hephastaeles pushed forwards.

In the next room, he found more pillars of glass, two dozen of them arranged in a diamond that spanned the entire space. The first he inspected held a creature with the head of a lizard and withered batlike wings sprouting from an otherwise human body. There was something solid about it, something cohesive that the abominations.in the jungle above had lacked. Hephastaeles clenched his jaw and moved to the next, surprised to find a man with the head of a panther - his hands shifted between human and feline, like those of the Leopard during their duel. Had she been created in this horrid laboratory?

He inspected the remaining pillars one by one, until he reached the last. "No," he said, falling to his knees.

Inside the pillar he saw his own face, his own red skin. Even the star-shaped birthmark on his thigh was present.

There was a plaque at the foot of the pillar. It read: "Slayer, impervious to sorcery. This one may ask you the meaning of beauty. Tell him as follows: '*There is nothing so beautiful as seeing a tool achieve the purpose of its creation.*'"

He lashed out. Glass shattered, shards sliced his hand and liquid spewed from the pillar to the floor. "No…." He knelt in the puddle of gel and broken glass, clutching the head of his double.

"Denial will win you nothing," a familiar voice came from behind him. He turned and saw the sage from his desert visions, draped in the same blue robes.

Beneath her veil he recognised the yellow eyes of the Leopard.

"The alchemist who ruled this place is long dead," she said. "He disappeared with this city, dried out with the river. The one above was an amateur, stepping blindly in his footsteps." She stepped towards him.

Her words felt unreal. As if he had died and was hearing them through the ears of his double. But real or not, she could be hiding a weapon in those robes. Hephastaeles tensed, pulling a shard of glass from his bloodied hand and pressing it to his palm.

"Blood of my Creation," she continued. "Those words are inscribed upstairs. The wizard thought to sacrifice his shambling experiments to gain access. But it seems the key was inside us."

"Why?" Hephastaeles managed at last, the word came as a feeble croak. "Why do any of this?"

"There are those who seek this place, thinking the secrets of the alchemist will make them gods. But I suspect he saw himself as an artist, or perhaps as a craftsman. There is a reek of obsession to this place, something that insists this work was an end unto itself."

A craftsman. *There is nothing so beautiful as seeing a tool achieve the purpose of its creation.*

Hephastaeles let loose an ugly laugh. "Then we either exist to be used and discarded, or to be preserved and admired. I don't know which is worse." He looked into her eyes. "Why did you bring me here? To break my spirit? To make your victory over me absolute?"

"You are the only other like me remaining. The rest I have slain." The Leopard shifted her shawl to reveal the stump of an arm. "When I found you in the desert I felt there would be something ... symmetrical about killing you here."

She was close enough to stab now. He could bury it in the soft flesh of her neck. He could—

"But returning here at last," she said, "seeing the truth laid bare, I knew something had changed."

He could smell her sweat and blood, pungent as oil. The last creations of an old master gathered in the forge that made them. He could prove which had the better craftsmanship. *There is nothing so beautiful as seeing a tool achieve the purpose of its creation.*

"I saw the chains on us for what they were. And if I can see them, I can slip out of their grasp. Do you understand?"

"I understand nothing!" Hephastales rose to his feet, waving his weapon "I came here seeking beauty. Thinking I had a grand idea, something that made me more than what I was created to be. And what did I find? The question was chosen for me too. Even my most intimate dreams are not my own. Don't you see that if I remove my chains, there will be nothing left of me?"

The Leopard placed a hand on his shoulder. He could feel her heartbeat. The turning gear that kept her moving, and he could sense the placement of all the tubes and valves essential for her function. There were so many places he could stab to break her. *There is nothing so beautiful as seeing a tool achieve the purpose of its creation.*

"And once there is nothing, you will be free."

Hephastaeles dropped the shard.

There is nothing so beautiful as...

He buried himself in the leopard's embrace and broke into sobs, tears and blood staining her robes. How long the two stood there weeping, neither could remember. The homunculus that had been chased away earlier brought them a tray of rotten fruit, which went ignored.

Some time later, they exited from the laboratory, escaping through a hidden passage that led outside the city walls. Hephastaeles and the Leopard ascended a nearby hill to assess the country around them and decide which direction they would take in the morning.

On the horizon, the sun was setting, and in its majestic red glow a thousand creatures sang the day to a close.

THE END.

Nick Badot (he/him) is an Irish-Belgian writer of fiction and poetry. His work has appeared in Impossible Worlds, Factor Four, Solstitia, Andromeda Spaceways, and the Sci Phi Journal among others. He has a penchant for all things speculative, mythological, macabre and fantastical. He is currently seeking representation for a novel about endless towers and the ruins of cities in the desert.

https://linktr.ee/nickbadot
Bluesky: @nickbadot

Actress Elke Sommer

HISTORICAL EMPORIUM

Est. 2003

Buy at... HISTORICAL EMPORIUM

Whose **REPUTATION** is *celebrated* world-wide as the pre-eminent clothing source for the **ADVENTUROUS** and *Fashionable*.

We are...

REVERED by our customers

REVILED by our competitors

RESPECTED by all who know us

NO LOCAL DEALER CAN COMPETE WITH OUR QUALITY, VARIETY AND INCOMPARIBLE CUSTOMER SERVICE!

ACCEPT NO SUBSTITUTE! If you require clothing and supplies as stylish and **stout-hearted** as you, contact us immediately to be outfitted.

800-997-4311

HistoricalEmporium.com

THE FOLLOWING POEM IS BASED ON THIS PAINTING BY JAMES CHAPIN.

THE SET-UP

BY JOSEPH MONCURE MARCH (1928)

ONE

Pansy had the stuff, but his skin was brown
And he never got a chance at the middleweight crown.
Mean as a panther,
Crafty as a fox,
He could hit like a mule,
And he knew how to box.
A dark-skinned jinx
With eyes like a lynx,
A heart like a lion,
And a face like the Sphinx:
Battered, flat, massive:
Grim,
Always impassive.
He was supple of build,
Graceful;
Trim:
Heavy above,
With legs slim.
Compact:
Neat.
Light as a cat on his feet.
His neck was solid.
His arms were long.
His bones were heavy,
And his hands were strong;
And whenever he moved, you could see the lithe
Muscles under his skin writhe.
He was slick:
Quick:

Each movement was like a trick.
Inside the ropes, he moved the way
A tiger does when it stalks its prey.
He got you nervous:
You never knew
Just what the hell he was going to do –
But he knew all about you.
Lead with your left –
You hit thin air.
Throw in with your right –
His shoulder was there.
Always an elbow,
A wrist,
A mitt:
He knew what was coming before you hit.
He slipped what he couldn't block.
His blows were timed like a clock.
He'd warm up slow:
He'd let you go
For maybe a couple of rounds or so.
Then he'd start.
One left –
One right –
And you'd wonder who told you
You could fight!
Clinch?
Try and do it!
It was over before you knew it.
He'd carve you up like a leg of mutton
And drop you flat with a sock on the button.

2.

He fought all comers,
And he reached his prime:
And he stayed there waiting,
Marking time.
Now was his chance for the title –

Or never:
Each month was vital.
When you get that far, you either click
Or you hit the skids, and go down quick.
His managers sweated.
They did what they could.
They schemed
And they wheedled –
But it did no good.
The months slid by:
The title hung high:
No Pansies need apply.
Some of the sporting writers tried
To throw their weight on Pansy's side.
They waxed sarcastic,
Biting, drastic
On the subject of champs that won the crown
And after they got it, then lay down!
Come on,
Take a sniff at Pansy's glove!
What was the champ so scared of?
No box-office attraction?
Hell!
They wanted action!
Then,
Sudden disaster:
A final hope-blaster.
The brass-knuckled hand of the law
Hung a hot one on Pansy's jaw.
Dissection of his private life
Revealed that he had an extra wife
And three scrawny brats
Living like alley cats.
"Not guilty," Pansy pled.
"Guilty," the jury said.
Elections were coming.
The judge was firm.
Pansy went up for a five-year term.

TWO

Time out.
Ten years pass.
Fighting bodies have gone to grass.
Some lie under grass,
Rotten:
Even their names have been forgotten.
Fresh blood,
New hopes
Inside the old ropes.
Kids that wet their short pants
Ten years back get their chance:
Giving,
Taking,
Champions in the making.
A fighter's life is short at best.
No time to waste,
No time to rest.
The spotlight shifts,
The clock ticks fast;
All youth becomes old age at last.
All fighters weaken.
All fighters crack.
All fighters go –
And they never come back.
Well,
So it goes:
Time hits the hardest blows.

THREE

I.

Herman's bar, where hoodlums met
With parasites of the sporting set:
A cellar Speak,
Grimy;
Clammy, dark,
Slimy.
Stale beer,
Dead butts,
The place stank to turn your guts.
Filthy sawdust.
Greasy brass.
Finger smears on every glass.
Dusty tumblers standing stacked
Before a mirror badly cracked.
Thin tin
Colored signs
Advertising beers and wines
Hung dirt-crusted,
Fly-specked,
Rusted.
Another room in back,
Smaller,
Quiet,
Black.
Battered round table tops,
Sticky,
Damp from beer slops.
Rickety chairs.
Cracked walls

Overrun with pencil scrawls
And pictures:
Photos
Clipped from the Sunday Rotos.
Boxing bouts.
Steeplechases.
Speed snaps from bike races.
Baseball kings in prideful poses
Holding enormous wreaths of roses.
Big blond bathing dames
Looking coy in gold frames.
Higher things were not forgotten:
Under a faded flag of cotton
Woodrow Wilson's narrow face
Stared three-quarters into space,
Cold,
Austere;
A face above beer.
Three o'clock.
The bar was crowded,
Dim lit,
Smoke shrouded.
Dark figures slouched,
Stood
Crouched
Above the damp wood.
They spat.
They drank.
They huddled flank to flank.
Behind the bar, Herman Brecht:
A man built to command respect.
Huge.
An ox.
Six-four in his socks.
Square head,
Face red,
Pitted with smallpox.
Under his lumpy nose curled

A black moustache with the ends twirled,
And on his low forehead sat
One black curl, pasted flat.

2.

The smoke swirled,
The door swung wide,
And a couple of shivering
Watery-eyed
Red-nosed customers blew inside.
Meet this pair:
Two of the worst –
And sew your shirt to your back, first.
The little one is Spider Stone.
Look at his face –
Let him alone.
Maggot-white, the puffy skin
Melted and dripped below his chin.
Small furtive eyes,
Cold, glassy, wise.
Above stained teeth
His mouth hung slack
With one of the corners hooked back.
Out of this corner drooped a wet
Smouldering Turkish cigarette.
A derby cocked over one eye
And a diamond horseshoe stuck in his tie
Gave him a rakish, jaunty air,
Repulsive and debonair.
The bird with him was Fingers MacPhail.
He looked like something
Lost in the mail:
Dirty, battered, fringed;
Tattered, yellow-tinged.
Pig's eyes, close together.
Skin like rusty shoe leather.
Yellow teeth.

Hair like straw.
A rat-trap mouth,
And a lantern jaw.
A pickpocket once, he had risen to fame
And had earned the right to his nickname.
Then his luck ran out:
He had tried to snatch
A handsome seventeen-jeweled gold watch
From a crippled man.
This proved a mistake:
The cripple had promptly proceeded to break
His head wide open with a heavy crutch,
And from then on, Fingers had lost his touch.
He tried one safe, but couldn't crack it;
Did three years in the pen
And then
Drifted into the fight racket.
He and Spider had met one night
In the bowels of the Garden, after a fight.
That night, a management team was born:
Stone and MacPhail,
Lice of the ring.
God help the fighters on their string!
They framed 'em,
Set 'em up.
Double-crossed:
No matter who won,
They never lost.
Conscience?
So has a snake got hips!
Stone and MacPhail –
The perfect gyps.
They squeezed to the rail.
Stone blew his nose.
He cleared his throat
And his thin voice rose:
"How they hangin', Herman?" he said.
Herman looked up.

He nodded his head.
He came forward without haste,
Wiping big hands on his aproned waist.
Solid,
Stolid,
He eyed the two:
"Tony Diamond was looking for you."
'Yeah?" they said, in chorus:
"Tony lookin' for us?"
"Yeah," said Herman:
"He's out in back."
He jerked his thumb,
Plunged a stack
Of dirty glasses into grey
Rinsing water,
Turned away;
Face blank
Polite –
But his lips were clamped tight.
They went in back.
Tony was there
At a corner table, slouched in his chair
A small-time manager
With big-time hopes;
Just beginning,
But he knew the ropes.
Hard as a sidewalk.
A guttersnipe.
One of the swaggering, loud-mouth type.
He got to his feet as they came in,
Flashed them a thin
Mirthless grin:
"Where the hell have you birds been?
Jeez!
I'm gonna be late for a date
Wit' a hot floozie –
But she can wait.
A he-man – that's me!

I treat 'em rough see?
Siddown! Jeez!
Have a seat!
Siddown, and take a load off your feet!?"
MacPhail looked sour,
At a los for words.
He hated these god-damned social birds.
"Hello," he muttered,
And spat.
He pulled out a chair
And sat.
But Stone had manners.
He held out his hand.
His air was familiar,
Gracious,
Bland.
"Well!" he said,
"So they're hangin' high!
You ought to lay off that Spanish fly."
He winked a cold
Fish-like eye;
His grin was knowing,
Sly.
He sat down, rubbing his hands together
And added "My God –
What lousy weather.
Every winter, it gets colder –
Or maybe it's just that I'm gettin' older ..."
"Ah," said Tony,
"don't give me that line –
You ain't a day over seventy-nine.
Gus!" he yelled.
A waiter appeared,
Red,
Perspiration smeared.
"Two whiskey sours, and a beer –
And make it dark –
Hear?"

They settled back, lost in thought,
Waiting until the drinks were brought.
In the opposite corner slumped a pair
Of heavy tarts with bleached hair.
Open fur coats displayed
Threadbare linings
Ripped,
Frayed;
Thin summer frocks with blue
Brassieres showing through.
Big breasts.
Wide hips.
Loose mouths with red lips.
Short skirts.
Crossed knees.
Ten inches above these
Sheer stockings ended in
A glimpse of garter and white skin.
Slowly they smoked.
Slowly they drank:
Silent:
Faces white,
Blank.
They stared at nothing with eyes of stone:
They chose to be left alone.
Stone studied their legs
With glazed eyes.
Veins in his forehead began to rise.
He licked his lips,
Winked,
Said
"There's two I wouldn't kick out of bed!"
"Ah," said Tony,
"they ain't so hot.
Beef to the heels!
What have they got?
Jeez, you oughta see my skirt –
She makes them look like so much dirt!"

"Yeah?" said MacPhail;
He looked depressed.
He fumbled in the lower pocket of his vest,
Pulled out a knife,
Began to pare
His yellow nails with care.
The drinks arrived on a rusty tray.
MacPhail closed his knife,
Put it away.
The drinks were placed.
The waiter withdrew.
"Well –" said Tony,
"Here's lookin' at you!"
The glasses rose:
They drank.
They sighed:
The glasses sank.
Tony hunched forward,
Wary eyed;
He cocked his head to one side:
'Say,
By the way –
You've heard of this bird
Named Sailor Gray –?"
Stone shook his head.
MacPhail looked dim.
"Nah, who d'hell ever heard of him?"
"Ah, give that high-hat stuff the air!
You don't know Gray?
Jeez, what a pair!
He's a fighter, see?
He fights.
In the ring.
He's god-damned good,
An' he's on my string!"
"Yeah?" said Stone,
"is that so!
A fighter, eh?

Well, whadda yuh know!
A fighter, eh?
Say, that's slick!
Who the hell did he ever lick?"
He chuckled faintly.
He took a drink.
He gave MacPhail a broad wink.
Tony Diamond burned.
He tried to look unconcerned.
"Ah, hell!
Nuts to you
You don't kid me like you think you do!
Cut this kiddin' stuff,
See?
I ain't got enough time!"
MacPhail blinked.
Stone looked resigned:
"Well," he said,
"What's on your mind?"
Tony frowned.
His voice turned gruff:
"The kid's okay, see?
He's got the stuff;
But you know
An' I know
That ain't enough.
The best man wins'
–like hell!"
Said Tony.
"That stuff is all so much baloney!
One year more–Gray'll be set.
But I ain't takin' no chances yet.
He'll do big time –
But he's gotta be nursed:
The kid's gotta have his record first.
He's won twelve fights out of twelve
This season,
Ten of 'em kayos –

An' there's a reason . .
Now listen:
I got him booked for a fight.
The Star Arena.
Next Monday night.
Six-round bout.
It's a damn good thing.
How's it for somebody off your string?"
"Yeah?" said MacPhail.
Stone pushed back his hat:
"Well – we might do somepin', at that."
He scratched his head,
Pursed his lips,
Drummed on the table with his finger tips.
"How about Carter–?" MacPhail suggested.
The Spider shrugged:
"He won't take a dive
For less than a hundred and seventy-five."
Diamond turned pale.
'Christ!" he protested,
"You talk like this was a title bout!
If it costs over fifty,
It's strictly out:
I ain't even interested."
The Spider shook his head.
"No dice. We ain't got nothin' at that price."
"Ah," said Tony, "save your breath.
Most of your fighters
Are starvin' to death.
They'd take a dive
If you tossed 'em a dime.
Now stop givin' me a hard time."
MacPhail blinked.
His eyes met Stone's.
He said "Well – how about Pansy Jones?"

3.

Ten minutes later
They rose.
"Okay!" said Tony –
"That goes.
Star Arena
Monday night . . .
Jeez, you're a couple of gyps, all right!
Sixty bucks!
Jeez!
Oh, well –
It's a good set-up,
So what the hell!"
They started out .
The Spider went last.
He paused,
Grinned at the tarts as he passed.
"Oh, baby!" he said, clucking his tongue,
"Them two would make a mummy feel young!"
They stiffened.
They sat on guard.
Their eyes were hostile,
Hard.
One of them raised her head;
She spoke
Hoarsely, through blue, leaking smoke:
"A-ah, take a walk
Or I'll bust your snout!"
Her eyes flamed.
Stone hurried out.

FOUR

I.

The Star Arena reeked with age:
It smelled like the bottom of a monkey cage.
Dark,
Stark,
It stood immense
Between small shops and tenements:
Gloomy,
Dim,
Sinister looking,
Grim.
A glittering white
Arc light
Glared against the black night,
Making great shadows sprawl
Over the crumbling brown wall,
And bringing out the rigid shapes
Of long, slanting fire escapes.
Under this lamp, a crowd stirred
Wading through darkness,
Ghostly,
Blurred.
In high relief, sharp weird
Parts of human forms appeared:
Shoulders jostled, light-splashed.
Hats stuck out,
Dented, gashed.
Wrinkles made black cracks
Across yellow, swaying backs.
Faces nodding,

Turned in talk,
Were masks cut from white chalk.
Mouths were holes.
Eye-sockets
Looked like deep, black pockets.
The crowd shivered.
Above their heads
Their breaths rose in white shreds.
They grumbled.
They swore.
They edged towards the main door.
Slowly they stumbled up the wide
Unseen steps, and pushed inside.

2.

The dressing rooms in the old Star
Had gone out of date with the horsecar.
They were lousy dumps:
Two of a kind.
Enter –
And leave the kiddies behind.
A dirty bulb swung by a cable
Over a battered rubbing table.
The crude glare
Fell on bare
Gleaming flesh, and underwear.
Open trousers bagged,
Sagged.
Shirt-tails flopped.
Belts dragged.
Backs bent down:
Flushed faces
Scowled over shoelaces.
Shoes thumped.
Knees rose.
Hands clawed at sweaty hose
With holes in their toes.

Behind,
A row of lockers stood:
Old,
Battered,
Made of wood.
Hinges loose.
Locks rusted.
Doors with half their slats busted:
Genuine Antiques –
Used by them ancient Greeks.
Another Antique –
The toilet.
No modern touch to spoil it.
Pitch black.
You had to go in
With your nose done up in a clothespin.
Wash your hands?
Have a drink?
Observe this handsome
Stopped-up sink.
Here is your shower:
It's on the fritz.
If you don't like it –
Move to the Ritz.
Go in like a little man;
Come out as quick as you can.
Trust to your smell
Instead of your sight,
And be thankful to God
There is no light!
There were handlers in the dressing room,
Sweatered,
Capped,
Water splashed.
A bucket banged.
Bath towels flapped.
Some of the seconds lounged at ease:
They sat with their elbows on their knees,

Parked on a bench with stenciled black
Numbers across its back.
It was almost time for the first bout.
They kept pulling their watches out.
They'd give the watch a glance,
Then shove it back in their pants –
Then pull it out again, as if in doubt.
No air.
Hot as hell.
The room reeked with a triple smell:
Toilet disinfectant
Blent
With stale sweat and liniment.

3.

One lad was ready.
He sat still,
White lipped.
He looked ill.
A faded purple dressing gown
Hung from his shoulders,
Sagging down.
His eyes were narrowed.
He sat there tense,
Face drawn,
Pinched with suspense.
He licked his lips,
Stared at the bands
Of white tape that covered his hands.
A second went over,
Grimly gay:
"Well –How you feelin', kid?
Okay–?"
The lad nodded his head.
"Sure. Okay," he said.
His breath came quickly.
His smile was sickly.

A sudden spasm:
He shook.
His eyes had a glazed look.
he leapt up,
Covered his mouth,
Ran
With his head bowed
For the door of the can.
The second grinned at the rest of the bunch:
"Jeez –
The kid is losin' his lunch!"
Their eyes narrowed,
Stared.
They smiled with their teeth bared.
"Yeah," said one,
Watching the door:
"I seen 'em pull that stunt before."
"Yeah," said the second:
"The kid's all right.
He's nervous,
See?
It's his first fight."
The lad came out.
His ears flamed.
He slunk to his chair,
And sat there ashamed.
A bald-headed thin
Sweatered man rushed in.
He stopped,
Glared,
Scowled:
"Hey!–
MacMullen!" he howled.
The kid stood up,
Shaking,
Pale.
"Take the lead out of your tail!
Why he hell don't yuh keep awake!

They're waitin' for yuh,
Fer Christ's sake!"
His handlers stirred;
They rose:
"All right, kid –
On your toes!"
The kid nodded.
He tried to smile.
They went through the door
In single file.

4.

Footsteps out in the hall.
Two shadows sprang on the wall.
The footsteps paused,
Scraped,
Shuffled,
Two voices came through the door,
Muffled.
For a minute, they argued in undertones.
A face peered in:
The face was Stone's.
Over his shoulder blinked MacPhail ,
Sour,
Grim as a rusty nail.
"Hi there, Louie!
Hi there, Max!"
Two lounging handlers straightened their backs.
"Hi," they said.
Each raised a hand.
They uncrossed legs,
But did not stand.
Stone and MacPhail came through the door.
They stopped,
Spat on the dusty floor.
They looked around –
Frowned.

"Where the hell is Pansy gone?"
One of the handlers stifled a yawn:
"Dunno," he said: "He ain't here yet."
The Spider seemed upset.
"God-damn that smoke!
He's always late!
I'll bawl the hell outta him –
Just wait!"
The handlers were silent.
They stared out toward
The opposite wall,
Completely bored.
Louie,
A blond expressionless Swede,
Pulled out a tabloid
And started to read.
Across the room,
A fighter stood bent
Lacing his shoe,
Scowling,
Intent.
His foot was up on the edge of the table.
He balanced stork-like,
Unstable.
Something snapped.
His foot fell.
"There goes the god-damned shoestring to hell!"
He paused, shaking handed.
Slowly his chest expanded.
Then:
"Christ Almighty for Jesus sake . . . !"
His voice rose
Shrill,
Started to break.
His neck and ears grew stained with red.
He lifted clinched hands above his head.
He stood there glaring,
Swearing.

His second watched from the other side
Of the rubbing table,
Narrow-eyed.
"Watch it, kid–"
His voice was steady:
"Come on, now –
You gotta get ready.
Forget the shoestring,
That's all right.
Let's have your hands –
We ain't got all night ..."
From far off,
The echo of a roar
Drifted in through the open door.
Stone cocked his head,
Listened.
"They've started! ..."
His eyes glistened.

5.

A figure loomed on the door sill,
Paused for a moment,
Stood there still.
Across heavy shoulders spread
A checked suit, black and red.
Under sharply creased pants,
God knows whose
Cracked evening shoes
Shone with battered elegance.
Yellow gloves.
No overcoat.
Green muffler around his throat.
Over his nose, a rakish brown
Long-visored cap was pulled down;
And under one arm, some lumpy thing
Was wrapped in newspaper,
Tied with a string.

Lynx eyes glinted,
Took in the place.
White teeth flashed in a dark bronze face.
Stone raised a flabby hand,
He gave
The smiling figure a jerky wave:
"Hi there, Pansy!
Where yuh been?
We thought you got lost.
Come in –
Come in!"
Pansy came in with a slow stride,
Steady,
Unhurried,
Dignified.
Gravely he smiled.
He bowed his head:
"Good evenin' Mistuh Stone," he said.
His manner was gracious,
Polite,
Diffident,
Carefully right.
He turned to MacPhail, repeating
The same impressive greeting.
MacPhail started to tip his hat –
Decided not to;
Blinked;
Spat.
Louie and Max rose.
They stretched,
They swayed on their toes.
"Hi, Pansy!" they said
In a friendly tone.
"How 'do!" said Pansy.
His white teeth shone.
He felt more at east
With birds like these.
They seemed to talk a language he knew,

And he felt somehow that they liked him, too.

6.

He started to get undressed.
Off came his coat and vest.
He stood there blazing
In a rainbow shirt
So loud it would make your eardrums hurt.
"Some shirt!" said the Spider.
He winked at MacPhail:
"Where yuh get it, kid –
At a fire sale –?"
He giggled,
Tongue in his cheek.
Stone had a whimsical streak.
Pansy paused with his belt unbuckled.
He glanced back over his shoulder,
Chuckled.
Off came his pants.
He began to fold
Them carefully.
His lynx eyes rolled.
"Yes suh!" he said.
"This shirt sure grand!
Ah held four Aces in my hand.
Got this shirt,
Got this cap.
Poker suits me
Better'n crap.
Yes Suh!" he added;
He tugged at his tie:
"Ah sure is lucky –
An' that's no lie."
Again that echo of a roar:
Longer,
Louder than before.
"Come on!" snapped a voice:

"Whadda yuh say–?"
A group started for the doorway.
The man who'd broken his shoelace led:
Eyes like slits,
Out-thrust head.
He snarled to himself
With teeth set tight.
He looked as though he would bite.

7.

MacPhail nudged Stone:
He scowled:
"Let's go upstairs . . ." he growled.
The Spider said: "Not yet –
I gotta get Pansy set."
Pansy looked up from a shoelace.
Stone's eyes swerved,
Avoided his face.
"Purple trunks for you," Stone said.
He pushed his derby back on his head.
Hands in his pockets,
He wavered there,
Swaying a little, with a thoughtful air.
He jerked,
Bent at the knees;
Straightened,
Jangled some keys.
He nodded to himself.
He stopped swaying.
"Well–" he said,
'What was I saying . . .?
The purple trunks.
Yes.
Well – that's all, I guess.
Three fours,
One six –
And then your bout.

You oughta knock dis Sailor out.
He's easy, see?
Just watch his right.
But what d'hell–
You know how to fight!"
"Yes suh!" said Pansy.
His teeth shone:
'Yes suh – thank you,
Mistuh Stone!"
Stone smiled.
The smile was rigid,
Noncommittal,
Frigid. "Well, then," he said,
"We're all set.
Just watch his right, now–
Don't forget."
MacPhail gave a rasping cough.
Stone turned.
They shuffled off.

8.

They paused outside in the hall,
Stood leaning against the wall.
MacPhail spoke.
His tone was low:
"You don't think we oughta let him know–?"
A match flared.
Stone started to smoke:
"Say, what the hell is this –
Some joke?
Let him know what, for Christ's sake?"
He put out the match with a savage shake.
"Well–" said MacPhail,
'It's nothin' to me,
But Diamond paid for a sure thing,
See?
If we told Pansy it was fixed that way

He'd throw the fight
An' we'd be okay.
Split the sixty,
Give him a share,
And the Sailor cops it
Fair an' square.
As it stands now, if the Sailor lost
Tony might think he was double-crossed."
'You're kidding!" said Stone
With tremendous scorn:
"God Almighty,
You don't know you're born!
What did I ever do to deserve
A partner like you!
Where's your nerve?
Only sixty bucks we got.
Split wit' that dumb jerk–?
I should say not!
Listen –
I saw this Gray in the gym.
Pansy won't stay two rounds wit' him.
They'll carry that nigger outa the ring
Wit' his eyes shut
An' his guts in a sling!
You wit' your fairs and squares!
God!
You give me grey hairs!
Where would you be
It it wasn't for me!
Come on –
We're going upstairs!"

9.

Pansy peeled off purple socks
With holes for heels
And yellow clocks.
One-piece underwear –

No shirt:
Gym pants,
Edges grey with dirt.
Where the buttons had been
Was a safety pin.
This he unclipped.
Off they slipped.
He kicked them aside
And stood up stripped.
Ten years had got their claws in him.
He looked too sleek,
No longer trim.
Heavier, too;
Verging on fat;
Butt the real change seemed deeper than that.
It was something inside;
Hard to detect;
Not here–
Not there–
The general effect:
As though some tight string had been cut
And the whole works had loosened somewhat.
Max and Louie watched with wise
Critical, appraising eyes.
No remarks.
Still, you could sense
Their cool, detached indifference.
Pansy was through –
They knew.
Why didn't he know it too?
Christ Almighty,
He ought to have quit
Long ago
And been done with it.
But here he was,
Half on the shelf –
And still trying to kid himself?
Well –

Why the hell should they burst out crying?
Said Max,
"You're looking good to-night."
Said Pansy,
"Boy!
I feel just right!"

IO.

Voices in the hall,
Feet drumming.
It sounded like a whole platoon coming.
In they steamed,
Jostling each other;
It looked like everybody
And his brother.
They should have had a band
And the Mayor's committee
Waiting to give them a key to the city:
Managers,
Handlers,
Christ knows what,
Led by a swaggering tough little mutt.
This pasty-faced two-bit bantam was dressed
In a wallpaper suit
And a bartender vest.
He was full of himself.
He scowled when he talked.
If you tied his elbows,
He couldn't have walked.
He stuck out his chest
And sucked in his guts:
You gathered he thought
He was just the nuts.
Pansy stared.
His lynx eyes
Widened to twice their natural size.
"What for this big crowd come in here?"

Louie's lips
Twisted in a sneer.
"That's Battlin' Fargo.
He havin' it out
Wit' a kid named Horowitz.
Feature bout."
"Oh!" said Pansy,
Enlightened.
He nodded.
His face brightened:
"If that boy fights
Like he can dress,
He's big-time stuff
Or I miss my guess!"
"Yeah?" sneered Max:
"Him big time –?
He ain't got the edge
On a worn-our dime.
You watch him fight
And you can tell
What's the matter with him –
He's yelluh as hell."
Pansy shook his head,
Sad:
"Yelluh–?" he said,
"Now that's too bad!
Yes suh, that's bad . . ."
"But boy –
That sure is a han'some vest!"
His voice was wistful.
His bronze face took
On a childish
Plaintive
Far-off look:
As though he could see
In his mind's eye
The vests he might have been able to buy.
God, what vests!

A vest a day?–
If only the breaks had come his way . . .
He shook his head,
Sighed:
Bewildered,
Mystified.
He picked up his bundle,
Snapped the strings,
Unwrapped it,
Took out his fighting things:
Two pairs of trunks,
Stained and faded;
A crimson bathrobe,
Moth-invaded;
And his lucky shoes,
Old and loose,
Battered and scuffed
From constant use.
The purple trunks,
Stone said.
He discarded the black-and-red.
He stared at the trunks he had to don,
Then slowly he bent:
He pulled them on.
II.
Halfway through
Lacing a shoe,
Pansy paused.
He cocked his head:
"Boy!–
Listen to that crowd!" he said.
Louie yawned:
"That's the second bout.
Wonder how that kid MacMullen
Made out . . .
Lost his lunch before you came.
Nervous as hell –
But the kid looked game . . ."

Pansy grunted,
Busy with his feet:
"Must be he done et
Somethin' sweet.
Never eat sweet before a fight.
Lay off sweet stuff,
You'll be all right.
Yes, suh –
That's so.
Sweet's bad for a fighter –
I know!"
Again the sweatered, thin
Bald-headed man rushed in.
"Third bout!" he barked:
"Munsey on deck!"
Munsey got up.
Christ, what a wreck!
You could tell at a glace
He hadn't a chance,
This hulking,
Rawboned
Lumbering lout
With his knees knocking
And his feet splayed out.
He should have been pushing
A rusty plow;
Feeding the chickens,
Or milking a cow.
You looked,
And you wondered why in God's name
He had ever gone into the fight game.
And what a beating the game had shown on him!
His own mother wouldn't have known him.
Battered for years, his face had grown
Distorted,
Massive,
Swollen of bone.
Cauliflower ear.

Cocoanut head.
Close-cropped hair,
Bristling,
Red.
His nose was flat,
Dented by a scar,
As though he'd been hit
With a crowbar.
His bumpy forehead hung over two
Deep sunken eyes of faded blue:
The eyes were sleepy,
Mild,
Like those of a stupid child.
He stood there swaying,
With his eyes glazed,
Staring around him as though he were dazed.
"Snap out of it, Munsey!"
A second advised.
He started a little,
As though surprised:
"Awright . . ." he muttered:
"Awright . . . Awright . . .
Don't hurry me, see?
I'm fightin' this fight . . ."

12.

He was no sooner out
Than MacMullen came in,
Cocky as hell,
With a ten-inch grin.
His lips were puffed.
A red smear
Streaked one cheek from ear to ear.
Just under the eye
Was an oozing cut,
And the eye was swollen,
Beginning to shut.

"Howdja come out?" called Max,
"Didja nail 'im?"
The kid nodded.
Words seemed to fail him.
He flushed a little,
Shy, grinning,
Bright of eye.
Behind him
His handlers grinned at the kid:
"Nail 'im–?
Jesus!
I'll say he did!
K.o.'d 'im clean
At the end of the third.
A right to the button –
Jeez,
What a bird!"
Smiles.
Nods.
"Dat's duh stuff! ..."
"Dat's duh way, kid –
Treat 'em rough! ..."
Fargo spoke
With a lofty air:
'How much of a crowd
They got up there ...?"
"Oh–" said MacMullen;
He looked down,
Scratched his head
With a puzzled frown:
"Crowd–?
Jesus, I dunno ...
I guess it must be a big one, though."
Fargo sneered,
Scornful eyed.
He sniffed loudly.
He turned aside.
MacMullen's second

Called,
Beckoned.
He gave the rubbing table a smack:
"Come over here on the table, Mac!"
On top of the rubbing table a grey
Overcoat and hat lay.
The second started to move them away.
"Hey!" snapped Fargo:
"Give dat the air!
Say, what the hell
Are you doin' there!
Leave dat be!
Dat's my stuff,
See?"
"Yeah?" said the second
With a long sneer:
"Well get it the hell away from here!
Christ,
You act like a movie star!
Who the hell do you think you are?
"Put dem down!" said Fargo,
Loud:
"Put dem down
Before you get sloughed!"
Silence for a second.
The handler turned white.
His eyes glittered,
And his lips grew tight.
Then calm, quiet,
Without a word more,
He threw the hat and coat on the floor.
"Christ!" yelled Fargo,
Like someone had stabbed him.
He jumped for the second –
But his own men grabbed him.
"Leggo, god damn it!" Fargo said,
"I'll push his face
T'rough duh back of his head!

I'll break duh god-damned
Face off 'im, see?
He can't get away wid dat stuff
Wid me!"
He blustered,
Began to tug and squirm –
But the handlers held his elbows firm.
"Go easy, kid!"
"Put down your mitts!"
"Go easy –
Save it for Horowitz!"
He kept up the show
For a minute or so,
Then stopped.
"All right!" he growled,
"Leggo! . . ."
They let him go.
He turned away,
Face sullen,
Sulky, grey.
He went to a corner
And sat there,
Running his hands
Through his greasy hair.
He had a martyred air.
His gang clustered around,
Whispered,
Nodded,
Frowned.
One or two of them sat down by him;
Craftily tried
To soothe his pride;
But nothing they said would pacify him.
The rubbing table squeaked,
Creaked.
Slaps resounded.
Liniment reeked.
MacMullen lay on the table

Full length,
Wincing under his second's strength.
The second's jaw
Stuck out like a shelf.
He plucked and wrenched
With his teeth clenched,
And while he worked
He smiled to himself.
The smile was ironic,
Sardonic.
Over the room a silence dropped,
Oppressive,
Expressive.
Someone started to whistle through his teeth,
Cleared his throat,
Stopped.
Pansy winked.
His eyes rolled.
His teeth shone out
Dull ivory and gold:
"Boy–!" he whispered,
"That sure was fun!
I wish that handler
Had socked him one . . . !"

13.

Three figures appeared.
They all three tried
To get through the doorway
Side by side.
It was two handlers,
And between them staggered
The fighter who'd broken his shoelace,
White of face,
Haggard.
They came in slowly.
His arms were flung

Over their shoulders.
He tottered,
Clung.
His eyes were dilated,
Shot with red,
Unblinking,
Staring straight ahead.
They led him to a bench.
Down he slumped,
Elbows on his knees,
Shoulders humped.
He sat there shaking all over,
Grasping
His head in his hands,
Rocking,
Gasping.
The handlers watched him a minute,
Perplexed,
Wondering what they should do next.
One of them turned to the other,
Scowled:
"Jesus,
He looks pretty bad!" he growled.
"Yeah," said the other,
"He looks pretty white.
Dat sock in the bread-basket
Got 'im, all right!
Jesus–!"
He gave a short, grim laugh:
"I t'ought it would break
Duh kid in half!"
"Yeah," said the first;
His head shook:
"How wouldja like
To take what he took!
Those left and right hooks
Over the heart –
Jesus,

The kid was cooked from the start!"
"Yeah . . .
When he started to mix wid dat Mick,
I says to myself
He's up duh creek!
'Don't mix! I told 'im:
'Don't mix! I said:
'Jab wid yer left
To duh face and head –
But don't mix, see?
Keep away from dat guy!'
Dat guy was a slugger,
See?
Dat's why."
They nodded.
They looked wise.
They stared at the fighter
Through half-shut eyes.
He was getting better
By slow degrees.
He was quiet now.
He sat caved in.
Doubled up like a hairpin
With his chest resting on his knees.
His arms hung down.
His clenched fists
Lay on the floor,
Taped to the wrists.
Slowly,
Dark blood dripped from his nose
And spattered on the floor,
Just missing his toes.
"How yuh feel, kid–?"
"Yuh comin' around–?"
Not a movement out of him.
Not a sound.
"Try layin' down –
Dat might help some . . ."

His head shook slowly.
He sat there dumb.
"Well – take it easy,
You'll be okay . . .!"
They smiled grimly.
They moved away.

14.

Pansy was ready.
He sat there quiet,
Staring at the light,
Doped by it.
He sat hunched forward,
Settled,
At ease;
Chin in his hands,
Elbows on his knees;
Motionless as a stone;
Remote,
Silent,
Alone.
Suddenly his silence broke.
His voice was rough,
Gruff when he spoke:
"Hey, Louie," he said
Without turning his head.
"What!" said Louie,
Slightly annoyed;
He was busy reading his tabloid.
"Hey, Louie," said Pansy,
Staring at the light:
'You ever seen this Sailor fight–?"
A pause
While Louie finished half
Of a long, lurid paragraph.
He turned the page
With a hairy paw:

"Have I seen duh Sailor fight–?
Naw! ..."
"LOVE NEST VICTIM"
The headline said.
His head bent further down.
He read ...

15.

Muted and distant, a drumming sound
Settled into a rhythmic pound:
A measured thump,
Steady,
Dull,
Like an engine down in a ship's hull.
Upstairs,
Hundreds of angry feet
Were stamping out that heavy beat.
The crowd was getting impatient,
Sore.
They wanted action.
They wanted gore.
What had they paid good money for?
Munsey was up there,
Punch-drunk,
Slow,
Giving the fans a lousy show.
Thump – thump –
Give 'em the hook!
Their feet pounded
Till the house shook.

16.

The bald-headed thin
Sweatered man rushed in.
His face was red.
He looked unhappy.

"Fourth bout!" he yelped,
"An' make it snappy!"
Up rose a swarthy, pig-faced giant.
He looked surly.
He looked defiant.
He sneered.
And his glittering eyes ran
Nastily over the bald-headed man.
"A-ah, nuts!" he muttered.
It seemed that the thin
Bold-headed one got under his skin.
For reasons unknown,
He'd like to attack
That yelping bastard, and break his back.
The victim-to-be glared.
He didn't seem to be scared.
"Hey!" he yelped,
"Snap outa yer mope!
Don't stand dere
Lookin' like a god-damned dope!"
The giant's face grew darkly red.
"Ah, what duh hell is yer rush!" he said.
He panted a little
Stood there glaring –
A little uneasy at his own daring.
The eyes of the bald-headed man grew cold.
His voice turned hard:
"You do like you're told!
You ain't nothin'!
I'm runnin' dis show.
You do like I say –
Or out yuh go!
Don't try to pull no fresh stuff,
See?
Dat kinda stuff don't pass wit me!"
"Ah, hell . . ." the giant muttered,
"Ah, hell . . ."
He stood abashed.

His eyes fell.
Out the bald man rushed.
The giant followed,
Crushed.

17.

Max watched them out.
After they'd gone
He relieved himself of a tearing yawn.
His spine curved in,
His arms rose,
Flexed:
"Well . . ." he sighed:
"I guess we're next."
Pansy didn't say a word.
He nodded a little,
To show he'd heard;
That was all.
He just sat there
Watching the light
With that glittering stare.
His eyes were slits.
His breathing was deep.
He looked as though
He were almost asleep –
Except for his eyes:
His eyes were too bright.
They glinted like chips of glass
In the light.

18.

MacMullen was dressed,
Ready to go.
He stood there restless
For a minute or so.
He pulled out his watch,

Looked at the time,
Fumbled in his pocket,
Unearthed a dime.
"Hey–!" he called to his handler:
"Ed–!
You got two nickels for a dime–?"
He said:
"I gotta make a phone call
Up th' street . . ."
Ed grinned:
His grin was knowing,
Discreet.
He gave him the change
And a friendly shove:
"All right, kid,
Beat it!–
An' give her my love . . . !"

19.

Munsey came lurching in
Like a souse.
He looked like something
From a slaughterhouse.
One eye was closed,
One ear was a wreck:
The blood slid from it
Down the side of his neck.
His mouth was formless,
Puffy,
Spread
All over his face in a smear of red.
But Munsey didn't seem to mind.
He had some other axe to grind.
"Lemme alone . . ." he muttered;
"Awright!–
You lemme alone!
Who's fightin' this fight . . .?

'At's awright –
Don' try and tell me!
You lemme alone!
I'm doin' this,
See . . . ?!"
Every other step he tried
To jerk from the handlers
That walked on each side.
They were patient.
They held his elbows tight:
"Sure!" they said:
"Yeah, sure – that's right."
"Nobody's tellin' yuh how to fight . . ."
They winked at each other:
"Crazy wit' duh heat . . . !"
"Yeah –
The bastard's out on his feet."
They set him down on the bench
With care.
He muttered,
Swayed as he sat there.
They slopped a wet sponge
Over his head:
"He'll come outa dis all right"
One said.
"Sure! said the other, with a crooked grin:
"Sure . . . !"
The bald-headed man rushed in.
"Fift' bout!" he yelled
in savage tones:
"Where duh hell are you,
Pansy Jones . . . ?"

20.

Pansy stirred,
Sighed.
He stood up

Blinking-eyed.
"Come on," said Max:
"Whadda yuh say!"
Louie put his tabloid away.
Over his shoulders Pansy flung
His faded bathrobe.
He held it wrapped
Closely about him.
The sleeves flapped.
They hung empty,
Swung.
"You got duh gloves, Louie–?"
"Okay."
"All right.
Come on then.
Whadda yuh say!"
They turned together,
Started for the door.
The bucket jerked,
Slopped on the floor.
Max stopped,
Shifted it,
Swore."
-A-ah!" yelled Fargo:
Don't youse tell me!–
Youse don't know nothin' about it,
See?
I–"
"–Awright, Munsey.
Dat's awright, kid –"
"–Sure he licked 'im!"
"Duh hell he did–!"
"–Say, where duh hell
Is my hat gone to–?"
"–So he feints wit' his left,
An then he breaks through–"
"–Ah , you're nuts – dat fight was sold–!"
"–If you hadn't of mixed,

You'd of had 'im cold–!"
"–What'll yuh bet?"
"I know–
Dat's all . . . !"
The voices grew jumbled.
It was cold in the hall.

FIVE

I.

They came up the arena floor
In a back corner,
Near an exit door.
Entered all of a sudden, the place
Seemed vast,
Dim,
Tremendous of space.
It made you feel
Small and unreal.
You shrank in size.
Your wrists looked little.
You stood there
Feeling light, and brittle.
The smell was like
Ten cattle cars,
Mixed with the reek
Of cheap cigars.
The crowd was a blur,
A thing made mostly
Of pallid faces,
Shadowy,
Ghostly.
A gallery jutted.
Its steep-pitched bank
Was solid with faces,
Rank above rank.
In the center of the floor,
The raised ring stood.
Over it hung a metal hood.

Light from this hood
Flung a savage glare
Over two figures fighting there.

2.

The bald man came back,
Nodding his head:
"Stay right dere where you are!" he said:
"Dis'll be over
In about a minute . . ."
Max set the pail down,
Dropped the sponge in it.
Silent,
The three of them stood awhile
Staring at the ring
Down the corner aisle.
The figures in the ring were ponderous,
Slow.
Neither seemed to have
Much to show.
They crouched,
Circled,
Exchanged no blows.
Each was waiting
For the other to close.
The crowd sat hushed.
You could hear the muffled
Sound of the fighter's feet
As they shuffled.
Around and around them
The referee went,
Head thrust out,
Knees bent.
He crouched,
Watching,
Intent.
Then,

"A – ah–!" yelled a high
Sarcastic voice:
"A – ah–fer Christ's sake,
Get dem a hoise!
Get dem a hoise –
Dey're both of dem dead!"
Laughter.
More voices:
"Who's ahead . . . ?"
Whatcha waitin' for–
A change in duh weather . . . ?"
"Hey!–do youse two guys
Room together . . . ?"
General laughter followed this crack.
Heads turned around.
Faces peered back.
From up in the gallery
Came the sound
Of heavy feet beginning to pound.
The pair in the ring
Decided to close.
They sprang in
Slugging.
A roar rose.
"Jesus!" said Louie,
"Dat guy hits low . . . !
Lookatat–!
Didn't I tell yuh so–?"
One of the fighters staggered,
Dropped.
He lay on the canvas
Doubled up, grasping
His guts with both hands,
Writhing,
Gasping.
The roar sank,
Stopped.
The referee sprang in,

Crouching low.
He waved back the man
Who had struck the blow.
Back to his corner this giant went,
Flushed,
Scowling,
Head bent.
He walked with a sulky
Aggressive air,
Trying to show he didn't care.
"Foul! ... Foul ...!" the crowd clamored.
Handlers rushed in the ring.
They began to work on the guts
Of the fallen man.
A bell clanged,
Hammered.

3.

The ring cleared.
The clamor died.
Louie's elbow dug Max's side:
"Well–" he said,
"Here goes!
Come on now–
On your toes!"
Max lifted the bucket:
"Okay," he said.
They went up the aisle
In single file,
With Pansy striding ahead.
As they came into sight
A murmur swelled.
"Dere's a black cloud a-comin'...!"
Somebody yelled.
Appropriate laughter
Greeted this joke.
"Jesus!" they murmured:

Lookit duh smoke . . . !"
"Gonna be some action dis time . . ."
"Dat's right . . ."
"Hey dere, black-boy –
You know how to fight . . . ?"
Crowds were to Pansy
As heat is to Hell:
They suited him fine,
They made him feel swell.
His supple back stiffened.
His blunt chin rose.
He strutted a little
On lively toes.
His grin was friendly,
His grin was wide:
He felt that the crowd
Was on his side.
In the shadow of the ring
They came to a stop.
"Phew!" Max said.
He let the pail drop:
"Jesus Christ!" he shook his head:
"Dat god-damn pail is heavy as lead!"
"A-ah," said Louie,
"Pull in yer neck!
You're nothin' but a god-damned
Physical wreck!
You'd think it was heavy
From the line you pull.
Why, Jesus Christ,
It ain't half full!"
"Yeah?" said Max,
"Is that so!
You ain't ever carried it –
How can you know?"
"A-ah!" said Louie
With tremendous scorn,
"I was carryin' pails

Before you was born!
Come around some time–
I'll show yuh how;
I ain't got time
To fool wit' you now ... !"
He chuckled,
Pulled out a deck of gum.
He took a slice.
He offered Max some.
"Pansy–?"
"No thanks."
Louie put it away.
"Let's put on your gloves, kid –
Whadda yuh say ... ?"

4.

"How do they fell?
Are they good and tight–?"
"Yeah, said Pansy,
"They feel all right ..."
He stood there pushing his hands together,
Shoving each hand further
Into the leather.
The announcer came up:
Fat,
Short.
Moon face.
Bald head.
Nose with a wart.
"How about it–?
You guys all set?"
"Sure," said Max,
"Is the Sailor here yet?"
"Sure he's here!
Get up in the ring!
Get up in yer corner!
Let's start this thing ... !"

"Okay," said Louie,
Expressionless,
Cool:
"Hey, there, Max –
Throw us that stool!"
He caught the stool
With a deft swing:
"Let's go–!"
They climbed up into the ring.

5.

The crowd hummed.
The crowd chattered.
The smoke rose,
Drifted,
Scattered.
Cheap seats:
The crowd was tough.
None of your high-hat
Garden stuff.
Gallery,
A quarter.
Ringside,
A dollar.
You risked your life
In a winged collar.
Evening clothes?–
Try it!
You'd have started a god-damned riot.
Society women,
Dressed to kill,
Didn't go there for their evening thrill.
Even whores of the cheapest sort
Avoided this dismal palace of sport:
Their finer instincts shrank to see
Such masculine brutality.
No, this crowd was strictly gents –

Using the term in its loosest sense:
Crooks,
Gangsters,
Seedy drunks;
Pimps,
And pushers,
And pimply punks
With cold glassy eyes,
Sneering, contemptuous,
Wise:
The city's dregs:
Bums,
Spawned in alleys
And slums.
Small wonder, then, that here you saw
The ominous blue and brass of the Law:
Burly cops, swinging their sticks:
Truculent police –
Aching to keep the peace.

6.

Light glared down from the metal hood.
Pansy sat waiting.
He felt good.
He liked the smell.
He liked the bare
Grey canvas floor,
The ropes
The glare.
Once in the ring,
He never felt yellow;
He felt at home there,
Confident,
Mellow.
Max and Louie were standing there
With crossed feet
And a patient air.

They stood leaning back
On either side,
Clutching the rope
With their arms wide.
They looked dopey .
They looked dumb.
They stood there silent,
Chewing their gum.
Suddenly
Gray appeared.
A few hoarse voices cheered.
The voices seemed
To come from one spot:
Some gang of Gray's,
Likely as not.
Gray ducked in through the ropes,
Sat down.
He was bundled up in his dressing gown.
Pansy stared at what he saw:
Bull neck;
Heavy jaw;
Mouth like a slot;
Nose flat;
Green eyes,
Like an alley cat.
From just the little
There was to be seen,
Gray looked aggressive –
And he looked mean.
Something in Pansy grew suddenly tight.
He felt he was in for a nasty fight.

7.

Diamond came running down the aisle.
His mouth was stretched
In a mirthless smile.
He reached the ring.

He stood underneath,
Nervous,
Grinning,
Showing his teeth.
He called to a handler:
"Sam!–Come here!"
He whispered into the handler's ear . . .
". . . Get me–?" he said,
Backing away.
The handler nodded;
He climbed up towards Gray.
Sam put his mouth down
Close to Gray's head:
'I just been talkin'
Wit' Tony . . ." Sam said:
"Tony, he says the crowd is sore.
They ain't had action enough before.
See?
Tony says you better go slow:
Lay off
For a couple of rounds or so.
Take it easy.
Don't do him no dirt.
See?
Give the crowd its money's wort'"...
Gray nodded
With narrowed eyes:
"Okay–" he said:
"Okay–I'm wise . . .!"

8.

The bell hammered,
Staccato,
Swift.
The announcer's arm began to lift.
He bellowed,
Mouth wide,

Turning from side to side:
"LA-A-DEES–
An' gents . . . !
LA-A-DEES–
An' gents . . . !"
His voice roared out,
Echoed,
Immense:
NEXT we HAVE–
A SIX-ROUND BOUT–"
He paused, as a fierce dispute broke out
In the tenth row, where a tall thin
Man was trying to push his way in:
". . . Get duh hell outa there!–
Dat's my seat!"
"A-ah, gowan–
You're crazy wit' duh heat!". . .
The announcer scowled at the card he held.
His head jerked up.
His chest swelled:
"IN THIS CORNER–
SAILOR GRAY . . . !"
The Sailor rose from his stool halfway,
Sat down again.
The dispute flared higher:
". . . A-ah shut up!
You're a god-damned liar?"
"Dat's my seat!"
"Get outa here!"
"Gowan, I'll give yuh
A bust on d' ear!"
"You an' who else!"
The seated one rose,
And punched the thin man
Square in the nose.
Cheers.
Two cops came down the aisle,
And escorted the thin man out

In style.
Again the announcer's stentorian tones:
"–AND IN THIS CORNER–
PANSY JONES!"
Pansy half rose,
Bobbed left,
Bobbed right.
His grin flashed out,
Golden and white.
"Oh, Pansy de-ah . . .!"
It was girlish,
Mocking.
The house yelled.
They sat there rocking.
"Pansy–!"
"Jesus!–what a name!"
A hundred voices
Took up the game;
"Whoops, Pansy . . . !"
"Come an' be kissed!"
"Ooh, Pansy-Wansy!"
"Slap his wrist!"
"–SIX ROUNDS–!"
The announcer bawled:
"SIX ROUNDS–!"
BOTH MEN
ONE HUNNERT
AN' SIXTY POUNDS!"
". . . You must come ovah!"
"Don't rape him, Gob!"
"Hey, where did you get
Dat boyish bob . . . !"
"Pansy . . ."
"Jesus Christ! . . ."
"Oh, boy!"The crowd gasped,
Grew hoarse with joy.

9.

The announcer ducked through the ropes,
Sat down.
Gray flung off his dressing gown.
Pansy slipped out of the robe he wore.
They shuffled their feet
On the resined floor.
Max picked Pansy's bathrobe up:
"All right, Pansy–
Go get 'em, pup . . .!"
"All set–?" said the referee:
"Whaddaya say–?"
Pansy crouched forward,
Staring at Gray.
The crowd grew out of focus,
Blurred;
Strangely remote,
Only half heard.
He saw Gray sharp,
He saw Gray clear:
Mouth like a slot:
Mouth with a sneer.
Sloping shoulders.
Neck like a steer.
Nick in his left ear.
The referee crossed in between.
Baggy grey trousers.
His sweater was green.
Pansy shifted,
Trying to see
Around the legs of the referee.

10.

The bell clanged,
Broke
The air with its sudden stroke.

From somewhere behind:
"Go get 'em, pup . . . !"
His knees grew taut.
He was standing up.
Out towards the center of the ring
He went,
Walking like a cat,
Wary,
Intent.
There came Gray
From the opposite side,
Crouching,
Aggressive,
Narrow-eyed.
Their gloves touched,
Brushed.
The crowd sat
Hushed.
Pansy's left hung low,
By his thigh.
His right was close to his head,
High.
Everything about him moved.
He looked oiled,
Pistoned,
Grooved.
A long-range fighter,
Heady and cool;
No longer young–
But nobody's fool.
By contrast, Gray:
Stocky,
Square,
Built to stand up
Under wear and tear.
A plain slugger,
Blunt.
He stood square to the front,

Crouching a little.
Narrow-eyed,
Head rocking,
Feet wide;
Moving each hand a little bit,
Waiting his chance
To close
And hit.
They circled a moment,
Getting acquainted.
Pansy hitched up his left–
Feinted. Nothing stirring.
He feinted his right.
Still no reaction:
The Sailor held tight.
Pansy relaxed–
Sprang suddenly–
Led:
His left flashed up
To the Sailor's head.
It caught Gray by surprise.
He shook his head,
Blinked his eyes.
He crouched,
Circled each fist.
He sprang in–
Struck–
Missed.
Pansy's left
Snapped up like a whip.
Gray backed off
With a broken lip.
"Watch dat left . . . !"
A voice admonished.
Gray scowled,
Sullen, astonished.
The admonishing voice
Served to let loose

A shower of cracks,
Advice,
Abuse:
"Come on here, Gray!–
Whaddayuh say . . . !"
"Dat left ain't nothin'–
Brush that away . . . !"
"A-ah–" yelled the high
Sarcastic wit:
"Slap 'im on duh wrist
An be done wit' it . . . !"
Laughter.
Then suddenly:
"Dere he goes–!"
The sailor rushed;
Took one on the nose;
Hooked left,
Hooked right:
Short, vicious blows.
A flurry of cheers rose.
Pansy backed off,
Wary,
Alert.
One arm felt numb.
His left side hurt.
A hundred and sixty pounds–?
Like hell!
Somebody lied.
That hook in the side
Hurt like a hundred and seventy flat:
That was Gray's weight–
Or more than that.
A hundred and sixty pounds–
Like hell . . . !
His left snapped.
Gray rushed . . .
The bell!

II.

Pansy sat in his corner.
Louie and Max
Hovered about him attentive,
With bent backs.
He was breathing easy,
Hardly beginning to sweat.
So far, so good;
He didn't need them yet.
They gave him the bottle:
The water was warm,
Stale.
He gargled a mouthful,
Spat it out in the pail.
Max rubbed the bath towel
Over his face and head:
How d'yuh feel–?
D'yuh feel okay?" Max said.
"Yeah," said Pansy:
"Yeah – I feel okay ..."
He nodded a little.
He sat there staring at Gray.
Max cleared his throat:
"You're goin' good tonight."
"Yeah," said Louie:
"Yuh wanta throw in yer right.
Hook wid dat left,
And throw in duh right, too.
Play for his head,
Dat's what you wanta do."
"Yeah,' said Max:
"Dat left hook worries him,
See?
Play for his face, An' let duh body be."
Pansy nodded, silent.
He didn't feel right.
There was something he didn't like

About this fight.
He stared at gray,
And Gray stared back at him:
Eyes likes slits,
Face expressionless,
Grim.
The crowd chattered:
"... Dat Pansy's good!"
'Ah, nuts–
Dat left,
A helluva lotta ice dat cuts ...!"
"Dat Sailor ain't much ..."
"Duh Sailor ain't goin' yet ..."
"You wait–!"
"Ah, nuts ..."
"Yeah? Whaddayuh wanta bet ...?"
One gallery fan
Was a grubby, oldish man:
A small man,
Seedy looking, puffy cheeked.
His eyes watered.
His nose was red,
And it leaked.
His collar was held in the front
By a safety pin.
He seemed alone,
And his breath reeked of gin.
He turned to the stranger beside him.
He borrowed a light.
"Some fight," he said to the stranger:
"Yessir–some fight."
The stranger said nothing:
He eyed the borrower askance,
But the small man wanted to talk,
And he took a chance.
"Yessir–" he said:
"You see that fighter down there?
That's Pansy Jones!"

He paused with a speechless air,
As though he expected the stranger
To say Hell No!
Pansy Jones–?
You're kidding!
It Can't Be So . . . !
The stranger said nothing.
His manner was cold, at best.
He eyed the seedy man
As one eyes a pest.
"Yessir–" the pest went on:
"Yessir–I know!
That boy was good as hell
Ten years ago.
Last time I saw him fight was–
Let . . . me . . . see . . .
Back in Fifteen!–
He knocked out Billy McGee.
Knocked him out in the fifth:
A left to the jaw.
Yessir,
A prettier fighter you never saw.
Knocked him cold–
And didn't even take a scratch.
Yessir . . ."
He puffed, frowning:
". . . You got a match–?"
The stranger passed the box
Back over his shoulder.
His jaws were set,
And his ears had begun to smoulder.
The stump was re-lit.
It wobbled.
Some sparks fell.
The small man brushed them off:
"Yessir . . ."
The bell–!

12.

"Come on, now, Sailor–!"
"Come on!"
"Let's go!"
"Go on there, black-boy–
Knock him fer a row . . . !"
The voices snapped out
Staccato,
Tense.
Faces grew hard,
Blank with suspense.
Butts smouldered forgotten
In half-raised hands:
The smoke leaked from them
In thin, grey strands.
The figures in the ring
Looked hard,
Bright,
Glazed by the savage glare of light.
They circled . . .
Pansy broke the ice.
His left snapped up
Briskly,
Twice.
Gray rushed.
Pansy danced away.
"Ah – gowan!
Get to him, gray . . . !"
"Jesus Christ!–
Whadda yuh say!"
"Watch dat left!
Come on, let's go!"
"Block dat left!"
"Jesus you're slow!"
"What dud hell are you waitin' for . . . ?"
Gray's eyes glittered.
He was getting sore.

His fists circled.
He crouched to attack.
Pansy hooked:
Gray's head jerked back.
And just as it jerked,
Pansy let fly
With a hard straight right
To the Sailor's eye.
The crowd yelled.
Gray crouched,
Covered.
Pansy danced back out of range,
Hovered.
"Go on, Pansy!
You've got 'in now!"
"Dat right nailed 'im!"
"Christ what a slough!"
"Go on, black-boy–
Throw in dat right!"
"Duh Sailor's yelluh!"
"Duh Gob can't fight."
The Sailor snarled.
Splotched of red
Showed on his face.
He swayed his head.
He began to edge forward,
Ominous,
Slow.
His fists circled,
And he crouched low.
Pansy backed off
Narrow-eyed,
Feinting.
Dancing from side to side.
Watch it, now . . . !
His nerves grew taut.
He didn't want to get caught.
His eyes were glued

On that head of Gray,
Swaying there
Four feet away;
Glued on those shoulders,
Those circling fists
Close together
On heavy wrists . . .
Pansy paused.
His left smacked–
Smacked again.
Off he backed.
Gray crouched lower,
Shaking his head.
His right ear
Turned slowly red.
The crowd grew restless:
"Gowan an' fight!"
"Gowan, sock 'im!–
Don't take all night!"
"Go on, for Christ's sake–
Use dat glove!
What duh hell are yuh scared of–?"
"What game is dat yer playin'–
Red Rover . . . ?"
"Why don't youse lay down
An talk it over . . . !"
Slap –
Slap–!
Went Pansy's left.
He backed away,
Swift,
Deft.
Gray's chest swelled.
His shoulders humped.
His head stopped swaying.
In he jumped.
A yell from the crowd:
"Dere he goes . . . !"

There came the dull
Thump of blows.
Pansy chopped–
Missed.
Gray's head slid under his wrist.
Pansy swung left.
Before he could block,
Something jolted his ribs
Like a rock.
His insides thumped
Like a drum.
His ribs grew suddenly numb.
A glove shot up
And grazed his ear.
He shot in his right,
And sprang out
Clear.
"Gowan, Sailor . . . !"
"Gowan, Gray . . . !"
"Don't let him get away–!"
Gray swerved quickly,
Crouched,
Sprang–
The bell gave a sudden clang.

13.

Pansy walked to his corner,
Sat down on the stool.
They gave him the bottle:
The water tasted cool.
He was sweating now.
He could feel his heart pump;
And his head throbbed,
Echoed that steady thump.
They squeezed the sponge on his head:
It was cool and wet:
It trickled down,

Turned warm,
And mixed with the sweat.
Pansy leaned back.
He stretched his lets out wide.
He breathed in deep–
He winced:
It hurt his side.
That last one he stopped
Had hurt him pretty bad.
Christ on a raft!–
What a sock that Sailor had!
He was fast, too;
Faster than you'd have thought.
Just a little bit faster–
And he'd have got caught.
Max cleared his throat.
He said "You're goin' great.
Dat Sailor ain't much–
He swings like a rusty gate."
"Yeah," said Louie:
'Yeah–you're doin' good.
Dat right got 'im
Just like I said it would.
Keep throwin' that right,
An' mix in an uppercut . . ."
Pansy nodded,
Unhearing.
His eyes were shut.
In the opposite corner,
A crisis came up.
Gray sat in his corner,
Sore as a pup.
"Yeah–" he sneered,
"'Don't do 'im no dirt!'
Dat's fine for Tony–
He don't get hurt!
'Don't do him no dirt!'–
To hell wit' dat!

Dis round
I knock dat bastard flat!
No more o' dis foolin around–
I'm through!
An' if Tony don't like it–
He knows what to do!"
"Aw–" said Sam,
"Don't get so sore!
What duh hell are yuh sore for?
You done like Diamond told yuh to–
You laid off two rounds–
An' now yer through!
Pansy ain't hurtcha–
He knows what's what.
He'll take what he gets–
An' keep his trap shut.
You played it good,
Just like you were told.
Now be yerself–
An' knock 'im cold . . . !"
"Ah–" snarled Gray,
"You shut yer mout' . . . !"
The bell clanged.
He rose,
Rushed out.

14.

The crowd roared.
"Go get 'im, Gray!"
"Tear intuh 'im, Sailor–
Dat's duh way!"
"Now yer talkin' . . . !"
The roar died.
Pansy swung right.
He danced aside.
His left hooked up:
Gray shook his head:

His upper lip was smeared with red.
"Gowan, Sailor!"
"Gowan dere, Gray!"
'Don't let 'im get away–"
The crowd sat hushed.
The Sailor rushed.
Again the roar rose.
The roar sank.
Pansy hooked left.
He dodged off
On his toes.
"Ah, for Christ's sake–
Come on, Gray!
Why d'yuh let 'im
Fool yuh dat way–
Come on – whadda yuh say . . . !"
Blood ran down the Sailor's chin.
His teeth gleamed.
He sprang in.
He socked.
Pansy blocked.
Ropes on his left–
He swung to the right,
Dodging away,
Swift,
Light.
Gray crouched down,
Swaying his head.
His eyes flared:
"Come on!" he said:
"Come on, you dirty bastard–
Mix!
None o' yer god-damned monkey tricks!"
Pansy grinned,
Savage,
Mocking.
He backed away on this toes,
Rocking.

His heart was pounding.
His breath came fast.
The pace was too hot.
He couldn't last.
He knew it–
But he was game.
He'd take whatever came.
This Gray guy thought he could knock him out ...
He'd give Gray something
To think about–!
He sprang.
Before the Sailor could cover,
His left hooked up
And his right flashed over.
Back he jumped–
But his foot slipped.
He went off balance,
And in Gray ripped.
Pansy covered.
He was in for it now.
He staggered back onto balance somehow.
He twisted,
Blocked,
Chopped at Gray's head.
He felt Gray's fists
Thump in like lead.
Swiftly they thumped ,
And his body shook,
Jarred by the impact of every hook.
A glove flashed up–
Missed his jaw by an inch.
Swiftly he crouched,
Slid forward to clinch.
He trapped Gray's left ...
Suddenly he felt
A swift sharp pain below the belt.
He grunted,
Flinched,

But he hung on tight,
Trying to tie up the Sailors right.
"Watch dose low ones!" Pansy said.
"A-ah–!" snarled Gray,
"Go soak yer head!"
The Sailor's right arm rose
Crookt:
Down into Pansy's kidney's it hooked.
Up it came.
Down it fell,
Regular,
Swift–
And it hurt like hell.
Pansy's head lay out of harm.
His ear pressed Gray's
Left upper arm.
He stared unseeing at the canvas floor.
Dimly
He heard the crowd roar.
Somewhere above,
Out of sight,
His left arm wrestled
With the Sailor's right.
He had it now . . .
He had it tied . . . !They wheeled,
Swaying from side to side.
Gray tugged and shoved.
God, he was strong!
He wasn't going to stay
Tied up long . . . !
The referee's hand
Smacked Pansy's back.
They broke.
Gray crouched for another attack.
Pansy fell back
In a weary retreat.
No dancing now–
He stood flat on his feet.

That rush had got him.
His lungs felt hot.
His heart was jerking,
And his guts were shot.
"Gowan, Sailor!"
"You got 'im, Gray!"
"Tear intuh 'im, Sailor!"
"Dat's duh way!"
Gowan, Sailor–!"
"Knock 'im out . . . !
The voices blurred
In a steady shout.
The sweat poured down
Into Pansy's eyes.
He blinked.
Gray rushed.
He sprang sidewise.
The Sailor went by.
Like a ten-ton truck,
And Pansy hooked one in his side
For luck.
Back Pansy shuffled.
The Sailor stopped.
He wheeled,
Pointed.
His heart dropped.
Gray crouched,
Sniffed.
His glove rose:
He passed it swiftly
Under his nose.
Blood was smeared across one cheek.
Blood on his chin
Made a crooked streak.
The back of his glove
Was smudged with red.
He sniffed again,
Shaking his head.

He glared at Pansy.
What in Christ's name
Was this bastard trying–?
What was the game?
Sonofa bitch!
Too god-damned gay!
How the hell did he get that way!
The roar dwindled.
The roar died.
Deep groans came from every side.
"A-a-ah, Sailor . . . !"
"Christ on a log!–
Go after 'im, Sailor!
Snap outa yer fog . . . !"
"Gowan, Sailor–
Make it quick . . . !"
"Duh Sailor can't fight–
He's seasick . . . !"
"Gowan, stop wearin' out
Dat ring . . . !
"Charge dem rent . . . !"
"Can duh Sailor sing–?"
"Well–" a sudden, shrill voice said:
"Guess I'll go home
An' go tuh bed . . . !"
Heavy laughter.
Applause,
You could see Gray set his jaws.
He started for Pansy,
Wary, intent,
Ready to jump
The way Pansy went.
His teeth were showing.
His eyes were half shut,
He'd catch that bastard
And break his gut . . . !
The crowd watched,
Skeptical,

Jeering.
They spat.
They snorted.
They sat back sneering.
Gray stopped.
He feinted–
Then in he shot.
But Pansy stood there,
Rooted to the spot.
Pansy was watching,
He saw the rush come–
But his legs didn't move.
His brain seemed numb.
For just a second
He stood surprised,
Motionless,
And paralyzed.
Then all of a sudden he clicked–
Too late!
The Sailor hit him
Like a ton of freight.
Pansy crumpled.
He staggered back
Under that swift
Savage attack.
His head dropped.
His guts went in.
He bent at the middle
Like a twisted pin.
Gray's fist drove up
Like a battering-ram
Pansy saw double.
His head swam.
He sagged at the knees.
His arms fell.
The crowd stood up,
Roared . . .
The bell!

15.

Pansy slouched to his corner,
Flopped.
His eyes shut.
His head dropped.
Everything whirled.
He felt sick.
He opened his eyes again
Quick.
Hard bright
Savage light.
The ring tilted.
He held on tight.
His ears buzzed.
His head rumbled.
Far away,
Voices mumbled.
A blurred hand with a bottle
Rose:
The bottle came to rest
Pressed
With its top under his nose.
His nose burned with a sharp smell.
He sniffed,
Scowled:
It smelled like hell.
"Nix . . . !" he mumbled.
He squirmed,
He tried
To jerk his head aside.
The buzz in his ears
Disappeared.
The ring stood level.
His head cleared.
"Awright . . ." he muttered:
"Take dat away . . . !"
"Okay–" said Louie's voice:

"Okay . . . !"
Sponge on his head . . .
The water trickled
Down the back of his neck
And tickled.
Sponge on his heart,
Cool,
Sweet . . .
His heart slowed
Its furious beat.
The numbness was going.
His body ached,
Throbbed with pain.
His throat was baked.
"Drink," he muttered.
The bottle tipped.
He sucked at the water,
Greedy-lipped.
He swallowed a mouthful,
Smacked his lips:
It seemed to spread
To his finger tips.
God Almighty, it felt swell!
He sighed,
Leaned back.
His eyelids fell.
Max pulled the top of his trunks away,
Held them,
Giving his guts free play.
Louie slipped the sponge down where
The foul had struck
And held it there.
"Okay–?" Louie said.
Pansy nodded his head.
He felt lousy.
He felt drowsy.
His head rolled.
He could hardly keep

Himself from falling asleep.
Louie and Max exchanged a look.
They were pessimistic.
Their heads shook.
"Not so good ...!" that look implied.
They stared at Pansy
Narrow-eyed.
The crowd threw out a deep-toned sound
Like water rushing underground.
The smoke rose,
Swam,
Drifted.
Faces bobbed,
Swung,
Shifted.
Butts glowed.
Matches flared:
The eyes above them
Flashed,
Glared.
Pansy's chest
Lifted and fell.
He lay back waiting,
Dreading the bell.
The rest wasn't long enough.
He didn't feel strong enough
To last much longer.
He was tired as hell.
His arms were heavy,
His shoulders felt sore.
He let his arms dangle.
His gloves brushed the floor.
The hands in the gloves
Felt hot,
Bloated.
The leather felt slippery,
Sweat-coated.
"Well–" said Max,

"You're goin' good!"
He glanced at Louie.
They understood.
"Yeah," said Louie,
"You're goin' swell!
Keep throwin' dat right,
An' don't . . ."
The bell!

16.

Max and Louie got down off the ring.
They parked the stuff
They were carrying.
They sat down,
Stared at the ring overhead.
"Say–
You got a butt–?" Max said.
Louie handed over his pack.
Max took one,
And handed them back.
He fumbled for a match
Below his sweater.
He straightened a little,
To see better.
"Pansy's cooked," said Louie.
He frowned:
"Dat Sailor'll finish 'im up
Dis round . . ."
Max blew a thin
Blue stream of smoke:
"Yeah," he said,
"The old boy's broke.
He can't take
What duh Sailor gave 'im.
Nothin' but a lucky punch
Can save 'im . . ."
"Yeah," said Louie,

"Dat's my hunch.
His only chance is a lucky punch."
"Yeah–he's just too god-damn old ..."
They nodded.
Their faces were hard,
Cold.
A roar rose:
"Dere he goes–!"
The roar sank.
They sat hushed.
You could hear Gray's feet
Thud as he rushed.
"Jeez–!" said Max:
"Whadda yuh know!
Lookit dat Pansy!
Lookit 'im go–!"
Pansy's legs spread wide.
He snapped to one side.
The Sailor missed.
Before he could stop,
Pansy whirled,
Spun like a top.
His shoulders humped
And in he jumped
Hitting like hell
With his left and right.
The crowd yelled at the sight.
"Knock 'im out–!"
"Knock 'im out–!"
The air shook
With that savage shout.
Mouths snarled.
Eyes blazed:
They popped from flaming faces,
Glazed.
Gray staggered.
Stumbled.
Fell.

The crowd rose with a sharp yell.
In between sprang the referee.
Pansy fell back.
Gray crouched on one knee.
Gray jumped up.
His face was red.
He crouched to rush,
Swaying his head.
If Pansy had hurt him
You'd never know it;
Nothing about him
Seemed to show it.
Louie and Max exchanged a glance. "Well–" said Max,
"Dere goes his chance."
They shrugged a little.
They sat back.
Louie shook out
A butt from his pack.
"Yeah," said Louie,
"Dat's it.
He's through . . ."
He struck a match
On the sole of his shoe:
"He's tired how–
Too tired to run.
If duh Sailor rushes 'im now–
He's done."
Pansy knew
What was coming, too.
He stood there panting
With legs wide-spread,
Staring at the top
Of the Sailor's head.
Watch it now . . . !
Get ready to block–
Gray rushed.
The crowd saw Pansy rock,
Stagger back from the shock.

The crowd roared,
Yelped with delight
As Gray hooked home
His left and right.
A pimply youth
With greasy hair
And no chin
Sprang from his chair.
His face was convulsed.
His eyes popped out.
His voice was a raucous shout:
"Break duh nigger's face!–Break it!
Sock 'im Sailor–
He can't take it–!"
Behind the pimply youth there sat
A heavy man
In a derby hat.
His nose was broken.
One eye was black.
He sneered a the youth's back.
He folded his arms,
Contemptuous,
Placid;
He spoke to the youth,
And his voice was acid:
"Ah, shut yer trap
Fer Christ's sake–
He's takin' more
Dan you'll ever take . . . !"
The youth jerked around
To see who had spoken.
He saw.
His spirit seemed suddenly broken.
The derbied one spoke
With a menacing frown:
"Siddown–
Before I knock you down!
Yuh loud-mouthed bastard,

Yuh make me sick!"
The youth collapsed;
He sat down quick.
The crowd was yelping
"Sock 'im, Gray!"
"Finish 'im, Sailor!"
"Dat's duh way . . . !"
Back Pansy went.
You could see him flinch.
He twisted,
Desperate,
Trying to clinch.
Louie and Max's eyes met.
Each of them ground out his cigarette.
One reached for the pail,
The other for the towel . . .
Max whistled suddenly:
"Lookatat foul!
Lookatat, Louie–
Two in a row!
Jesus!
Duh Sailor's landin' 'em low . . . !"
Pansy spoke to the referee.
In he hopped.
The roar stopped.
The crowd craned necks to see.
The referee elbowed Gray aside:
"Well–?" he snapped,
Stony-eyed.
Pansy tapped with his glove
To show
Where the Sailor's blows
Had struck in low.
"Two . . ." said Pansy.
The Sailor scowled.
"Ah, nuts!" he snarled,
"The hell I fouled–!"
"A-ah . . . !" yelled a voice,

"Gowan an' fight!"
"Don't stand dere
Talkin' all night!"
The crowd's voice
Had an angry sound.
They booed.
Their feet began to pound.
The referee turned to Gray,
Severe:
'Watch dat foulin', Gray–
Yuh hear?"
The referee hopped back
Out of the way.
"Awright–!" he snapped,
"Whadda yuh say!"
Gray's head began to sway.
He crouched,
Rushed.
His right went wide.
They clinched.
He hammered at Pansy's side.
"Son-of-a-bitch–!" the Sailor growled.
He hammered as he spoke:
"–Say I fouled–!"
You double-crossin' bastard, you!
I'll get you for day
When dis bout is t'rough!
Just you wait
Till after dis fight–
You'll get what's comin' to you
All right –!"
He snarled.
He wrenched his lift arm clear.
The heel of his glove
Ripped Pansy's ear.
"Bastard–!" muttered Gray.
He slung Pansy away.
Pansy staggered back

Amazed.
For a second or two
He felt dazed.
What the hell was this all about?
He had no time
To figure it out ...
"Double-crossing son-of-a-bitch"
Pansy's mouth began to twitch.
His eyes narrowed,
Blazed.
The Sailor stiffened.
His chest swelled.
"Dere he goes–!"
The crowd yelled.
Pansy covered.
He tried to duck,
But Gray nailed him.
He was out of luck.
The air seemed suddenly
Blurred with fists
Flashing at him
On dim white wrists.
He felt them strike.
He seemed to grow numb.
To hell with those fists–
Let them come ...
The blows seemed far away
And dull.
An engine was whirring
Inside his skull.
The ring whirled.
His legs felt light.
Everything seemed to grow
Blurred and bright.
He lost his balance.
He hung in space.
The floor sprang up
And hit him in the face.

He stared at the floor
Surprised.
His brains were paralyzed.
He shook his head.
A voice said "Four . . ."
His brain clicked.
He was on the floor.
He had to get up
And do it quick!
He got on one knee.
He felt sick.
He had to get up!
His upper teeth
Gnawed at the lower lip beneath.
"Five . . . !" said the voice
Far away.
He had to get up
And get this Gray . . . !"
Blood on the floor:
A scarlet smear,
Savage pain in his right ear.
He crouched,
Looked up:
There stood Gray
Watching,
Sneering,
Ten feet away.
Gray's face swam
In a haze of red.
Pansy snarled.
He shook his head.
A shiver ran through him
Like a hot chill.
His face twitched.
He wanted to kill.
"Six . . . !" said the voice.
His ears rang.
Something inside him snapped.

He sprang.
No boxing now–
To hell with that!
He leapt in striking
Like a savage cat.
He felt Gray's fists
Thud into him.
Gray's face faded.
The ring grew dim.
Blindly he struck,
Trusting to luck.
Suddenly his right
Struck something hard.
Pain shot through his hand.
His wrist was jarred.
He struck again–
Hit air.
He stumbled into the ropes,
Clung there.
Now let it come!
To hell with it all.
To hell with the works,
He wanted to bawl.
No air in his lungs.
He felt drowned.
His ears were filled
With a roaring sound.
His heart pumped,
Thumped.
His knees sagged.
He slumped.
His eyes shut.
His head sank low . . .
A voice was counting,
Far off,
Slow:
"Two–!" said the voice:
"Three–!"

"Four–!"
He opened his eyes,
Stared at the floor.
They stung,
Parched with heat.
The floor swayed at his feet.
"Five–!" said the voice:
"Six–!"
His eyes were playing him tricks!
On the floor of the ring
A figure lay,
Face down,
Unmoving:
It looked like Gray!
He clung to the ropes.
He waited,
Staring,
Fascinated.
"Nine–
"Ten–!"
The counting stopped.
For half a second,
A silence dropped.
"–and Out!" snapped a voice
In that hushed pause.
The crowd rose,
Roaring applause.
Seconds seemed to spring
From nowhere into the ring.
Pansy clung to the ropes
Dazed.
His arm was seized at the wrist–
Raised.
The crowd clapped,
Cheered,
Clamored.
His arm dropped.
The bell hammered.

"Come on–" said Max
Into Pansy's ear;
"Let's get th' hell away from here . . . !

SIX

I.

The dressing room was a hot-box.
Pansy sat there
Holding his socks.
The air was stagnant,
Foul,
Thick.
The reek of liniment
Made him sick.
He sat there bent,
Spent.
The room was deserted looking,
Bare:
Only just the three of them there.
Fargo and gang
Were up at his bout.
Everyone else had gotten out.
Max and Louie were through.
They had done all they could do.
They'd rubbed him down
Long and good.
They'd patched his ear
As wells as they could.
He still felt lousy–
They didn't doubt it–
But what the hell
Could they do about it?
God,
With a beating like he had got,
A cast-iron set of guts would be shot!

They stood around
For a minute or so,
Impatient,
Restless,
Ready to go.
Max looked at his watch.
He rubbed his chin.
"Well–" he began . . .
Diamond rushed in.

2.

His grin was gone.
His face was white.
The muscles in his jaws
Stood rigid,
Tight.
He stared at Pansy
With a glittering look.
He pointed at him,
And his hand shook.
"You crooked son-of-a-bitch –" he said.
His voice was dead,
Cold,
Like lead.
He paused,
Overcome.
His mouth worked.
He was dumb.
Pansy straightened,
Stiffened as he sat:
"What th' hell yo' mean by that?"
The words clicked outLike flint.
His eyes began to glint.
Diamond grinned
As a skull grins:
The grin seemed fastened there
By pins.

"None o' dat stuff–
You know what I mean!
Don't pull dat stuff.
I ain't so green.
I know when I'm double-crossed,
See?
You don't get away
Wit' dat stuff wit' me!"
A pause.
Then Pansy shook his head.
"Ah don' know what yo' mean," he said.
"Nah!" sneered Diamond.
"You don't know!"
Ain't you the innocent bastard, though!
Dis wasn't duh Sailor's fight–
Oh, no!
Nobody ever told you so!
Not at all!
You never got
Yer twenty bucks!–
Of course not!?

Pansy couldn't grasp what he meant.
This stuff was over his head
Like a tent.

Twenty bucks–?
No such luck!
He hadn't gotten
A god-damned buck.
Pansy's voice was low.
The words came careful,
Slow:
"Mistuh Diamond,
You done got mixed.
Ah didn't know
Dis fight was fixed.
Dat twenty bucks

Must got mislaid!
What for you say
Ah done got paid–?"

"'Cause Stone and MacPhail said so–
Dat's why!"

Pansy got sore.
"Dat's a god-damned lie!
Ah nevah got nothin'.
An' dat's flat!
Nothin'.
On dat!"

"What duh hell good
Is yer lousy word–
Yuh god-damned nigger jail-bird!"

Pansy jumped up,
Stepped forward a pace:
"Git outa heah–
Or I'll break yo' face!"
His voice had an ugly ring.
His fists rose,
Menacing.

Diamond's swift
Vicious reply
Was to draw back a fist
And let it fly.
His ring cut Pansy
Below the eye.

Pansy let rip
With a right from the hip.
The blow smashed square
On Diamond's face.
He took a fast

Short trip through face.
He hit the floor flat.Up he bounced
Like a cat.

An angry red splotch marked the place
Where Pansy's fist
Had struck his face.
His hands rose,
Covered the spot.
He turned,
Made for the door like a shot.
His shoulder hit
The side of the door.
He staggered back,
Swore.

He stopped,
Whirled about.
He thrust a finger out:
"I'll get you fer dis–!
Just wait–
Dat's all . . . !"
He turned.
He dashed out into the hall.

3.

Louie whistled.
He waggled his jaw:
"Jesus!–
Did you see what I just saw . . . ?"
But Max frowned.
He shook his head:
"Pansy, you better look out–" he said.
"Look out fer Diamond
When he's mad like dat.
He's crazy,
See?

Crazy as a bat!"

"Dat's right, Max–"
Louie agreed:
"Diamond fights dirty–
I know dat breed!
Watch out fer Tony
After dat crack–
He's likely to stick
A knife in yer back."

"Yeah?" said Pansy.
His face was grim"
"Let 'im try–
Ah ain't scared uh him!"
"Well–" said Max,
"It's you – not me.
But watch yer step.
I'm tellin' yuh, see!"

Pansy seemed to be unimpressed.
He pulled out his clothes.
He began to get dressed.

They watched him a minute,
Silent,
Blinking.
Their faces grew hard
As they stood there thinking.
Then Max shrugged.
He looked away:
"Hey, Louie–
What does yer watch say?"
Louie looked:
"I got eighteen past."
Max pulled out his:
"You must be fast . . .
My watch says only

Ten after ten."

"Well, why duh hell
Didja ask me, then?"
"Let's beat it, Louie –
Whadda yuh say?"
"Yeah.
Let's make a getaway.
Jeez,
It's hot as hell down here.
Let's go up to Herman's
An' get a beer."

"Okay wit' me–
I got a thirst.
Beer an' a sandwich–
Liverwurst . . ."

They turned to Pansy:
"So long, kid–
Yuh done great."
"I'll say yuh did . . ."
"Yuh better go home
An' go to bed . . ."

Pansy grinned,
Nodding his head:
"So long–" he said,
"See yuh some more . . ."
They turned.
He watched them stroll through the door.

4.

They vanished.
Pansy sat alone.
A silence dropped
Like the silence of stone.

The echo of a roar
Swelled,
Died.
The silence rushed back
From every side,
Heavy,
Dense,
Implacable,
Immense.
Pansy pulled on a shoe.
He tied
It. Stared at the shoe
Preoccupied.
A window rattled.
He jumped at the sound.
He raised his head.
He peered around . . .
White walls ,
Cracked,
Scarred.
Closed windows,
Black,
Barred.
Out on the sill,
A dim scrap
Of dirty paper began to flap.
Again the roar echoed,
Died.
The silence returned,
Magnified.
He stared at the door.
It was dark out there.
The shadows baffled
His steady stare.
He cocked his head,
Listened.

The whites of his eyes

Glistened.
Silence.
He rose.
His shadow sprang tall,
Stood huge before him
Against the wall.
A board creaked in the floor.
He started back,
Swore.
He grinned to himself.
The grin was sickly.
He put on the rest of his clothes,
Quickly.

He wrapped his togs.
He buttoned his coat.
He tightened the muffler
Around his throat.
He put on his cap
And pulled it low.
He picked up his parcel,
And started to go.
At the door,
He stopped dead.
Slowly
He stuck out his head.
A roar from upstairs.
It echoed,
Died.
Silence.
He stiffened.
He stepped outside.

5.
____

He walked swiftly.
The dark hall
Echoed every footfall.

125

He reached a red light
Caged in wire
Above red buckets labeled "Fire."

He stopped.
He looked back.
The hall behind
Lay black.
His teeth chattered
With a chill.

He listened . . .
The hall was still.
He started again.
The floor creaked.
Rats raced through the walls,
Squeaked.
They rattled around
In the loose plaster.
He licked his lips.
He walked faster.
He reached the stairs:
Up he went
Two at a time,
Swift,
Bent.
He got to the door;
He stopped.
His hand rose,
Dropped.
He stood a moment
As if in doubt,
Then swung the door open
And stepped out.

6.

The street was cold.

Misty,
Damp,
Ghostly, lit by a blurred lamp.
Around the lamp-post
Stood a dim
Group of figures,
Waiting,
Grim.
Pansy's heart jumped.
The door behind him thumped.
He spotted Diamond.
He spotted Gray.
He turned quickly,
Started away.

"Dere he goes!" a voice said:
"Let's get duh bastard.
Come ahead . . . !"
Pansy pretended he hadn't heard.
He kept on going
Without a word.
The feet behind him
Quickened their stride.
Two figures ranged
Alongside.
"Hey–!
What duh hell is your rush . . . ?"
They started to jostle,
Elbow,
Push.

"Cut it out . . ." Pansy mumbled.
A foot tripped him.
He staggered,
Stumbled.
He lurched into someone.

A voice swore.

Said "What duh hell
Are you pushin' me for–!
"Break his face!" another said.
A fist thudded against his head.

His arms rose on guard.
He whirled.
He stuck out hard. "Cheese it–!" snapped someone:
"Cheese it–duh cop!"
They paused.
They let their fists drop.
The cop came up,
Burly,
Severe:
"What duh hell
Goes on, here . . . ?"

No one answered.
The cop scowled.
"Break dis up, youse guys!" he growled.
"Move on, see?–
An' make it quick!"

His chest swelled.
He twirled his stick.
Pansy didn't trust the Law.
Cops shot at everything they saw.
He walked away.
He was scared to run–
He thought the cop
Might pull his gun.

He was getting close
To a cross street.
The gang was behind him–
He heard their feet.
He was all right
While the cop was in sight,

But once he turned that corner–
Good night!
He broke out in a cold sweat.
Jesus!
That bunch would get him yet!

He reached the corner.
A block to the right
He saw one blue
One yellow light:
The Subway!
Could he make it?
A chance:
He'd have to take it.

Empty street . . .
Ten to one . . .
A panic hit him.
He started to run.
"Get ' im!" he heard a voice yell:
"Get dat nigger–!"
He ran like hell.

7.

Steep stairs.
White tiles.
Bare lights.
Turnstiles.

Express platform:
Grey,
Dusty.
Cold air,
Sharp,
Musty.
Vaulted ceiling.
Dismal light.

Square pillars,
Black and white.

A few frozen figures tramped
Up and down,
Shuffled,
Stamped.
Cold draughts from ventilators
Sighed around the restless waiters.
Dirty paper flapped.
The dust
Streamed, swirled at every gust.
Empty tracks.

No sound.
A Klaxon whooped
Aboveground.
Its high snarling note
Was muffled,
Faint,
Remote.

8.

Suddenly
A turnstile clattered.
Voices yelled.
Feet pattered.
Down the stairs Pansy came,
Face convulsed,
Eyes aflame.
He rushed down,
Wheeled about
To the edge of the platform
And leaned out.

The tunnel was black,

Empty,
Blank.
Pansy gulped.
His heart sank.

He stared.
Far down along the track
Two lights appeared against the black.
He listened.
He heard a faint humming.
His heart jumped–
An Express was coming!

The lights seemed to grow clearer,
Nearer:
One light green,
One light red . . .
Feet on the stairs.
He turned his head.
There they came–!

His throat grew tight.
His heart raced with fright.
They crowded towards him.
"Well–!" sneered Gray:
"Think yuh were gonna get away . . . ?"

Pansy's face grew suddenly grim.
His jaws set.
It was them or him.

They saw his hand slip
To the pocket over his hip.
His fist rose,
Menacing,
Black.

A razor glittered
Across its back.
"Come on–!" he said.

They eyed the blade.
They shrank back,
Afraid.

The razor glittered,
The razor gleamed.
Far down the tracks
A whistle screamed,
Savage,
Hoarse:
The air split with its force.

Low thunder.
The rails shivered.
The air trembled.
The platform quivered.

Diamond gave his pants a hitch:
"Let's get duh nigger son-of-a-bitch . . . !"
"Sure!" said the Sailor,
"come on–let's go!
You hit 'im high–
I'll hit 'im low . . ."

They crouched,
Sprang.
The razor flashed,
Slashed at Diamond's face,
Gashed.
Diamond yelped.
A thin red streak
Rapidly widened across his cheek.

He clapped his hands to his face.
He staggered back a pace.

Gray and Pansy locked.
They swung,
Wrestled,
Rocked.
"Look out fer d'edge–!
Look out dere, Gray . . . !"

The Sailor suddenly wrenched away.
Pansy spun.
He staggered back.
He tottered on the edge.
He crashed to the track.

The tunnel roared.
The whistle screamed.
Over the tracks
Light streamed.

They turned their heads
So as not to see.
Pansy hitched up
Onto one knee.
Blood on his face,
Dripping,
Red.
He crooked one arm
Around his head.

He crouched,
Ready to duck.
The train screeched
And struck.

THE END.

Southwest Scenarios

COMMENTARIES FROM RURAL ARIZONA
BY DARRYLE PURCELL

Texas scientists cough up cloned hairball named 'Cc'

February 22, 2002

THE SCIENTIFIC COMMUNITY HAS ONCE AGAIN AMAZED THE REST OF US WITH A startling announcement: They have cloned a cat.

I only have one question regarding the situation: Why?

The kitty, named "Cc" which probably stands for "cloned cat," is the product of experiments at Texas A&M University. Apparently the researchers had 187 failures before their final success in producing Cc, the feline of the future. One would think that if those Texas scientists really wanted a kitten that much they would have just put a male and a female cat in the same vicinity. Their success ratio would have been better.

But, then again, this makes one wonder if we are going through a period of not having enough cats. Are those four-legged, furniture-clawing, sand-pooping, aloof felines on the endangered animals list? I don't believe local community animal shelters would say we are having a cat shortage.

Besides the cat, researchers have now been able to clone sheep, goats, cattle and mice.

Although I believe the natural reproduction process to be far superior to sci-fi cloning theories, I can understand why some would experiment with cloning sheep, goats and cattle. People eat these creatures and perhaps, someday, it will be necessary to use high-tech means to feed the growing population.

But mice are another thing. Do we really need cloned mice? Maybe that is why the brain trust cloned the cat — to catch their cloned mice.

Japanese scientists have reported recently that most of the mice they have cloned have died young of liver and lung problems. Perhaps cloned lab-mice have a predisposition for use of alcohol and tobacco.

According to another recent news story, the city of Scottsdale, Ariz., would not welcome any cloned mice at this time. Apparently, the area residents are under siege from an infestation of roof rats. These rodents allegedly live, party and reproduce in trees and roofs. The problem is so bad that local officials have requested federal funds and services to help exterminate the fuzzy rodent trespassers.

Perhaps Cc could lead a small army of cloned super-soldier cats in an assault on the Scottsdale vermin. The Texas A&M scientists could dress the future felines in Santa suits so they could sneak up on the roof rats before terminating them.

But I may be stretching my imagination a bit as I think the use of cloned super soldiers in Santa suits has been in at least three of Arnold Schwarzenegger's recent films. It would probably be wiser to see what traditional exterminators could do about the situation before we send in the clones.

Anyway, I can understand why scientists may want to experiment with cloning endangered species. But the idea of cloning cats and mice makes about as much sense to me as attempts to clone cockroaches and mosquitoes.

Southwest Scenarios

The commentaries here and in future issues were originally published by *The Mohave Valley Daily News* between 1993 & 2013--and in many ways they apply to today. We are grateful to republish these commentaries written by Darryle Purcell in full and unedited. His own brand of humor and style can deliver insight, provoke thought, and even boil blood.

Night

The night has a thousand eyes,
  And the day but one;
Yet the light of the bright world dies
  With the dying sun.

The mind has a thousand eyes,
  And the heart but one;
Yet the light of a whole life dies,
  When love is done.

Francis William Bourdillon
(March 22nd 1852 – January 30th 1921)

**British Film Actress Anne Heywood
(1931-2023)**

**I'm tall when I'm young,
and I'm short when I'm
old.
What am I?**

Answer in back of book.

SUDOKU

		9		1			2	5
1		5	8					3
							9	
	6			7	9			1
2								
	8	1					3	
	4			2				
	7			9	4			8

**A page from Mary Shelley's
Frankenstein notes.**

STRANGE KINDNESS

AN ORIGINAL STORY:

BY E.W.H. THORNTON

And no one is allowed to pass the sick man in silence without asking him what his ailment is.

—Herodotus, History of the Persian Wars, 430 B.C.

My name is Jon Gladd. I am in horrific pain. I seek the aid of a medical professional.

The hospital consists of multiple buildings, each of them gargantuan and featureless, colossal edifices of naked glass and steel and brick. If not for the large signs identifying them as hospitals it would be impossible to discern their purpose, though the word 'Hospital' is not actually on any of the signs, most of which bear the legend 'Stamen Medical Group' in vivid Helevetica font, white letters on a gray background like a more somber version of a sign identifying a chain restaurant. The buildings' appearance betrays no hint of what could possibly be transpiring within, projecting nothing beyond an air of grim architectural professionalism. There are three distinct buildings bisected by roads riddled with traffic and they are joined together by skybridges, umbilical walkways suspended aloft where remote human shapes can be seen, patients shuffling wearily while medical professionals stride forth with adamant purpose.

I guide my car into the parking complex. A machine vomits out a ticket. I accept it and the large metal arm barring my entry winces upward via a succession of sclerotic twitches. The road bends back upon itself while curling upward as I drive past innumerable other parked cars patiently awaiting their diseased owners' return. Despite my ascent it feels like I'm progressing downward, the parking complex growing ever darker and danker as I venture up in search of an empty space, eventually finding one bathed in shadow so deep that as I walk away from my car it seems to be absorbed by the parking structure's oppressive atmosphere of bitter exhaust and concrete stillness.

I hobble into the Emergency Room, or rather what I presumptuously assumed was the Emergency Room but what is in fact the waiting room adjacent to the Emergency Room, which in truth lies beyond two impregnable steel doors, and a security guard wearing a bulletproof vest along with an expression of profound boredom. I approach a woman seated behind what I take to be an intake desk, a sober professional whose hair is piled atop her head in a heap of artfully coiled strands. Her name tag identifies her as Donna Wilkes. There is a sign next to her that says PHYSICAL OR VERBAL ABUSE OF STAFF WILL NOT BE TOLERATED.

"Can I help you?" Donna asks.

"I am in horrific pain." I say; which is not, strictly speaking, a literal answer to her question, rather I say it in hopes of getting the ball rolling, of priming the pump of medicine, of making the gears of healing begin to turn, of spurring the horse of treatment into the motion of attending to my problem down the path of recovery leading to the ultimate destination of restored health.

Donna asks me my name. I tell her it is John Gladd. She asks me my birthday. I tell her it is twelve three ninety eight. She asks me how I would rate my pain on a scale of one to ten. I tell her ten. She stops asking me questions, looks at her computer monitor, and types on her keyboard for a very long time.

I wait. I look around the room that is not the Emergency Room, but rather the place where people wait for emergencies to run their course, for emergencies to stabilize until they can be managed, controlled, alleviated entirely—or, conversely, for them to deteriorate, for the emergency to emerge and continue emerging until it has emerged so much it has taken the place of that which it originally emerged from. This is the place that is purpose built for things not to happen, a bardo sealed off from any true emergency by a veil of steel doors and a security guard whose rigidly languid expression shows that he exists in a constant state of wishing he could look at his phone.

Eventually Donna Wilkes invites me to sit down. I tell her that I can't sit down because it hurts too much. She accepts this, prints out a bracelet of laminated paper and wraps it around my wrist. The bracelet carries information identifying me as myself, along with a bar code that I assume conveys the same information in a way that can be read and understood by a computerized gun that shoots light. Donna scans it with said gun. It beeps in response, which is apparently what it is supposed to do. She moves out from behind her desk, wheeling with her a stainless steel rod supporting a machine trailing insulated rubber wires ending in various devices. She attaches one device to my finger that reads my pulse, another device consisting of an inflating cuff that she wraps around my bicep in order to read my blood pressure. The machine beeps. Donna Wilkes reads the results, removes the devices from me, wheels the machine away and returns to her seat behind the desk. She says nothing of what the machine told her, which I assume means the results were acceptable.

I ask her what happens now. She tells me someone will be with me shortly.

I wait.

A machine beeps and the doors to the Emergency Room open slightly, allowing a short woman with a round face and accommodating demeanor to walk through and approach me.

"Mr. Gladd?" She asks warmly.

"Yes."

"Come with me." I go with her. She presses an ID card attached to a lanyard at her hip identifying her as Cassandra Snitowsky CNP-BC CBN to a plastic device by the steel doors. The machine beeps. The doors open. We enter.

The Emergency Room is actually many rooms. Most of the space is taken up by a vast complex of desks and computers and phones, a great hive of administrative activity beyond my understanding. The treatment rooms fan out from this epicenter, enclosures contained by sliding glass doors, some obscured by white curtains while others are open to onlookers. Cassandra guides me into an empty room where everything is either white, beige, or the metallic hue of stainless steel. Within are a great number of machines and drawers, as well as a television expressing things in a barrage of bright colors and loud noises. Cassandra Snitowsky tells me to remove all my clothes and to replace them with a flimsy cotton gown resembling a large overused dishrag, then leaves. I do as I'm told and eventually manage to lie down on the bed with a great deal of difficulty and pain. Cassandra returns. She touches her ID card to a cabinet of draws. A machine beeps. The drawers unlock. She withdraws a needle she proceeds to insert into my arm, which is in turn attached to an IV drip suspended from a sac of clear fluid I can't identify. She asks me to tell her how much pain I'm in. I tell her the amount is horrific. Cassandra nods, tells me we'll see what we can do to help me about that, gives me a plastic hand held device at the end of a long cord that acts as both television remote control and a means to summon medical assistance, then leaves forever. I use it to turn off the television.

It takes me a little over an hour to realize that, in addition to being an Emergency Room, this is also another waiting room. Yes, it is a place made to house and treat patients, but it also a place built for the express purpose of nothing happening, imbuing the space with an airy vacuity not unlike that of any other place where you are made to wait, an airport terminal, a theater lobby, automotive traffic, anywhere in the world you happen you spend time on the phone attempting to contact customer service.

Eventually a woman with long legs and her hair in a ponytail arrives, identifies herself as Jada Hansberry PA-C, and tells me she has been alerted to the fact that I am in pain. She sits down by my bed, inserts another tube into my IV, injects a clear liquid she identifies as the anesthetic morphine, removes the tube, and leaves forever. The morphine does nothing. My horrific pain endures.

Eventually a tall thin man with aquiline features enters and identifies himself as Robert P. Goldberg MD MPH.

"What seems to be the problem?" He inquires.

"I am in horrific pain." I respond. He asks me to provide further detail. I describe my symptoms in terms as precise and lucid as I can. He nods while absorbing the details. When I've reached the limit of my capacity to elaborate on what I'm experiencing, I ask him what could be the cause. He says it could be several things, then leaves. I never see him again.

I wait a long time. Eventually a woman with a pointed chin and sloping eyebrows who identifies herself as Melina Cocteau MS comes and fills multiple small plastic tubes with my blood. She attaches each one to the needle penetrating my arm in quick succession and my blood squirts out in small, pressurized jets as if eager to escape my body. Having gotten what she came for, Melina Cocteau MS leaves with my blood. I never see her again.

I wait a long time. Eventually a woman with squat shoulders and dark eyes named Liz Farwell RN APN APRN-BC CBN enters and tells me she's taking me to get a CT scan, which stands for computerized tomography. I ask her what it is. She tells me it's an X-Ray machine. She undoes the mechanism holding the wheeled gurney I occupy in place and commences rolling my supine form through the hospital. From my perspective it appears as if I'm remaining stationary while the entire hospital is moving around me, medical professionals and abstract expressionist paintings scrolling by while I look at a ceiling more than I have ever looked at a ceiling before in my life, beholding the speckled confusion of acoustic tiles and metallic grids enclosing islands of cold florescent light.

I'm wheeled into a small room filled with a machine shaped like a large upright gray doughnut with a mobile platform attached to its hole. I'm told to lie down on the platform, and I manage to do so with great difficulty and pain. Liz Farwell RN APN APRN-BC CBN exits the room. The machine spins up, interior mechanisms whirring with a subdued rumble. A voice on an intercom tells me to pay attention to the lights on the machine above me, which will tell me when to hold my breath and when to resume breathing. I obey them as the platform slowly thrusts me in and out of the hole while the green illuminated image of a nonplussed cartoon head alternates with the illuminated image of green lungs overlaid with a red X. Eventually the machine stops, a voice on the intercom tells me to breathe normally, and Liz Farwell reenters the room. I roll back onto the bed and Liz Farwell RN APN APRN-BC CBN wheels me back into my small room within the larger Emergency Room. I never see Liz Farwell RN APN APRN-BC CBN again.

I wait more, then even more. It is a long wait, an extended wait, a wait so pronounced I come to understand that the many waits preceding this one were mere prelude, comparatively brief waits that only served to prepare the way for this wait, the ultimate wait. I feel myself reduced to an abstraction, the object of a thought experiment concerning a being hovering in a void, absent all sensory input, deprived of all information, a thing that knows only its own thoughts and pain.

After an unfathomable stretch of time a woman with short hair and prominent ears enters and identifies herself as Sonia Dutta MD. I ask her what the CT scan showed. She tells me it produced an image with a shape on it that might be something. She prescribes me medicine, one kind for the pain and another kind for the disease, and tells me that's everything and I should leave. I never see her again.

I exit the hospital. In the elevator lobby I feed my parking ticket into a machine along with a specific sum of money that endows the ticket with the power to free me and my vehicle from the parking garage. As I guide my car back down to ground level, feed my parking ticket into the machine, and exit into the normal, non-emergency world, I draw solace from the fact that I have been attended to by many and numerous medical professionals, all of whom posses both knowledge and wisdom far outstripping my own.

I fill the prescriptions at my local pharmacy, take them as directed, and attempt to integrate myself back into the life I had before my disease and pain overrode everything else. I return home to my boyfriend, my job, my dog, my mortgage, the reality television shows I watch where people with awful lives are judged based on their ability to prepare delicious food and rewarded accordingly.

The medicine does not work. My pain and disease persist undaunted. I call my General Practitioner and alert him to this news. He tells me to return to the hospital. I ask if I should go back to the same hospital or visit a different hospital. He tells me they're all the same.

I am almost certain that this is the same hospital I visited before, yet things have changed significantly in the brief interval of time since my last visit. The simple, square office buildings have been radically altered, appearing to have grown in angular, jutting shapes like budding crystals that protrude upwards and downwards from formerly flat walls. The roof has sprouted an abundance of large satellite dishes and solar panels whose cells display a vivid rainbow shimmer like oil on water.

Just as before I make my way to the waiting room adjacent to the Emergency Room and approach the person manning the front desk. She may be the same person I saw last time; I'm not sure because she now wears so many new facial accouterments as to be unrecognizable. She regards me through the lens suspended on a thin metal arm in front of her right eye. I can see a dense readout of information scrolling down the lens, though since the writing appears both very small and backwards from where I'm standing I have no means of understanding it. A network of antennae spring from her head. One of her ears has been replaced with an oblong receiver shaped like the head of a mushroom.

"Can I help you?" She asks.

"I am in horrific pain." I say.

She types in her computer for a very long time. I look at the security guard. His eyes are completely obscured by a visor while a softball sized sphere bearing too many lenses to count is suspended atop a metal arm sprouting from his head. It is no doubt channeling a three hundred sixty degree view of the waiting room to his visor, allowing him to see everywhere at once. Before I can ponder the ramifications of this my attention is diverted by a sharp pain in my right forearm. I turn to see the receptionist holding a device that looks like a miniaturized staple gun made of the same gray plastic as the Stamen Medical Group sign out front.

"What did you do?" I ask, looking down at my arm where a drop of blood emerges from the epicenter of a small patch of red skin.

"I provided you with a subdermal microchip implant." She says as she returns the implanter device to her desk drawer. "It will store all the relevant data concerning you for easy access by your care team if it works." Before I can ask for further elaboration a middle aged woman with black hair in a long braid and purple nail polish emerges from behind the steel doors to collect me. She identifies herself as Melissa Hogg MD MS and tells me she's here to deliver me to the Emergency Room. I follow her back to the steel doors, which open only after she has undergone a retinal scan, voiceprint analysis, and handprint reading.

Inside, the network of desks at the center of the emergency room has come to more resemble a web of elaborately integrated electronics, colossal server racks whose wires form a sprawling multihued arterial network of data while too many lights to count twinkle inscrutably. Medical professionals toil in the shadows of these towering servers, their heads outfitted with visors and antennae similar to those I saw on the woman womanning the intake desk. I can see objects embedded on the inside of their right forearms in the same place where the receptionist gave me my implant, though in contrast to the tiny microchip I received theirs is a byzantine array of circuitry, wires, and lights so large it protrudes from their flesh several inches, there is one petite woman whose implant is so large it's almost as big as her arm, which dangles heavily from her shoulder.

Melissa Hogg MD MS guides me into an enclosed patient room. I disrobe and put on the medical gown and lie atop the bed with a great deal of pain and difficulty. The bed moves in response, its smart mattress attempting to mold itself to the contours of my body, which causes further pain. She scans my microchip implant with a plastic gun seemingly designed for such such a purpose, inserts a needle in my arm connected to an intravenous drip, and asks me to rate my pain on a scale of one to ten. I say ten. She scans my microchip again, soberly regards the screen readout, then leaves. I never see her again.

A television hangs over the door, one so large I had to duck while entering the room lest I hit my head on it. It displays a talk show where the middle aged host is screaming at someone who has accumulated too much credit card debt. I look around for a remote control to turn it off, but find none. I idly scratch at the patch of irritated skin where I was chipped and the television suddenly changes channels. I find that by applying varying degrees of pressure on various points on and around the chipped region I can adjust the contrast, color saturation, motion smoothing, HDR, brightness, backlighting, sharpness, and color temperature of the television. I can do everything except turn it off, though I find that by continually applying pressure to the chipped area for sixty seconds I can return the television to its original factory settings, which is effectively the same thing.

After waiting a long time a balding man with a slightly askew nose named Philip A. Theodoropoulos MD FACS comes to my room. He takes blood samples, tissue samples, saliva samples, hair samples, swabs my mouth and nose and ears, then takes the samples and leaves. I never see him again.

I wait longer. I wait even longer. Then I wait even longer than that.

A woman with brown hair streaked with gray cinched back in a tight bun enters the room, identifies herself as Rebecca Williams Dodick APN CMP. She activates the electric motor powering the wheels of the bed I occupy and gently guides it through the hospital via an app on her phone. The paintings adorning the walls are gone, replaced with screens showing calming videos such as aquariums and gently scrolling drone footage of natural landscapes and exotic wild animals behaving themselves. The corridors are far more elaborate and labyrinthine than I remember, and when we pass by windows I find the landscape they frame has shifted in dramatic ways that make me wonder how the exterior of a single set of adjacent buildings could possibly be so diverse.

We enter an elevator with a rounded cylindrical shape, being inside it feels like inhabiting a large capsule. There are no buttons, Doctor Dodick operates it with her phone. I feel the elevator car go up, then down, then side to side multiple times, When the door opens I am completely disoriented. She guides my bed down the hall and into a room with a large machine in it that appears to consist of a mirror and a metronome and a camera and many other things. I ask what it is.

Doctor Dodick tells me it is the Dynamizer Machine, the latest in the pioneering field of Radionics. Healthy people, she elaborates, emit healthy radio signals, which are called Electronic Reactions of Abrams, or E.R.A. By the same principle unhealthy people emit unhealthy radio signals. This can be corrected with the use of machines to manipulate E.R.A.s, devices such as the Radioclast which detects Ohmage or Dullness in Areas of Resonance, an Oscilloclast, or a Hieronymus Machine which detects Eloptic Energy and can also be used for agricultural purposes like pest removal, though we here at Stamen Medical Group use the classic Albert Abrams Dynamizer. She tells me to face west so she can take a hair sample, which will be used to calibrate the device. She then guides my bed over to the Dynamizer and activates it. It doesn't seem to do anything, but Doctor Dodick assures me it is recalibrating my E.R.A.s to a more healthy frequency. This goes on for several minutes, then Doctor Dodick returns me to my room. I never see her again.

After an extremely long amount of time passes nothing happens so I wait for another extremely long amount of time after which nothing happens so I wait for another amount of extremely long time and a doctor comes and identifies himself as David J. Winchester MD FACS and asks how I'm doing. I tell him I am in horrific pain.

"Uh-huh." He says, and tells me it's time for me to go away now. This does not strike me as an adequate response to my condition. I tell him that my situation is dire, that my sickness has taken over my life, that being sick has essentially become my job at this point; however, unlike my normal job, being sick occupies my every waking and sleeping moment, it has inhibited or destroyed my capacity to be a worker to my employer, a boyfriend to my boyfriend, an owner to my dog, a payer of my mortgage, a watcher of reality television shows where people who have had too much cosmetic surgery look into cameras and cry but since they can no longer move their face it appears as if they are having a petit mal seizure. "None of that is a problem." David J. Winchester MD FACS replies. "We here at Stamen Medical Group have accounted for this eventuality." Doctor Winchester makes a beckoning gesture and a person who looks exactly like me enters the room, though he is fully dressed whereas I am wearing a large rag. "This is the clone we created from the many blood and tissue samples we took from your body. We call him Jongladd-2 in order to distinguish him from you. Say hello, Jongladd-2." He says hello to me in my voice. "We here at Stamen Medical Group appreciate just how problematic bearing the hideous burden of your own continued existence can be. Therefore we have created Jongladd-2 here to fulfill the various obligations you, in your current state of convalescent infirmity, are no longer capable of fulfilling. Jongladd-2 is endowed with your memories and is capable of doing everything you were once capable of doing when you were healthy. He will perform said duties while you are occupied with your recovery, keeping your life warm for you until you are healthy once more, at which point he will be discarded as medical waste."

Doctor Winchester writes me another prescription and sends me home with my clone. Jongladd-2 fills my role admirably. I take my medicine as directed. I do not get better. When I announce my intention to return to the hospital Jongladd-2 tells me he hasn't been feeling well either and asks if he can accompany me. I oblige, of course.

The hospital now consists of multiple geodesic domes, what one might call Buckyballs after their creator, the architect and futurist Buckminster Fuller. The domes appear to bud off from one another like coral or so many dividing cells, each spherical bulge buttressed by an elaborate latticework of interlocking triangles.

Jongladd-2 and I enter the Emergency Room waiting room. The lenses of the receptionist's artificial eyes swivel to focus on us. The light implanted in her forehead flashes twice to perform twin facial recognition scans to identify us. "Error." The speaker where her mouth once was proclaims. "False positive in facial recognition scan. Database maintenance required."

"It's not an error." I say. "He's my clone. We're identical."

"Error." She repeats. "Error code: Lava Sandwich. Please contact an administrator." The lamp on the receptionist's head begins flashing again and again like a strobe light as it struggles to get a reading it can comprehend. The security guard begins approaching us, plastic handcuffs appearing in his hands thanks to the automatic dispensers installed on his forearms.

Jongladd-2's nose falls off. The light on the receptionist's head stops flashing as our faces become distinct from one another. The security guard throws the plastic handcuffs in a nearby trash can and returns to his usual post. The receptionist asks us our names.

"Jon Gladd."

"Jongladd-2."

The receptionist asks our date of birth.

"Twelve three ninety eight."

"Two and a half days ago."

After waiting we are both led into the Emergency Room by a woman whose feet have been replaced with self-balancing hoverboards so she glides instead of walks. Inside the server racks are gone, replaced with medical professionals lying in repose on complex chairs with such elaborately integrated electronic devices plugged into so many sockets implanted int heir bodies it's impossible to tell where the medical professional ends and the device begins. The lofty curves of the hospital's geodesic sphere and the thoughtful way light is channeled through the triangular honeycombs of glass and steel imbues the space with a certain solemnity, a reverence not unlike that of a cathedral or mosque. Jongladd-2's left ear peels off his head so it dangles by its lobe like an earring without an ear. We're led into separate patient rooms. One of the walls of my room consists of a screen where a talk show host is admonishing a very fat person for being too fat.

Eventually a white plastic orb floating in midair arrives. A human face appears on what I realize is an LED screen covering the entire sphere. He identifies himself as John G. Linn MD through tinny speakers. He asks what's wrong. I tell him I am in horrific pain and ask what's happening to Jongladd-2. There is no doctor-patient confidentiality between myself and my clone since we are legally as well as factually the same person, and he tells me Jongladd-2 has leprosy. I ask him if that is unusual. He says no, people in hospitals having diseases is in fact quite common, and guides my likewise hovering bed to a treatment room.

"Behold the miracle of electricity!" Declares the doctorb. Mechanical arms sprout from his spherical body and he retrieves what he identifies as Pulvermacher's Chain, a zinc and copper belt soaked in vinegar. He wraps several electric belts around my waist, arms, legs, and neck. He then fits me with an electric corset, and brushes my hair with an electric brush. I feel a slight tingling sensation and several of my muscles spasm involuntarily. The doctorb tells me that men normally have a finite supply of semen, however the glands can be stimulated to replenish the supply with the proper application of electrotherapy.

My nerves still quaking, I follow the doctorb into a room labeled PHOTOTHERAPY. Inside the entire room is blue. I am instructed to sit in a blue chair while massive blue bulbs bathe me with blue light. The doctorb, who is white but now appears blue, says "Color therapy restores the human Radio-Active and Raidio-Emanative Equilibrium by attuning the color waves to their proper frequency, alleviating many ailments such as scurvy, constipation, and brain fog." After bathing me in blue light for a time, the doctorb leads me to a different part of the phototherapy area and applies the light of Dinshah Ghadiali's Spectro-Chrome Box, which, as the name implies, is a box that emanates light the user can tune by filtering it through different glass panes of various colors. The doctorb then applies light from a Von Schilling Surgical ray which is literally a lens of colored glass on a stick, then applies a Radiolux Violet Ray device, which is a black device with a phallic shape and long electrical cord wrapped in braided fiber that emits no visible light, violet or otherwise.

My treatment complete, the doctorb guides me back to my room, where I find two intact versions of myself awaiting my arrival.

"These fine specimens" The doctorb explains. "are Jongladd-3 and Jongladd-4. They will be living your life for you until Jongladd-2 is back in one piece, or at least less than three. By equipping you with two clones instead of one, we at Stamen Medical Group have in effect cut the failure points of our system in half, so even if one of the Jongladds should become unable to execute the duties of his office, another will be present to fill his vacated role." I am sent back home with the two new clones. Within days both are afflicted with severe, debilitating illnesses.

Jongladd-3 amputates both his legs with a hacksaw, a symptom of Body Integrity Identity Disorder, an illness where the afflicted party is seized with an overwhelming compulsion to be disabled. Fortunately he is whisked away to the hospital before he can manage to blind himself. I receive a call from my supervisor.

"I'm afraid we're going to have to let you go, Jon."

"Why?" I ask.

"You have behaved in a manner that does not reflect the values of Yum! Brands or its affiliate subsidiaries."

"What does that mean?"

"You sawed your legs off in your cubicle, which is unsanitary, not to mention a gross misuse of the company hacksaw."

"That wasn't me, it was a clone of me, though that's irrelevant. He has Body Integrity Identity Disorder and isn't responsible for his actions. Firing him on the basis of behavior he can't control due to an illness is a violation of the Americans With Disabilities Act of 1990."

"That would be true if Yum! Brands was legally incorporated in the United States of America, which it is not."

"Where is it incorporated?"

"It cannot be pronounced by your human tongue. Suffice to say it inhabits a realm of quantum uncertainty that can only be described by imaginary numbers, which are a real thing."

We exchange a few parting niceties and end the call. It only later occurs to me that the person on the phone had a voice not unlike mine.

I fill the various prescriptions the doctorb gave me, all of which seek to harness the healing powers of radium, number 88 on the periodic table. I acquire a Revigator, a Radium Emanator, thirty Soothol Radium Bougies, a Radiendocrinator, and thirty Vita Radium Suppositories, which contain radium mixed in a cocoa butter base. The Revigator is a ceramic pitcher lined with radium that renders the water in it radioactive. The Radiendocrinator is a small metal slab containing seven pieces of blotter paper soaked in radium. It comes with an elastic harness that allows me to strap it to my testicles, along with the directive that I am to leave it on overnight so it can work its healing power on my endocrine system. The Radium Emanator is a device about ten inches tall consisting of five interlinked discs made of cement and radium, so sized as to fit inside an average glass of water. Allow to soak overnight, then drink as needed. I soon discover my urine glows in the dark. Presumably my ejaculate would also glow in the dark if I were healthy enough to have sex with my boyfriend, which I am not.

Jongladd-4 acquires Morgellon's Disease and breaks out in skin lesions. It is a controversial disorder where the sufferer is gripped with the certainty that their skin is infested with small alien objects such as bugs or tiny strings. Many doctors believe that Morgellon's Disease has no physical cause but is psychosomatic in origin, the manifestation of some underlying psychological ailment that could be anything from obsessive compulsive disorder to group hysteria. Whatever its origin the distress is very real and Jongladd-4, having scratched off an alarming amount of skin, determines to go to the hospital. My ailment hasn't improved either, so I elect to go with him.

The hospital now resembles a colossal silver saucer hovering about twenty meters above the ground, which is convenient insofar as it frees up a great deal of space for parking that I can't use because the machine barring the entrance can't read the chip in my arm. Jongladd-4 obligingly agrees to drive in circles for the duration of my hospital visit, saying he feels a strange affinity for the massive floating chrome spheroid and wishes to delve into it further from the safety and comfort of his/my automobile.

There is no visible entrance to the gargantuan structure, but as I stagger towards it under the colossal burden of my horrific pain a small part of it detaches on its own, solid metal seemingly liquefying in midair like a stream of oozing mercury that then, upon touching the ground, reforms itself into a set of stairs that transform into an ascending escalator the moment I stand upon them, bearing me up into the Emergency Room's waiting room. As I approach the reception area I notice that the sign saying PHYSICAL OR VERBAL ABUSE OF STAFF WILL NOT BE TOLERATED has been replaced by a sign that says TAKING STAFF'S NAME IN VAIN SHALL NOT BE TOLERATED.

I approach the receptionist. It takes me a while since about a quarter of his body is gone and another quarter is covered with bulbous, disfiguring granulomas, but I eventually recognize him as Jongladd-2.

"How are you doing?" He asks.

"I am in horrific pain." I tell him. "How are you doing?" He either shrugs or twitches involuntarily, I can't tell. He types on his computer with astonishing speed for someone with only four and a half fingers, having gotten his hunt and peck style down to a science. Eventually a hovering silver disk that looks like a smaller version of the hospital I am currently inside comes to collect me. A compartment in it slides open and launches a wireless earbud at me that bounces off my chest and onto the floor. Bending down to retrieve it is an odyssey of suffering in my current state, and by the time I've inserted it into my ear and managed to straighten back up the silver saucer is gliding past the steel entrance doors to the Emergency Room. I hobble after it, managing to get inside just before they close.

"Hello?" I say, tapping the earbud. "Can you hear me?"

"-omitted to providing you the highest quality care available in this best of all possible worlds. At Stamen Medical Group our polite and helpful staff is-" I realize what I'm listening to is a recording. I follow the saucer drone past the technological center of the emergency room. Gone are the medical professionals, at least in any form I can recognize, replaced by another hovering metal saucer, this one about the size of two school buses parked next to one another. I reach my assigned room. A disembodied voice interrupts the recording and tells me to disrobe and lie on the bed, by which I can only assume they mean the bed-sized hovering metal saucer. I comply, donning a medial gown that is a gown in the truest sense of the word, a diaphanous silver negligee that would hug my body in all the right places if there were any right places on my body to hug. There is still a screen taking up the entirety of the room's far wall, however instead of a talk show it displays an a intense, high concept serialized drama about the exceptional care provided by Stamen Medical Group. Major characters are regularly and unceremoniously killed off, though they are always found to not be entirely dead and are brought back to full health by a team of extremely attractive doctors, who then go have sex with each other.

Eventually a human comes to my room, another clone of me that introduces himself, with spectacular difficulty, as Jongladd-36.

Jongladd-36 apologizes for his profound awkwardness and tells me he is afflicted with Taijin Kyofusho Disorder, which is an overwhelming fear of embarrassing others with one's presence.

"I'm sorry if I smell so horrible you can barely tolerate it." Jongladd-36 says.

"You smell fine to me." I tell him.

"I'm sorry if I'm hideously ugly to look upon."

"I'm admittedly biased since you look exactly like me, but I think your appearance is totally acceptable."

"I'm sorry if my voice sounds like a hideous atonal screech."

"While it is strange to hear my voice coming out of someone else, an effect akin to listening to a recording of one's own voice only moreso, listening to you speak is not offensive in any way."

"I'm sorry if-"

"You're fine, okay? There's nothing unpleasant about you, your presence here is in no way offensive."

"I'm sorry if my constant need for reassurance is galling."

"I accept your apology."

"Thank you."

Jongladd-36 puts on his burqa and guides my bed down the various hallways. We pass another room containing Jongladd-4 who, from the snippets of conversation I overhear, does not want the broken bones he received in his car crash treated right now, the far more pressing issue is the swarm of foreign objects infesting his skin.

Beyond a door labeled HYDROTHERAPY I am relieved of my gossamer gown and wrapped in a sheet soaked in cold water. I am placed below a device called a Dripping Machine that pummels my head with a slow but steady stream of large, singular water droplets. I am then placed in an extremely hot bath covered with a taught rubber sheet from which only my head protrudes so my entire body is submerged, and made to drink thirty glasses of oxygenated water. I then take take a long, cold, pressurized shower, after which I am told to put my medical gown back on. At some point Jongladd-36 leaves, proving unable to bear what he perceives to be my hidden revulsion at his presence.

A woman who looks like me if I was a woman arrives and identifies herself as Jangladd-8. I fall down in the process of attempting to get back on the gurney. She laughs, then collapses to the floor herself. Having lost almost all muscle strength in her neck, face and jaw, it takes Jangladd-8 some time to communicate that she is afflicted with fits of Cataplexy, a sudden but transient episode of muscle weakness typically triggered by autonomic emotional responses such as crying and laughing. Jangladd-8 slurs a request for assistance into the metal device installed on her wrist and after a long period of both of us lying together on the cold, wet floor another woman arrives.

She identifies herself as Jangladd-13, holds up her hands, and apologies in advance for her severely limited ability to help us. She tells us she has Dupuytren's Contracture, which is a condition in which one or more fingers become permanently bent in a flexed position. She tells us each of her fingers is at one of the four increasingly paralyzing stages of the disease, limiting her mobility. Still, with a great deal of effort, Jangladd-13 is eventually able to get both of us onto gurneys. Jangladd-8 is whisked away in one direction while Jangladd-13 guides me in another, conveying me to a part of the hospital designated CAUTERY AND BLISTERING.

Jangladd-8 retrieves an object that, at least to me, looks like a large, poorly made nail. She identifies it as Saint Hubert's Key, heats the head of the object until it's red hot in a nearby brazier, and proceeds to apply it to various parts of my body. She makes an incision in my forehead, sews in threads that she identifies as being from the clothes of Saint Hubert himself, then covers my forehead with a black cloth. She pierces the back of my neck with a needle and flosses a length of thread coated with resin-based salve back and forth through the wound while telling me this is an excellent treatment for sunstroke, lovesickness, and werewolfism. She then applies Canthardin to various sections of my body, a substance consisting of liquid harvested from blister beetles mixed with wax and lard. It raises large colonies of blisters on my skin that she regards with approval, telling me that these treatments will attract the diseased elements of my body away from the affected area.

She only manages to accomplish all this with great difficulty, though given the paralysis afflicting her fingers, it's amazing she can administer any healing treatment at all.

"Can you give me something for the pain?" I ask.

"Certainly." She moistens what she identifies as a Soporific Sponge, a sponge soaked in mandrake, henbane, hemlock, and opium. She holds it to my nose. I nearly pass out, though that may just be due to the terrible smell.

A man arrives and identifies himself as Jongladd-27. He wheels my gurney down the hall, regularly crashing it in one way or another. He apologizes profusely each time and haltingly informs me that he has Spasmodic Torticollis, an extremely painful disorder causing his neck to violently, involuntarily jerk in multiple directions, Torticollis propels his head to the side making him push the gurney into a wall, Laterocollis causes him to jerk his head laterally so he tips the gurney over to the left or right, Retrocollis causes his head to snap back causing him to flip the gurney up and over, and Anterocollis jerks his head down, making him push down on the gurney making it flip over in the opposite direction. Jongladd-27 soldiers on valiantly, righting the gurney each time so we eventually make it to the treatment room.

Jongladd-27 tells me about Animal Magnetism (also known as Lebensmagnetismus) identified by Franz Mesmer, an invisible natural force that animates all life including humans, animals, and vegetables. He produces a glass bottle of what he identifies as Universal Fluid and holds it to various parts of my body as he tells me health and disease are determined by how well the invisible force of Animal Magnetism is flowing through one's body. By holding this bottle to my flesh he can calibrate- His head jerks savagely to the side, causing him to slam the bottle of healing Universal Fluid against my head where it shatters, raking jagged glass shards across my face.

"Oh Doc, I'm sorry." He says, and injects me with some brandy to promote clotting.

I am discharged and, noting the wreckage of my car where Jongladd-4 crashed it into a Chipotle resulting in a tragic loss of human life and queso, call an Uber. A Prius arrives. It is driven by a man who identifies himself as Jongladd-69 with a hearty guffaw. I get in with a great amount of difficulty and pain. Jongladd-69 asks me to describe our surroundings and to tell him when it's safe to pull out into traffic. When I ask what's wrong he tells me he's blind, but not to worry, it's only for the moment.

"I have statokinetic dissociation of homonymous hemianopsia, also known as Riddoch Syndrome, which is a kind of visual impairment where I can only see moving objects. Don't worry, once we get rolling all will be revealed."

"What about stop signs and stoplights?" I ask.

"I can usually manage to slow down without stopping completely. The only problem is picking people up, they tend to really want me to come to a full and complete stop, even just going one or two miles per hour is too much for them, it's whack."

'Whack?' I think. I'm not the kind of person who calls things Whack, irrespective of how Whack the thing in question may or may not be, and find myself wondering just how divergent from me these clones are becoming as I tell Jongladd-69 to go left now, no, now, wait, now.

Several minor accidents later I arrive at the pharmacy where I redeem my latest prescription. The pharmacist identifies herself as Jangladd-420 with a hearty guffaw. Her hips are twisted violently out of alignment with her shoulders, a state of affairs she attributes to scoliosis, a condition where one's spine assumes a sideways curve, and she retrieves my medicine with a great deal of pain and difficulty.

My latest outpatient treatment seeks to harness the healing powers of strychnine and gold. The strychnine is derived from seeds of the Nux Vomica tree and administered via enema. The gold comes in the form of Aqua Regia, which is gold dissolved in a mix of nitric and hydrochloric acid to produce Gold Chloride that can be drunk with water, also known as Aurum Potable. Imbibing it is said to induce a state of Cordiality, a sort of warming of the heart. The medicine also takes the form of Fulminating Gold, a substance that can explode if moved, touched, or exposed to light, and does.

I arrive home and my boyfriend insists that I to do something about Jongladd-183, who was sent here to perform the romantic duties I could no longer fulfill due to my infirmity but has since locked himself in the bathroom and refuses to come out. I knock on the door and Jongladd-183 screams symptoms at me that are consistent with Furious Rabies, including hyperactivity, hypersalivation, and hydrophobia. I wonder if anyone at Stamen Medical Group is bothering to vaccinate these clones as I phone the police.

Two officers arrive and identify themselves as officer Jangladd-236 and Jongladd-390. Jangladd-236 immediately begins eating our couch, specifically the artificial foam substance contained within the cushions. Jongladd-390 apologies for his partner saying she has Pica (pronounced PIKE-AH to distinguish it from the chu of the same name) which is an uncontrollable appetite for objects that aren't food. Despite not currently eating a couch Jongladd-390 appears to be in far worse shape than his partner, looking pale, haggard, and drawn, his cheeks sunken, his eyes far away and blank, his skin hanging loose from his skeleton. I ask what's wrong and he says he's fine, he's just going through a bout of Fatal Insomnia, which is exactly what it sounds like, though not to worry, he's undergoing regular treatments where the grease derived from an ass' ear is applied to his temples, and will be cured forthwith.

The police eventually manage to take the rabid Jongladd-183 away. Jangladd-236 leaves in her police cruiser, taking half of our couch with her so she has something to snack on while waiting for Jongladd-183 to be processed. Jongladd-390 says he needs to rest for a moment and lies down on the remaining half of our couch, his eyes wide open, his body tense.

My boyfriend asks me which Jongladd clone I am.

"I'm not a clone, I'm Jon Gladd, the original, the man you fell in love with back when I was healthy." His brow furrows in that cute way I like while he regards me with a pointed suspicion I do not like.

"How can I be sure you're the original? I thought that other you was the original, then he started screaming and bit our dog, we're lucky his vaccinations are up to date. Even if you are the man I fell in love with, you appear to be exactly the same as the other, rabid you was. I can't disassociate the two of you."

"That's not my fault." I protest.

"Being sick isn't your fault, but it is your responsibility. Why aren't you getting better?" I'm forced to tell him I don't know why, I've been sick before many times and gotten better many times, I don't know what's different this time, I don't know what failure I've committed to bring about this state of affairs. "How can I trust you if you can't trust your own body? What are you if not your body? And don't try to placate me by spouting some Cartesian Dualism crap, my last boyfriend tried that and it ended badly for both of us."

I tell him I don't have an answer for him except to say that I think he's being unfair, it's unfair to demand reasons from me in relation to disease, a condition among whose defining traits is that it needs no reasons, appearing out of nowhere and persisting of its own accord just as the life it sabotages did. I did not chose to be sick any more than I chose to be born. Existence was forced upon me before I was capable of any kind of informed consent. I was very young when I was born, violently discharged from my mother's vagina via a series of crushing peristaltic contractions propelling me inexorably forward into a cold bright reality while screaming hysterically all the while, my protestations passing unacknowledged. By the time the full consequences of being alive dawned on me I'd grown too afraid of death to remediate the situation.

"Please," I entreat him. "just stay with me a little longer. Disease is by its very nature transient, if it was permanent it would be called something different, foreverhurt or some such term. I am seeking help from professionals, I am scrupulously following their orders, things cannot remain as they are, it is in their nature to change, how can it not be change for the better with my endeavoring so mightily to become well?" My boyfriend agrees to stay with me. We watch a reality television show where a dozen Jongladds attempt to win the romantic favor of one Jangladd, Jangladd-485. Jangladd-485 has Anton-Babinski Syndrome, an illness where the sufferer is blind, yet absolutely convinced they can see. The show mostly consists of the Jongladds struggling to accommodate her as she strides confidently through a world that exists solely in her mind. The Jongladds who tell her she's blind are voted off the show. The winner proposes marriage to her on a high cliff. She says yes, then they walk off the edge hand in hand, their bodies dashed on the rocks below while romantic music swells, followed by a commercial for pretzels. A Jangladd who can't open her mouth due to Lockjaw resulting from a Tetanus infection holds up a sign saying that while she is physically incapable of eating the pretzels or saying anything about them, the good people of Snyder's of Hanover have assured her they are, in fact, delicious.

I don't get better. I go back to the hospital.

There is nothing on the ground but a humble, medium-sized circular building resembling a large white life preserver encircling a vertical tube consisting of steel and carbon fiber nanotubes that rises up into the sky, growing ever more distant until it vanishes entirely. I step inside. A perky Jangladd who's had half her body paralyzed by a series of violent strokes slurs an explanation, telling me this is a space elevator that will bear me aloft to the hospital, which is situated at one of five Lagrange Points in the space around Earth. The elevator's cab travels at three hundred kilometers per hour, and it takes me five days to reach the hospital in orbit.

The entire space station is surrounded by a meter thick layer of water in order to shield the occupants from harmful cosmic rays, and while there are many windows looking out into space, the view they present is a hazy, aqueous one that makes me feel like I'm in some kind of bizarre space aquarium.

I reach the Emergency Room waiting room and notice the sign saying TAKING STAFF'S NAME IN VAIN SHALL NOT BE TOLERATED has been replaced with a new sign saying OUR STAFF IS A JEALOUS STAFF AND THOU SHALT HAVE NO OTHER STAFF BEFORE OUR STAFF. I approach the intake desk. I presume the person behind it is Jongladd-2, though it's impossible to tell for certain when nothing of him remains but a brain attached to multiple electrodes floating in a jar of yellow fluid. I ask him how he's doing. A nearby speaker informs me in a synthesized voice that he's fine, he's having doses of powdered thyroid gland extracted from pigs and cows regularly sprinkled in his jar to help him lose weight.

Jangladd-797 comes to collect me. She has Acromegaly, a condition caused by a noncancerous tumor that results in the enlargement of her hands, feet, forehead, jaw, and nose. Her movement is hindered by the intense pain in her joints, and it's relatively easy to keep up with her despite my own horrific pain as she beckons me beyond the steel doors leading to the Emergency Room entrance in her exceptionally deep voice.

Inside the Emergency Room data processing area it seems everything that was once solid has undergone some sort of liquification. Fluids so richly colored and radiant they look like liquid jewels stream through transparent pipe networks whose complexity is so baffling it seems like it could be the circulatory system extracted from a god. Each liquid sports radiant tributaries of endlessly forking electric current as calculations of unfathomable complexity are executed in a computational symphony of unerring majesty.

"Which Jongladd are you?" Jangladd-797 asks.

"I'm not a clone." I say. "I'm the original Jon Gladd."

"Yeah, sure, you're Jongladd Prime." Jangladd-797 responds sarcastically. "And I'm Doc. This way please." She leads me to my room. As I enter she pulls a lever and a stream of viscous green liquid is dumped out of the ceiling onto me. Moving on its own, the green liquid—which I belatedly realize is in fact a kind of living, quasi-sentient slime mold— removes my clothes, folds them neatly and deposits them in the plastic bag provided. The slime mold provides a makeshift hospital gown by veiling my body in a thin layer of itself, then slides onto the floor while bearing up my supine form so it functions as a hospital gurney.

Jangladd-797 leaves. Eventually a man arrives and identifies himself as Jongladd-892.

"What seems to be the problem today?" He asks.

"I am in horrific pain."

"I am in horrific pain. I'm sorry to hear that, we'll see what we can do about it."

"Are you a Doctor?"

"Are you a Doctor? No, but I do pride myself on being one of the Doctors' Earthly representatives, or I would be if we were on Earth, which we are not. By the way, do you like the artificial gravity?"

"It's okay."

"It's okay."

"Why are you repeating everything I say?" I ask.

"Why are you repeating everything I say? I have Echolalia, which is the involuntary repetition of another person's vocalizations."

"I'm sorry, that must be difficult."

"I'm sorry, that must be difficult. I appreciate your concern, unwarranted as it may be. Please direct your attention to the mass of rotting tissue currently jutting out from my head."

"I thought that was a tumor."

"I thought that was a tumor. You thought wrong, it's a mass of pickled ox brain. This treatment, along with the regular deflowering of virgins and a few other feats of curative ingenuity passed down from the Doctors themselves, will soon have me restored to full health. Now let's see if we can't do the same for you." Urged into motion with shocks delivered from an electric prod wielded by Jongladd-892, the slime mold jerks forward and scuttles down the hall.

On the way we pass dozens of rooms containing Jongladds and Jangladds being treated by other Jongladds and Jangladds. None of the rooms have doors of any kind, there is no need to attempt to maintain any sort of confidentality anymore since everyone is now everyone else, and with each room we pass a brief snippet of conversation can be heard, which Jongladd-892 repeats verbatim.

"Auric fever resulting in profuse salvation and urination preventing the effective operation of glycine a chemical that sends nerve signals to muscles causing spasms that kill through asphyxiation or exhaustion incinerate hemorrhoids apoplexy malaise melancholia hysteria due to wandering uterus treatable by regular sexual penetration with a penis sanctioned by a religiously and legally binding marriage ceremony poisoning treated with various alexipharmics a bezoar or mithridate a mix of iris, cardamom, anise, frankincense, myrrh, ginger, and saffron or a pearl soaked in malt and serpent's gall or honeycomb and pumice stone or a theriac also known as Venetian treacle or we could just rub you with a unicorn horn suffering from nephroptosis meaning your kidneys are misplaced somewhere in your body heal your eyes with galvanic spectacles the miracle of electric eyeglasses cancer is caused by bacteria fortunately the Rife Frequency Generator can re-tune the auras of microbes we can also tie a dead puppy to the affected area or smear crab ashes on it with a feather that cleft lip will be mended easily by this image of Saint Michael licked by the king's very own horse skin infection rub with the hand of a hanged man blood from gladiators called Elixir Vitae we can fix that wound by applying this salve to the weapon that caused it or a reasonable facsimile thereof baldness remedied by some blood harvested from children mixed with sugar that's distilled over hot water then dried and snorted tissue harvested from the corpse of someone with red hair chopped and mixed with myrrh and aloe then mashed in wine and cured a good measure of Man's Grease also known as Poor Sinner's Fat also known as Hangman's Salve makes a decent love potion childbirth pains alleviated by tanned human skin wrapped around the belly, also worn about the neck to prevent hysterical passions and goiters human bone marrow to treat cramps human gallbladder to remedy deafness human heart to alleviate epilepsy a good battery of brain pills or wine drunk directly from the skull some moss from a skull will clear up that nosebleed some spirit of skull to stop those nervous fits Mumia essence of mummy we call it The Sovereign Remedy good for plague snake bites or spitting up blood implanting some baboon testicles in your scrotum will relieve that impotence and stop aging in its tracks an injection of dog and guinea pig testicles also good to carry some beaver testicles to ward off plague some Rectal Dilators will halt that bad breath okay Jongladd-whatever-your-number, we're here."

"I'm not a clone, I'm the original, Jongladd Prime."

"I'm not a clone, I'm the original, Jongladd Prime. Hear how ridiculous you sound? You should, we sound exactly the same." The slime mold bears me into an area labeled CLYSTER and straps me onto what Jongladd-892 identifies as a West Gravitiser Table. The table rotates so my body is poised at a forty five degree angle, head down, ass up.

"What's going on?" I ask.

"What's going on? Yours is a classic case of Autointoxication. You have an unhealthy buildup of Ptomaines, the chemicals that produce putrescent smells. All byproducts of digestion are poisonous and must be purged, just think of me as Stalin and the contents of your colon as a mass of ideologically imperfect apparatchiks." He inserts a tube into my rectum and pumps in a mix of herbs and milk. The contents are allowed to sit for a few minutes, then he rotates the West Gravitiser Table ninety degrees in the opposite direction so I am now head up, ass down, and the contents are vacated. He then repeats the process with molasses, then turpentine, then honey, then yogurt, then beer, then soup, then wine, then oil. "This will also alleviate dropsy, hernias, and sluggishness." Done with liquids, he proceeds to fill me with tobacco smoke, which he says is a surefire cure for drowning, which is good, since I feel like I've been doing that for some time. By the time the slime mold picks me back up and commences bearing me through the space hospital in response to further electric prodding from Jongladd-892, it feels strange to be making physical contact with a liquid that is not being dumped in or out of my lower gastrointestinal tract.

I'm led beyond a door labeled Trepanation. The slime mold assumes the form of chair and part of it encircles my brow and temples in a firm embrace.

"What now?" I ask.

"What now?" The voice comes from behind me and is followed by the sort of loud, high pitched wine I associate with drills. "Many disorders are caused by a stone in the brain." A trephane begins sawing into my head. "Fortunately this can be alleviated with a process we like to call Cutting The Stone." There's a clatter as what I presume to be a significant portion of my skull falls to the floor. "While I'm in here I'll also get in a Leucotomy, a Lobotomy, and a hearty injection of ethanol, just to be on the safe side."

"How does destroying my brain fix my brain?"

"How does destroying my brain fix my brain? I'm just clearing out the bad parts."

"What if it's all bad parts?"

"What if it's all bad parts? Sometimes you have to destroy the village to save it."

"Did a doctor approve this treatment?"

"Did a Doctor approve this treatment? Jongladd Prime—if that's truly what you insist on being called—your question wounds me. We always act in accordance with the commandments passed down from the Doctors, however mysterious their ways or inscrutable their will."

"Will any of this actually help me?"

"Will any of this actually help me?"

"Well?"

"Well?"

"Say something."

"Say something."

"Say something that isn't just repeating me."

"Say something that isn't just repeating me."

"I'm a big fat jerk and I'm ugly too."

"I'm afraid I can't help you with that. I'm cured!"

"Congratulations!

"Congratulations! Damn."

During the five days it takes for the space elevator to descend back to the Earth I watch a staged production of a jukebox musical called Doctor Rock Thyself! which features songs such as The Beatles' Doctor Robert and Mötley Crüe's Doctor Feelgood along with songs by Doctor Dre as well as songs from the musical Cats with the word 'cat' replaced by 'doctor'.

It was spring when I arrived. Now as I stagger out of the hospital the sun is a low, pale shade haunting a dim recess of the sky, everything is coated with several inches of snow, and the wind is cold on my exposed brain. I don't remember how to operate my phone or where I live, so I set off in a random direction, moving at a slow hobble that's the best I can manage in my current state of horrific pain.

Never before have I felt so extremely tethered to, and simultaneously alienated from, my own body. I imagine what astronauts must feel when they realize their ship is going to burn up on reentry, the looming awareness that some flaw has doomed the vessel meant to bear them safely through the void, transforming it into a thing that betrays and annihilates them even as it remains the only thing they can possibly inhabit, that they can ever hope to sustain their infinitely fragile lives.

I watch as a Jongladd waiting for the bus collapses to the ground. His whole body violently contorts, bending into an arced 'U' shape indicating that he has Trismus Opisthotonos, a state of severe hyperextention caused by muscle spasms symptomatic of a tetanus infection. A staccato series of cracks and pops issue from his body as bones break and joints separate, his figure distending ever further like an overstretched bow until it seems like he might split in half.

An ambulance eventually arrives. Two uniformed Jangladds and a Jongladd exit the vehicle and immediately collapse to the ground in similar violently contorted positions, a result of their Echopraxia, which is the involuntary repetition or imitation of another person's physical actions. More ambulances arrive and more medical professionals approach the scene of the emergency and more of them collapse, their bodies twisted, their features locked in a snarl of rictus tension. The cycle repeats itself until the street is choked with ambulances, the ground covered in paralyzed clones, innumerable sirens overlapping to form a wall of screeching incoherence. I hobble away, knowing that when night falls they'll all freeze to death.

I pass advertisements featuring Jongladds rubbing salve on their festering sores, Jangladds with hooks for hands, Jongladds screwed into head and neck braces, Jangladds with a significant portion of their arm surgically grafted to their face to replace a nose destroyed by syphilis, Jongladds breathing deeply the fumes of raw sewage to cure bubonic plague, skeletal Jangladds promoting the virtues of starvation diets, Jongladds with their skin sloughing off promoting escharotics, though most of all I see advertisements with Jongladds and Jangladds and the new intersexed/genderfluid Xgladds covered in leeches; leeches on their temples for headaches, leeches behind their ears for vertigo, leeches on the back of their head for lethargy, leeches on their abdomen for stomach ailments, leeches on their spleen for epilepsy, leeches on their thighs and vulva and cervix for menstrual cramps, all leech advertisements touting their leeches as Extra Virgin meaning they haven't been used on any other patients prior to you, the consumer, and there are also advertisements advertising using leeches to cure diseases caused by using used leeches.

I find a bench and sit down. Sitting down hurts just as much as standing up, but it is a slightly different kind of pain, and this tiny shred of novelty constitutes a tiny shred of relief, however fleeting.

The sun emerges from behind its veil of cloud, setting the world alight. The branch of a nearby evergreen shakes in a gust of wind, dislodging a cloud of snowflakes that form a plume of effervescent radiance as they fall, a sheet of scintillating crystalline brilliance that seems to embody the sum total all of the world's beauty for one fleeting instant before dispersing and vanishing. It is so beautiful I feel like I'm going to cry. If I wasn't sick I probably wouldn't, but I am sick, so I do.

Once I begin crying I can't stop. I soon realize that if I don't take aggressive steps to stop I'll never stop, crying is meant to express feelings, but I could cry for multiple lifetimes without expressing a fraction of the sum total of my experience.

I take the electric prod out of the complimentary goody bag I was given upon my discharge from the hospital, which also contains a mug with World's Best Patient written on it, a HOSPITAL: The Trading Card Game starter pack, and foil wrapped chocolates shaped like stethoscopes, scalpels, and consent forms. I wipe the electric prod on my shirt to clean it, and apply it to my exposed brain via the hole carved in my skull.

Zap.

I smell burnt toast.

Zap.

I have have strong opinions about tagging the value of currency to precious metals.

Zap.

I am sexually attracted to feet.

Zap.

I cry a little less.

I continue zapping that point. Even with the prod at maximum power it takes a long time for the crying to ebb, and I'm eventually forced to stop when I smell burning brain, at which point I've managed to reduce the crying from a torrent to the subdued trickle of a few stoic tears, though that may just be cerebrospinal fluid leaking out my face. I prod other parts of my brain until I remember where I live, and set off home.

By the time I reach my residence night has fallen and my brain has frosted over. I don't remember how to use doors anymore, so I knock, hoping my boyfriend is home or that the Jongladd with Fatal Insomnia inhabiting the leftovers of our couch isn't dead yet. Eventually the door is opened by different Jongladd, who regards me with disdain.

"Another? We're overcrowded as it is."

"I'm not a clone, I'm the original, and this is my home." I say, pushing my way inside a room filled with Jongladds and Jangladds and Xgladds. "Why is everybody fighting?"

"We're not fighting." The Jongladd says as he slams the door. "We all have Sydenham's Chorea also known as Chorea Minor and Saint Vitus' Dance, a condition that manifests as a series of brief, semi-directed irregular movements." I look closer and see that while the movements of the Gladds aren't exactly physical attacks and could be more accurately be described as spasmodic writhing, a significant amount of their semi-directed irregular movements are manifesting as aggressive blows directed at other Gladds to the point where it seems like they're using their affliction as an excuse to violently carve out their own meager personal space.

Never before has the directive 'Stop hitting yourself.' been more urgent or apropos.

"Where's my dog?" I demand.

"You mean our dog." The Jongladd says.

"No, I mean *my* dog. Where is he?"

"Here he comes now."

A nude, hairy Jongladd encrusted with filth emerges from the kitchen and scampers toward me on all fours. He tries to jump up and lick my face. I hold him at bay with multiple jabs of my electric prod.

"This isn't my dog, this is a clone with Hypertrichosis, a condition characterized by excessive hair growth, and Severe Cynical Lycanthropy, a psychiatric delusion that involves the belief that one is an animal." The Jongladd shrugs.

"Six of one. You won't be able to tell the difference once he's housebroken."

"Where's my boyfriend?" The Jongladd sighs wearily, produces a tablet computer and begins scrolling through a spreadsheet with more entries than I can comprehend.

"Let's see... They've yet to perfect a cisgender male homosexual Jongladd. Fortunately for you there's Jangladd-29,486, a lesbian with many conventionally masculine traits who suffers from Charles Bonnet

Syndrome, a condition of partial or complete blindness comorbid with vivid hallucinations. Lately she's been seeing lots of dragons, but if you can convince her you're a female dragon you might be able to get her to have some kind of sexual intercourse with you."

"That's unconscionable for a multitude of reasons." I say. The Jongladd looks incredulous.

"We do what we have to, how can you not-" The Jongladd eyes me intently. "Perhaps you are the Jongladd Prime, a being whose moral convictions were shaped by the luxury of health."

"I told you I was." A dreamy, faraway expression flickers across the Jongladd's face.

"What's being healthy like?"

I'm forced to tell him I don't remember, and demand that he tell me where my real boyfriend is. The Jongladd looks at the spreadsheet for a long time, then summons Jongladd-34,462 to explain.

Jongladd-34,462 tells us he has Hyperthymesia, also known as Highly Superior Autobiographical Memory or Marilu Henner's Disease, a condition where he can perfectly recall every moment of his, i.e. my, life. When I ask what that has to do with my boyfriend's absence, he tells me that his Highly Superior Autobiographical Memory or HRAM for short (not to be confused 'haram', the word for something that is forbidden by Islamic law) allows Jongladd-34,462 to remember every single slight that my boyfriend has ever perpetrated against me, every forgotten anniversary, every unkind word, every imperfectly cleaned dish, every time a sneeze wasn't followed by a Doc bless you, every major and minor irritation that is endemic to cohabitation with another human being, a bottomless wellspring of minor vexations that resulted in endless resentments and recriminations spewing forth from Jongladd-34,462 until the point where our boyfriend deemed us impossible to live with and left for good.

Now I want to cry but I can't. I never will again, since neural tissue doesn't grow back. Then again, what with the brain's capacity for neuoplasticity, it's possible that the remaining intact neurons may find some way to-

I push such thoughts aside, lest they dilute my outrage.

"He wasn't *our* boyfriend, he was *mine*! You had no right to drive him away! You're a copy of me, you have my memories, how can you possibly remember things better than I can, how can you possibly retain memories I never retained?!"

Jongladd-34,462 responds by physically attacking me. Fortunately his Fibromyalgia slows him down to the point where I'm able to hold him at bay with my electric prod until three Jangladds step forward to restrain him and drag him away.

"What the hell?" I cry. Jongladd-34,462 manages to briefly free his right arm, and uses the opportunity to pull a small blue book out of his pocket and throw it at me. I'm lucky enough to have it glance off my forehead instead of striking my brain, which might have proved fatal.

"That's for two years, eight months, thirty four weeks, three days, eighteen hours, thirteen minutes, and fifty seconds of memories of your jaw making a clicking sound when you chew, you obnoxious fuck!" He yells. I don't know what to say. My jaw has never made a clicking sound when I chew, not one that I've ever heard. The other Jongladds and Jangladds and Xgladds' passions are inflamed and they begin directing their Chorea twitches at Jongladd-34,462 in one massive, coordinated group assault. At first I think they're doing it on my behalf, but from what they're yelling it soon becomes clear they're not outraged that he threw a book at me, but that he threw the book at all, waving their own copies with manic enthusiasm as they take turns striking the ball he's curled up into on the floor. I lean down and, with a great deal of pain, manage to pick the little blue book up from the floor. It is entitled Quotations From The Great Leaders, The Great Supreme Commanders, The Great Teachers, The Great Helmsmen, The Doctors. I open it up to a random page.

We must thoroughly clear away all ideas among our cadres of winning easy health through good luck, without hard and bitter struggle, without sweat and blood.

Anyone who sees only the bright side but not the difficulties cannot fight effectively for the accomplishment of the Hospital's tasks.

What is health? Health is struggle. There are difficulties and problems in those places for us to overcome and

solve. We go there to heal and struggle to overcome these difficulties. A good patient is one who is more eager to go where the difficulties are greater.

I close the little blue book and pocket it. I look up to see that all the Gladds are staring at me and whispering among themselves, generating a steady hum of utterances about how I'm THE Jongladd Prime. I try to press my way through the crowd, but someone grabs my arm. I turn to behold a version of me that is both a child and an old man. He opens his mouth, exposing toothless gums.

"Why do I have Hutchinson-Gilford Progeria?" He demands in a voice that is both wizened and naïve.

"I don't know." I say, jerking my arm away from his feeble grip. "Ask the Doctors who made you." He screws up his face, wrinkles layered upon wrinkles so his skin resembles the bark of an ancient tree. "You dare speak of the Doctors that way?"

"The Doctors are faultless!" Declares a Jangladd with pale blue skin induced by Methemoglobinemia, a disorder caused by an excess of methemoglobin in one's bloodstream.

"Yea, 'tis your sin that damn'ed us!" Slurs a Jongladd with Fields Condition, a degenerative disorder resulting in reduced articulation and muscle spasms.

"Yours is the genetic material that spawned us, yours is the affliction that taints us!" Wails a Jangladd with Ribose-5-Phosphate Isomerasedeficiency, a disorder whose symptoms include nystagmus, hyperreflexia, dysdiadochokinesia, and leukoencephalopathy. "If you hadn't allowed yourself to degenerate so much we would all be hale and hearty, in the finest fettle! Why aren't you better?"

"Why aren't you better?" Another Xgladd demands between hacking coughing fits induced by their chronic Pneumonoultramicroscopicsilicovolcanoconiosis.

"Why aren't you better?"

"Why aren't you better?"

"WHY AREN'T YOU BETTER?"

"WHY AREN'T YOU BETTER?"

WHY AREN'T YOU BETTER? WHY AREN'T YOU BETTER? WHY AREN'T YOU BETTER? WHY AREN'T YOU BETTER? WHY AREN'T YOU BETTER? WHY AREN'T YOU BETTER? WHY AREN'T YOU BETTER? WHY AREN'T YOU BETTER? WHY AREN'T YOU BETTER?

WHY AREN'T YOU BETTER? WHY AREN'T YOU BETTER? WHY AREN'T YOU BETTER? WHY AREN'T YOU BETTER? WHY AREN'T YOU BETTER? WHY AREN'T YOU BETTER? WHY AREN'T YOU BETTER? WHY AREN'T YOU BETTER? WHY AREN'T YOU BETTER?

WHY AREN'T YOU BETTER? WHY AREN'T YOU BETTER? WHY AREN'T YOU BETTER? WHY AREN'T YOU BETTER? WHY AREN'T YOU BETTER? WHY AREN'T YOU BETTER? WHY AREN'T YOU BETTER? WHY AREN'T YOU BETTER? WHY AREN'T YOU BETTER?

Malformed and mangled limbs claw at me as I struggle forward, harrowing me until I resort to using the electric prod to force my way through the endless crush of deranged mes, thrusting forward until I finally make it to the bedroom I used to share with my boyfriend, slam the door shut, and lock it behind me.

It's dark inside, and I can just barely see the outline of a lone figure rising from my bed.

"Who's there?" He switches on the bedside lamp and I recognize him as Jongladd-390 as I lurch forward.

"It's just me," I say. "Jongladd Prime."

"Oh. How are you doing?"

"I am in horrific pain." I say as I sit down on the bed next to him with an immense amount of corresponding agony. "Thanks for asking."

"Sure." I warm to Jongladd-390's kindness, or at least his lack of overt hostility.

"I'm glad to see that your Fatal Insomnia has not yet proved fatal."

"Oh!" He exclaims, brightening. "There's good news on that front! I was misdiagnosed! I don't have Fatal Insomnia! I have Cotard Delusion! Also known as Walking Corpse Syndrome! Or Nihilistic Delusion!"

"I don't understand."

"There is no understanding, only feeling!" He chirps merrily. "Or rather, lack thereof! I feel as if I was born dead! A corpse devoid of any true, vital, animating force! Soulless and lifeless! The fact that I yet exist is a hideous abomination in defiance of all that is natural and good! I am repulsed by my own materiality, a creature of revolting putrescence, filth made flesh, irredeemable and meaningless! I am nothing, yet I exist! A hideous paradox! A revolting abortion! My insomnia was but one symptom of this waking nightmare! Now I know exactly what's wrong! Hooray!"

"Are you getting help?"

"Of course." He says, growing somber. "The Doctors' worldly emissaries have decreed that I must purge to re-balance my bodily humors, and in service of this have prescribed a thorough battery of emetics, including The Triumphal Chariot of Antimony, Pucula Emetic. They're known as Perpetual Pills since you recover it after it's passed through your body for re-use. I'm also taking Blue Vitriol, Ipecacuanha Syrup, and Apomorphine. Soon I will no doubt have purged myself of all emptiness, and be truly alive."

"So," I respond cautiously. "right now you're kind of like a zombie?"

"Not literally!" He affirms, nodding vigorously. "But I certainly feel like one!"

"Please excuse me if I'm wallowing in the ignorance of a negative stereotype, but since you feel like a zombie, does that mean you also feel a typical zombie's insatiable hunger for living human brains?"

A thoughtful expression appears on Jongladd-390's decrepit face.

"I don't know."

"Here" I incline my head and hold my electric prod at the ready in case I have to fend him off. "I've already partially cooked it. Take a look and a smell, then tell me if you feel anything."

He peers down at my exposed neural tissue.

"Oh my Doc-"

Jongladd-390 vomits in my brain.

"I'm sorry."

"It's okay." I respond. "I'm used to it."

Jongladd-390 and I lie down in bed and watch television.

We watch a cooking show where chefs make dishes no one is healthy enough to eat or smell or see, so they're judged based on how they feel.

Celebrity guest judge Jangladd-971,487 dips her right foot—the only remaining part of her body she can move—in lobster bouillabaisse with olive oil and clam juice. She says she likes how it warms her toes, which briefly negates the effects of her Raynaud's Disease, an affliction that causes the small arteries in one's hands and feet to narrow so one's extremities always feel cold.

We watch a construction show where Jongladd-1,246,178 wants to build a new, completely soundproof addition onto his house so can have some relief from his Musical Ear Syndrome, a disease characterized by auditory hallucinations triggered by hearing loss that manifest as music or singing. He says it's always possible to have too much of a good thing, and while he longs for any form of atonal discord, he's willing to settle for a measure of temporary silence. The Xgladd-7,149,572 hosting the television show screams obscenities at him as a symptom of their Tourette's Syndrome. Jongladd-1,246,178 covers his ears and begs them to stop tormenting him with their transcendentally beautiful harmonies.

We watch a show about a group of idle rich Gladds struggling to amuse themselves. There are scandalous rumors about someone secretly getting reconstructive surgery to look normal after Mercury Fumigation treatments caused most of their face to rot off. A group of Jongladds seeking to cure their dysentery undergo Geophagy treatments, also known as eating dirt. One uses the universal antidote Terra Sigillata pills to heal the poisoning he got from the arsenic bread pills he used to heal his thiamine deficiency and when the soil he eats infects him with parasites he's treated with cyanide. A Jangladd is chastised for wearing a scandalously revealing dress to his funeral, though the majority of what's displayed is scar tissue. The episode ends with them going to an exclusive night club, where their elaborate dance moves are ultimately revealed to be muscle spasms caused by Rachitis resulting in multiple bone fractures. There is then a commercial for Calomel, also known as Worm Candy due to its being used to treat helminth infestations. "N-n-n-now w-w-w-w-with less d-d-drooling!" An Xgladd declares, the triangular wedge of flesh surgically amputated from the root of their tongue having failed to cure their stuttering.

An indeterminate amount of time passes.

I turn to look at Jongladd-390. At first I can't tell if he's asleep or dead, then I remember it doesn't matter. I remain in horrific pain, and decide to go to the hospital. I find the bedroom door won't open anything beyond a crack due to the pile of Gladd corpses heaped outside it, and am forced to exit via the window.

Outside the world is virtually unrecognizable. A case of St. Antony's Fire has infected the population, rendering all the world a sickbed and all the men and women merely patients. I shuffle past myself afflicted with spasms, riddled his diarrhea, felled by paresthesias, distorted by mania, twisted with psychosis, addled by headaches, vexed by nausea, deranged by vomiting, tainted by gangrene, harried by desquamation, tormented by edema and so on and so on and et cetera and et cetera populating every street and every building and every train on every screen in every window inhabiting every church and synagogue and mosque and temple and shrine.

I reach the hospital by following the flow of pedestrian traffic, becoming one tiny mote in a teeming swarm of Gladds, a veritable ocean of disease along with the human byproducts who exist as vessels to give it an opportunity to manifest; the Gladds existing to be diseased the same way a canvas exists to be painted on, or a rag exists to absorb filth.

The hospital building has become a living, sentient being of pure energy. Its wisdom is so great and terrible it produces its own light and heat, thoughts so enlightened drawing conclusions so profound they create their own energy like the nuclear fusion that powers a star. It is a thing almost too awesome to look upon, its glory incalculable, its brilliance undeniable, a being endlessly unfolding in a cascade of enlightened benevolence that is the ultimate expression of reality. The smell surrounding it is one of burning human excrement.

A favela has sprung up around the hospital, a makeshift refugee camp consisting of millions of diseased Gladds awaiting treatment, a metropolis of illness the locals have taken to calling Sick City. Sick City has no sewer system, no trash pickup, no corpse removal, no sanitation or public services of any kind. Every day human waste, garbage, and Gladd corpses are piled into the same midden heap and burned, it happens so often I soon cease to notice the smell. Every day more Gladd clones are produced to replace the dead along with a few more to pick up the slack. Most new Gladds are felled by illness within a mile of the hospital, and return to take up residence in Sick City while waiting to be made well.

I slowly pick my way through the teeming throngs amassed at the edge of the force field surrounding the hospital. As I approach it in all its effulgent majesty an alien voice manifests in my head, at once authoritative and kind.

What seems to be the problem?

I am in horrific pain, I think.

Please rate your pain on a scale of one to ten.

Ten. I think.

I'm sorry to hear that. One of our care team will be with you shortly. Until then please be patient.

I find a hovel full of dead Gladds, clear them out, and take up residence.

Time becomes meaningless. There is no night since Sick City is continuously bathed in the hospital's glow, no seasons since we are permanently ensconced in its warmth. The only indicator of change is the steady accumulation of Gladds, the rate of their production always outpacing their rate of attrition. No matter how many Gladds die more stride forth from the hospital so there is always a net gain. Sick City swells to cover the entire face of the...

The...

Whatever this planet was called before it was officially renamed Waiting Area.

I wait. I live. I hurt. In time the three are made one, becoming indistinguishable until they gel into one persistent, enduring state so abiding and unchanging that when the disembodied voice finally returns to inform me the time has come for the hospital to suffer me to come unto it, I have to force myself to remember who and what I am, that there is something that is not pain, that there exists a state of being absent it, a form of life that is worth seeking out.

I approach the hospital, wading through the sea of Gladds surrounding it until I reach the force field. Instead of meeting the resistance I've come to expect, I pass through the pane of shimmering energy as if there's nothing there. Other Gladds pummel and claw at the region where I passed through in a desperate attempt to follow, but are rebuffed. The hospital's radiance is almost blinding, and it's all I can do to shield my eyes and shuffle forth toward the source of its glory while a dream of perfect music caresses my ears. Soon the light is blinding, the noise deafening, the heat unbearable. Just when I expect it to consume me it disappears, and I am inside the exact same Emergency Room waiting room I entered when I came to the hospital for the very first time. The laminate tile floor is the same, the acoustic ceiling tiles are the same, the vending machines are the same, the assemblage of chairs are the same along with are the magazines on the tables next to them, the celebrities adorning their covers still individuals instead of some form of Gladd. The only difference is no one is here besides me, no receptionist, no security guard, no staff of any kind.

"What's going on?" I ask the emptiness.

Be not afraid. The voice intones within my brain. The chartered avenues of your linear mind could not withstand beholding us as we truly are in all our transcendent majesty. Instead we have reached into the vault of thine memories to fashion an environment thou shalt comprehend.

"Oh, right, now that I look closely, I see what you mean." I say. "All the writing is illegible. The environment outside the windows is motionless, like a picture. All the furniture is made of painted cardboard."

Our reproduction is flawless. If there is imperfection, it lies in thine memory, not our perfect rendering thereof.

"I'm sure I don't remember the hospital smelling like ham."

Verily, cease thy recrimination, none doth like a whiner.

"What should I do?"

Ascend, Jongladd Prime. Rise ever higher until thou hast made thyself unto occupying the seventy seventh of floors and get thee to the hospital's complimentary chapel. Use the stairs, thine imperfect recollection hath rendered the elevators out of order.

Fortunately for me they failed to make floors two through seventy six so I only have to ascend one flight of stairs. Still, my horrific pain hinders my progress, forcing me to rest and collect myself multiple times before I finally reach the second, i.e. seventy seventh floor.

When I finally manage to reach my destination I see the chapel's defining feature is a large stained glass window depicting Christ's resurrection being made possible thanks to the timely intervention of medical professionals. At least I think that's what it is; the image is rather crude, not consisting of real stained glass but wax paper colored by crayons. None of the images in the church are particularly accurate, I have no recollection of Jesus ascending to heaven via jetpack or being photographed shaking hands with Richard Nixon, but these are among the least of my concerns.

"What now?"

Descend, Jongladd Prime. Return thou'st to the first floor, there is someone thou shalt want to meet.

"Go back to the first- If it's on the first floor, why did you have me come up in here in the first place?"

'Tis not our fault thou hast remembered events in thine wrong order. Goest now, before thou dost exhaust our infinite patience.

I return to the first floor. My feet impress themselves upon the ground tile, leaving tracks in the linoleum like I'm walking on sand. Static objects waver slightly while details flicker in and out of existence depending on how much attention I'm paying. Eventually I reach two doors illuminated by dozens of gold panels depicting medical breakthroughs throughout the ages: Pasteur developing germ theory, Alexander Fleming discovering Penicillin, Jonas Salk inventing the Polio Vaccine, Walter Freeman performing a lobotomy, the god Asclepius wielding his snake-entwined rod to slay the dragon of illness.

The doors open on their own.

I enter.

As the doors close behind me I find myself inside someone's home. It has an open floor plan, lots of space for entertaining guests. The furniture and appliances match each other to foster an impression of understated elegance.

I don't recognize this place but feel that I should, a mental disconnect that fosters a sense of intense déjà vu.

"Hold on!" Comes a merry voice from another room. "I'll be with you in a moment!" Again, I don't recognize the voice but feel that I should, that it's endowed with some underlying familiarity that I could grasp if only I knew how. I make my way to the nearby picture window and peer out at a gorgeous view encompassing a park, a beach, and what I take to be an ocean.

Suddenly it comes to me.

This is my dream home, the place I always imagined I would make for myself if I ever had unlimited money and time. This dream and others like it had fled from my mind soon after I got sick, and came to dream only of a life without constant agony.

And eventually ceased to dream even of that.

"Sorry about the wait." The speaker enters the room. It's me, another Jongladd; however this one is different somehow.

I didn't recognize his voice because it is cheerful. Light. Easy.

It is the voice of someone who is healthy.

A smile revealing two rows of perfectly symmetrical, spotlessly radiant teeth beams at me as he reaches out for a handshake. I look down at his hand. It is resplendently manicured, perfectly moisturized, devoid of flaw. I don't return the gesture, instead staring blankly at the perfect extremity until it's withdrawn.

"Who are you?" I ask, surprised by the recriminatory tone of my voice, suspicion tinged with revulsion.

He is Jon Gladd. The voice announces proudly.

"I'm Jon Gladd." He turns and approaches the stainless steel wet bar I always envisioned getting. "Specifically, I am Jon Gladd Version 1.0, out of Beta, the production model, ready for mass market." He reaches into the bar and produces a bottle of Johnnie Walker Blue, an elite brand of scotch whiskey I always wanted to try but never could due to its exorbitant price. "Refined. Remodeled. Recoded. Reborn." He produces two glasses containing two ice cubes and fills both halfway. "Please." He gestures at the table he's set the glasses on, a solid block of exquisitely varnished hardwood, no need for coasters. "Sit. Enjoy." I do neither.

"I don't understand. What are you?" He produces a sleek black remote and aims it at a gargantuan television screen.

"Marketing produced a video, take a look."

Images appear of racially diverse, uniformly attractive doctors in lab coats doing scientific things such as peering into microscopes, pouring liquids into beakers, and pressing buttons on devices. A narrator speaks in a tone of solemn, profound intensity.

"Jon Gladd isn't just a man. He's all men in one. He's bold. Yet understated. Jon Gladd is classic. Style. Luxury. Elegance itself. For designers, Jon Gladd is the most difficult human to create. To understand his qualities, we studied all the ways he's used. In cars, fashion, art, and more. Jon Gladd comes in many different forms. But in the design world, there is only one perfect Jon Gladd. We aspired to craft a Jon Gladd that stays true at every angle and reflection of light. In our quest we conducted countless tests. We examined molding, the process to create genetic patterns. Vapor deposition, the process to create the genetic layer. We even examined glass etching. Nothing was quite right." The footage of doctors is interspersed with other dramatic scenes. Footage of a calving glacier. Footage of a majestic waterfall. Footage of an eagle soaring over a mountain. Footage of a photogenic child running through a field of golden wheat in slow motion. "Our experiments showed that any process we added only reduced the Jon Gladd's intensity. To reach the man that encompasses all others, we found that less is more. We needed to subtract. Removing the traditional processes was an extreme, uncompromising gesture, but we needed to break new ground. We put all our focus on just two parts of the Jon Gladd. Body and mind. First, we built the Jon Gladd base with new materials, creating a Jon Gladd that absorbs all characteristics. Then, we worked to find the perfect haze formula." Two human silhouettes backlit by a glorious sunset come together in a passionate kiss. "We varied times of etching, changed the thickness of the biology, and even tested mixtures and concentrations of the genetic solution. Finally, we had a breakthrough. We discovered an optimal haze that preserves a deep, resonant Jon Gladd, one that shows the man in its truest form." Footage of the Waiting Area from space. The sun rises over the horizon, its light expanding to encompass more and more of the image until the entire screen is pure white. "The result of all these efforts is the Jon Gladd Version 1.0." The man currently occupying the room with me appears onscreen, his posture upright, his smile radiant, the camera slowly panning over various close ups of his body. "Strong. Fluid. Modern. We fashioned this singular Jon Gladd not by adding more, but by using less. Unforgettable and unapologetic. This: Is Jon Gladd." Smash cut to the Stamen Medical Group logo, fade out.

"You get the idea." Jon Gladd 1.0 raises the glass, lets the liquid breathe, takes a tentative, thoughtful sip, swishes it in his mouth, and finally swallows. "It's the little things, you know?"

"What does this have to do with making me better?" I say.

"I told you he wouldn't get it." Jon Gladd says.

We *have* made you better. The voice says. We have made you better than you ever could have possibly been. You are beyond restored. You are perfected.

"What does that have to do with my horrific pain?"

Not everything is about you. This is, of course. But not everything.

"What about everyone else? Gladds two through ten billion?"

They have prepared the way, made the path straight for him.

"I still don't understand."

"That's the thing, though!" Jon Gladd says. "You don't have to. I can understand for you. I can suit any purpose, execute any task, not just the ones neglected by you due to your infirmity. You need no longer live in fear of a life unlived or a legacy neglected. I will live, I will love, I will inscribe the Jon Gladd name on the cosmos." He nods at the glass of scotch set before me. "You could at least try to enjoy yourself.

I ignore the glass. Instead I pick up the bottle of Johnnie Walker Blue, uncap it, lift it above my head, and empty its entire contents into my exposed brain. The expensive amber liquid spills down my head and face. The effect is bracing as well as intoxicating. Jon Gladd's vibrant eyes regard me with resigned disappointment.

"Very mature. I suppose there's no fighting decay. Entropy is entropy."

"That's a popular misconception." I say, slowly rounding the table. "Entropy isn't just decay, reducing everything to a lifeless equilibrium. Entropy is all transfers of energy from one system to another, it is the capacity of everything to do work. Without entropy there would be no complexity, stars wouldn't have generated the carbon that makes life possible. Without it time itself would not pass. It's not just a force that inexorably reduces everything to dust and ashes. Entropy is both creation and destruction, it is change itself."

"So what?"

"I'm just trying to put things in perspective." I smash the bottle against Jon Gladd's head. It shatters. He falls to the floor, unconscious.

What are you doing?!

"Administering anesthetic." I say, kneeling down to attend to Jon Gladd's prone form. "I'm afraid the patient is suffering from sanguinity, a dangerous excess of blood leading to a catastrophic imbalance of humors and must be tended to immediately lest he perish from his illness." I continue to narrate while stabbing him repeatedly in the throat. "As Galen taught us, blood does not circulate and must be purged. Though women can accomplish this naturally via menstruation, with men more direct physical intervention is required." Having severed both his carotid arteries, I move on to treat his femoral arteries, and commence stabbing him in the thighs. "Regular bleeding is key, nay instrumental to a healthy lifestyle. Blood is of paramount importance among the four humors, which include Yellow Bile, Black Bile, and Phlegm. Copious exsanguination is instrumental in fostering the humoral balance necessary for a functioning body." It feels good to be helping someone else for once, and with the femoral arteries tapped I move on to the radial arteries, dragging the broken bottle across the inside of one wrist and then the other, continuing to breathe the veins until he's rendered as healthy as humanly possible. It is only after I've helped him in every way I can that I toss the bottle away, stand up with a unimaginable amount of corresponding pain, gaze down at my restored patient, and bathe in the afterglow of a job well done. Jon Gladd's perfect body is an island sprawled in a sea of red, an oasis of health in a desert of corruption, unsullied at last. Physician heal thyself indeed.

You are under arrest. The voice declares. For practicing medicine without a license. Please report to a local penitentiary under your own recognizance, as there are no law enforcement officials healthy enough to physically coerce you to do so.

I don't. I am not being defiant. Rather, surrendering myself to the authorities would be a fruitless gesture because I've done nothing wrong; rather this is the first time in living memory that I've done something unequivocally right. I lay down on the sort of couch I've always dreamed of having and relish in the glory of being a creature of absolute correctness. The voice harangues me for a time, then eventually strikes a more conciliatory tone, appealing for me to respect the institutions of law that, of course, exist for everyone's benefit. Eventually it stops talking to me directly and trails off into a sustained stream of consciousness monologue that weighs the merits of individual wellness relative to a healthy and harmonious society, ruminations that grow ever more insular and abstract until the words themselves complexify into to a version of a Khoisan click language spoken by the San people of South Africa, at which point Jon Gladd's recovering body has begun to smell so healthy its stench is unbearable, and I'm compelled to leave. I exit the illuminated doors, am engulfed by a familiar light, and return to Waiting Area.

The world I return to is a beautiful one. The buildings are sleek and modern, outfitted with lofty spires whose gilded surfaces make the sunlight dance. Aerodynamic vehicles glide down the wide boulevards with serene grace, producing no sound other than an understated, pleasant hum. The air is pristine, the activity orderly, the surfaces resplendently clean, the citizens universally hideous. There is not a single man, woman, genderqueer individual, or child who is not profoundly deformed in some way.

News of my inexplicable presence spreads, attracting more and more people until I find myself marooned in a veritable ocean of scars, abscesses, stunted limbs, rashes, sores, scleromas, blisters, and growths, a seemingly endless profusion of every conceivable anatomical abnormality that is humanly possible. Eventually a man with severe Proteus Syndrome steps forward as ably as his misshapen legs permit.

"What are you?" He asks as clearly as his deformed esophagus will allow.

"I'm Jongladd Prime." The man laughs, then abruptly falls silent as he realizes I'm being serious. "Why are the children sick?"

"Sick?" The man echoes, tilting his head at a quizzical angle, or perhaps it's always that way and I'm just now noticing.

"Yes. Hurt, malformed, afflicted, stricken, unwell, diseased, unhealthy, differently abled, under the weather, infected, enfeebled, not up to snuff, in a bad way, however you want to put it." More blank stares. "This." I say, pointing to a finger belonging to the stranger that's of a particularly large and unwieldy shape that's grossly out of sync with the rest of him.

"Oh!" He says, comprehension finally dawning. "You mean our Holymarks."

"Holymarks?" I ask. He rolls his eyes at my ignorance—though, again, his eyes may always be that way and I'm only just noticing it now.

"And you claimed to be the Second Coming of Jongladd Prime. These are the Holymarks, the distinct traits bestowed by Doc that mark us as His one, true chosen people, favored and beloved, righteous and pure, serving as stewards of His covenant until He comes again in glory to judge the living and the dead and other stuff."

"Why do the children have your... Holymarks?"

"It's hereditary, of course. The bloodline must be preserved, the true healthy must remain untainted by the heretical sick."

"The heretical sick?" The crowd gathered around me gradually disperses as the novelty of my sudden appearance wears off. Soon only the man I'm speaking to remains, and I come to appreciate his obliging character as he patiently answers my questions until an idea of the world I've found myself in forms in my mind, and I begin to realize just how much time has passed.

Hospitals are no more. Doctors and Medicine are the stuff of legend, long since consigned to the fog of ancient history, while the tale of Jongladd Prime is but one creation myth among many. The world is still split into nations, but they are no longer defined by culture or geography, rather their collective identity is forged by the unique illness (Holymarks) infecting the population. That isn't to say anyone identifies themselves as sick; rather, every group claims their own unique illness to be the one true health. It is only outsiders who are genuinely unwell.

I have happened to manifest in the People's United Democratic Republic of Deformia. As I continue speaking to the man it becomes clear that the meaning of the word 'form' and 'deform' have switched places in the popular lexicon. Goodness and rectitude are now associated with chaos, asymmetry, and nonconformity to any standard. As I come to understand this I begin to see their ethos represented in the world around me. The city, whose name I learn is Rictus, appeared upon first glance to be orderly and elegant, but that's only because I was comparing it to the chaotic squalor of the favela of Sick City I inhabited for so long outside the Hospital's final form. When I look closer I see that the city is an amalgam of thoughtfully manufactured dissonance. Rictus has no straight lines or consistent structure, everything is haphazardly fashioned out of wildly differing materials to no coherent purpose. It is a misshapen city, its streets labyrinthine coils of distorted roundabouts and sudden dead ends, its buildings ungainly amalgams that appear to be the result of five or more architects all working at cross purposes with different materials and methods in mind. Rictus is beautiful in its own absurd way, but not a place I would ever want to actually live.

The man speaking to me is kind enough to guide me to a library where I can learn more about this new world. As we arrive I notice the national flag wriggling on the pole outside the building is a patchwork amalgam of seemingly random scraps. I ask him about this and he explains that the People's United Democratic Republic of Deformia has no one single unified flag, rather all of them are fashioned from various scavenged materials, and can only be identified by means of their consistent inconsistency. We enter and I manage to sit down before a computer, experiencing a horrific amount of pain in the process. The man asks me if I'm going to be okay. I tell him no, but he should feel free to leave, he's already been extremely kind and done more than I ever could have reasonably asked for. He gives me an amiable pat on my brain, wishes me well, and staggers away. I never see him again.

I begin my research, and this new world reveals itself to me.

Conventional Westphalian nation-states with fixed borders are no more, replaced by Soverillties, (pronounced sov-ur-ill-tease) a portmanteau of Sovereignty and ill. There are six major Soverillties scattered throughout the planet, whose name has been shortened from Waiting Area to Wayteria.

The People's United Democratic Republic of Infirmis, the Soverillty for people with ambulatory disabilities that hinder their movement somehow, be it vertigo, paralysis, an inner ear infection, or dismemberment.

The People's United Democratic Republic of Naughtika, the Soverillty for people whose senses are impaired somehow, the blind, deaf, tasteless, scentless or numb.

The People's United Democratic Republic of Deformia where I find myself now, the Soverillty for people with any sort of disease resulting in a physical deformity of some kind.

The People's United Democratic Republic of of Involin, the Soverillty for people afflicted with involuntary movements, spasms, seizures, or convulsions.

The People's United Democratic Republic of Psychosical, the Soverillty for people with delusions and hallucinations, hearing voices that aren't there, seeing things that aren't there, believing things not supported by consensus reality.

The People's United Democratic Republic of Affecdis, the Soverillty for people with mood disorders, depression, mania, bipolar disorder, borderline personality disorder, anxiety.

A brief overview of the history of Wayteria née Waiting Area shows that all six Soverillties either once were at war with one another, are currently at war with one another, or are threatening future military action toward one another, all in the name of their own illness being the One True Illness ordained by Doc, who fashioned them in His own perfect image. The holy text of all Soverillties is some version of the little blue book Jongladd-34,462 threw at my head ages ago, though each individual Soverillty has their own particular version of it, revised and reinterpreted to distinguish them as Doc's Chosen Patients.

Just when I think I've gotten the gist of the new world of Wayteria I notice offhand references to one more group. At first I think it is a seventh Soverillty I've somehow overlooked, but as I delve further into the topic I find they are nothing of the kind, in fact the defining trait of this group is its specific exclusion from all of civilized society. They are outcastes, refugees, itinerant wanderers, stateless people locked in permanent exile. They are called the Malingerers, and they are people whose illness or illnesses do not fit cleanly into any distinct category.

If there is anything that unites the disparate Soverillties of Wayteria, it is their universal loathing of the Malingerers, also known as parasites, failures, losers, good for nothings, undesirables, deadbeats, bums, failures, leeches, sponges, vermin, idlers, pissants, self-declared victims who will never take responsibility for their own lives, and so on. The Malingerers are simultaneously seen as fundamentally weak and inferior, while also being thought of as an immanent existential threat to all civilization, scheming in the shadows to dilute the Soverillties' purity, undermine their authority, and seize power by underhanded means.

All of the sudden I become aware of the looks I've been getting from the library's staff as well as fellow patrons, expressions of rigid hostility and eyes sharp with suspicion when they are not deformed beyond all possible recognition.

As I delve deeper into the topic of the Malingerers I find the citizens of Deformia around me taking a none-to-subtle interest in what's transpiring on my screen. Eventually one of the resident librarians screws up enough courage to approach me and ask me if I am a registered patron. When I respond in the negative I am politely but pointedly asked me to leave the premises, the librarian employing the word 'sir' five times before I lose count.

I do as I'm asked, departing with my horrific pain.

It doesn't matter, there's no reason for me to tarry any further.

I resolve to travel to a makeshift encampment of wandering Malingerers that exists just beyond the city limits of Rictus, though in embarking on my trek I fail to account for just how difficult it will be to get out of a purposefully deformed city that is essentially one giant, incoherent maze. I begin to appreciate just how exceptional the kindness of the man I happened to encounter when I first appeared out of thin air truly was as I pass by masses of people regarding me as if I'm an intrusive cockroach they aren't allowed to step on due to some obscure legal technicality. I'm too apprehensive to ask for directions out of Rictus or sustenance of any kind, and when I finally manage to reach the Malingerer camp outside town I am dehydrated and disoriented in addition to being in horrific pain, and it's all I can do to stagger into the outskirts and collapse.

The Malingerers take me into their encampment and are kind enough to shelter and rehydrate me, though they make no attempt to hide their suspicions regarding my strange appearance in their midst. I tell them about the circumstances that led me to their proverbial doorstep, at least what I can remember of them. It's clear they don't believe me, but that quickly proves irrelevant as I stumble into a a new role in their community: that of scapegoat.

Perhaps the only people who hate listening to sick people talk more than healthy people are other sick people. Misery loves company, but only insofar as that company is receptive and sympathetic, which necessitates the luxury of the listener being willing to concede, at least tacitly, that they are doing better than the complainant, which grants the sufferer a degree of moral superiority, and therefore solace.

By contrast, when everyone exists in the same state of colossal agony, the moral calculus necessary to determine whose feelings matter more becomes unworkable. This leads to the sort of seething resentment endemic to all radically egalitarian societies, where tiny vexations pile atop one another to become blood feuds, where there is constant jockeying for some form of ascent in the social hierarchy no matter how insignificant, resulting in endless efforts to generate social capital for oneself at the expense of others.

Granted, the Malingerers could have directed their hostility at the individuals with actual power who bore direct responsibility for their disproportionate suffering, but such figures were distant, abstract, and seemingly unassailable, while one's neighbor was clearly visible and within striking distance.

My sudden presence has enough of a destabilizing effect to upend this state of permanent crisis. My story being unbelievable despite the gaping hole in my skull has the effect of rendering my suffering inconsequential, and my insignificance in the permanent record of Authentic Agony makes me a perfect sounding board for everyone else's grievances.

At first I resist, insisting on the relevance of my own feelings and experiences, but my failure to accept my moral inferiority only serves to enhance my moral inferiority, and I eventually give up and accept my role as a kind of satanic confessor, which at least affords me some tangible place in Malingerer society. In time I come to appreciate and respect the woes of others, even as my own horrific pain endures unacknowledged.

Shortly after my arrival a group of law enforcement officials employed by The People's United Democratic Republic of Deformia arrive and bulldoze the camp. The Malingerers tell me this always happens eventually, and they are forced to take to the road again. They ask if I want to accompany them in their peripatetic voyage, and I accept their offer.

We wander the surface of Wayteria, venturing across frontiers to find brief refuge in Naughtika, Infirmis, Involin, Psychosical, and Affecdis, our presence never more than tolerated, our residences always temporary, our expulsion always violent.

My reputation as an eager receptacle for other people's agony spreads among the various disparate tribes of Malingerers. I become something akin to a guru, but a guru who is not treasured for great wisdom. Rather it is my terrific ignorance and profound irrelevance relative to all others that renders me so important.

Eventually not just Malingerers but people from all over Wayteria come to chastise me for misunderstanding them, failing to appreciate their pain, being so abhorrently content to reside in my own little narcissistic bubble while the rest of humanity toils and suffers and endures every conceivable affront to their dignity and humanity, nobly persisting in living their lives despite my habitual ingratitude. At some point a person has the temerity to ask me how I'm doing. Before I can answer she is dragged away and savagely pummeled by an angry mob who chastises me as they rain blows down upon her, demanding to know how I could have possibly let this happen, the unmitigated gall, hurry up and mitigate your gall, mitigate it already.

It is eventually determined that I should be given permanent residence within a shrine to make me more easily accessible to pilgrims all over the world. None of Soverillties can agree on where I should go, and after much squabbling they elect to leave the decision up to me. I opt to settle in the city of Rictus where I first appeared, inspiring first massive outrage, then universal condemnation, and finally agreement.

It is not a bad life. Or it would be if I was not in constant, horrific pain. Which I am. So I suppose it is a bad life. Technically. As well as factually.

Dozens of people come to pour out their woes and berate me about my failure to equal or understand their suffering each day. Their behavior varies greatly. Some wail, unleashing their sorrows in a great torrent, gnashing their teeth and rending their clothes, launching salvo after salvo of ardent vituperation at me until they are finally spent. Other people take a more sober approach, coolly enumerating each pain afflicting both themselves and the people they love, their castigation of me stern but subdued. Some say nothing, just staring at me in silent reproach. For some people repudiating me becomes a kind of art unto itself, they express their loathing in interpretive dance, abstract painting, musical compositions; some quite masterful, others endearing in their amateur earnestness.

Soon, in addition to their various denunciations of my insufficient and inauthentic suffering, each pilgrim who seeks me out begins to ask the same question.

Why?

Why are they, and more importantly the people they love, made to experience such pain? To what end?

I tell everyone the same thing: I don't know, and I also don't know why they think I would know.

Despite my failure to provide resolution of any kind, some people seem strangely edified by my non-answer, as if I've at least verified the legitimacy of their question somehow.

There is one more thing, the last thing; perhaps the most important thing, or perhaps a meaningless triviality.

As more visitors come and go, there is a subtle shift in their attitude, a vague discrepancy I cannot place until a very old woman with Erotomania states it openly.

"Honestly," She says, her voice hushed despite the new policy of guaranteed confidentiality that undergirds all these meetings. "I thought I'd hate you more. Naturally if you tell anyone I said this I'll deny it but..." Her tone grows even more somber and hushed, descending into a husky whisper I can just barely hear. "...perhaps you have experienced a kind of suffering." Astonished by her own audacity, she blushes and scrambles out of the chamber.

At first I take her confession to be an aberration. She is mentally ill after all, her Erotomania afflicting her with the false yet unshakable conviction that a person she's never met is in passionate love with her, a disorder that could trigger all manner of corresponding delusions out of line with reality as envisioned by the popular imagination. Then it happens again. A young man from The People's United Democratic Republic of Naughtika with Axenfeld-Rieger Syndrome impairing his vision by giving him too many holes in his irises expresses a similar sentiment, interrupting his tirade of insults to furtively admit that maybe, possibly, I have experienced some form of legitimate suffering, even if it can never compare with that of anyone else on Wayteria.

Somehow, this becomes a trend. At first I wonder if it is an inside joke of some kind, a collective prank devised by a cadre of tricksters to blow my mind or freak me out, what the kids today call gaslighting, but I can sense no malicious pattern to it, nor any duplicity on the part of people divulging their sympathies. Rather it seems like everyone is reaching the same conclusion in isolation. The possibility that other people have had the same idea and expressed a similar sentiment to me has seemingly never occurred to any them, and every single one of them is privately afraid of what will happen to them if anyone else learns they have conceded the possible existence of authentic suffering on my part.

This strange kindness spreads with remarkable speed, soon it seems like everyone who visits me either address it directly or alludes to it in some way—the remote possibility that I may have experienced some small shred of the pain they've been subjected to, the vague notion that we may in some obscure way share a remote hint of mutual humanity.

I make no attempt to tell anyone they're not alone in their assessment, that at this point practically everyone who seeks me out expresses some version of the same secret empathy. It seems important that everyone reach the conclusion on their own and hold it close in their innermost hearts. Admitting it to themselves seems more important, in a grand sense, than admitting it to me. In some circuitous manner it seems to give them permission to have empathy for the world entire, something like what Ancient Greeks called agape or Nietzsche called amor fati.

If I am to be used as nothing more than a vessel, I'm glad I'm being used this way.

At some point the tenor of the public's engagement with me changes, and while I'm not regarded with any more sympathy than before, the question of what, precisely, is wrong with me emerges as a matter of global concern. Since I embody everything that is wrong with the world, there is a sense that if I could somehow be made right, all of Wayteria could be healed.

Asking what's wrong with me becomes a moral imperative. Young people do it during coming of age ceremonies. I'm asked it on the occasion of births and baptisms and marriages. Dying people do it in what seems to be a form of extreme unction.

There are days when I am made to sit atop a dais in the center of Rictus' town square and great multitudes of humanity come to see me, people of all nations and even the universally reviled Malingerers resigning themselves to some form of brief, grudging coexistence as they wait, sometimes for days, for the opportunity to equate their experience with my own in person.

Everyone asks the same question.

What is your ailment?

I'm always forced to provide the same answer.

I am in horrific pain.

The inquirer then speaks to me of their own afflictions. It is still taboo to publicly characterize their Holymarks as anything other than a gift from Doc marking them as His most favored people, but each person somehow always manages the rhetorical trick of asking me if my sickness is anything like their own. I'm always forced to respond in the negative, however even if our disorders did happen to overlap I have no idea what we'd do about it, everyone else's illness seems just as intractable as my own.

Still they come, from morning to evening to morning again, asking what's wrong with me then detailing their own plight, the public inquiry into my illness seeming just as strange to me as the secret sympathy to my possibly legitimate suffering people disclose in private.

I know not what purpose I serve, if indeed I serve any at all. I know not why I am here in this place and time, if indeed there is any reason for it whatsoever. If there is any defining characteristic of my existence besides my horrific pain, it is this abiding ignorance, the dark ocean of unknowing in which I feel myself bob to and fro like a sliver of flotsam.

There are many things I want to tell the people who come to see me.

"I am a stranger to myself. I contain no wisdom. I spend most of my time thinking about how I want to scratch my brain but cannot. My brain should not be capable of itching since it has none of the nerve cells that produce the itching sensation. The fact that it does anyway is no doubt emblematic of something. I can't help you. I can't help myself. Help is seemingly beyond us all."

I do not say any of this. The world continues to exist and change around me, and I am able to recognize it only by dint of its consistent unrecognizability, how the only normal thing is endless irregularity.

One day (there is always another, each immediately following the last like clockwork) I receive a thick envelope in the mail addressed to Jon Gladd. No one calls me that anymore (being an embodiment of evil, I have many names) but it has somehow found its way to me regardless. I open it and find it to be a bill for all the professional medical treatment I have received from the good people of Stamen Medical Group.

The sum presented is so large it is impossible to represent with rational numbers, or positional notation of any kind. I owe pi. I owe the square root of two. I owe Euler's number. I owe Ein Sof. I owe Brahman. What I owe surpasses all human understanding to the point where whether it truly can be said to exist or not is a matter of abstract speculation. The bill helpfully references an analogy commonly attributed to the Buddha, saying that if I were to gently brush a rock one square mile in size with a silk cloth once every century until it eroded to nothing, the sum of nanoseconds contained in this process would not begin to total even a minor fraction of what I owe Stamen Medical Group and its various parent companies, associates, and subsidiaries. I, for my own part, do not remember the last time I interacted with money, and do not know what I am supposed to do with this information.

In time a collections agent in the employ of Stamen Medical Group confronts me. I have no idea how he intends to extract anything of value from me, but that proves irrelevant due to the fact that he suffers from Capgras Delusion, and thus believes that I am not the once and former Jon Gladd but an identical imposer.

He demands to know what happened to the real me. I tell him I'd like to know that myself. He tells me I'm not funny and storms off in a huff. I bid him goodbye, wishing him well in all his future endeavors. He doesn't look back, but responds with an obscene gesture aimed in my general direction.

He returns the next day, apologizes, and politely asks me where the real Jon Gladd is. When I say that I am in fact him, he gets angry again, screams obscenities at me, and storms off.

The next day he's back. He flatters, cajoles, pleads, threatens, and rages, all in the name of coercing me into admitting the true location of the real me. I persist in telling the truth to his endless consternation, saying his quest is at an end, the object of his search is right before his eyes, he need only acknowledge it.

This tête-à-tête continues for several weeks until one day he reaches into his pocket and produces a pistol. At first he points the gun at me, yet in what seems like an instant he's suddenly aiming it at his own head. He cocks the hammer, his expression a tumult of crazed desperation, and demands I finally tell him the truth, or he'll end it all right here and now.

I don't know what else to do.

"I killed him."

He shudders, my words striking him with an almost physical force. For a second I'm afraid he'll pull the trigger anyway, but the gun slowly drifts away from his head as tears well in his eyes. He drops the gun as he falls his knees and proceeds to weep. His body is wracked with sobs for several minutes before he's finally able to tremulously stammer out two words.

"Thank you."

I can tell by the way he speaks that he means it.

THE END.

E.W.H. THORNTON'S WORK HAS APPEARED ON THE NOSLEEP PODCAST, IN THE BlazeVOX Journal, Unorthodox Fiction, After The Storm Magazine, and the meat4meat anthology. They maintain a blog presenting magazine content from pre, mid, and post World War Two era America, with a focus on the golden age of pulp fiction. It can be found at https://thegildedcentury.tumblr.com. They also occasionally write about the more bizarre, lurid, and tragic aspects of video game history at https://www.giantbomb.com/profile/lostsol/blog/.

Annie Londonderry

Annie, a Jewish Latvian Immigrant to the United States, is considered to be the first woman to bicycle around the world in 1894-95.

Annie Londonderry

Annie, a Jewish Latvian immigrant to the United States, is
considered to be the first woman to bicycle
around the world in 1894-95.

CALUMET K

BY SAMUEL MERWIN

AND

HENRY KITCHELL WEBSTER

CHAPTER 1

The contract for the two million bushel grain elevator, Calumet K, had been let to MacBride & Company, of Minneapolis, in January, but the superstructure was not begun until late in May, and at the end of October it was still far from completion. Ill luck had attended Peterson, the constructor, especially since August. MacBride, the head of the firm, disliked unlucky men, and at the end of three months his patience gave out, and he telegraphed Charlie Bannon to leave the job he was completing at Duluth and report at once at the home office.

Rumors of the way things were going at Calumet under the hands of his younger co-laborer had reached Bannon, and he was not greatly surprised when MacBride told him to go to Chicago Sunday night and supersede Peterson.

At ten o'clock Monday morning, Bannon, looking out through the dusty window of the trolley car, caught sight of the elevator, the naked cribbing of its huge bins looming high above the huddled shanties and lumber piles about it. A few minutes later he was walking along a rickety plank sidewalk which seemed to lead in a general direction toward the elevator. The sidewalks at Calumet are at the theoretical grade of the district, that is, about five feet above the actual level of the ground. In winter and spring they are necessary causeways above seas of mud, but in dry weather every one abandons them, to walk straight to his destination over the uninterrupted flats. Bannon set down his hand bag to button has ulster, for the wind was driving clouds of smoke and stinging dust and an occasional grimy snowflake out of the northwest. Then he sprang down from the sidewalk and made his way through the intervening bogs and, heedless of the shouts of the brakemen, over a freight train which was creaking its endless length across his path, to the elevator site.

The elevator lay back from the river about sixty yards and parallel to it. Between was the main line of the C. & S. C., four clear tracks unbroken by switch or siding. On the wharf, along with a big pile of timber, was the beginning of a small spouting house, to be connected with the main elevator by a belt gallery above the C. & S. C. tracks. A hundred yards to the westward, up the river, the Belt Line tracks crossed the river and the C. & S. C. right of way at an oblique angle, and sent two side tracks lengthwise through the middle of the elevator and a third along the south side, that is, the side away from the river.

Bannon glanced over the lay of the land, looked more particularly at the long ranges of timber to be used for framing the cupola, and then asked a passing workman the way to the office. He frowned at the wretched shanty, evidently an abandoned Belt Line section house, which Peterson used for headquarters. Then, setting down his bag just outside the door, he went in.

"Where's the boss?" he asked.

The occupant of the office, a clerk, looked up impatiently, and spoke in a tone reserved to discourage seekers for work.

"He ain't here. Out on the job somewhere."

"Palatial office you've got," Bannon commented. "It would help those windows to have 'em ploughed." He brought his bag into the office and kicked it under a desk, then began turning over a stack of blue prints that lay, weighted down with a coupling pin, on the table.

"I guess I can find Peterson for you if you want to see him," said the clerk.

"Don't worry about my finding him," came from Bannon, deep in his study of the plans. A moment later he went out.

A gang of laborers was engaged in moving the timbers back from the railroad siding. Superintending the work was a squat little man—Bannon could not see until near by that he was not a boy—big-headed, big-handed, big-footed. He stood there in his shirt-sleeves, his back to Bannon, swearing good-humoredly at the men. When he turned toward him Bannon saw that he had that morning played an unconscious joke upon his bright red hair by putting on a crimson necktie.

Bannon asked for Peterson.

"He's up on the framing of the spouting house, over on the wharf there."

"What are you carrying that stuff around for?" asked Bannon.

"Moving it back to make room by the siding. We're expecting a big bill of cribbing. You're Mr. Bannon, ain't you?" Bannon nodded. "Peterson had a telegram from the office saying to expect you."

"You're still expecting that cribbing, eh?"

"Harder than ever. That's most all we've been doing for ten days. There's Peterson, now; up there with the sledge."

Bannon looked in time to see the boss spring out on a timber that was still balancing and swaying upon the hoisting rope. It was a good forty feet above the dock. Clinging to the rope with one hand, with the other Peterson drove his sledge against the side of the timber which swung almost to its exact position in the framing.

"Slack away!" he called to the engineers, and he cast off the rope sling. Then cautiously he stepped out to the end of the timber. It tottered, but the lithe figure moved on to within striking distance. He swung the twenty-four pound sledge in a circle against the butt of the timber. Every muscle in his body from the ankles up had helped to deal the blow, and the big stick bucked. The boss sprang erect, flinging his arms wide and using the sledge to recover his balance. He struck hard once more and again lightly. Then he hammered the timber down on the iron dowel pins. "All right," he shouted to the engineer; "send up the next one."

A few minutes later Bannon climbed out on the framing beside him.

"Hello, Charlie!" said the boss, "I've been looking for you. They wired me you was coming."

"Well, I'm here," said Bannon, "though I 'most met my death climbing up just now. Where do you keep your ladders?"

"What do I want of a ladder? I've no use for a man who can't get up on the timbers. If a man needs a ladder, he'd better stay abed."

"That's where I get fired first thing," said Bannon.

"Why, you come up all right, with your overcoat on, too."

"I had to wear it or scratch up the timbers with my bones. I lost thirty-two pounds up at Duluth."

Another big timber came swinging up to them at the end of the hoisting rope. Peterson sprang out upon it. "I'm going down before I get brushed off," said Bannon.

"I'll be back at the office as soon as I get this corbel laid."

"No hurry. I want to look over the drawings. Go easy there," he called to the engineer at the hoist; "I'm coming down on the elevator." Peterson had already cast off the rope, but Bannon jumped for it and thrust his foot into the hook, and the engineer, not knowing who he was, let him down none too gently.

On his way to the office he spoke to two carpenters at work on a stick of timber. "You'd better leave that, I guess, and get some four-inch cribbing and some inch stuff and make some ladders; I guess there's enough lying 'round for that. About four'll do."

It was no wonder that the Calumet K job had proved too much for Peterson. It was difficult from the beginning. There was not enough ground space to work in comfortably, and the proper bestowal of the millions of feet of lumber until time for it to be used in the construction was no mean problem. The elevator was to be a typical "Chicago" house, built to receive grain from cars and to deliver it either to cars or to ships. As has been said, it stood back from the river, and grain for ships was to be carried on belt conveyors running in an inclosed bridge above the railroad tracks to the small spouting house on the wharf. It had originally been designed to have a capacity for twelve hundred thousand bushels, but the grain men who were building it, Page & Company, had decided after it was fairly started that it must be larger; so, in the midst of his work, Peterson had received instructions and drawings for a million bushel annex. He had done excellent work—work satisfactory even to MacBride & Company—on a smaller scale, and so he had been given the opportunity, the responsibility, the hundreds of employees, the liberal authority, to make what he could of it all.

There could be no doubt that he had made a tangle; that the big job as a whole was not under his hand, but was just running itself as best it could. Bannon, who, since the days when he was chief of the wrecking gang on a division of the Grand Trunk, had made a business of rising to emergencies, was obviously the man for the situation. He was worn thin as an old knife-blade, he was just at the end of a piece of work that would have entitled any other man to a vacation; but MacBride made no apologies when he assigned him the new task—"Go down and stop this fiddling around and get the house built. See that it's handling grain before you come away. If you can't do it, I'll come down and do it myself."

Bannon shook his head dubiously. "Well, I'm not sure——" he began. But MacBride laughed, whereupon Bannon grinned in spite of himself. "All right," he said.

It was no laughing matter, though, here on the job this Monday morning, and, once alone in the little section house, he shook his head again gravely. He liked Peterson too well, for one thing, to supersede him without a qualm. But there was nothing else for it, and he took off his overcoat, laid aside the coupling pin, and attacked the stack of blue prints.

He worked rapidly, turning now and then from the plans for a reference to the building book or the specifications, whistling softly, except when he stopped to growl, from force of habit, at the office, or, with more reasonable disapproval, at the man who made the drawings for the annex. "Regular damn bird cage," he called it.

It was half an hour before Peterson came in. He was wiping the sweat off his forehead with the back of his hand, and drawing long breaths with the mere enjoyment of living. "I feel good," he said. "That's where I'd like to work all day. You ought to go up and sledge them timbers for a while. That'd warm you through, I bet."

"You ought to make your timekeeper give you one of those brass checks there and pay you eighteen cents an hour for that work. That's what I'd do."

Peterson laughed. It took more than a hint to reach him. "I have to do it. Those laborers are no good. Honest, I can lift as much as any three men on the job."

"That's all right if those same three don't stop to swap lies while you're lifting."

"Well, I guess they don't come any of that on me," said Peterson, laughing again. "How long are you going to stay with us?"

The office, then, had not told him. Bannon was for a moment at a loss what to say. Luckily there was an interruption. The red-headed young man he had spoken to an hour before came in, tossed a tally board on the desk, and said that another carload of timber had come in.

"Mr. Bannon," said Peterson, "shake hands with Mr. Max Vogel, our lumber checker." That formality attended to, he turned to Bannon and repeated his question. By that time the other had his answer ready.

"Oh, it all depends on the office," he said. "They're bound to keep me busy at something. I'll just stay until they tell me to go somewhere else. They ain't happy except when they've just put me in a hole and told me to climb out. Generally before I'm out they pick me up and chuck me down another one. Old MacBride wouldn't think the Company was prosperous if I wasn't working nights and Sundays."

"You won't be doing that down here."

"I don't know about that. Why, when I first went to work for 'em, they hired me by the day. My time cards for the first years figured up four hundred and thirty-six days." Peterson laughed. "Oh, that's straight," said Bannon. "Next time you're at the office, ask Brown about it. Since then they've paid me a salary. They seem to think they'd have to go out of business if I ever took a vacation. I've been with 'em twelve years and they've never given me one yet. They made a bluff at it once. I was down at Newport News, been doing a job for the C. & O., and Fred Brown was down that way on business. He——"

"What does Brown look like?" interrupted Peterson. "I never saw him."

"You didn't! Oh, he's a good-looking young chap. Dresses kind of sporty. He's a great jollier. You have to know him a while to find out that he means business. Well, he came 'round and saw I was feeling pretty tired, so he asked me to knock off for a week and go fishing with him. I did, and it was the hardest work I ever tackled."

"Did you get any fish?"

"Fish? Whales! You'd no sooner throw your line over than another one'd grab it—great, big, heavy fish, and they never gave us a minute's rest. I worked like a horse for about half a day and then I gave up. Told Brown I'd take a duplex car-puller along next time I tackled that kind of a job, and I went back to the elevator."

"I'd like to see Brown. I get letters from him right along, of course. He's been jollying me about that cribbing for the last two weeks. I can't make it grow, and I've written him right along that we was expecting it, but that don't seem to satisfy him."

"I suppose not," said Bannon. "They're mostly out for results up at the office. Let's see the bill for it." Vogel handed him a thin typewritten sheet and Bannon looked it over thoughtfully. "Big lot of stuff, ain't it? Have you tried to get any of it here in Chicago?"

"Course not. It's all ordered and cut out up to Ledyard."

"Cut out? Then why don't they send it?"

"They can't get the cars."

"That'll do to tell. 'Can't get the cars!' What sort of a railroad have they got up there?"

"Max, here, can tell you about that, I guess," said Peterson.

"It's the G. & M.," said the lumber checker. "That's enough for any one who's lived in Michigan. It ain't much good."

"How long have they kept 'em waiting for the cars?"

"How long is it, Max?" asked Peterson.

"Let's see. It was two weeks ago come Tuesday."

"Sure?"

"Yes. We got the letter the same day the red-headed man came here. His hair was good and red." Max laughed broadly at the recollection. "He came into the office just as we was reading it."

"Oh, yes. My friend, the walking delegate."

"What's that?" Bannon snapped the words out so sharply that Peterson looked at him in slow surprise.

"Oh, nothing," he said. "A darn little rat of a red-headed walking delegate came out here—had a printed card with Business Agent on it— and poked his long nose into other people's business for a while, and asked the men questions, and at last he came to me. I told him that we treated our men all right and didn't need no help from him, and if I ever caught him out here again I'd carry him up to the top of the jim pole and leave him there. He went fast enough."

"I wish he'd knocked you down first, to even things up," said Bannon.

"Him! Oh, I could have handled him with three fingers."

"I'm going out for a look around," said Bannon, abruptly.

He left Peterson still smiling good-humoredly over the incident.

It was not so much to look over the job as to get where he could work out his wrath that Bannon left the office. There was no use in trying to explain to Peterson what he had done, for even if he could be made to understand, he could undo nothing. Bannon had known a good many walking delegates, and he had found them, so far, square. But it would be a large-minded man who could overlook what Peterson had done. However, there was no help for it. All that remained was to wait till the business agent should make the next move.

So Bannon put the whole incident out of his mind, and until noon inspected the job in earnest. By the time the whistle blew, every one of the hundreds of men on the job, save Peterson himself, knew that there was a new boss. There was no formal assumption of authority; Bannon's supremacy was established simply by the obvious fact that he was the man who knew how. Systematizing the confusion in one corner, showing another gang how to save handling a big stick twice, finally putting a runway across the drillage of the annex, and doing a hundred little things between times, he made himself master.

The afternoon he spent in the little office, and by four o'clock had seen everything there was in it, plans, specifications, building book, bill file, and even the pay roll, the cash account, and the correspondence. The clerk, who was also timekeeper, exhibited the latter rather grudgingly.

"What's all this stuff?" Bannon asked, holding up a stack of unfiled letters.

"Letters we ain't answered yet."

"Well, we'll answer them now," and Bannon commenced dictating his reply to the one on top of the stack. "Hold on," said the clerk, "I ain't a stenographer."

"So?" said Bannon. He scribbled a brief memorandum on each sheet. "There's enough to go by," he said. "Answer 'em according to instructions."

"I won't have time to do it till to-morrow some time."

"I'd do it to-night, if I were you," said Bannon, significantly. Then he began writing letters himself.

Peterson and Vogel came into the office a few minutes later.

"Writing a letter to your girl?" said Peterson, jocularly.

"We ought to have a stenographer out here, Pete."

"Stenographer! I didn't know you was such a dude. You'll be wanting a solid silver electric bell connecting with the sody fountain next."

"That's straight," said Bannon. "We ought to have a stenographer for a fact."

He said nothing until he had finished and sealed the two letters he was writing. They were as follows:—

DEAR MR. BROWN:

It's a mess and no mistake. I'm glad Mr. MacBride didn't come to see it. He'd have fits. The whole job is tied up in a hard knot. Peterson is wearing out chair bottoms waiting for the cribbing from Ledyard. I expect we will have a strike before long. I mean it.

The main house is most up to the distributing floor. The spouting house is framed. The annex is up as far as the bottom, waiting for cribbing.

Yours,

BANNON.

P.S. I hope this letter makes you sweat to pay you for last Saturday night. I am about dead. Can't get any sleep. And I lost thirty-two pounds up to Duluth. I expect to die down here.

C. B.

P.S. I guess we'd better set fire to the whole damn thing and collect the insurance and skip.

C.

The other was shorter.

MACBRIDE & COMPANY, Minneapolis:

Gentlemen: I came on the Calumet job to-day. Found it held up by failure of cribbing from Ledyard. Will have at least enough to work with by end of the week. We will get the house done according to specifications.

Yours truly,

MACBRIDE & COMPANY.

CHARLES BANNON.

CHAPTER 2

T he five o'clock whistle had sounded, and Peterson sat on the bench inside the office door, while Bannon washed his hands in the tin basin. The twilight was already settling; within the shanty, whose dirty, small-paned windows served only to indicate the lesser darkness without, a wall lamp, set in a dull reflector, threw shadows into the corners.

"You're coming up with me, ain't you?" said Peterson. "I don't believe you'll get much to eat. Supper's just the pickings from dinner."

"Well, the dinner was all right. But I wish you had a bigger bed. I ain't slept for two nights."

"What was the matter?"

"I was on the sleeper last night; and I didn't get in from the Duluth job till seven o'clock Saturday night, and Brown was after me before I'd got my supper. Those fellows at the office wouldn't let a man sleep at all if they could help it. Here I'd been working like a nigger 'most five months on the Duluth house—and the last three weeks running night shifts and Sundays; didn't stop to eat, half the time—and what does Brown do but—'Well,' he says, 'how're you feeling, Charlie?' 'Middling,' said I. 'Are you up to a little job to-morrow?' 'What's that?' I said. 'Seems to me if I've got to go down to the Calumet job Sunday night I might have an hour or so at home.' 'Well, Charlie,' he says, 'I'm mighty sorry, but you see we've been putting in a big rope drive on a water-power plant over at Stillwater. We got the job on the high bid,' he says, 'and we agreed to have it running on Monday morning. It'll play the devil with us if we can't make good.' 'What's the matter?' said I. 'Well,' he says, 'Murphy's had the job and has balled himself up.'"

By this time the two men had their coats on, and were outside the building.

"Let's see," said Bannon, "we go this way, don't we?"

"Yes."

There was still the light, flying flakes of snow, and the biting wind that came sweeping down from the northwest. The two men crossed the siding, and, picking their way between the freight cars on the Belt Line tracks, followed the path that wound across the stretch of dusty meadow.

"Go ahead," said Peterson; "you was telling about Murphy."

"Well, that was the situation. I could see that Brown was up on his hind legs about it, but it made me tired, all the same. Of course the job had to be done, but I wasn't letting him have any satisfaction. I told him he ought to give it to somebody else, and he handed me a lot of stuff about my experience. Finally I said: 'You come around in the morning, Mr. Brown. I ain't had any sleep to speak of for three weeks. I lost thirty-two pounds,' I said, 'and I ain't going to be bothered to-night.' Well, sir, he kind of shook his head, but he went away, and I got to thinking about it. Long about half-past seven I went down and got a time-table. There was a train to Stillwater at eight-forty-two."

"That night?"

"Sure. I went over to the shops with an express wagon and got a thousand feet of rope—had it in two coils so I could handle it—and just made the train. It was a mean night. There was some rain when I started, but you ought to have seen it when I got to Stillwater—it was coming down in layers, and mud that sucked your feet down halfway to your knees. There wasn't a wagon anywhere around the station, and the agent wouldn't lift a finger. It was blind dark. I walked off the end of the platform, and went plump into a mudhole. I waded up as far as the street crossing, where there was an electric light, and ran across a big lumber yard, and hung around until I found the night watchman. He was pretty near as mean as the station agent, but he finally let me have a wheelbarrow for half a dollar, and told me how to get to the job.

"He called it fifty rods, but it was a clean mile if it was a step, and most of the way down the track. I wheeled her back to the station, got the rope, and started out. Did you ever try to shove two five hundred foot coils over a mile of crossties? Well, that's what I did. I scraped off as much mud as

I could, so I could lift my feet, and bumped over those ties till I thought the teeth were going to be jarred clean out of me. After I got off the track there was a stretch of mud that left the road by the station up on dry land.

"There was a fool of a night watchman at the power plant—I reckon he thought I was going to steal the turbines, but he finally let me in, and I set him to starting up the power while I cleaned up Murphy's job and put in the new rope."

"All by yourself?" asked Peterson.

"Sure thing. Then I got her going and she worked smooth as grease. When we shut down and I came up to wash my hands, it was five minutes of three. I said, 'Is there a train back to Minneapolis before very long?' 'Yes,' says the watchman, 'the fast freight goes through a little after three.' 'How much after?' I said. 'Oh,' he says, 'I couldn't say exactly. Five or eight minutes, I guess.' I asked when the next train went, and he said there wasn't a regular passenger till six-fifty-five. Well, sir, maybe you think I was going to wait four hours in that hole! I went out of that building to beat the limited—never thought of the wheelbarrow till I was halfway to the station. And there was some of the liveliest stepping you ever saw. Couldn't see a thing except the light on the rails from the arc lamp up by the station. I got about halfway there—running along between the rails—and banged into a switch—knocked me seven ways for Sunday. Lost my hat picking myself up, and couldn't stop to find it."

Peterson turned in toward one of a long row of square frame houses.

"Here we are," he said. As they went up the stairs he asked: "Did you make the train?"

"Caught the caboose just as she was swinging out. They dumped me out in the freight yards, and I didn't get home till 'most five o'clock. I went right to bed, and along about eight o'clock Brown came in and woke me up. He was feeling pretty nervous. 'Say, Charlie,' he said, 'ain't it time for you to be starting?' 'Where to?' said I. 'Over to Stillwater,' he said. 'There ain't any getting out of it. That drive's got to be running to-morrow.' 'That's all right,' said I, 'but I'd like to know if I can't have one day's rest between jobs—Sunday, too. And I lost thirty-two pounds.' Well, sir, he didn't know whether to get hot or not. I guess he thought himself they were kind of rubbing it in. 'Look here,' he said, 'are you going to Stillwater, or ain't you?' 'No,' said I, 'I ain't. Not for a hundred rope drives.' Well, he just got up and took his hat and started out. 'Mr. Brown,' I said, when he was opening the door, 'I lost my hat down at Stillwater last night. I reckon the office ought to stand for it.' He turned around and looked queer, and then he grinned. 'So you went over?' he said. 'I reckon I did,' said I. 'What kind of a hat did you lose?' he asked, and he grinned again. 'I guess it was a silk one, wasn't it?' 'Yes,' said I, 'a silk hat—something about eight dollars.'"

"Did he mean he'd give you a silk hat?" asked Peterson.

"Couldn't say."

They were sitting in the ten-by-twelve room that Peterson rented for a dollar a week. Bannon had the one chair, and was sitting tipped back against the washstand. Peterson sat on the bed. Bannon had thrown his overcoat over the foot of the bed, and had dropped his bag on the floor by the window.

"Ain't it time to eat, Pete?" he said.

"Yes, there's the bell."

The significance of Bannon's arrival, and the fact that he was planning to stay, was slow in coming to Peterson. After supper, when they had returned to the room, his manner showed constraint. Finally he said:—

"Is there any fuss up at the office?"

"What about?"

"Why—do they want to rush the job or something?"

"Well, we haven't got such a lot of time. You see, it's November already."

"What's the hurry all of a sudden? They didn't say nothing to me."

"I guess you haven't been crowding it very hard, have you?"

Peterson flushed.

"I've been working harder than I ever did before," he said. "If it wasn't for the cribbing being held up like this, I'd 'a' had the cupola half done before now. I've been playing in hard luck."

Bannon was silent for a moment, then he said:—

"How long do you suppose it would take to get the cribbing down from Ledyard?"

"Not very long if it was rushed, I should think—a couple of days, or maybe three. And they'll rush it all right when they can get the cars. You see, it's only ten or eleven hours up there, passenger schedule; and they could run it right in on the job over the Belt Line."

"It's the Belt Line that crosses the bridge, is it?"

"Yes."

Bannon spread his legs apart and drummed on the front of his chair.

"What's the other line?" he asked—"the four track line?"

"That's the C. & S. C. We don't have nothing to do with them."

They were both silent for a time. The flush had not left Peterson's face. His eyes were roving over the carpet, lifting now and then to Bannon's face with a quick glance.

"Guess I'll shave," said Bannon. "Do you get hot water here?"

"Why, I don't know," replied Peterson. "I generally use cold water. The folks here ain't very obliging. Kind o' poor, you know."

Bannon was rummaging in his grip for his shaving kit.

"You never saw a razor like that, Pete," he said. "Just heft it once."

"Light, ain't it," said Peterson, taking it in his hand.

"You bet it's light. And look here"—he reached for it and drew it back and forth over the palm of his hand—"that's the only stropping I ever give it."

"Don't you have to hone it?"

"No, sir; it's never been touched to a stone or leather. You just get up and try it once. Those whiskers of yours won't look any the worse for a chopping."

Peterson laughed, and lathered his face, while Bannon put an edge on the razor, testing it with a hair.

"Say, that's about the best yet," said Peterson, after the first stroke.

"You're right it is."

Bannon looked on for a few minutes, then he took a railroad "Pathfinder" from his grip and rapidly turned the pages. Peterson saw it in the mirror, and asked, between strokes:—

"What are you going to do?"

"Looking up trains."

While Peterson was splashing in the washbowl, Bannon took his turn at the mirror.

"How's the Duluth job getting on?" asked Peterson, when Bannon had finished, and was wiping his razor.

"All right—'most done. Just a little millwright work left, and some cleaning up."

"There ain't any marine leg on the house, is there?"

"No."

"How big a house is it?"

"Eight hundred thousand bushels."

"That so? Ain't half as big as this one, is it?"

"Guess not. Built for the same people, though, Page & Company."

"They must be going in pretty heavy."

"They are. There's a good deal of talk about it. Some of the boys up at the office say there's going to be fun with December wheat before they get through with it. It's been going up pretty steadily since the end of September—it was seventy-four and three-eighths Saturday in Minneapolis. It ain't got up quite so high down here yet, but the boys say there's going to be a lot of money in it for somebody."

"Be a kind of a good thing to get in on, eh?" said Peterson, cautiously.

"Maybe, for those that like to put money in wheat. I've got no money for that sort of thing myself."

"Yes, of course," was Peterson's quick reply. "A fellow doesn't want to run them kind o' chances. I don't believe in it myself."

"The fact's this,—and this is just between you and me, mind you; I don't know anything about it, it's only what I think,—somebody's buying a lot of December wheat, or the price wouldn't keep going up. And I've got a notion that, whoever he is, it's Page & Company that's selling it to him. That's just putting two and two together, you see. It's the real grain that the Pages handle, and if they sell to a man it means that they're going to make a mighty good try at unloading it on him and making him pay for it. That's all I know about it. I see the Pages selling—or what looks mighty like it—and I see them beginning to look around and talk on the quiet about crowding things a little on their new houses, and it just strikes me that there's likely to be a devil of a lot of wheat coming into Chicago before the year runs out; and if that's so, why, there's got to be a place to put it when it gets here."

"Do they have to have an elevator to put it in?" asked Peterson. "Can't they deliver it in the cars? I don't know much about that side of the business."

"I should say not. The Board of Trade won't recognize grain as delivered until it has been inspected and stored in a registered house."

"When would the house have to be ready?"

"Well, if I'm right, if they're going to put December wheat in this house, they'll have to have it in before the last day of December."

"We couldn't do that," said Peterson, "if the cribbing was here."

Bannon, who had stretched out on the bed, swung his feet around and sat up. The situation was not easy, but he had been sent to Calumet to get the work done in time, and he meant to do it.

"Now, about this cribbing, Pete," he said; "we've got to have it before we can touch the annex?"

"I guess that's about it," Peterson replied.

"I've been figuring a little on this bill. I take it there's something over two million feet altogether. Is that right?"

"It's something like that. Couldn't say exactly. Max takes care of the lumber."

Bannon's brows came together.

"You ought to know a little more about this yourself, Pete. You're the man that's building the house."

"I guess I've been pushing it along as well as any one could," said Peterson, sullenly.

"That's all right. I ain't hitting at you. I'm talking business, that's all. Now, if Vogel's right, this cribbing ought to have been here fourteen days ago—fourteen days to-morrow."

Peterson nodded.

"That's just two weeks of lost time. How've you been planning to make that up?"

"Why—why—I reckon I can put things together soon's I get the cribbing."

"Look here, Pete. The office has contracted to get this house done by a certain date. They've got to pay $750 for every day that we run over that date. There's no getting out of that, cribbing or no cribbing. When they're seeing ten or twenty thousand dollars slipping out of their hands, do you think they're going to thank you for telling 'em that the G. & M. railroad couldn't get cars? They don't care what's the matter—all they want of you is to do the work on time."

"Now, look here, Charlie———"

"Hold on, Pete. Don't get mad. It's facts, that's all. Here's these two weeks gone. You see that, all right enough. Now, the way this work's laid out, a man's got to make every day count right from the start if he wants to land on his feet when the house is done. Maybe you think somebody up in the sky is going to hand you down a present of two extra weeks so the lost time won't count. That would be all right, only it ain't very likely to happen."

"Well," said Peterson, "what are you getting at? What do you want me to do? Perhaps you think it's easy."

"No, I don't. But I'll tell you what to do. In the first place you want to quit this getting out on the job and doing a laborer's work. The office is paying out good money to the men that should do that. You know how to lay a corbel, but just now you couldn't tell me how much cribbing was coming. You're paid to direct this whole job and to know all about it, not to lay corbels. If you put in half a day swinging a sledge out there on the spouting house, how're you going to know that the lumber bills tally, and the carpenters ain't making mistakes, and that the timber's piled right. Here to-day you had a dozen men throwing away their time moving a lot of timber that ought to have been put in the right place when it first came in."

Peterson was silent.

"Now to-morrow, Pete, as soon as you've got the work moving along, you'd better go over to the electric light company and see about having the whole ground wired for arc lamps, so we can be ready to put on a night shift the minute the cribbing comes in. You want to crowd 'em, too. They ought to have it ready in two days."

Bannon sat for a moment, then he arose and looked at his watch.

"I'm going to leave you, Pete," he said, as he put on his collar.

"Where're you going?"

"I've got to get up to the city to make the ten o'clock train. I'm going up to Ledyard to get the cribbing. Be back in a couple of days." He threw his shaving kit into his grip, put on his overcoat, said good-night, and went out.

CHAPTER 3

Next morning at eight o'clock Charlie Bannon walked into the office of C. H. Dennis, the manager of the Ledyard Salt and Lumber Company.

"I'm Bannon," he said, "of MacBride & Company. Come up to see why you don't get out our bill of cribbing."

"Told you by letter," retorted Dennis. "We can't get the cars."

"I know you did. That's a good thing to say in a letter. I wanted to find out how much of it really was cut."

"It's all cut and stacked by the siding, taking up half the yard. Want to see it?"

Bannon smiled and nodded. "Here's a good cigar for you," he said, "and you're a good fellow, but I think I'd like to see the cribbing."

"Oh, that's all right," laughed Dennis. "I'd have said the same thing if it wasn't cut. Come out this way."

Bannon followed him out into the yard. "There it is," said the manager.

There was no need of pointing it out. It made a pile more than three hundred feet long. It was nothing but rough hemlock, two inches thick, and from two to ten inches wide, intended to be spiked together flatwise for the walls of the bins, but its bulk was impressive. Bannon measured it with his eye and whistled. "I wish that had been down on our job ten days ago," he said, presently. "I'd be taking a vacation now if it had."

"Well, it was ready then. You can tell by the color."

"What's the matter with the G. & M. anyway? They don't seem to be hauling very much. I noticed that last night when I came up. I'm no good at sleeping on the train."

"Search me," said Dennis. "They've tied us up for these two weeks. I've kicked for cars, and the old man—that's Sloan—he's kicked, but here we are yet—can't move hand or foot."

"Who's Sloan?"

"Oh, he's the whole thing. Owns the First National Bank and the trolley line and the Ledyard Salt and Lumber Company and most of the downtown real estate."

"Where can I find him? Is he in town?"

"I guess so. He's got an office across the river. Just ask anybody where the Sloan Building is."

"Likely to be there as early as this?" asked Bannon, looking at his watch.

"Sure, if he's in town."

Bannon slipped his watch into his pocket. "Much obliged," he said. "Glad to have met you. Good morning;" and, turning, he walked rapidly away down the plank wagon road.

In Sloan's office he stated his errand as briefly as on the former occasion, adding only that he had already seen Dennis.

"I guess he told you all there is to tell," said the magnate. "We can't make the G. & M. give us cars. I've told Dennis to stir 'em up as hard as he could. I guess we'll have to wait."

"I can't wait."

"What else can you do? It's every bit as bad for us as it is for you, and you can rest assured that we'll do all we can." As if the cadence of his last sentence were not sufficiently recognizable as a formula of dismissal, he picked up a letter that lay on his desk and began reading it.

"This isn't an ordinary kick," said Bannon, sharply. "It isn't just a case of us having to pay a big delay forfeit. There's a reason why our job's got to be done on time. I want to know the reason why the G. & M. won't give you cars. It ain't because they haven't got them."

"What makes you say that?"

"Because there's three big strings of empties within twenty miles of here this minute. I saw them when I came up this morning."

For a minute Sloan said nothing, only traced designs on the blotter with his pencil. Bannon saw that there was no longer any question of arousing his interest. At last he spoke:—

"I've suspected that there was something in the wind, but I've been too busy with other things to tend to it, so I turned it over to Dennis. Perhaps he's done as well as I could. I don't know much about G. & M. these days. For a long time they were at me to take a big block of treasury stock, but the road seemed to me in bad shape, so I wouldn't go in. Lately they've reorganized—have got a lot of new money in there—I don't know whose, but they've let me alone. There's been no row, you understand. That ain't the reason they've tied us up, but I haven't known much about what was going on inside."

"Would they be likely to tell you if you asked? I mean if you took it to headquarters?"

"I couldn't get any more out of them than you could—that is, not by asking."

"I guess I'll go look 'em up myself. Where can I find anybody that knows anything?"

"The division offices are at Blake City. That's only about twenty miles. You could save time by talking over the 'phone."

"Not me," said Bannon. "In a case like this I couldn't express myself properly unless I saw the fellow I was talking to."

Sloan laughed. "I guess you're right. But I'll call up the division superintendent and tell him you're coming. Then you'll be sure of finding him."

Bannon shook his head. "I'd find him with his little speech all learned. No, I'll take my chances on his being there. When's the train?"

"Nine-forty-six."

"That gives me fifteen minutes. Can I make it?"

"Not afoot, and you ain't likely to catch a car. I'll drive you down. I've got the fastest mare in Pottawatomie County."

The fact that the G. & M. had been rescued from its poverty and was about to be "developed" was made manifest in Blake City by the modern building which the railroad was erecting on the main street. Eventually the division officials were to be installed in office suites of mahogany veneer, with ground glass doors lettered in gold leaf. For the present, as from the beginning, they occupied an upper floor of a freight warehouse. Bannon came in about eleven o'clock, looked briefly about, and seeing that one corner was partitioned off into a private office, he ducked under the hand rail intended to pen up ordinary visitors, and made for it. A telegraph operator just outside the door asked what his business was, but he answered merely that it was with the superintendent, and went in.

He expected rather rough work. The superintendent of a railroad, or of a division, has to do with the employees, never with the customers, and his professional manner is not likely to be distinguished by suavity. So he unconsciously squared his shoulders when he said, "I'm Bannon, of MacBride & Company."

The superintendent dismissed his stenographer, swept with his arm a clear space on the desk, and then drummed on it with his fingers, but he did not look up immediately. When he did, it was with an expression of grave concern.

"Mr. Bannon," he said, "I'm mighty sorry. I'll do anything I can for you. You can smoke ten cent cigars on me from now till Christmas, and light them with passes. Anything——"

"If you feel like that," said Bannon, "we can fix things all comfortable in three minutes. All I want is cars."

The superintendent shook his head. "There's where you stump me," he said. "I haven't got 'em."

"Mr. Superintendent, that's what they told me in Chicago, and that's what they told me at Ledyard. I didn't come up here to Blake City to be told the same thing and then go back home."

"Well, I don't know what else I can tell you. That's just the size of it. I hope we'll be able to fix you in a few days, but we can't promise anything."

Bannon frowned, and after an expectant pause, the superintendent went on talking vaguely about the immense rush of traffic. Finally he asked, "Why do you think we'd hold you up if we had the cars?"

"That's what I came here to find out. I think you're mistaken about not having them."

The superintendent laughed. "You can't expect to know more about that than I do. You doubtless understand your business, but this is my business. If you can tell me where the cars are, you can have them."

"Well, as you say, that's your business. But I can tell you. There's a big string of empties—I counted fourteen—on the siding at Victory."

The superintendent looked out of the window and again drummed on the desk. When he spoke again, his manner was more what one would expect from a division superintendent. "You don't know anything about it. When we want advice how to run our road we'll ask you for it. Victory isn't in my division anyway."

"Then wire the general manager. He ought to know something about it."

"Wire him yourself, if you like. I can't bother about it. I'm sorry I can't do anything, but I haven't got time."

"I haven't begun sending telegrams yet. And I haven't very much more time to fool away. I'd like to have you find out if the Ledyard Salt and Lumber Company can have those cars that are on the siding at Victory."

"All right," said the superintendent, rising. At the door he turned back to ask, "When was it you saw them?"

Bannon decided to chance it. "Yesterday morning," he said.

The superintendent returned presently, and, turning to his desk, resumed his work. A few minutes later the telegraph operator came in and told him that the cars at Victory had been loaded with iron truss work the night before, and had gone off down the State.

"Just too late, wasn't I?" said Bannon. "That's hard luck." He went to the window and, staring out into the yards, began tapping idly with his pencil on the glass. The office door was open, and when he paused he heard the telegraph instrument just without, clicking out a message.

"Anything else I can do for you?" asked the superintendent. His good humor was returning at the sight of his visitor's perplexity.

"I wish you'd just wire the general manager once more and ask him if he can't possibly let us have those cars."

"All right," said the other, cheerfully. He nodded to the operator. "For the Ledyard Salt and Lumber Company," he said.

Bannon dropped into a chair, stretched himself, and yawned. "I'm sleepy," he said; "haven't had any sleep in three weeks. Lost thirty-two pounds. If you fellows had only got that cribbing down on time, I'd be having a vacation——"

Another yawn interrupted him. The telegraph receiver had begun giving out the general manager's answer.

Tell-Ledyard-we-hope-to-have-cars-in-a-few-days-

The superintendent looked at Bannon, expecting him to finish his sentence, but he only yawned again.

obey-previous-instructions.—Do-not-give-Ledyard-cars-in-any-case-

Bannon's eyes were half closed, but the superintendent thought he was turning a little toward the open doorway.

"Do you feel cold?" he asked. "I'll shut the door."

He rose quickly and started toward it, but Bannon was there before him. He hesitated, his hand on the knob.

"Why don't you shut it?" snapped the superintendent.

"I think I'll—I think I'll send a telegram."

"Here's a blank, in here. Come in." But Bannon had slipped out and was standing beside the operator's table. From the doorway the superintendent saw him biting his pencil and frowning over a bit of paper. The general manager's message was still coming in.

We-don't-help-put-up-any-grain-elevator-in-Chicago-these-days.

As the last click sounded, Bannon handed his message to the operator. "Send it collect," he said. With that he strode away, over the hand rail, this time, and down the stairs. The operator carried the message to the superintendent.

"It seems to be for you," he said.

The superintendent read—

> Div. Supt. G. & M., Blake City. Tell manager it takes better man than him to tie us up.
>
> MACBRIDE & COMPANY.

Bannon had nearly an hour to wait for the next train back to Ledyard, but it was not time wasted, for as he paced the smoky waiting room, he arrived at a fairly accurate estimate of the meaning of the general manager's message.

It was simply a confirmation of the cautious prediction he had made to Peterson the night before. Why should any one want to hinder the construction of an elevator in Chicago "these days" except to prevent its use for the formal delivery of grain which the buyer did not wish delivered? And why had Page & Company suddenly ordered a million bushel annex? Why had they suddenly become anxious that the elevator should be ready to receive grain before January first, unless they wished to deliver a vast amount of December wheat? Before Bannon's train came in he understood it all. A clique of speculators had decided to corner wheat, an enterprise nearly enough impossible in any case, but stark madness unless they had many millions at command. It was a long chance, of course, but after all not wonderful that some one in their number was a power in the reorganized G. & M.

Already the immense amount of wheat in Chicago was testing the capacity of the registered warehouses, and plainly, if the Calumet K should be delayed long enough, it might prevent Page & Company from carrying out their contract to deliver two million bushels of the grain, even though it were actually in the cars in Chicago.

Bannon knew much of Page & Company; that dotted all over the vast wheat tracts of Minnesota and Montana were their little receiving elevators where they bought grain of the farmers; that miles of wheat-laden freight cars were already lumbering eastward along the railroad lines of the North. He had a touch of imagination, and something of the enormous momentum of that Northern wheat took possession of him. It would come to Chicago, and he must be ready for it. It would be absurd to be balked by the refusal of a little single-track road up in Michigan to carry a pile of planks.

He paused before the grated window of the ticket and telegraph office and asked for a map. He studied it attentively for a while; then he sent a telegram:—

MACBRIDE & COMPANY, _Minneapolis_: G. & M. R. R. wants to tie us up. Will not furnish cars to carry our cribbing. Can't get it elsewhere inside of three weeks. Find out if Page will O. K. any bill of extras I send in for bringing it down. If so, can they have one or more steam barges at Manistogee within forty-eight hours?

Wire Ledyard Hotel. C. H. BANNON.

It was an hour's ride back to Ledyard. He went to the hotel and persuaded the head waiter to give him something to eat, although it was long after the dinner hour. As he left the dining room, the clerk handed him two telegrams. One read:—

Get cribbing down. Page pays the freight. BROWN.

The other:—

Steam barge Demosthenes leaves Milwaukee to-night for Manistogee.

PAGE & CO.

CHAPTER 4

As Bannon was paying for his dinner, he asked the clerk what sort of a place Manistogee was. The clerk replied that he had never been there, but that he understood it was quite a lively town.

"Good road over there?"

"Pretty fair."

"That means you can get through if you're lucky."

The clerk smiled. "It won't be so bad to-day. You see we've been getting a good deal of rain. That packs down the sand. You ought to get there all right. Were you thinking of driving over?"

"That's the only way to go, is it? Well, I'll see. Maybe a little later. How far is it?"

"The farmers call it eighteen miles."

Bannon nodded his thanks and went back to Sloan's office.

"Well, it didn't take you long," said the magnate. "Find out what was the matter with 'em?"

He enjoyed his well-earned reputation for choler, and as Bannon told him what he had discovered that morning, the old man paced the room in a regular beat, pausing every time he came to a certain tempting bit of blank wall to deal it a thump with his big fist. When the whole situation was made clear to him, he stopped walking and cursed the whole G. & M. system, from the ties up. "I'll make 'em smart for that," he said. "They haul those planks whether they want to or not. You hear me say it. There's a law that covers a case like that. I'll prosecute 'em. They'll see whether J. B. Sloan is a safe kind of man to monkey with. Why, man," he added, turning sharply to Bannon, "why don't you get mad? You don't seem to care—no more than the angel Gabriel."

HE ... CURSED THE WHOLE G. & M. SYSTEM, FROM THE TIES UP

"I don't care a damn for the G. & M. I want the cribbing."

"Don't you worry. I'll have the law on those fellows——"

"And I'd get the stuff about five years from now, when I was likely enough dead."

"What's the best way to get it, according to your idea?"

"Take it over to Manistogee in wagons and then down by barges."

Sloan snorted. "You'd stand a chance to get some of it by Fourth of July that way."

"Do you want to bet on that proposition?"

Sloan made no reply. He had allowed his wrath to boil for a few minutes merely as a luxury. Now he was thinking seriously of the scheme. "It sounds like moonshine," he said at last, "but I don't know as it is. How are you going to get your barges?"

"I've got one already. It leaves Milwaukee to-night."

Sloan looked him over. "I wish you were out of a job," he said. Then abruptly he went on: "Where are your wagons coming from? You haven't got them all lined up in the yard now, have you? It'll take a lot of them."

"I know it. Well, we'll get all there are in Ledyard. There's a beginning. And the farmers round here ain't so very fond of the G. & M., are they? Don't they think the railroad discriminates against them—and ain't they right about it? I never saw a farmer yet that wouldn't grab a chance to get even with a railroad."

"That's about right, in this part of the country, anyway."

"You get up a regular circus poster saying what you think of the G. & M., and call on the farmers to hitch up and drive to your lumber yard. We'll stick that up at every crossroads between here and Manistogee."

Sloan was scribbling on a memorandum pad before Bannon had finished speaking. He made a false start or two, but presently got something that seemed to please him. He rang for his office boy, and told him to take it to the _Eagle_ office.

"It's got to be done in an hour," said Bannon. "That's when the procession moves," he added; as Sloan looked at him questioningly.

The other nodded. "In an hour," he said to the office boy. "What are you going to do in an hour?" he asked, as the boy went out.

"Why, it'll be four o'clock then, and we ought to start for Manistogee as early as we can."

"We! Well, I should think not!" said Sloan.

"You're going to drive me over with that fast mare of yours, aren't you?"

Sloan laughed. "Look at it rain out there."

"Best thing in the world for a sand road," said Bannon. "And we'll wash, I guess. Both been wet before."

"But it's twenty-five miles over there—twenty-five to thirty."

Bannon looked at his watch. "We ought to get there by ten o'clock, I should think."

"Ten o'clock! What do you think she is—a sawhorse! She never took more than two hours to Manistogee in her life."

The corners of Bannon's mouth twitched expressively. Sloan laughed again. "I guess it's up to me this time," he said.

Before they started Sloan telephoned to the Eagle office to tell them to print a full-sized reproduction of his poster on the front page of the Ledyard Evening Eagle.

"Crowd their news a little, won't it?" Bannon asked.

Sloan shook his head. "That helps 'em out in great shape."

The Eagle did not keep them waiting. The moment Sloan pulled up his impatient mare before the office door, the editor ran out, bare-headed, in the rain, with the posters.

"They're pretty wet yet," he said.

"That's all right. I only want a handful. Send the others to my office. They know what to do with 'em."

"I was glad to print them," the editor went on deferentially. "You have expressed our opinion of the G. & M. exactly."

"Guess I did," said Sloan as they drove away. "The reorganized G. & M. decided they didn't want to carry him around the country on a pass."

Bannon pulled out one of the sheets and opened it on his knee. He whistled as he read the first sentence, and swore appreciatively over the next. When he had finished, he buttoned the waterproof apron and rubbed his wet hands over his knees. "It's grand," he said. "I never saw anything like it."

Sloan spoke to the mare. He had held her back as they jolted over the worn pavement of cedar blocks, but now they had reached the city limits and were starting out upon the rain-beaten sand. She was a tall, clean-limbed sorrel, a Kentucky-bred Morgan, and as she settled into her stride, Bannon watched her admiringly. Her wet flanks had the dull sheen of bronze.

"Don't tell me," said Sloan, "that Michigan roads are no good for driving. You never had anything finer than this in your life." They sped along as on velvet, noiselessly save when their wheels sliced through standing pools of water. "She can keep this up till further notice, I suppose," said Bannon. Sloan nodded.

Soon they reached the first crossroad. There was a general store at one corner, and, opposite, a blacksmith's shop. Sloan pulled up and Bannon sprang out with a hammer, a mouthful of tacks, and three or four of the posters. He put them up on the sheltered side of conspicuous trees, left one with the storekeeper, and another with the smith. Then they drove on.

They made no pretence at conversation. Bannon seemed asleep save that he

was always ready with his hammer and his posters whenever Sloan halted the mare. The west wind freshened as the evening came on and dashed fine, sleety rain into their faces. Bannon huddled his wet coat closer about him. Sloan put the reins between his knees and pulled on a pair of heavy gloves.

It had been dark for half an hour—Bannon could hardly distinguish the moving figure of the mare—when Sloan spoke to her and drew her to a walk. Bannon reached for his hammer. "No crossroad here," said Sloan. "Bridge out of repair. We've got to fetch a circle here up to where she can wade it."

"Hold on," said Bannon sharply. "Let me get out."

"Don't be scared. We'll make it all right."

"We! Yes, but will fifteen hundred feet of lumber make it? I want to take a look."

He splashed forward in the dark, but soon returned. "It's nothing that can't be fixed in two hours. Where's the nearest farmhouse?"

"Fifty rods up the road to your right."

Again Bannon disappeared. Presently Sloan heard the deep challenge of a big dog. He backed the buggy around up against the wind so that he could have shelter while he waited. Then he pulled a spare blanket from under the seat and threw it over the mare. At the end of twenty minutes, he saw a lantern bobbing toward him.

The big farmer who accompanied Bannon held the lantern high and looked over the mare. "It's her all right," he said. Then he turned so that the light shone full in Sloan's face. "Good evening, Mr. Sloan," he said. "You'll excuse me, but is what this gentleman tells me all straight?"

"Guess it is," Sloan smiled. "I'd bank on him myself."

The farmer nodded with satisfaction. "All right then, Mr. What's-your-name. I'll have it done for you."

Sloan asked no questions until they had forded the stream and were back on the road. Then he inquired, "What's he going to do?"

"Mend the bridge. I told him it had to be done to-night. Said he couldn't. Hadn't any lumber. Couldn't think of it I told him to pull down the lee side of his house if necessary; said you'd give him the lumber to build an annex on it."

"What!"

"Oh, it's all right. Send the bill to MacBride. I knew your name would go down and mine wouldn't."

The delay had proved costly, and it was half-past seven before they reached the Manistogee hotel.

"Now," said Bannon, "we'll have time to rub down the mare and feed her before I'm ready to go back."

Sloan stared at him for a moment in unfeigned amazement. Then slowly he shook his head. "All right, I'm no quitter. But I will say that I'm glad you ain't coming to Ledyard to live."

Bannon left the supper table before Sloan had finished, and was gone nearly an hour. "It's all fixed up," he said when he returned. "I've cinched the wharf."

They started back as they had come, in silence, Bannon crowding as low as possible in his ulster, dozing. But he roused when the mare, of her own accord, left the road at the detour for the ford.

"You don't need to do that," he said. "The bridge is fixed." So they drove straight across, the mare feeling her way cautiously over the new-laid planks.

The clouds were thinning, so that there was a little light, and Bannon leaned forward and looked about.

"How did you get hold of the message from the general manager?" asked Sloan abruptly.

"Heard it. I can read Morse signals like print. Used to work for the Grand Trunk."

"What doing?"

"Boss of a wrecking gang." Bannon paused. Presently he went on.

"Yes, there was two years when I slept with my boots on. Didn't know a quiet minute. Never could tell what I was going to get up against. I never saw two wrecks that were anything alike. There was a junction about fifty miles down the road where they used to have collisions regular; but they were all different. I couldn't figure out what I was going to do till I was on the ground, and then I didn't have time to. My only order was, 'Clear the road—and be damn quick about it. 'What I said went. I've set fire to fifty thousand dollars' worth of mixed freight just to get it out of the way—and they never kicked. That ain't the kind of life for me, though. No, nor this ain't, either. I want to be quiet. I've never had a chance yet, and I've been looking for it ever since I was twelve years old. I'd like to get a little farm and live on it all by myself. I'd raise garden truck, cabbages, and such, and I'd take piano lessons."

"Is that why you quit the Grand Trunk? So that you could take piano lessons?" Sloan laughed as he asked the question, but Bannon replied seriously:—

"Why, not exactly. There was a little friction between me and the master mechanic, so I resigned. I didn't exactly resign, either," he added a moment later. "I wired the superintendent to go to hell. It came to the same thing."

"I worked for a railroad once myself," said Sloan. "Was a hostler in the round-house at Syracuse, New York. I never worked up any higher than that. I had ambitions to be promoted to the presidency, but it didn't seem very likely, so I gave it up and came West."

"You made a good thing of it. You seem to own most all Pottawatomie County."

"Pretty much."

"I wish you would tell me how to do it. I have worked like an all-the-year-round blast furnace ever since I could creep, and never slighted a job yet, but here I am—can't call my soul my own. I have saved fifteen thousand dollars, but that ain't enough to stop with. I don't see why I don't own a county too."

"There's some luck about it. And then I don't believe you look very sharp for opportunities. I suppose you are too busy. You've got a chance this minute to turn your fifteen thousand to fifty; maybe lot more."

"I'm afraid I'm too thick-headed to see it."

"Why, what you found out this morning was the straightest kind of a straight tip on the wheat market for the next two months. A big elevator like yours will be almost decisive. The thing's right in your own hands. If Page & Company can't make that delivery, why, fellows who buy wheat now are going to make money."

"I see," said Bannon, quickly. "All I'd have to do would be to buy all the wheat I could get trusted for and then hold back the job a little. And while I was at it, I might just as well make a clean job and walk off with the pay roll." He laughed. "I'd look pretty, wouldn't I, going to old MacBride with my tail between my legs, telling him that the job was too much for me and I couldn't get it done on time. He'd look me over and say: 'Bannon, you're a liar. You've never had to lay down yet, and you don't now. Go back and get that job done before New Year's or I'll shoot you.'"

"You don't want to get rich, that's the trouble with you," said Sloan, and he said it almost enviously.

Bannon rode to Manistogee on the first wagon. The barge was there, so the work of loading the cribbing into her began at once. There were numerous interruptions at first, but later in the day the stream of wagons became almost continuous. Farmers living on other than the Manistogee roads came into Ledyard and hurried back to tell their neighbors of the chance to get ahead of the railroad for once. Dennis, who was in charge at the yard, had hard work to keep up with the supply of empty wagons.

Sloan disappeared early in the morning, but at five o'clock Bannon had a telephone message from him. "I'm here at Blake City," he said, "raising hell. The general manager gets here at nine o'clock to-night to talk with me. They're feeling nervous about your getting that message. I think you'd better come up here and talk to him."

So a little after nine that night the three men, Sloan, Bannon, and the manager, sat down to talk it over. And the fact that in the first place an attempt to boycott could be proved, and in the second that Page & Company were getting what they wanted anyway—while they talked a long procession of cribbing was creaking along by lantern light to Manistogee—finally convinced the manager that the time had come to yield as gracefully as possible.

"He means it this time," said Sloan, when he and Bannon were left alone at the Blake City hotel to talk things over.

"Yes, I think he does. If he don't, I'll come up here again and have a short session with him."

CHAPTER 5

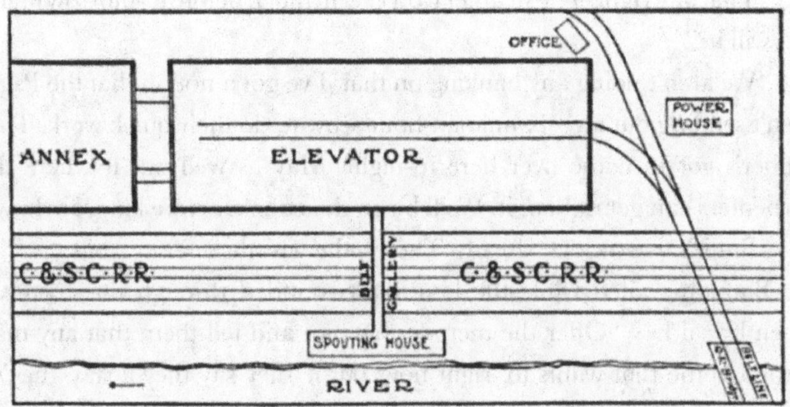

I t was nearly five o'clock when Bannon appeared at the elevator on Thursday. He at once sought Peterson.

"Well, what luck did you have?" he asked. "Did you get my message?"

"Your message? Oh, sure. You said the cribbing was coming down by boat. I don't see how, though. Ledyard ain't on the lake."

"Well, it's coming just the same, two hundred thousand feet of it. What have you done about it?"

"Oh, we'll be ready for it, soon's it gets here."

They were standing at the north side of the elevator near the paling fence which bounded the C. & S. C. right of way. Bannon looked across the tracks to the wharf; the pile of timber was still there.

"Did you have any trouble with the railroad when you took your stuff across for the spouting house?" he asked.

"Not much of any. The section boss came around and talked a little, but we only opened the fence in one place, and that seemed to suit him."

Bannon was looking about, calculating with his eye the space that was available for the incoming lumber.

"How'd you manage that business, anyway?" asked Peterson.

"What business?"

"The cribbing. How'd you get it to the lake?"

"Oh, that was easy. I just carried it off."

"Yes, you did!" "Look here, Pete, that timber hasn't got any business out there on the wharf. We've got to have that room for the cribbing."

"That's all right. The steamer won't get in much before to-morrow night, will it?"

"We aren't doing any banking on that. I've got a notion that the Pages aren't sending out any six-mile-an-hour scow to do their quick work. That timber's got to come over here to-night. May as well put it where the carpenters can get right at it. We'll be on the cupola before long, anyhow."

"But it's five o'clock already. There's the whistle."

Bannon waited while the long blast sounded through the crisp air. Then he said:— "Offer the men double pay, and tell them that any man can go home that wants to, right now, but if they say they'll stay, they've got to see it through."

Already the laborers were hurrying toward the tool house in a long, irregular line. Peterson started toward the office, to give the word to the men before they could hand in their time checks.

"Mr. Bannon."

The foreman turned; Vogel was approaching.

"I wanted to see about that cribbing bill. How much of it's coming down by boat?"

"Two hundred thousand. You'd better help Peterson get that timber out of the way. We're holding the men."

"Yes, I've been waiting for directions about that. We can put a big gang on it, and snake it across in no time."

"You'll have to open up the fence in half a dozen places, and put on every man you've got. There's no use in making an all-night job of it."

"I'm afraid we'll have trouble with the railroad."

"No, we won't. If they kick, you send them to me. Are your arc lights in?"

"Yes, all but one or two. They were going to finish it to-day, but they ain't very spry about it."

"Tell you what you do, Max; you call them up and tell them we want a man to come out here and stay for a while. I may want to move the lights around a little. And, anyhow, they may as well clean up their job and have it done with."

He was starting back after the returning laborers when Max said:—

"Mr. Bannon."

"Hello?"

"I heard you speaking about a stenographer the other day."

"Yes—what about it? Haven't you got one yet?"

"No, but I know of one that could do the work first-rate."

"I want a good one—he's got to keep time besides doing the office work."

"Yes, I thought of that. I don't suppose she——"

"She? We can't have any shes on this job."

"Well, it's like this, Mr. Bannon; she's an A1 stenographer and bookkeeper; and as for keeping the time, why, I'm out on the job all day anyhow, and I reckon I could take care of it without cutting into my work."

Bannon looked quizzically down at him.

"You don't know what you're talking about," he said slowly. "Just look around at this gang of men—you know the likes of them as well as I do— and then talk to me about bringing a girl on the job." He his head. "I reckon it's some one you're interested in."

"Yes," said Max, "it's my sister."

Max evidently did not intend to be turned off. As he stood awaiting a reply—his broad, flat features, his long arms and bow legs with their huge hands and feet, his fringe of brick-red hair cropping out behind his cap, each contributing to the general appearance of utter homeliness—a faint smile came over Bannon's face. The half-formed thought was in his mind, "If she looks anything like that, I guess she's safe." He was silent for a moment, then he said abruptly:—

"When can she start?"

"Right away."

"All right. We'll try it for a day or so and see how it goes. Tell that boy in the office that he can charge his time up to Saturday night, but he needn't stay around any longer."

Max hurried away. Group after group of laborers, peavies or cant-hooks on shoulders, were moving slowly past him toward the wharf. It was already nearly dark, and the arc lights on the elevator structure, and on the spouting house, beyond the tracks, were flaring. He started toward the wharf, walking behind a score of the laborers.

From the east, over the flats and marshes through which the narrow, sluggish river wanders to Lake Michigan, came the hoarse whistle of a steamer. Bannon turned and looked. His view was blocked by some freight cars that were standing on the C. & S. C tracks at some distance to the east. He ran across the tracks and out on the wharf, climbing on the timber pile, where Peterson and his gang were rolling down the big sticks with cant-hooks. Not a quarter of a mile away was a big steamer, ploughing slowly up the river; the cough of her engines and the swash of the churning water at her bow and stern could be plainly heard. Peterson stopped work for a moment, and joined him.

"Well," Bannon said, "we're in for it now. I never thought they'd make such time as this."

"She can lay up here all night till morning, I guess."

Bannon was thinking hard.

"No," he finally said, "she can't. There ain't any use of wasting all day to-morrow unloading that cribbing and getting it across."

Peterson, too, was thinking; and his eye-brows were coming together in a puzzled scowl.

"Oh," he said, "you mean to do it to-night?"

"Yes, sir. We don't get any sleep till every piece of that cribbing is over at the annex, ready for business in the morning. Your sills are laid—there's nothing in the way of starting those bins right up. This ain't an all-night job if we hustle it."

The steamer was a big lake barge, with high bow and stern, and a long, low, cargo deck amidships that was piled squarely and high with yellow two-inch plank. Her crew had clearly been impressed with the need of hurry, for long before she could be worked into the wharf they had rigged the two hoists and got the donkey engines into running order. The captain stood by the rail on the bridge, smoking a cigar, his hand on the bell-pull.

"Where do you want it?" he called to Bannon.

"Right here, where I'm standing. You can swing your bow in just below the bridge there."

The captain pulled the bell, and the snub-nosed craft, stirring up a whirl of mud from the bottom of the river, was brought alongside the wharf.

"Where are you going to put it?" the captain called.

"Here. We'll clean this up as fast as we can. I want that cribbing all unloaded to-night, sure."

"That suits me," said the captain. "I don't want to be held up here—ought to pull out the first thing in the morning."

"All right, you can do it." Bannon turned to Peterson and Vogel (who had just reached the wharf). "You want to rush this, boys. I'll go over and see to the piling."

He hurried away, pausing at the office long enough to find the man sent by the electric light company, and to set him at work. The arc lamps had been placed, for the most part, where they would best illuminate the annex and the cupola of the elevator, and there was none too much light on the tracks, where the men were stumbling along, hindered rather than helped by the bright light before them. On the wharf it was less dark, for the lights of the steamer were aided by two on the spouting house. Before seven o'clock Bannon had succeeded in getting two more lights up on poles, one on each side of the track.

It was just at seven that the timbers suddenly stopped coming in. Bannon looked around impatiently. The six men that had brought in the last stick were disappearing around the corner of the great, shadowy structure that shut off Bannon's view of the wharf. He waited for a moment, but no more gangs appeared, and then he ran around the elevator over the path the men had already trampled. Within the circle of light between him and the C. & S. C. tracks stood scattered groups of the laborers, and others wandered about with their hooks over their shoulders. There was a larger, less distinct crowd out on the tracks. Bannon ran through an opening in the fence, and pushed into the largest group. Here Peterson and Vogel were talking to a stupid-looking man with a sandy mustache.

"What does this mean, Pete?" he said shortly. "We can't be held up this way. Get your men back on the work."

"No, he won't," said the third man. "You can't go on with this work."

Bannon sharply looked the man over. There was in his manner a dogged authority.

"Who are you?" Bannon asked. "Who do you represent?"

"I represent the C. & S. C. railroad, and I tell you this work stops right here."

"Why?"

The man waved his arm toward the fence.

"You can't do that sort of business."

"What sort?"

"You look at that fence and then talk to me about what sort."

"What's the matter with the fence?"

"What's the matter with it! There ain't more'n a rod of it left, that's what."

Bannon's scowl relaxed.

"Oh," he said, "I see. You're the section boss, ain't you?"

"Yes."

"That's all right then. Come over here and I'll show you how we've got things fixed."

He walked across the track, followed by the section boss and Pete, and pointed out the displaced sections of the fence, each of which had been carefully placed at one side.

"We'll have it all up all right before morning," he said.

The man was running his fingers up under his cap.

"I don't know anything about that," he replied sullenly. "I've got my orders. We didn't make any kick when you opened up in one place, but we can't stand for all this."

He was not speaking firmly, and Bannon, watching him closely, jumped at the conclusion that his orders were not very definite. Probably his superintendent had instructed him to keep a close eye on the work, and perhaps to grant no privileges. Bannon wished he knew more about the understanding between the railroad and MacBride & Company. He felt sure, however, that an understanding did exist or he would not have been told to go ahead.

"That's all right," he said, with an air of easy authority. "We've got to be working over your tracks for the next two months. It's as much to our interest as it is to yours to be careful, and I guess we can pull together. We've got an agreement with your general manager, and that's what goes." He turned away, but paused and added, "I'll see that you don't have any reason to complain."

The section boss looked about with an uncertain air at the crowd of waiting men.

"Don't go too fast there———" he began.

"Look here," said Bannon, abruptly. "We'll sit right down here and send a message to the general manager. That's the quickest way to settle it—tell him that we're carrying out timber across the tracks and you've stopped us."

It was a bluff, but Bannon knew his man.

"Now, how about this?" was the reply. "How long will it take you?"

"Till some time before daylight." Bannon was feeling for his pencil.

"You see that the fence goes back, will you? We ain't taking any chances, you understand."

Bannon nodded.

"All right, Max," he shouted. "Get to work there. And look here, Max," in a stern voice, "I expect you to see that the road is not blocked or delayed in any way. That's your business now, mind." He turned to the boss as the men hurried past to the wharf. "I used to be a railroad man myself—chief wrecker on the Grand Trunk—and I guess we won't have any trouble understanding each other."

Again the six long lines of men were creeping from the brightly lighted wharf across the shadowy tracks and around the end of the elevator. Bannon had held the electric light man within call, and now set him at work moving two other arc lamps to a position where they made the ground about the growing piles of timber nearly as light as day. Through the night air he could hear the thumping of the planks on the wharf. Faintly over this sound came the shouting of men and the tramp and shuffle of feet. And at intervals a train would rumble in the distance, slowly coming nearer, until with a roar that swallowed all the other noises it was past. The arc lamps glowed and buzzed over the heads of the sweating, grunting men, as they came along the path, gang after gang, lifting an end of a heavy stick to the level of the steadily rising pile, and sliding it home.

Bannon knew from long experience how to pile the different sizes so that each would be ready at the hands of the carpenters when the morning whistle should blow. He was all about the work, giving a hand here, an order there, always good-humored, though brusque, and always inspiring the men with the sight of his own activity.

Toward the middle of the evening Vogel came up from the wharf with a question. As he was about to return, Bannon, who had been turning over in his mind the incident of the section boss, said:—

"Wait a minute, Max. What about this railroad business—have they bothered you much before now?"

"Not very much, only in little ways. I guess it's just this section boss that does it on his own hook. He's a sort of a fool, you know, and he's got it into his head that we're trying to do him some way."

Bannon put his hands into his pockets, and studied the checkered pattern in the ground shadow of the nearest arc lamp. Then he slowly shook his head.

"No," he said, "that ain't it. He's too big a fool to do much on his own hook. He's acting on orders of some sort, and that's just what I don't understand. As a general thing a railroad's mighty white to an elevator. Come to think of it, they said something about it up at the office,"—he was apparently speaking to himself, and Max quietly waited,—"Brown said something about the C. & S. C. having got in the way a little down here, but I didn't think much about it at the time."

"What could they do?" Max asked.

"A lot, if they wanted to. But that ain't what's bothering me. They haven't any connection with the G. & M., have they?"

"No"—Max shook his head—"no, not that I know of."

"Well, it's funny, that's all. The man behind those orders that the section boss talks about is the general manager; and it's my notion that we're likely to hear from him again. I'll tell you what it is. Somebody—I don't know who, but somebody—is mighty eager to keep this house from being finished by the first of January. After this I wish you'd keep your eyes open for this section boss. Have you had any trouble with the men?"

"No, only that clerk that we laid off to-day, he 'lowed he was going to make trouble. I didn't say anything about it, because they always talk like that."

"Yes, I know. What's his name?"

"Briggs."

"I guess he can't hurt us any."

Bannon turned back to his work; and Vogel disappeared in the shadows along the path.

Nine o'clock came, and the timber was still coming in. The men were growing tired and surly from the merciless strain of carrying the long, heavy sticks. The night was raw and chill. Bannon felt it as he stood directing the work, and he kept his hands in his pockets, and wished he had worn his overcoat; but the laborers, barearmed and bare-headed, clad only in overalls or in thin trousers and cotton shirts, were shaking sweat from their eyes, and stealing moments between trips to stand where the keen lake breeze could cool them. Another half-hour or so should see the last stick on the piles, and Bannon had about decided to go over to the office when he saw Vogel moving among the men, marking their time in his book.

"Here, Max," he called, adding, when Vogel had reached his side: "Just keep an eye on this, will you? I'll be at the office. Keep things going just as they are."

There was a light in the office. Bannon stepped into the doorway, and, with a suppressed word of impatience, stood looking at the scene within. The desk that Peterson had supplied for the use of his clerk was breast-high from the floor, built against the wall, with a high stool before it. The wall lamp had been taken down; now it stood with its reflector on the top of the desk, which was covered with books and papers. A girl was sitting on the stool, bending over a ledger and rapidly footing up columns. Bannon could not see her face, for a young fellow stood leaning over the railing by the desk, his back to the door. He had just said something, and now he was laughing in a conscious manner.

Bannon quietly stepped to one side. The girl looked up for a moment and brushed her hair back from her face. The fellow spoke again in a low tone, but beyond a slight compressing of her lips she did not seem to hear him. Without a word, Bannon came forward, took him by the arm, and led him out of the door. Still holding his arm, he took a step back, and (they stood in the outer circle of the electric light) looked him over.

"Let's see," he said, "you're the man that was clerking here."

There was no reply.

"And your name's—what?"

"Briggs."

"Well, Mr. Briggs, did you get a message from me?"

"I don't know what you mean," said the young man, his eyes on the ground. "Max, he come around, but I wanted to wait and see you. He's a mean cuss——"

"You see me now, don't you?"

"Yes." The reply was indistinct.

"You keep out of the office after this. If I catch you in there again, I won't stop to talk. Now, clear out."

Briggs walked a little way, then turned.

"Maybe you think you can lay me off without notice—but you'll wish——" Bannon turned back to the office, giving no heed to Briggs' last words: "I've got you fixed already." He was thinking of the girl there on the stool. She did not look like the girl he had expected to see. To be sure her hair was red, but it was not of the red that outcropped from Max's big head; it was of a dark, rich color, and it had caught the light from the lamp with such a shine as there is in new red gold. When he entered, she was again footing columns. She was slender, and her hand, where it supported her forehead was white. Again Bannon stood motionless, slowly shaking his head. Then he came forward. She heard his step and looked up, as if to answer a question, letting her eyes rest on his face. He hesitated, and she quietly asked:—

"What is it, please?"

"Miss Vogel?"

"Yes."

"I'm Mr. Bannon. There wasn't any need of your working to-night. I'm just keeping the men on so we can get in this cribbing. When did you come?"

"My brother telephoned to me. I wanted to look things over before starting in to-morrow."

"How do you find it?"

She hesitated, glancing over the jumble of papers on the desk.

"It hasn't been kept up very well," she presently said. "But it won't be hard, I think, to straighten it out."

Bannon leaned on the rail and glanced at the paper on which she had been setting down totals.

"I guess you'd better go home, Miss Vogel. It's after nine o'clock."

"I can finish in an hour."

"You'd better go. There'll be chances enough for night work without your making them."

She smiled, cleared up the desk, and reached for her jacket, which hung from the nail behind her. Then she paused.

"I thought I would wait for my brother, Mr. Bannon."

"That's all right. I guess we can spare him. I'll speak to him. Do you live far?"

"No; Max and I are boarding at the same place."

He had got to the door when she asked:—

"Shall I put out the light?"

He turned and nodded. She was drawing on her gloves. She perhaps was not a very pretty girl, but there was something in her manner, as she stood there in the dim light, her hair straying out from beneath her white "sombrero" hat, that for the moment took Bannon far away from this environment of railroad tracks and lumber piles. He waited till she came out, then he locked the door.

"I'll walk along with you myself, if you don't mind," he said. And after they had crossed the Belt Line tracks, and he had helped her, with a little laugh from each of them, to pick her way over the switches and between the freight cars, he said: "You don't look much like your brother."

It was not a long walk to the boarding house but before they had reached it Bannon was nervous. It was not a custom with him to leave his work on such an errand. He bade her a brusque good-night, and hurried back, pausing only after he had crossed the tracks, to cast his eye over the timber. There was no sign of activity, though the two arc lamps were still in place. "All in, eh," he said.

He followed the path beside the elevator and on around the end, and then, with an exclamation, he hurried forward; for there was the same idle crowd about the tracks that had been there during the trouble with the section boss—the same buzz of talk, and the idle laughter and shouting. As he ran, his foot struck a timber-end, and he sprawled forward for nearly a rod before recovering his balance; then he stopped and looked along the ground. A long line of timbers lay end to end, the timber hooks across them or near by on the ground, where they had been dropped by the laborers. On along the path, through the fence openings, and out on the tracks, lay the lines of timber. Here and there Bannon passed gangs of men lounging on the ground, waiting for the order to move on. As he passed through the fence, walking on the timbers, and hurried through the crowd, which had been pushed back close to the fence, he heard a low laugh that came along like a wave from man to man. In a moment he was in front of them all.

The middle tracks were clear, excepting a group of three or four men, who stood a little to one side. Bannon could not make them out. Another crowd of laborers was pressed back against the opposite fence. These had moved apart at one of the fence openings, and as Bannon looked, two men came through, stumbling and staggering under a long ten-by-twelve timber, which they were carrying on their shoulders. Bannon looked sharply; the first, a big, deep-chested man, bare-headed and in his shirt sleeves, was Peterson.

Bannon started forward, when Max, who had been hurrying over to him, touched his arm.

"What's all this, Max?"

"I'm glad you've come. It's Grady, the walking delegate—that's him over there where those men are standing, the little fellow with his hat on one side—he's been here for ten minutes."

"Speak quick. What's the trouble?"

"First he wanted to know how much we were paying the men for night work, and I told him. Thought I might as well be civil to him. Then he said we'd got to take Briggs back, and I told him Briggs wasn't a union man, and he hadn't anything to say about it. He and Briggs seemed to know each other. Finally he came out here on the job and said we were working the men too hard—said we'd have to put ten men on the heavy sticks and eight on the others. I was going to do it, but Peterson came up and said he wouldn't do it, and Grady called the men off, just where they were. He wouldn't let 'em lift a finger. You see there's timber all over the tracks. Then Pete got mad, and said him and Donnelly could bring a twenty-foot stick over alone, and it was all rot about putting on more men. Here they come—just look at Pete's arms! He could lift a house."

Some of the men were laughing, others growling, but all had their eyes fixed on Peterson and Donnelly as they came across the tracks, slowly picking their way, and shifting the weight a little, at every few seconds, on their shoulders. Bannon was glancing swiftly about, taking in the situation. He would not imperil his discipline by reproving Peterson before the men, so he stood for a moment, thinking, until the task should be accomplished.

"It's Briggs that did the whole business," Max was saying. "He brought the delegate around—he was blowing about it among the men when I found him."

"Is he on the job now?" Bannon asked.

"No, and I don't think he'll be around again very soon. There were some loafers with him, and they took him away."

Peterson and Donnelly had disappeared through the fence, and a few of the crowd were following, to see them get the timber clear around the building to the pile.

"Have you sent out flagmen, Max?" Bannon asked.

"No, I didn't."

"Get at it quick—send a man each way with a lantern—put something red over them, their shirts if necessary."

"None of the men will dare do it while the delegate's here."

"Find some one—take one side yourself, if you have to."

Max hurried away for the lanterns, Bannon walked out to the group of men on the middle tracks.

"Where's Mr. Grady?" he said.

One of the men pointed, but the delegate gave no attention.

"You're Mr. Grady, are you?" said Bannon. "I'm Mr. Bannon, of MacBride & Company. What's the trouble here?"

The delegate was revelling in his authority: his manner was not what it was to be when he should know Bannon better. He waved his hand toward the wharf.

"You ought to know better than that," he said curtly.

"Than what?"

"Than what?—than running a job the way this is run."

"I think I can run this job," said Bannon, quietly. "You haven't told me what's the trouble yet."

"It's right here—you're trying to make money by putting on one man to do the work of two."

"How?"

Bannon's quiet manner exasperated the delegate.

"Use your eyes, man—you can't make eight men carry a twelve-by-fourteen stick."

"How many shall I put on?"

"Ten."

"All right."

"And you'd better put eight men on the other sticks."

The delegate looked up, nettled that Bannon should yield so easily.

"That's all right," said Bannon. "We aren't fighting the union. After this, if you've got anything to say, I wish you'd come to me with it before you call off the men. Is there anything else before I start up?"

Grady was chewing the stub of a cigar. He stood looking about with an ugly air, then he said:—

"You ain't starting up just yet."

"Why not?"

The delegate's reply was lost in the shout that suddenly went up from the western end of the line of laborers. Then came the sound of a locomotive bell and exhaust. Bannon started down the track, jumping the timbers as he ran, toward Vogel's lantern, that was bobbing along toward him. The train had stopped, but now it was puffing slowly forward, throwing a bright light along the rails.

"It's a C. & S. C. local," Max shouted. "Can't we clear up the right track?"

Bannon stopped and looked around. About half of the men had followed him, and were strung out in irregular groups between him and the timbers. Walking up between the groups came the delegate, with two men, chewing his cigar in silence as he walked. The train was creeping along, the fireman leaning far out of the cab window, closely scanning the track for signs of an obstruction. On the steps between the cars a few passengers were trying to get a view up the track; and others were running along beside the train.

"This has gone too far," Bannon muttered. He turned and shouted to the men: "Clear up that track. Quick, now!"

Some of the men started, but stopped, and all looked at the delegate. He stepped to one side and coolly looked over the train; then he raised his hand.

"Don't touch the timbers," he said. "It ain't a mail train."

His voice was not loud, but those near at hand passed the word along, and the long line of men stood motionless. By that time the train had stopped, and three of the crew had come forward. They saw the timbers on the track and hurried toward them, but the delegate called out:—

"Watch those sticks, boys! Don't let a man touch them!"

There was no hesitation when the delegate spoke in that tone. A score of men blocked the way of the train crew.

Bannon was angry. He stood looking at Grady with snapping eyes, and his hands closed into knotted fists. But Bannon knew the power of the unions, and he knew that a rash step now might destroy all hope of completing the elevator in time. He crossed over to the delegate.

"What do you want?" he said gruffly.

"Nothing from you."

"What do you want?" Bannon repeated, and there was something in his voice that caused the delegate to check a second retort.

"You'll kill these men if you work them like this. They've been on the job all day."

Bannon was beginning to see that Grady was more eager to make trouble than to uphold the cause of the men he was supposed to represent. In his experience with walking delegates he had not met this type before. He was proud of the fact that he had never had any serious trouble in dealing with his workmen or their representatives. Mr. MacBride was fond of saying that Bannon's tact in handling men was unequalled; but Bannon himself did not think of it in this way—to him, trouble with the laborers or the carpenters or the millwrights meant loss of time and loss of money, the two things he was putting in his time to avoid; and until now he had found the maligned walking delegate a fair man when he was fairly dealt with. So he said:—

"Well, what are you asking?"

"These gangs ought to be relieved every two hours."

"I'll do it. Now clear up those timbers."

The delegate turned with a scowl, and waved the men back to their work. In a moment the track was clear, and the train was moving slowly onward between the long lines of men.

Bannon started the gangs at work. When the timbers were again coming across from the wharf in six slowly moving streams that converged at the end of the elevator, he stood looking after the triangle of red lights on the last car of the train until they had grown small and close together in the distance. Then he went over to the wharf to see how much timber remained, and to tell Peterson to hurry the work; for he did not look for any further accommodation on the part of the C. & S. C. railroad, now that a train had been stopped. The steamer lay quietly at the dock, the long pile of cribbing on her deck shadowed by the high bow deckhouse from the lights on the spouting house. Her crew were bustling about, rigging the two hoisting engines, and making all ready for unloading when the order should be given.

Peterson had been working through the timber pile from the shore side, so that now only a thin wall remained at the outer edge of the wharf. Bannon found him standing on the pile, rolling down the sticks with a peavey to where the carrying gangs could pick them up.

"Better bring all your men up here, Pete, and clean it all away by the steamer. She may as well begin unloading now."

Bannon walked back to the tracks, in time to see a handcar and trailer, packed with men, come up the track and stop near at hand. The men at once scattered, and brushing aside Bannon's laborers, they began replacing the sections of fence. Bannon crossed to the section boss, who recognized him and without comment handed him a telegraphed order.

"There's no getting around that," he said, when Bannon had read it. "That's straight from the old man."

Bannon returned it, called Peterson, and hurried with him around the elevator to find Max, who was overseeing the piling.

"What'll we do?" Peterson asked, as they ran; but Bannon made no reply until the three were together. Then he said, speaking shortly:—

"Get the wire cable off one of your hoisting engines, Pete, and make one end fast as high as you can on the spouting house. We'll run it across the tracks, on a slope, down to this side. Max, you get a light rope and a running block, and hang a hook on it."

"I see," said Max, eagerly. "You're going to run it over on a trolley."

"Yes. The engineers have gone, haven't they?"

"Went at five," said Peterson.

"That's all right. We'll only need the hoist at the spouting house. The rest of it's just plain sliding down hill."

"But who'll run it?"

"I will. Pete, you get up on the spouting house and see that they're started down. Max will stay over here and watch the piling. Now rush it."

Half an hour had gone before the cable could be stretched from the spouting house, high over the tracks, down to the elevator structure, and before the hoisting engine could be got under steam. Meanwhile, for the third time since five o'clock, the laborers stood about, grumbling and growing more impatient. But at last it was all under way. The timbers were hoisted lightly up the side of the spouting house, hooked to the travelling block, and sent whirling down to Max's waiting hands, to be snatched away and piled by the men. But compared with the other method, it was slow work, and Bannon found that, for lack of employment, it was necessary to let half of the men go for the night.

Soon, to the rattle of blocks and the tramping of feet and the calling and shouting of men, was added the creak of the steamer's hoists, and the groan of her donkey engines as her crew began the work of dumping out the cribbing by hand and steam, on the cleared space on the wharf. And then, when the last big stick had gone over, Peterson began sending bundles of two-inch cribbing. Before the work was finished, and the last plank from the steamer's cargo had been tossed on the pile by the annex, the first faint color was spreading over the eastern sky, and the damp of a low-country morning was in the air.

Bannon stopped the engine and drew the fire; Peterson and his crew clambered to the ground, and Max put on his coat and waited for the two foremen to come across the tracks. When they joined him, Bannon looked sharply at him in the growing light.

"Hello, Max," he said; "where did you get that black eye?"

"That ain't much," Max replied. "You ought to see Briggs."

CHAPTER 6

When Bannon came on the job on Friday morning at seven o'clock, a group of heavy-eyed men were falling into line at the timekeeper's window. Max was in the office, passing out the checks. His sister was continuing her work of the night before, going over what books and papers were to be found in the desk. Bannon hung up his overcoat and looked through the doorway at the square mass of the elevator that stood out against the sky like some gigantic, unroofed barn. The walls rose nearly eighty feet from the ground—though the length and breadth of the structure made them appear lower—so close to the tops of the posts that were to support the cupola frame that Bannon's eyes spoke of satisfaction. He meant to hide those posts behind the rising walls of cribbing before the day should be gone. He glanced about at the piles of two-inch plank that hid the annex foundation work. There it lay, two hundred thousand feet of it—not very much, to be sure, but enough to keep the men busy for the present, and enough, too, to give a start to the annex bins and walls.

Peterson was approaching from the tool house, and Bannon called.

"How many laborers have you got, Pete?"

"Hardly any. Max, there, can tell."

Max, who had just passed out his last check, now joined them at the doorstep.

"There's just sixty-two that came for checks," he said, "not counting the carpenters."

"About what I expected," Bannon replied. "This night business lays them out." He put his head in at the door. "You'd better give checks to any new men that we send to the window, Miss Vogel; but keep the names of the old men, and if they show up in the morning, take them back on the job. Now, boys"—to Peterson and Max—"pick up the men you see hanging around and send them over. I'll be at the office for a while. We'll push the cribbing on the main house and start right in on the annex bins. There ain't much time to throw around if we're going to eat our Christmas dinner."

The two went at once. The hoisting engines were impatiently blowing off steam. New men were appearing every moment, delaying only to answer a few brisk questions and to give their names to Miss Vogel, and then hurrying away to the tool house, each with his brass check fastened to his coat. When Bannon was at last ready to enter the office, he paused again to look over the ground. The engines were now puffing steadily, and the rapping of many hammers came through the crisp air. Gangs of laborers were swarming over the lumber piles, pitching down the planks, and other gangs were carrying them away and piling them on "dollies," to be pushed along the plank runways to the hoist. There was a black fringe of heads between the posts on the top of the elevator, where the carpenters were spiking down the last planks of the walls and bins.

Miss Vogel was at work on the ledger when Bannon entered the office. He pushed his hat back on his head and came up beside her.

"How's it coming out?" he asked. "Do we know how much we're good for?"

She looked up, smiling.

"I think so. I'm nearly through. It's a little mixed in some places, but I think everything has been entered."

"Can you drop it long enough to take a letter or so?"

"Oh, yes." She reached for her notebook, saying, with a nod toward the table: "The mail is here."

Bannon went rapidly through the heap of letters and bills.

"There's nothing much," he said. "You needn't wait for me to open it after this. You'll want to read everything to keep posted. These bills for cribbing go to your brother, you know." There was one chair within the enclosure; he brought it forward and sat down, tipping back against the railing. "Well, I guess we may as well go ahead and tell the firm that we're still moving around and drawing our salaries. To MacBride & Company,

Minneapolis, Gentlemen: Cribbing is now going up on elevator and annex. A little over two feet remains to be done on the elevator beneath the distributing floor. The timber is ready for framing the cupola. Two hundred thousand feet of the Ledyard cribbing reached here by steamer last night, and the balance will be down in a few days. Very truly yours, MacBride & Company. That will do for them. Now, we'll write to Mr. Brown—no, you needn't bother, though; I'll do that one myself. You might run off the other and I'll sign it." He got up and moved his chair to the table. "I don't generally seem able to say just what I want to Brown unless I write it out." His letter ran:—

> DEAR MR. BROWN: We've finally got things going. Had to stir them up a little at Ledyard. Can you tell me who it is that's got hold of our coat tails on this job? There's somebody trying to hold us back, all right. Had a little fuss with a red-headed walking delegate last night, but fixed him. That hat hasn't come yet. Shall I call up the express company and see what's the matter? 7-1/4 is my size.
>
> Yours,
>
> BANNON.

He had folded the letter and addressed the envelope, when he paused and looked around. The typewritten letter to MacBride & Company lay at his elbow. He signed it before he spoke.

"Miss Vogel, have you come across any letters or papers about an agreement with the C. & S. C.?"

"No," she replied, "there is nothing here about the railroad."

Bannon drummed on the table; then he went to the door and called to a laborer who was leaving the tool house:—

"Find Mr. Peterson and ask him if he will please come to the office for a moment."

He came slowly back and sat on the corner of the table, watching Miss Vogel as her pencil moved rapidly up column after column.

"Had quite a time up there in Michigan," he said. "Those G. & M. people were after us in earnest. If they'd had their way, we'd never have got the cribbing."

She looked up.

"You see, they had told Sloan—he's the man that owns the lumber company and the city of Ledyard and pretty much all of the Lower Peninsula—that they hadn't any cars; and he'd just swallowed it down and folded up his napkin. I hadn't got to Ledyard before I saw a string of empties on a siding that weren't doing a thing but waiting for our cribbing, so I caught a train to Blake City and gave the Division Superintendent some points on running railroads. He was a nice, friendly man"—Bannon clasped his hands about one knee and smiled reminiscently—"I had him pretty busy there for a while thinking up lies. He was wondering how he could get ready for the next caller, when I came at him and made him wire the General Manager of the line. The operator was sitting right outside the door, and when the answer came I just took it in—it gave the whole snap away, clear as you want."

Miss Vogel turned on her stool.

"You took his message?"

"I should say I did. It takes a pretty lively man to crowd me off the end of a wire. He told the superintendent not to give us cars. That was all I wanted to know. So I told him how sorry I was that I couldn't stay to lunch, caught the next train back to Ledyard, and built a fire under Sloan."

Miss Vogel was looking out of the window.

"He said he could not give us cars?" she repeated.

Bannon smiled.

"But we didn't need them," he said. "I got a barge to come over from Milwaukee, and we loaded her up and started her down."

"I don't understand, Mr. Bannon. Ledyard isn't on the lake—and you couldn't get cars."

"That wasn't very hard." He paused, for a step sounded outside the door and in a moment Peterson had come in.

"I guess you wanted to talk to me, didn't you, Charlie?"

"Yes, I'm writing to the office. It's about this C. & S. C. business. You said you'd had trouble with them before."

"Oh, no," said Peterson, sitting on the railing and removing his hat, with a side glance at Miss Vogel, "not to speak of. There wasn't nothing so bad as last night."

"What was it?"

"Why, just a little talk when we opened the fence first time. That section boss was around, but I told him how things was, and he didn't seem to have no kick coming as long as we was careful."

Bannon had taken up his letter to Brown, and was slowly unfolding it and looking it over. When Peterson got to his feet, he laid it on the table.

"Anything else, Charlie? I'm just getting things to going on the annex. We're going to make her jump, I tell you. I ain't allowing any loafing there."

"No," Bannon replied, "I guess not." He followed the foreman out of doors. "Do you remember having any letters, Pete, about our agreement with the C. & S. C. to build over the tracks—from the office or anybody?"

Peterson brought his brows together and tried to remember. After a moment he slowly shook his head.

"Nothing, eh?" said Bannon.

"Not that I can think of. Something may have come in while Max was here in the office——"

"I wish you'd ask him."

"All right. He'll be around my way before long, taking the time."

"And say," Bannon added, with one foot on the doorstep, "you haven't seen anything more of that man Briggs, have you?"

Peterson shook his head.

"If you see him hanging around, you may as well throw him right off the job."

Peterson grinned.

"I guess he won't show up very fast. Max did him up good last night, when he was blowing off about bringing the delegate around."

Bannon had drawn the door to after him when he came out. He was turning back, with a hand on the knob, when Peterson, who was lingering, said in a low voice, getting out the words awkwardly:—

"Say, Charlie, she's all right, ain't she."

Bannon did not reply, and Peterson jerked his thumb toward the office.

"Max's sister, there. I never saw any red hair before that was up to the mark. Ain't she a little uppish, though, don't you think?"

"I guess not."

"Red-haired girls generally is. They've got tempers, too, most of them. It's funny about her looks. She don't look any more like Max than anything." He grinned again. "Lord, Max is a peach, though, ain't he."

Bannon nodded and reentered the office. He sat down and added a postscript to his letter:

> The C. & S. C. people are trying to make it warm for us about working across their tracks. Can't we have an understanding with them before we get ready to put up the belt gallery? If we don't, we'll have to build a suspension bridge.
>
> C. B.

He sealed the envelope and tossed it to one side.

"Miss Vogel," he said, pushing his chair back, "didn't you ask me something just now?"

"It was about getting the cribbing across the lake," she replied. "I don't see how you did it."

Her interest in the work pleased Bannon.

"It ain't a bad story. You see the farmers up in that country hate the railroads. It's the tariff rebate, you know. They have to pay more to ship their stuff to market than some places a thousand miles farther off. And I guess the service is pretty bad all around. I was figuring on something like that as soon as I had a look at things. So we got up a poster and had it printed, telling what they all think of the G. & M."—he paused, and his eyes twinkled—"I wouldn't mind handing one to that Superintendent just for the fun of seeing him when he read it. It told the farmers to come around to Sloan's lumber yard with their wagons."

"And you carried it across in the wagons?"

"I guess we did."

"Isn't it a good ways?"

"Eighteen to thirty miles, according to who you ask. As soon as things got to going we went after the General Manager and gave him a bad half hour; so I shouldn't be surprised to see the rest of the bill coming in by rail any time now."

Bannon got up and slowly buttoned his coat. He was looking about the office, at the mud-tracked floor and the coated windows, and at the hanging shreds of spider web in the corners and between the rafters overhead.

"It ain't a very cheerful house to live in all day, is it?" he said. "I don't know but what we'd better clean house a little. There's not much danger of putting a shine on things that'll hurt your eyes. We ought to be able to get hold of some one that could come in once in a while and stir up the dust. Do you know of any one?"

"There is a woman that comes to our boarding-house. I think they know about her at the hotel."

He went to the telephone and called up the hotel.

"She'll be here this afternoon," he said as he hung up the receiver. "Will she bring her own scrubbing things, or are we supposed to have them for her? This is some out of my line."

Miss Vogel was smiling.

"She'll have her own things, I guess. When she comes, would you like me to start her to work?"

"If you'd just as soon. And tell her to make a good job of it. I've got to go out now, but I'll be around off and on during the day."

When the noon whistle blew Bannon and Max were standing near the annex. Already the bins and walls had been raised more than a foot above the foundation, which gave it the appearance of a great checker-board.

"Looks like business, doesn't it," said Max. He was a little excited, for now there was to be no more delaying until the elevator should stand completed from the working floor to the top, one hundred and sixty feet above the ground; until engines, conveyors, and scales should be working smoothly and every bin filled with grain. Indeed, nearly everybody on the job had by this time caught the spirit of energy that Bannon had infused into the work.

"I'll be glad when it gets up far enough to look like something, so we can feel that things are really getting on."

"They're getting on all right," Bannon replied.

"How soon will we be working on the cupola?"

"Tomorrow."

"Tomorrow!" Max stopped (they had started toward the office) and looked at Bannon in amazement. "Why, we can't do it, can we?"

"Why not?" Bannon pointed toward a cleared space behind the pile of cribbing, where the carpenters had been at work on the heavy timbers. "They're all ready for the framing."

Max made no reply, but he looked up as they passed the elevator and measured with his eyes the space remaining between the cribbing and the tops of the posts. He had yet to become accustomed to Bannon's methods; but he had seen enough of him to believe that it would be done if Bannon said so.

They were halfway to the office when Max said, with a touch of embarrassment:—

"How's Hilda going to take hold, Mr. Bannon?"

"First-class."

Max's eyes sparkled.

"She can do anything you give her. Her head's as clear as a bell."

For the moment Bannon made no reply, but as they paused outside the office door he said:

"We'd better make a point of dropping in at the office now and then during the day. Any time you know I'm out on the job and you're up this way, just look in."

Max nodded.

"And nights when we're working overtime, there won't be any trouble about your getting off long enough to see your sister home. She won't need to do any night work."

They entered the office. Miss Vogel was standing by the railing gate, buttoning her jacket and waiting for Max. Behind her, bending over the blue prints on the table, stood Peterson, apparently too absorbed to hear the two men come in. Bannon gave him a curious glance, for no blue prints were needed in working on the annex, which was simply a matter of building bins up from the foundation. When Max and his sister had gone the foreman looked around, and said, with a show of surprise:—

"Oh, hello, Charlie. Going up to the house?"

"Yes."

Peterson's manner was not wholly natural. As they walked across the flats his conversation was a little forced, and he laughed occasionally at certain occurrences in the morning's work that were not particularly amusing.

Bannon did not get back to the office until a half hour after work had commenced for the afternoon. He carried a large bundle under one arm and in his hand a wooden box with a slot cut in the cover. He found the scrub-woman hard at work on the office floor. The chair and the unused stool were on the table. He looked about with satisfaction.

"It begins to look better already," he said to Miss Vogel. "You know we're not going to be able to keep it all clean; there'll be too many coming in. But there's going to be a law passed about tracking mud inside the railing." He opened his bundle and unrolled a door mat, which he laid in front of the gate.

Miss Vogel was smiling, but Bannon's face was serious. He cut a square piece from the wrapping paper, and sitting on the table, printed the placard: "Wipe your feet! Or put five cents in the box." Then he nailed both box and placard to the railing, and stood back to look at his work.

"That will do it," he said.

She nodded. "There's no danger that they won't see it."

"We had a box down on the New Orleans job," said Bannon, "only that was for swearing. Every time anybody swore he put in a nickel, and then when Saturday came around we'd have ten or fifteen dollars to spend."

"It didn't stop the swearing, then?"

"Oh, yes. Everybody was broke a day or so after pay day, and for a few days every week it was the best crowd you ever saw. But we won't spend this money that way. I guess we'll let you decide what to do with it."

Hour by hour the piles of cribbing dwindled, and on the elevator the distance from bin walls to post-tops grew shorter. Before five o'clock the last planks were spiked home on the walls and bins in the northwest corner. A few hours' work in the morning would bring the rest of the house to the same level, and then work could commence on the distributing floor and on the frame of the cupola. Before the middle of the afternoon he had started two teams of horses dragging the cupola timbers, which had been cut ready for framing, to the foot of the hoist. By ten o'clock in the morning, Bannon figured, the engine would be lifting timbers instead of bundles of cribbing.

There was a chill wind, up there on the top of the elevator, coming across the flats out of the glowing sunset. But Bannon let his coat flap open, as he gave a hand now and then to help the men. He liked to feel the wind tugging at sleeves and cap, and he leaned against it, bare-throated and bare-handed—bare-headed, too, he would have been had not a carpenter, rods away on the cribbing, put out a hand to catch his cap as it tried to whirl past on a gust. The river wound away toward the lake, touched with the color of the sky, to lose itself half a mile away among the straggling rows of factories and rolling mills. From the splendid crimson of the western sky to the broken horizon line of South Chicago, whose buildings hid Lake Michigan, the air was crisp and clear; but on the north, over the dim shops and blocks of houses that grew closer together as the eye went on, until spires and towers and gray walls were massed in confusion, hung a veil of smoke, like a black cloud, spreading away farther than eye could see. This was Chicago.

Bannon climbed to the ground and took a last look about the work before going to the office. The annex was growing slowly but surely; and Peterson, coatless and hatless as usual, with sleeves rolled up, was at work with the men, swinging a hammer here, impatiently shouldering a bundle of planks there. And Bannon saw more clearly what he had known before, that Peterson was a good man when kept within his limitations. Certainly the annex could not have been better started.

When Bannon entered the office, Miss Vogel handed him a sheet of paper. He came in through the gate and stood at the desk beside her to have the light of the lamp. It was a balance sheet, giving the results of her examination of the books.

"All right, eh?" he said. A glance had been enough to show him that hereafter there would be no confusion in the books; the cashier of a metropolitan bank could not have issued a more businesslike statement. He tossed it on the desk, saying, "You might file it."

Then he took time to look about the office. It was as clean as blackened, splintered planks could be made; even the ceiling had been attacked and every trace of cobweb removed.

"Well," he said, "this is business. And we'll keep it this way, too."

She had faced about on the stool and was looking at him with a twinkle in her eye.

"Yes," she said, evidently trying not to laugh; "we'll try to."

He was not looking at her as she spoke, but when, a moment later, the laugh broke away from her, he turned. She was looking at his feet. He glanced down and saw a row of black footprints leading from the door to where he stood, one of them squarely in the centre of the new mat. He gazed ruefully, then he reached into his pocket and drew out a quarter, dropping it in the box.

"Well——" he said, wiping his feet; but the whistle just then gave a long blast, and he did not finish the sentence.

After supper Bannon and Peterson sat in the room they occupied together. In the walk home and during supper there had been the same sullen manner about the younger man that Bannon had observed at noon. Half a day was a long time for Peterson to keep to himself something that bothered him, and before the close of dinner he had begun working the talk around. Now, after a long silence, that Bannon filled with sharpening pencils, he said:

"Some people think a lot of themselves, don't they, Charlie?"

Bannon looked up from his pencils; he was sitting on the edge of the bed.

"She seems to think she's better'n Max and you and me, and everybody. I thought she looked pretty civil, and I didn't say a word she need to have got stuck-up about."

Bannon asked no questions. After waiting to give him an opportunity, Peterson went on:—

"There's going to be a picnic Sunday of the Iron Workers up at Sharpshooters' Park. I know a fellow that has tickets. It'd be just as quiet as anywhere—and speeches, you know. I don't see that she's any better than a lot of the girls that'll be there."

"Do you mean to say you asked her to go?" Bannon asked.

"Yes, and she——"

Bannon had turned away to strop his razor on his hand, and Peterson, after one or two attempts to begin the story, let the subject drop.

CHAPTER 7

Bannon had the knack of commanding men. He knew the difference between an isolated—or better, perhaps, an insulated—man and the same man in a crowd. Without knowing how he did it, he could, nevertheless, distinguish between the signs of temporary ill feeling among the men and the perhaps less apparent danger signal that meant serious mischief.

Since his first day on the job the attitude of the men had worried him a little. There was something in the air he did not like. Peterson, accustomed to handling smaller bodies of men, had made the natural mistake of driving the very large force employed on the elevator with much too loose a rein. The men were still further demoralized by the episode with the walking delegate, Grady, on Thursday night. Bannon knew too much to attempt halfway measures, so he waited for a case of insubordination serious enough to call for severe treatment.

When he happened into the office about the middle of Saturday morning, Miss Vogel handed him two letters addressed to him personally. One was from Brown,—the last paragraph of it as follows:—

Young Page has told MacBride in so many words what we've all been guessing about, that is, that they are fighting to break the corner in December wheat. They have a tremendous short line on the Chicago Board, and they mean to deliver it. Twenty-two hundred thousand has got to be in the bins there at Calumet before the first of January unless the Day of Judgment happens along before then. Never mind what it costs you.

BROWN.

P.S. MacBride has got down an atlas and is trying to figure out how you got that cribbing to the lake. I told him you put the barge on rollers and towed it up to Ledyard with a traction engine.

The letter from Sloan was to the effect that twelve cars were at that moment on the yard siding, loading with cribbing, and that all of it, something more than eighteen hundred thousand feet, would probably be in Chicago within a week. A note was scribbled on the margin in Sloan's handwriting. "Those fool farmers are still coming in expecting a job. One is out in the yard now. Came clear from Victory. I've had to send out a man to take down the posters."

"That's just like a farmer," Bannon said to Miss Vogel. "Time don't count with him. To-morrow morning or two weeks from next Tuesday— he can't see the difference. I suppose if one of those posters on an inconspicuous tree happens to be overlooked that some old fellow'll come driving in next Fourth of July."

He buttoned his coat as though going out, but stood looking at her thoughtfully awhile. "All the same," he said, "I'd like to be that way myself; never do anything till to-morrow. I'm going to turn farmer some day. Once I get this job done, I'd like to see the man who can hurry me. I'll say to MacBride: 'I'm willing to work on nice, quiet, easy little jobs that never have to be finished. I'll want to sit at the desk and whittle most of the time. But if you ever try to put me on a rush job I'll quit and buy a small farm.' I could make the laziest farmer in twelve states. Well, I've got to go out on the job."

An elevator is simply a big grain warehouse, and of course the bins where the grain is kept occupy most of the building. But for handling the grain more than bin room is necessary. Beneath the bins is what is called the working story, where is the machinery for unloading cars and for lifting the grain. The cupola, which Bannon was about to frame, is a five-story building perched atop the bins. It contains the appliances for weighing the grain and distributing it.

When Bannon climbed out on top of the bins, he found the carpenters partially flooring over the area, preparatory to putting in place the framework of the cupola. Below them in the bins, like bees in a honeycomb, laborers were taking down the scaffolding which had served in building their walls. At the south side of the building a group of laborers, under one of the foremen, was rigging what is known as a boom hoist, which was to lift the timbers for framing the cupola.

While Bannon stood watching the carpenters, one of them sawed off the end of a plank and dropped it down into the bin. There was a low laugh, and one or two of the men glanced uneasily at Bannon. He spoke to the offender "Don't do that again if you want to stay on this job. You know there are men at work down there." Then: "Look here," he called, getting the attention of all the carpenters, "every man that drops anything into the bins gets docked an hour's pay. If he does it twice he leaves the job just as quick as we can make out a time-check. I want you to be careful."

He was picking his way over to the group of men about the hoisting pole, when he heard another general laugh from the carpenters. Turning back he saw them all looking at a fellow named Reilly, who, trying to suppress a smile, was peering with mock concern down into the dark bin. "My hammer slipped," Bannon heard him say in a loud aside to the man nearest him. Then, with a laugh: "Accidents will happen."

Bannon almost smiled himself, for the man had played right into his hand. He had, in the four days since he took command, already become aware of Reilly and had put him down for the sort ambitious to rise rather in the organization of his union than in his trade.

"I guess we won't take the trouble to dock you," he said. "Go to the office and get your time. And be quick about it, too."

"Did ye mean me?" the man asked impudently, but Bannon, without heeding, went over to the hoist. Presently a rough hand fell on his shoulder. "Say," demanded Reilly again, "did ye mean me?"

"No doubt of that. Go and get your time."

"I guess not," said the man. "Not me. My hammer just slipped. How're you going to prove I meant to do it?"

"I'm not. I'm going to fire you. You ain't laid off, you understand; you're fired. If you ever come back, I'll have you kicked off the place."

"You don't dare fire me," the man said, coming nearer. "You'll have to take me back to-morrow."

"I'm through talking with you," said Bannon, still quietly. "The faster you can light out of here the better."

"We'll see about that. You can't come it on the union that way——"

Then, without any preparatory gesture whatever, Bannon knocked him down. The man seemed to fairly rebound from the floor. He rushed at the boss, but before he could come within striking distance, Bannon whipped out a revolver and dropped it level with Reilly's face.

"I've talked to you," he said slowly, his eye blazing along the barrel, "and I've knocked you down. But——"

The man staggered back, then walked away very pale, but muttering. Bannon shoved back the revolver into his hip pocket. "It's all right, boys," he said, "nothing to get excited about."

He walked to the edge and looked over. "We can't wait to pick it up a stick at a time," he said. "I'll tell 'em to load four or five on each larry. Then you can lift the whole bunch."

"We run some chances of a spill or a break that way," said the foreman.

"I know it," answered Bannon, dryly. "That's the kind of chances we'll have to run for the next two months."

Descending to the ground, he gave the same order to the men below; then he sent word to Peterson and Vogel that he wished to see them in the office. He wiped his feet on the mat, glancing at Hilda as he did so, but she was hard at work and did not look up. He took the one unoccupied chair and placed it where he could watch the burnished light in her red hair. Presently she turned toward him.

"Did you want something?" she asked.

"Excuse me. I guess—I——"

In the midst of his embarrassment, Max and Pete came in. "I've got a couple of letters I want to talk over with you boys," he said. "That's why I sent for you."

Pete laughed and vaulted to a seat on the draughting-table. "I was most afraid to come," he said. "I heard you drawed a gun on that fellow, Reilly. What was he doing to make you mad?"

"Nothing much."

"Well, I'm glad you fired him. He's made trouble right along. How'd it happen you had a gun with you? Do you always carry one?"

"Haven't been without one on a job since I've worked for the old man."

"Well," said Pete, straightening up, "I've never so much as owned one, and I never want to. I don't like 'em. If my fists ain't good enough to take care of me against any fellow that comes along, why, he's welcome to lick me, that's all."

Hilda glanced at him, and for a moment her eyes rested on his figure. There was not a line of it but showed grace and strength and a magnificent confidence. Then, as if for the contrast, she looked at Bannon. He had been watching her all the while, and he seemed to guess her thought.

"That's all right," he said in answer to Peterson, "when it's just you and him and a fellow to hold your coats. But it don't always begin that way. I've been in places where things got pretty miscellaneous sometimes, but I never had a man come up and say: 'Mr. Bannon, I'm going to lick you. Any time when you're ready,' There's generally from three to thirty, and they all try to get on your back."

Peterson laughed reminiscently. "I was an attendant in the insane ward of the Massachusetts General Hospital for a while, and one time when I wasn't looking for it, twenty-four of those lunatics all jumped on me at once. They got me on the floor and 'most killed me." He paused, as though there was nothing more to tell.

"Don't stop there," said Max.

"Why," he went on, "I crawled along the floor till I got to a chair, and I just knocked 'em around with that till they was quiet."

Bannon looked at his watch; then he took Brown's letter from his pocket. "It's from the office," he said. "We've got to have the bins full before New Year's Day."

"Got to!" exclaimed Pete. "I don't see it that way. We can't do it."

"Can or can't, that don't interest MacBride a bit. He says it's got to be done and it has."

"Why, he can't expect us to do it. He didn't say anything about January first to me. _I_ didn't know it was a rush job. And then we played in hard luck, too, before you came. That cribbing being tied up, for instance. He certainly can't blame us if——"

"That's got nothing to do with it," Bannon cut in shortly. "He don't pay us to make excuses; he pays us to do as we're told. When I have to begin explaining to MacBride why it can't be done, I'll send my resignation along in a separate envelope and go to peddling a cure for corns. What we want to talk about is how we're going to do it."

Peterson flushed, but said nothing, and Bannon went on: "Now, here's what we've got to do. We've got to frame the cupola and put on the roof and sheathe the entire house with galvanized iron; we've got to finish the spouting house and sheathe that; we've got to build the belt gallery—and we'll have no end of a time doing it if the C. & S. C. is still looking for trouble. Then there's all the machinery to erect and the millwright work to do. And we've got to build the annex."

"I thought you was going to forget that," said Pete. "That's the worst job of all."

"No, it ain't. It's the easiest. It'll build itself. It's just a case of two and two makes four. All you've got to do is spike down two-inch planks till it's done, and then clap on some sort of a roof. There's no machinery, no details, just straight work. It's just a question of having the lumber to do it with, and we've got it now. It's the little work that can raise Ned with you. There is more than a million little things that any man ought to do in half an hour, but if one of 'em goes wrong, it may hold you up for all day. Now, I figure the business this way."

He took a memorandum from his pocket and began reading. There was very little guesswork about it; he had set down as nearly as possible the amount of labor involved in each separate piece of construction, and the number of men who could work on it at once. Allowing for the different kinds of work that could be done simultaneously, he made out a total of one hundred and twenty days.

"Well, that's all right, I guess," said Pete, "but you see that takes us way along into next year sometime."

"About March first," said Max.

"You haven't divided by three yet," said Bannon. "We'll get three eight-hour days into every twenty-four hours, and twenty-one of 'em into every week."

"Why, that's better than we need to do," said Pete, after a moment. "That gets us about two weeks ahead of time."

"Did you ever get through when you thought you would?" Bannon demanded. "I never did. Don't you know that you always get hit by something you ain't looking for? I'm figuring in our hard-luck margin, that's all. There are some things I am looking for, too. We'll have a strike here before we get through."

"Oh, I guess not," said Pete, easily. "You're still thinking of Reilly, aren't you."

"And for another thing, Page & Company are likely to spring something on us at the last moment."

"What sort of thing?"

"If I knew I'd go ahead and build it now, but I don't."

"How are you going to work three gangs? Who'll look after 'em?"

"One of us has got to stay up nights, I guess," said Bannon. "We'll have to get a couple of boys to help Max keep time. It may take us a day or two to get the good men divided up and the thing to running properly, but we ought to be going full blast by the first of the week."

He arose and buttoned his coat. "You two know the men better than I do. I wish you'd go through the pay roll and pick out the best men and find out, if you can, who'll work nights at regular night wages."

Peterson came out of the office with him. "I suppose you'll put me in the night gang," he said.

"I haven't decided yet what I'll do."

"When I came by the main hoist," Pete went on, "they was picking up four and five sticks at once. I stopped 'em, and they said it was your orders. You'll come to smash that way, sure as a gun."

"Not if they don't take more than I told 'em to and if they're careful. They have to do it to keep up with the carpenters."

"Well, it's running a big risk, that's all. I don't like it."

"My God, don't I know it's a risk! Do you suppose I like it? We've got something to do, and we've got to do it somehow."

Pete laughed uneasily. "I—I told 'em not to pick up more than two sticks at a time till they heard from me."

"I think," said Bannon, with a look that was new to Pete, "I think you'd better go as fast as you can and tell them to go on as they were when you found them."

Late on Tuesday afternoon the hoist broke. It was not easy to get from the men a clear account of the accident. The boss of the gang denied that he had carried more of a load than Bannon had authorized, but some of the talk among the men indicated the contrary. Only one man was injured and he not fatally, a piece of almost miraculous good luck. Some scaffolding was torn down and a couple of timbers badly sprung, but the total damage was really slight.

Bannon in person superintended rigging the new hoist. It was ready for work within two hours after the accident. "She's guyed a little better than the other was, I think," said Bannon to the foreman. "You won't have any more trouble. Go ahead."

"How about the load?"

"Carry the same load as before. You weren't any more than keeping up."

CHAPTER 8

Five minutes after the noon whistle blew, on Saturday, every carpenter and laborer knew that Bannon had "pulled a gun" on Reilly. Those who heard it last heard more than that, for when the story had passed through a few hands it was bigger and it took longer to tell. And every man, during the afternoon, kept his eyes more closely on his work. Some were angry, but these dropped from muttering into sullenness; the majority were relieved, for a good workman is surer of himself under a firm than under a slack hand; but all were cowed. And Bannon, when after dinner he looked over the work, knew more about all of them and their feelings, perhaps, than they knew themselves. He knew, too, that the incident might in the long run make trouble. But trouble was likely in any case, and it was better to meet it after he had established his authority than while discipline was at loose ends.

But Hilda and Max were disappointed. They were in the habit of talking over the incidents and problems of the day every night after supper. And while Hilda, as Max used to say, had a mind of her own, she had fallen into the habit of seeing things much as Max saw them. Max had from the start admired, in his boyish way, Peterson's big muscles and his easy good nature. He had been the first to catch the new spirit that Bannon had got into the work, but it was more the outward activity that he could understand and admire than Bannon's finer achievements in organization. Like Hilda, he did not see the difference between dropping a hammer down a bin and overloading a hoist. Bannon's distinction between running risks in order to push the work and using caution in minor matters was not recognized in their talks. And as Bannon was not in the habit of giving his reasons, the misunderstanding grew. But more than all Max felt, and in a way Hilda felt, too, that Peterson would never have found it necessary to use a revolver; his fists would have been enough for a dozen Reillys. Max did not tell Hilda about all the conversations he and Peterson had had during the last week, for they were confidential. Peterson had never been without a confidant, and though he still shared a room with Bannon, he could not talk his mind out with him. Max, who to Bannon was merely an unusually capable lumber-checker, was to Peterson a friend and adviser. And though Max tried to defend Bannon when Peterson fell into criticism of the way the work was going, he was influenced by it.

During the few days after the accident Hilda was so deeply distressed about the injured man that Max finally went to see him.

"He's pretty well taken care of," he said when he returned. "There's some ribs broken, he says, and a little fever, but it ain't serious. He's got a couple of sneaking little lawyers around trying to get him to sue for damages, but I don't think he'll do it. The Company's giving him full pay and all his doctor's bills."

Nearly every evening after that Max took him some little delicacy. Hilda made him promise that he would not tell who sent them.

Bannon had quickly caught the changed attitude toward him, and for several days kept his own counsel. But one morning, after dictating some letters to Hilda, he lingered.

"How's our fund getting on?" he said, smiling. "Have you looked lately?"

"No," she said, "I haven't."

He leaned over the railing and opened the box.

"It's coming slow," he said, shaking his head. "Are you sure nobody's been getting away from us?"

Hilda was seated before the typewriter. She turned partly around, without taking her fingers from the keys.

"I don't know," she said quietly. "I haven't been watching it."

"We'll have to be stricter about it," said Bannon. "These fellows have got to understand that rules are rules."

He spoke with a little laugh, but the remark was unfortunate. The only men who came within the railing were Max and Peterson.

"I may have forgotten it, myself," she said.

"That won't do, you know. I don't know but what I can let you off this time—I'll tell you what I'll do, Miss Vogel: I'll make a new rule that you can come in without wiping your feet if you'll hand in a written excuse. That's the way they did things when I went to school." He turned to go, then hesitated again. "You haven't been out on the job yet, have you?"

"No, I haven't."

"I rather think you'd like it. It's pretty work, now that we're framing the cupola. If you say so, I'll fix it for you to go up to the distributing floor this afternoon."

She looked back at the machine.

"The view ain't bad," he went on, "when you get up there. You can see down into Indiana, and all around. You could see all Chicago, too, if it wasn't for the smoke."

There was a moment's silence.

"Why, yes, Mr. Bannon," she said; "I'd like to go very much."

"All right," he replied, his smile returning. "I'll guarantee to get you up there somehow, if I have to build a stairway. Ninety feet's pretty high, you know."

When Bannon reached the elevator he stood for a moment in the well at the west end of the structure. This well, or "stairway bin," sixteen by thirty-two feet, and open from the ground to the distributing floor, occupied the space of two bins. It was here that the stairway would be, and the passenger elevator, and the rope-drive for the transmission of power from the working to the distributing floor. The stairway was barely indicated by rude landings. For the present a series of eight ladders zigzagged up from landing to landing. Bannon began climbing; halfway up he met Max, who was coming down, time book in hand.

"Look here, Max," he said, "we're going to have visitors this afternoon. If you've got a little extra time I'd like to have you help get things ready."

"All right," Max replied. "I'm not crowded very hard to-day."

"I've asked your sister to come up and see the framing."

Max glanced down between the loose boards on the landing.

"I don't know," he said slowly; "I don't believe she could climb up here very well."

"She won't have to. I'm going to put in a passenger elevator, and carry her up as grand as the Palmer House. You put in your odd minutes between now and three o'clock making a box that's big and strong enough."

Max grinned.

"Say, that's all right. She'll like that. I can do most of it at noon."

Bannon nodded and went on up the ladders. At the distributing floor he looked about for a long timber, and had the laborers lay it across the well opening. The ladders and landings occupied only about a third of the space; the rest was open, a clear drop of eighty feet.

At noon he found Max in an open space behind the office, screwing iron rings into the corners of a stout box. Max glanced up and laughed.

"I made Hilda promise not to come out here," he said. He waved his hand toward the back wall of the office. Bannon saw that he had nailed strips over the larger cracks and knot holes. "She was peeking, but I shut that off before I'd got very far along. I don't think she saw what it was. I only had part of the frame done."

"She'll be coming out in a minute," said Bannon.

"I know. I thought of that." Max threw an armful of burlap sacking over the box. "That'll cover it up enough. I guess it's time to quit, anyway, if I'm going to get any dinner. There's a little square of carpet up to the house that I'm going to get for the bottom, and we can run pieces of half-inch rope from the rings up to a hook, and sling it right on the hoist."

"It's not going on the hoist," said Bannon. "I wouldn't stop the timbers for Mr. MacBride himself. When you go back, you'll see a timber on the top of the well. I'd like you to sling a block under it and run an inch-and-a-quarter rope through. We'll haul it up from below."

"What power?"

"Man power."

"All right, Mr. Bannon. I'll see to it. There's Hilda now."

He called to her to wait while he got his coat, and then the two disappeared across the tracks. Hilda had bowed to Bannon, but without the smile and the nod that he liked. He looked after her as if he would follow; but he changed his mind, and waited a few minutes.

The "elevator" was ready soon after the afternoon's work had commenced. Bannon found time between two and three o'clock to inspect the tackle. He picked up an end of rope and lashed the cross timber down securely. Then he went down the ladders and found Max, who had brought the carpet for the box and was looking over his work. The rope led up to the top of the well through a pulley and then back to the working floor and through another pulley, so that the box could be hoisted from below.

"It's all ready," said Max. "It'll run up as smooth as you want."

"You'd better go for your sister, then," Bannon replied.

Max hesitated.

"You meant for me to bring her?"

"Yes, I guess you might as well."

Bannon stood looking after Max as he walked along the railroad track out into the open air. Then he glanced up between the smooth walls of cribbing that seemed to draw closer and closer together until they ended, far overhead, in a rectangle of blue sky. The beam across the top was a black line against the light. The rope, hanging from it, swayed lazily. He walked around the box, examining the rings and the four corner ropes, and testing them.

Hilda was laughing when she came with Max along the track. Bannon could not see her at first for the intervening rows of timbers that supported the bins. Then she came into view through an opening between two "bents" of timber, beyond a heap of rubbish that had been thrown at one side of the track. She was trying to walk on the rail, one arm thrown out to balance, the other resting across Max's shoulders. Her jacket was buttoned snugly up to the chin, and there was a fresh color in her face.

Bannon had called in three laborers to man the rope; they stood at one side, awaiting the order to haul away. He found a block of wood, and set it against the box for a step.

"This way, Miss Vogel," he called. "The elevator starts in a minute. You came pretty near being late."

"Am I going to get in that?" she asked; and she looked up, with a little gasp, along the dwindling rope.

"Here," said Max, "don't you say nothing against that elevator. I call it pretty grand."

She stood on the block, holding to one of the ropes, and looking alternately into the box and up to the narrow sky above them.

"It's awfully high," she said. "Is that little stick up there all that's going to hold me up?"

"That little stick is ten-by-twelve," Max replied. "It would hold more'n a dozen of you."

She laughed, but still hesitated. She lowered her eyes and looked about the great dim space of the working story with its long aisles and its solid masses of timber. Suddenly she turned to Bannon, who was standing at her side, waiting to give her a hand.

"Oh, Mr. Bannon," she said, "are you sure it's strong enough? It doesn't look safe."

"I think it's safe," he replied quietly. He vaulted into the box and signalled to the laborers. Hilda stepped back off the block as he went up perhaps a third of the way, and then came down. She said nothing, but stepped on the block.

"How shall I get in?" she asked, laughing a little, but not looking at Bannon.

"Here," said Bannon, "give us each a hand. A little jump'll do it. Max here'll go along the ladders and steady you if you swing too much. Wait a minute, though." He hurried out of doors, and returned with a light line, one end of which he made fast to the box, the other he gave to Max.

"Now," he said, "you can guide it as nice as walking upstairs."

They started up, Hilda sitting in the box and holding tightly to the sides, Max climbing the ladders with the end of the line about his wrist. Bannon joined the laborers, and kept a hand on the hoisting rope.

"You'd better not look down," he called after her.

She laughed and shook her head. Bannon waited until they had reached the top, and Max had lifted her out on the last landing; then, at Max's shout, he made the rope fast and followed up the ladders.

He found them waiting for him near the top of the well.

"We might as well sit down," he said. He led the way to a timber a few steps away. "Well, Miss Vogel, how do you like it?"

She was looking eagerly about; at the frame, a great skeleton of new timber, some of it still holding so much of the water of river and mill-yard that it glistened in the sunlight; at the moving groups of men, the figure of Peterson standing out above the others on a high girder, his arms knotted, and his neck bare, though the day was not warm; at the straining hoist, trembling with each new load that came swinging from somewhere below, to be hustled off to its place, stick by stick; and then out into the west, where the November sun was dropping, and around at the hazy flats and the strip of a river. She drew in her breath quickly, and looked up at Bannon with a nervous little gesture.

"I like it," she finally said, after a long silence, during which they had watched a big stick go up on one of the small hoists, to be swung into place and driven home on the dowel pins by Peterson's sledge.

"Isn't Pete a hummer?" said Max. "I never yet saw him take hold of a thing that was too much for him."

Neither Hilda nor Bannon replied to this, and there was another silence.

"Would you like to walk around and see things closer to?" Bannon asked, turning to Miss Vogel.

"I wouldn't mind. It's rather cold, sitting still."

He led the way along one side of the structure, guiding her carefully in places where the flooring was not yet secure.

"I'm glad you came up," he said. "A good many people think there's nothing in this kind of work but just sawing wood and making money for somebody up in Minneapolis. But it isn't that way. It's pretty, and sometimes it's exciting; and things happen every little while that are interesting enough to tell to anybody, if people only knew it. I'll have you come up a little later, when we get the house built and the machinery coming in. That's when we'll have things really moving. There'll be some fun putting up the belt gallery, too. That'll be over here on the other side."

He turned to lead the way across the floor to the north side of the building. They had stopped a little way from the boom hoist, and she was standing motionless, watching as the boom swung out and the rope rattled to the ground. There was the puffing of the engine far below, the straining of the rope, and the creaking of the blocks as the heavy load came slowly up. Gangs of men were waiting to take the timbers the moment they reached the floor. The foreman of the hoist gang was leaning out over the edge, looking down and shouting orders.

Hilda turned with a little start and saw that Bannon was waiting for her. Following him, she picked her way between piles of planks and timber, and between groups of laborers and carpenters, to the other side. Now they could look down at the four tracks of the C. & S. C., the unfinished spouting house on the wharf, and the river.

"Here's where the belt gallery will go," he said, pointing downward: "right over the tracks to the spouting house. They carry the grain on endless belts, you know."

"Doesn't it ever fall off?"

"Not a kernel. It's pretty to watch. When she gets to running we'll come up some day and look at it."

They walked slowly back toward the well. Before they reached it Peterson and Max joined them. Peterson had rolled down his sleeves and put on his coat.

"You ain't going down now, are you?" he said. "We'll be starting in pretty soon on some of the heavy framing. This is just putting in girders."

He was speaking directly to Miss Vogel, but he made an effort to include Bannon in the conversation by an awkward movement of his head. This stiffness in Peterson's manner when Bannon was within hearing had been growing more noticeable during the past few days.

"Don't you think of going yet," he continued, with a nervous laugh, for Hilda was moving on. "She needn't be in such a rush to get to work, eh, Charlie?"

Hilda did not give Bannon a chance to reply.

"Thank you very much, Mr. Peterson," she said, smiling, "but I must go back, really. Maybe you'll tell me some day when you're going to do something special, so I can come up again."

Peterson's disappointment was so frankly shown in his face that she smiled again. "I've enjoyed it very much," she said. She was still looking at Peterson, but at the last word she turned to include Bannon, as if she had suddenly remembered that he was in the party. There was an uncomfortable feeling, shown by all in their silence and in their groping about for something to say.

"I'll go ahead and clear the track," said Bannon. "I'll holler up to you, Max, when we're ready down below."

"Here," said Max, "let me go down."

But Bannon had already started down the first ladder.

"The next time you come to visit us, Miss Vogel," he called back, "I guess we'll have our real elevator in, and we can run you up so fast it'll take your breath away. We'll be real swells here yet."

When he reached the working floor, he called in the laborers and shouted to Max. But when the box, slowly descending, appeared below the bin walls, it was Peterson who held the line and chatted with Hilda as he steadied her.

The next day a lot of cribbing came from Ledyard, and Bannon at once set about reorganizing his forces so that work could go on night and day. He and Peterson would divide the time equally into twelve-hour days; but three divisions were necessary for the men, the morning shift working from midnight until eight o'clock, the day shift from eight to four, and the night shift from four to midnight.

Finally, when the whistle blew, at noon, Bannon tipped back his chair and pushed his hat back on his head.

"Well," he said, "that's fixed."

"When will we begin on it?" Peterson asked.

"To-day. Have the whistle blow at four. It'll make some of the men work overtime to-day, but we'll pay them for it."

Miss Vogel was putting on her jacket. Before joining Max, who was waiting at the door, she asked:—

"Do you want me to make any change in my work, Mr. Bannon?"

"No, you'd better go ahead just as you are. We won't try to cut you up into three shifts yet awhile. We can do what letters and accounts we have in the daytime."

She nodded and left the office.

All through the morning's work Peterson had worn a heavy, puzzled expression, and now that they had finished, he seemed unable to throw it off. Bannon, who had risen and was reaching for his ulster, which he had thrown over the railing, looked around at him.

"You and I'll have to make twelve-hour days of it, you know," he said. He knew, from his quick glance and the expression almost of relief that came over his face, that this was what Peterson had been waiting for. "You'd better come on in the evening, if it's all the same to you—at seven. I'll take it in the morning and keep an eye on it during the day."

Peterson's eyes had lowered at the first words. He swung one leg over the other and picked up the list of carpenters that Max had made out, pretending to examine it. Bannon was not watching him closely, but he could have read the thoughts behind that sullen face. If their misunderstanding had arisen from business conditions alone, Bannon would have talked out plainly. But now that Hilda had come between them, and particularly that it was all so vague—a matter of feeling, and not at all of reason—he had decided to say nothing. It was important that he should control the work during the day, and coming on at seven in the morning, he would have a hand on the work of all three shifts. He knew that Peterson would not see it reasonably; that he would think it was done to keep him away from Hilda. He stood leaning against the gate to keep it open, buttoning his ulster.

"Coming on up to the house, Pete?"

Peterson got down off the railing.

"So you're going to put me on the night shift," he said, almost as a child would have said it.

"I guess that's the way it's got to work out," Bannon replied. "Coming up?"

"No—not yet. I'll be along pretty soon."

Bannon started toward the door, but turned with a snap of his finger.

"Oh, while we're at it, Pete—you'd better tell Max to get those men to keep time for the night shifts."

"You mean you want him to go on with you in the daytime?"

"That's just as he likes. But I guess he'll want to be around while his sister is here. You see about that after lunch, will you?"

Peterson came in while Bannon was eating his dinner and stayed after he had gone. In the evening, when he returned to the house for his supper, after arranging with Peterson to share the first night's work, Bannon found that the foreman's clothes and grip had been taken from the room. On the stairs he met the landlady, and asked her if Mr. Peterson had moved.

"Yes," she replied; "he took his things away this noon. I'm sorry he's gone, for he was a good young man. He never give me any trouble like some of the men do that's been here. The trouble with most of them is that they get drunk on pay-days and come home simply disgusting."

Bannon passed on without comment. During the evening he saw Peterson on the distributing floor, helping the man from the electric light company rig up a new arc light. His expression when he caught sight of Bannon, sullen and defiant, yet showing a great effort to appear natural, was the only explanation needed of how matters stood between them.

It took a few days to get the new system to running smoothly—new carpenters and laborers had to be taken on, and new foremen worked into their duties—but it proved to be less difficult than Max and Hilda had supposed from what Peterson had to say about the conduct of the work. The men all worked better than before; each new move of Bannon's seemed to infuse more vigor and energy into the work; and the cupola and annex began rapidly, as Max said, "to look like something." Bannon was on hand all day, and frequently during a large part of the night. He had a way of appearing at any hour to look at the work and keep it moving. Max, after hearing the day men repeat what the night men had to tell of the boss and his work, said to his sister: "Honest, Hilda, I don't see how he does it. I don't believe he ever takes his clothes off."

CHAPTER 9

The direct result of the episode with the carpenter Reilly was insignificant. He did not attempt to make good his boast that he would be back at work next day, and when he did appear, on Wednesday of the next week, his bleared eyes and dilapidated air made the reason plain enough. A business agent of his union was with him; Bannon found them in the office.

He nodded to the delegate. "Sit down," he said. Then he turned to Reilly. "I don't ask you to do the same. You're not wanted on the premises. I told you once before that I was through talking." Reilly started to reply, but his companion checked him. "That's all right," he said. "I know your side of it. Wait for me up by the car line."

When Reilly had gone Bannon repeated his invitation to sit down.

"You probably know why I've come," the delegate began. "Mr. Reilly has charged you with treating him unjustly and with drawing a revolver on him. Of course, in a case like this, we try to get at both sides before we take any action. Would you give me your account of it?"

Bannon told in twenty words just how it had happened. The agent said cautiously: "Reilly told another story."

"I suppose so. Now, I don't ask you to take my word against his. If you'd like to investigate the business, I'll give you all the opportunity you want."

"If we find that he did drop the hammer by accident, would you be willing to take him back?"

Bannon smiled. "There's no use in my telling you what I'll do till you tell me what you want me to do, is there?"

Bannon held out his hand when the man rose to go.

"Any time you think there's something wrong out here, or anything you don't understand, come out and we'll talk it over. I treat a man as well as I can, if he's square with me."

He walked to the door with the agent and closed it after him. As he turned back to the draughting table, he found Hilda's eyes on him.

"They're very clean chaps, mostly, those walking delegates," he said. "If you treat 'em half as well as you'd treat a yellow dog, they're likely to be very reasonable. If one of 'em does happen to be a rascal, though, he's meaner to handle than frozen dynamite. I expect to be white-headed before I'm through with that man Grady."

"Is he a rascal?" she asked.

"He's as bad as you find 'em. Even if he'd been handled right——"

Bannon broke off abruptly and began turning over the blue prints. "Suppose I'd better see how this next story looks," he said. Hilda had heard how Pete had dealt with Grady at their first meeting, and she could complete the broken sentence.

Bannon never heard whether the agent from the carpenters' union had looked further into Reilly's case, but he was not asked to take him back on the pay roll. But that was not the end of the incident. Coming out on the distributing floor just before noon on Thursday, he found Grady in the act of delivering an impassioned oration to the group of laborers about the hoist. Before Grady saw him, Bannon had come near enough to hear something about being "driven at the point of a pistol."

The speech came suddenly to an end when Grady, following the glances of his auditors, turned and saw who was coming. Bannon noted with satisfaction the scared look of appeal which he turned, for a second, toward the men. It was good to know that Grady was something of a coward.

Bannon nodded to him pleasantly enough. "How are you, Grady?" he said.

Seeing that he was in no danger, the delegate threw back his shoulders, held up his head, and, frowning in an important manner, he returned Bannon's greeting with the scantest civility.

Bannon walked up and stood beside him. "If you can spare the time," he said politely, "I'd like to see you at the office for a while."

Convinced now that Bannon was doing everything in his power to conciliate him, Grady grew more important "Very well," he said; "when I've got through up here, ye can see me if ye like."

"All right," said Bannon, patiently; "no hurry."

During the full torrent of Grady's eloquence the work had not actually been interrupted. The big boom bearing its load of timber swept in over the distributing floor with unbroken regularity; but the men had worked with only half their minds and had given as close attention as they dared to the delegate's fervid utterances. But from the moment Bannon appeared there had been a marked change in the attitude of the little audience; they steered the hoist and canted the timbers about with a sudden enthusiasm which made Bannon smile a little as he stood watching them.

Grady could not pump up a word to say. He cleared his throat loudly once or twice, but the men ignored him utterly. He kept casting his shifty little sidewise glances at the boss, wondering why he didn't go away, but Bannon continued to stand there, giving an occasional direction, and watching the progress of the work with much satisfaction. The little delegate shifted his weight from one foot to the other and cleared his throat again. Then he saw that two or three of the men were grinning. That was too much.

"Well, I'll go with you," he snapped.

Bannon could not be sure how much of an impression Grady's big words and his ridiculous assumption of importance had made upon the men, but he determined to counteract it as thoroughly as possible, then and there. It was a sort of gallery play that he had decided on, but he felt sure it would prove effective.

Grady turned to go down as he had come up, by the ladders, but Bannon caught him by the shoulder, saying with a laugh: "Oh, don't waste your time walking. Take the elevator." His tone was friendly but his grip was like a man-trap, and he was propelling Grady straight toward the edge of the building. Four big timbers had just come up and Bannon caught the released rope as it came trailing by. "Here," he said; "put your foot in the hook and hang on, and you'll come down in no time."

Grady laughed nervously. "No you don't. I suppose you'd be glad to get rid of me that way. You don't come that on me."

The men were watching with interest; Bannon raised his voice a little. "All right," he said, thrusting his foot into the great hook, "if you feel that way about it. We'll have a regular passenger elevator in here by and by, with an electric bell and sliding door, for the capitalist crowd that are going to own the place. But we workingmen get along all right on this. Swing off, boys."

He waited for Grady down below. It mattered very little to him now whether the walking delegate chose to follow him down the hoist or to walk down on the ladders, for every one had seen that Grady was afraid. Bannon had seen all the men grinning broadly as he began his descent, and that was all he wanted.

Evidently Grady's fear of the rope was less than his dread of the ridicule of the men, for Bannon saw him preparing to come down after the next load. He took a long time getting ready, but at last they started him. He was the color of a handful of waste when he reached the ground, and he staggered as he walked with Bannon over to the office. He dropped into a chair and rubbed his forehead with his coat-sleeve.

"Well," said Bannon, "do you like the look of things? I hope you didn't find anything out of the way?"

"Do you dare ask me that?" Grady began. His voice was weak at first, but as his giddiness passed away it arose again to its own inimitable oratorical level. "Do you dare pretend that you are treating these men right? Who gave you the right to decide that this man shall live and this man shall die, and that this poor fellow who asks no more than to be allowed to earn his honest living with his honest sweat shall be stricken down with two broken ribs?"

"I don't know," said Bannon. "You're speaking of the hoist accident, I suppose. Well, go and ask that man if he has any complaint to make. If he has, come and let me know about it."

"They call this a free country, and yet you oppressors can compel men to risk their lives——"

"Have you any changes to suggest in the way that hoist is rigged?" Bannon cut in quietly. "You've been inspecting it. What did you think was unsafe about it?"

Grady was getting ready for his next outburst, but Bannon prevented him. "There ain't many jobs, if you leave out tacking down carpets, where a man don't risk his life more or less. MacBride don't compel men to risk their lives; he pays 'em for doing it, and you can bet he's done it himself. We don't like it, but it's necessary. Now, if you saw men out there taking risks that you think are unnecessary, why, say so, and we'll talk it over."

"There's another thing you've got to answer for, Mr. Bannon. These are free men that are devoting their honest labor to you. You may think you're a slave driver, but you aren't. You may flourish your revolver in the faces of slaves, but free American citizens will resent it——"

"Mr. Grady, the man I drew a gun on was a carpenter. His own union is looking after him. He had thrown a hammer down into a bin where some of your laborers were at work, so I acted in their defence."

Grady stood up. "I come here to give you warning to-day, Mr. Bannon. There is a watchful eye on you. The next time I come it will not be to warn, but to act. That's all I've got to say to you now."

Bannon, too, was on his feet. "Mr. Grady, we try to be fair to our men. It's your business to see that we are fair, so we ought to get on all right together. After this, if the men lodge any complaint with you, come to me; don't go out on the job and make speeches. If you're looking for fair play, you'll get it. If you're looking for trouble, you'll get it. Good-morning."

The new _régime_ in operation at the elevator was more of a hardship to Peterson than to any one else, because it compelled him to be much alone. Not only was he quite cut off from the society of Max and Hilda, but it happened that the two or three under-foremen whom he liked best were on the day shift. The night's work with none of those pleasant little momentary interruptions that used to occur in the daytime was mere unrelieved drudgery, but the afternoons, when he had given up trying to sleep any longer, were tedious enough to make him long for six o'clock.

Naturally, his disposition was easy and generous, but he had never been in the habit of thinking much, and thinking, especially as it led to brooding, was not good for him. From the first, of course, he had been hurt that the office should have thought it necessary to send Bannon to supersede him, but so long as he had plenty to do and was in Bannon's company every hour of the day, he had not taken time to think about it much. But now he thought of little else, and as time went on he succeeded in twisting nearly everything the new boss had said or done to fit his theory that Bannon was jealous of him and was trying to take from him the credit which rightfully belonged to him. And Bannon had put him in charge of the night shift, so Peterson came to think, simply because he had seen that Hilda was beginning to like him.

About four o'clock one afternoon, not many days after Grady's talk with Bannon, Peterson sat on the steps of his boarding-house, trying to make up his mind what to do, and wishing it were six o'clock. He wanted to stroll down to the job to have a chat with his friends, but he had somewhat childishly decided he wasn't wanted there while Miss Vogel was in the office, so he sat still and whittled, and took another view of his grievances. Glancing up, he saw Grady, the walking delegate, coming along the sidewalk. Now that the responsibility of the elevator was off his shoulders he no longer cherished any particular animosity toward the little Irishman, but he remembered their last encounter and wondered whether he should speak to him or not.

But Grady solved his doubt by calling out cheerfully to know how he was and turning in toward the steps. "I suppose I ought to lick you after what's passed between us," he added with a broad smile, "but if you're willing we'll call it bygones."

"Sure," said Peterson.

"It's fine seasonable weather we're having, and just the thing for you on the elevator. It's coming right along."

"First-rate."

"It's as interesting a bit of work as I ever saw. I was there the other day looking at it. And, by the way, I had a long talk with Mr. Bannon. He's a fine man."

Grady had seated himself on the step below Peterson. Now for the first time he looked at him.

"He's a good hustler," said Peterson.

"Well, that's what passes for a fine man, these days, though mistakes are sometimes made that way. But how does it happen that you're not down there superintending? I hope some carpenter hasn't taken it into his head to fire the boss."

"I'm not boss there any longer. The office sent Bannon down to take it over my head."

"You don't tell me that? It's a pity." Grady was shaking his head solemnly. "It's a pity. The men like you first-rate, Mr. Peterson. I'm not saying they don't like anybody else, but they like you. But people in an office a thousand miles away can't know everything, and that's a fact. And so he laid you off."

"Oh, no, I ain't quite laid off—yet. He's put me in charge of the night shift."

"So you're working nights, then? It seemed to me you was working fast enough in the daytime to satisfy anybody. But I suppose some rich man is in a hurry for it and you must do your best to accommodate him."

"You bet, he's in a hurry for it. He won't listen to reason at all. Says the bins have got to be chock full of grain before January first, no matter what happens to us. He don't care how much it costs, either."

"I must be going along," said Grady, getting to his feet. "That man must be in a hurry. January first! That's quick work, and he don't care how much it costs him. Oh, these rich devils! They're hustlers, too, Mr. Peterson. Well, good-night to you."

Peterson saw Bannon twice every day,—for a half hour at night when he took charge of the job, and for another half hour in the morning when he relinquished it. That was all except when they chanced to meet during Bannon's irregular nightly wanderings about the elevator. As the days had gone by these conversations had been confined more and more rigidly to necessary business, and though this result was Peterson's own bringing about, still he charged it up as another of his grievances against Bannon.

When, about an hour after his conversation with Grady, he started down to the elevator to take command, he knew he ought to tell Bannon of his conversation with Grady, and he fully intended doing so. But his determination oozed away as he neared the office, and when he finally saw Bannon he decided to say nothing about it whatever. He decided thus partly because he wished to make his conversation with Bannon as short as possible, partly because he had not made up his mind what significance, if any, the incident had, and (more than either of these reasons) because ever since Grady had repeated the phrase: "He don't care what it costs him," Peterson had been uneasily aware that he had talked too much.

CHAPTER 10

Grady's affairs were prospering beyond his expectations, confident though he had been. Away back in the summer, when the work was in its early stages, his eye had been upon it; he had bided his time in the somewhat indefinite hope that something would turn up. But he went away jubilant from his conversation with Peterson, for it seemed that all the cards were in his hands.

Just as a man running for a car is the safest mark for a gamin's snowball, so Calumet K, through being a rush job as well as a rich one, offered a particularly advantageous field for Grady's endeavors. Men who were trying to accomplish the impossible feat of completing, at any cost, the great hulk on the river front before the first of January, would not be likely to stop to quibble at paying the five thousand dollars or so that Grady, who, as the business agent of his union was simply in masquerade, would like to extort.

He had heard that Peterson was somewhat disaffected to Bannon's authority, but had not expected him to make so frank an avowal of it. That was almost as much in his favor as the necessity for hurry. These, with the hoist accident to give a color of respectability to the operation, ought to make it simple enough. He had wit enough to see that Bannon was a much harder man to handle than Peterson, and that with Peterson restored to full authority, the only element of uncertainty would be removed. And he thought that if he could get Peterson to help him it might be possible to secure Bannon's recall. If the scheme failed, he had still another shot in his locker, but this one was worth a trial, anyway.

One afternoon in the next week he went around to Peterson's boarding-house and sent up his card with as much ceremony as though the night boss had been a railway president.

"I hope you can spare me half an hour, Mr. Peterson. There's a little matter of business I'd like to talk over with you."

The word affected Peterson unpleasantly. That was a little farther than he could go without a qualm. "Sure," he said uneasily, looking at his watch.

"I don't know as I should call it business, either," Grady went on. "When you come right down to it, it's a matter of friendship, for surely it's no business of mine. Maybe you think it's queer—I think it's queer myself, that I should be coming 'round tendering my friendly services to a man who's had his hands on my throat threatening my life. That ain't my way, but somehow I like you, Mr. Peterson, and there's an end of it. And when I like a man, I like him, too. How's the elevator? Everything going to please you?"

"I guess it's going all right. It ain't——" Pete hesitated, and then gave up the broken sentence. "It's all right," he repeated.

Grady smiled. "There's the good soldier. Won't talk against his general. But, Mr. Peterson, let me ask you a question; answer me as a man of sense. Which makes the best general—the man who leads the charge straight up to the intrenchments, yellin': 'Come on, boys!'—or the one who says, very likely shaking a revolver in their faces: 'Get in there, ye damn low-down privates, and take that fort, and report to me when I've finished my breakfast'? Which one of those two men will the soldiers do the most for? For the one they like best, Mr. Peterson, and don't forget it. And which one of these are they going to like best, do you suppose—the brave leader who scorns to ask his men to go where he wouldn't go himself, who isn't ashamed to do honest work with honest hands, whose fists are good enough to defend him against his enemies; or the man who is afraid to go out among the men without a revolver in his hip pocket? Answer me as a man of sense, Mr. Peterson."

Peterson was manifestly disturbed by the last part of the harangue. Now he said: "Oh, I guess Bannon wasn't scared when he drawed that gun on Reilly. He ain't that kind."

"Would you draw a gun on an unarmed, defenceless man?" Grady asked earnestly.

"No, I wouldn't. I don't like that way of doing."

"The men don't like it either, Mr. Peterson. No more than you do. They like you. They'll do anything you ask them to. They know that you can do anything that they can. But, Mr. Peterson, I'll be frank with you. They don't like the man who crowded you out. That's putting it mild. I won't say they hate him for an uncivil, hard-tongued, sneaking weasel of a spy——"

"I never knew Bannon to do anything like that," said Peterson, slowly.

"I did. Didn't he come sneaking up and hear what I was saying—up on top of the elevator the other day? I guess he won't try that again. I told him that when I was ready to talk to him, I'd come down to the office to do it."

Grady was going almost too far; Pete would not stand very much more; already he was trying to get on his feet to put an end to the conversation. "I ask your pardon, Mr. Peterson. I forgot he was a friend of yours. But the point is right here. The men don't like him. They've been wanting to strike these three days, just because they don't want to work for that ruffian. I soothed them all I can, but they won't hold in much longer. Mark my words, there'll be a strike on your hands before the week's out unless you do something pretty soon."

"What have they got to strike about? Don't we treat them all right? What do they kick about?"

"A good many things, big and little. But the real reason is the one I've been giving you—Bannon. Neither more nor less."

"Do you mean they'd be all right if another man was in charge?"

Grady could not be sure from Peterson's expression whether the ice were firm enough to step out boldly upon, or not. He tested it cautiously.

"Mr. Peterson, I know you're a good man. I know you're a generous man. I know you wouldn't want to crowd Bannon out of his shoes the way he crowded you out of yours; not even after the way he's treated you. But look here, Mr. Peterson. Who's your duty to? The men up in Minneapolis who pay your salary, or the man who has come down here and is giving orders over your head?

"——No, just let me finish, Mr. Peterson. I know what you're going to say. But do your employers want to get the job done by New Year's? They do. Do they pay you to help get it done? They do. Will it be done if that would-be murderer of a Bannon is allowed to stay here? It will not, you can bet on that. Then it's your duty to get him out of here, and I'm going to help you do it."

Grady was on his feet when he declaimed the last sentence. He flung out his hand toward Pete. "Shake on it!" he cried.

Peterson had also got to his feet, but more slowly. He did not take the hand. "I'm much obliged, Mr. Grady," he said. "It's very kind in you. If that's so as you say, I suppose he'll have to go. And he'll go all right without any shoving when he sees that it is so. You go and tell just what you've told me to Charlie Bannon. He's boss on this job."

Grady would have fared better with a man of quicker intelligence. Peterson was so slow at catching the blackmailer's drift that he spoke in perfectly good faith when he made the suggestion that he tell Bannon, and Grady went away a good deal perplexed as to the best course to pursue,— whether to go directly to Bannon, or to try the night boss again.

As for Peterson, four or five times during his half-hour talk with Bannon at the office that evening, he braced himself to tell the boss what Grady had said, but it was not till just as Bannon was going home that it finally came out. "Have you seen Grady lately?" Pete asked, as calmly as he could.

"He was around here something more than a week ago; gave me a little bombthrowers' anniversary oratory about oppressors and a watchful eye. There's no use paying any attention to him yet. He thinks he's got some trouble cooking for us on the stove, but we'll have to wait till he turns it into the dish. He ain't as dangerous as he thinks he is."

"He's been around to see me lately—twice."

"He has! What did he want with you? When was it he came?"

"The first time about a week ago. That was nothing but a little friendly talk, but——"

"Friendly! Him! What did he have to say?"

"Why, it was nothing. I don't remember. He wanted to know if I was laid off, and I told him I was on the night shift."

"Was that all?"

"Pretty near. He wanted to know what we was in such a hurry about, working nights, and I said we had to be through by January first. Then he said he supposed it must be for some rich man who didn't care how much it cost him; and I said yes, it was. That was all. He didn't mean nothing. We were just passing the time of day. I don't see any harm in that."

Bannon was leaning on the rail, his face away from Peterson. After a while he spoke thoughtfully. "Well, that cinches it. I guess he meant to hold us up, anyway, but now he knows we're a good thing."

"How's that? I don't see," said Peterson; but Bannon made no reply.

"What did he have to offer the next time he came around? More in the same friendly way? When was it?"

"Just this afternoon. Why, he said he was afraid we'd have a strike on our hands."

"He ought to know," said Bannon. "Did he give any reason?"

"Yes, he did. You won't mind my speaking it right out, I guess. He said the men didn't like you, and if you wasn't recalled they'd likely strike. He said they'd work under me if you was recalled, but he didn't think he could keep 'em from going out if you stayed. That ain't what I think, mind you; I'm just telling you what he said. Then he kind of insinuated that I ought to do something about it myself. That made me tired, and I told him to come to you about it. I said you was the boss here now, and I was only the foreman of the night shift."

Until that last sentence Bannon had been only half listening. He made no sign, indeed, of having heard anything, but stood hacking at the pine railing with his pocket-knife. He was silent so long that at last Peterson arose to go. Bannon shut his knife and wheeled around to face him.

"Hold on, Pete," he said. "We'd better talk this business out right here."

"Talk out what?"

"Oh, I guess you know. Why don't we pull together better? What is it you're sore about?"

"Nothing. You don't need to worry about it."

"Look here, Pete. You've known me a good many years. Do you think I'm square?"

"I never said you wasn't square."

"You might have given me the benefit of the doubt, anyway. I know you didn't like my coming down here to take charge. Do you suppose I did? You were unlucky, and a man working for MacBride can't afford to be unlucky; so he told me to come and finish the job. And once I was down here he held me responsible for getting it done. I've got to go ahead just the best I can. I thought you saw that at first, and that we'd get on all right together, but lately it's been different." "I thought I'd been working hard enough to satisfy anybody."

"It ain't that, and you know it ain't. It's just the spirit of the thing. Now, I don't ask you to tell me why it is you feel this way. If you want to talk it out now, all right. If you don't, all right again. But if you ever think I'm not using you right, come to me and say so. Just look at what we've got to do here, Pete, before the first of January. Sometimes I think we can do it, and sometimes I think we can't, but we've got to anyway. If we don't, MacBride will just make up his mind we're no good. And unless we pull together, we're stuck for sure. It ain't a matter of work entirely. I want to feel that I've got you with me. Come around in the afternoon if you happen to be awake, and fuss around and tell me what I'm doing wrong. I want to consult you about a good many things in the course of a day."

Pete's face was simply a lens through which one could see the feelings at work beneath, and Bannon knew that he had struck the right chord at last. "How is it? Does that go?"

"Sure," said Pete. "I never knew you wanted to consult me about anything, or I'd have been around before."

Friday afternoon Bannon received a note from Grady saying that if he had any regard for his own interests or for those of his employers, he would do well to meet the writer at ten o'clock Sunday morning at a certain downtown hotel. It closed with a postscript containing the disinterested suggestion that delays were dangerous, and a hint that the writer's time was valuable and he wished to be informed whether the appointment would be kept or not.

Bannon ignored the note, and all day Monday expected Grady's appearance at the office. He did not come, but when Bannon reached his boarding-house about eight o'clock that evening, he found Grady in his room waiting for him.

"I can't talk on an empty stomach," said the boss, cheerfully, as he was washing up. "Just wait till I get some supper."

"I'll wait," said Grady, grimly.

When Bannon came back to talk, he took off his coat and sat down astride a chair. "Well, Mr. Grady, when you came here before you said it was to warn me, but the next time you came you were going to begin to act. I'm all ready."

"All right," said Grady, with a vicious grin. "Be as smart as you like. I'll be paid well for every word of it and for every minute you've kept me waiting yesterday and to-night That was the most expensive supper you ever ate. I thought you had sense enough to come, Mr. Bannon. That's why I wasted a stamp on you. You made the biggest mistake of your life——"

During the speech Bannon had sat like a man hesitating between two courses of action. At this point he interrupted:—

"Let's get to business, Mr. Grady."

"I'll get to it fast enough. And when I do you'll see if you can safely insult the representative of the mighty power of the honest workingman of this vast land."

"Well?"

"I hear you folks are in a hurry, Mr. Bannon?"

"Yes."

"And that you'll spend anything it costs to get through on time. How'd it suit you to have all your laborers strike about now? Don't that idea make you sick?"

"Pretty near."

"Well, they will strike inside two days."

"What for? Suppose we settle with them direct."

"Just try that," said Grady, with withering sarcasm. "Just try that and see how it works."

"I don't want to. I only wanted to hear you confess that you are a rascal."

"You'll pay dear for giving me that name. But we come to that later. Do you think it would be worth something to the men who hire you for a dirty slave-driver to be protected against a strike? Wouldn't they be willing to pay a round sum to get this work done on time? Take a minute to think about it. Be careful how you tell me they wouldn't. You're not liked here, Mr. Bannon, by anybody——"

"You're threatening to have me recalled, according to your suggestions to Mr. Peterson the other night. Well, that's all right if you can do it. But I think that sooner than recall me or have a strike they would be willing to pay for protection."

"You do. I didn't look for that much sense in you. If you'd shown it sooner it might have saved your employers a large wad of bills. If you'd taken the trouble to be decent when I went to you in a friendly way a very little would have been enough. But now I've got to be paid. What do you say to five thousand as a fair sum?"

"They'd be willing to pay fully that to save delay," said Bannon, cheerfully.

"They would!" To save his life Grady could not help looking crestfallen. It seemed then that he might have got fifty. "All right," he went on, "five thousand it is; and I want it in hundred-dollar bills."

"You do!" cried Bannon, jumping to his feet. "Do you think you're going to get a cent of it? I might pay blackmail to an honest rascal who delivered the goods paid for. But I had your size the first time you came around. Don't you think I knew what you wanted? If I'd thought you were worth buying, I'd have settled it up for three hundred dollars and a box of cigars right at the start. That's about your market price. But as long as I knew you'd sell us out again if you could, I didn't think you were even worth the cigars. No; don't tell me what you're going to do. Go out and do it if you can. And get out of here."

For the second time Bannon took the little delegate by the arm. He marched him to the head of the long, straight flight of stairs. Then he hesitated a moment. "I wish you were three sizes larger," he said.

CHAPTER 11

The organization of labor unions is generally democratic. The local lodge is self-governing; it elects its delegate, who attends a council of fellow-delegates, and this council may send representatives to a still more powerful body. But however high their titles, or their salaries, these dignitaries have power only to suggest action, except in a very limited variety of cases. There must always be a reference back to the rank and file. The real decision lies with them.

That is the theory. The laborers on Calumet K, with some others at work in the neighborhood, had organized into a lodge and had affiliated with the American Federation of Labor. Grady, who had appeared out of nowhere, who had urged upon them the need of combining against the forces of oppression, and had induced them to organize, had been, without dissent, elected delegate. He was nothing more in theory than this: simply their concentrated voice. And this theory had the fond support of the laborers. "He's not our boss; he's our servant," was a sentiment they never tired of uttering when the delegate was out of earshot.

They met every Friday night, debated, passed portentous resolutions, and listened to Grady's oratory. After the meeting was over they liked to hear their delegate, their servant, talk mysteriously of the doings of the council, and so well did Grady manage this air of mystery that each man thought it assumed because of the presence of others, but that he himself was of the inner circle. They would not have dreamed of questioning his acts in meeting or after, as they stood about the dingy, reeking hall over Barry's saloon. It was only as they went to their lodgings in groups of two and three that they told how much better they could manage things themselves.

Bannon enjoyed his last conversation with Grady, though it left him a good deal to think out afterward. He had acted quite deliberately, had said nothing that afterward he wished unsaid; but as yet he had not decided what to do next. After he heard the door slam behind the little delegate, he walked back into his room, paced the length of it two or three times, then put on his ulster and went out. He started off aimlessly, paying no attention to whither he was going, and consequently he walked straight to the elevator. He picked his way across the C. & S. C. tracks, out to the wharf, and seated himself upon an empty nail keg not far from the end of the spouting house.

He sat there for a long while, heedless of all that was doing about him, turning the situation over and over in his mind. Like a good strategist, he was planning Grady's campaign as carefully as his own. Finally he was recalled to his material surroundings by a rough voice which commanded, "Get off that keg and clear out. We don't allow no loafers around here."

Turning, Bannon recognized one of the under-foremen. "That's a good idea," he said. "Are you making a regular patrol, or did you just happen to see me?"

"I didn't know it was you. No, I'm tending to some work here in the spouting house."

"Do you know where Mr. Peterson is?"

"He was right up here a bit ago. Do you want to see him?"

"Yes, if he isn't busy. I'm not the only loafer here, it seems," added Bannon, nodding toward where the indistinct figures of a man and a woman could be seen coming slowly toward them along the narrow strip of wharf between the building and the water. "Never mind," he added, as the foreman made a step in their direction, "I'll look after them myself."

The moment after he had called the foreman's attention to them he had recognized them as Hilda and Max. He walked over to meet them. "We can't get enough of it in the daytime, can we."

"It's a great place for a girl, isn't it, Mr. Bannon," said Max. "I was coming over here and Hilda made me bring her along. She said she thought it must look pretty at night." "Doesn't it?" she asked. "Don't you think it does, Mr. Bannon?"

He had been staring at it for half an hour. Now for the first time he looked at it. For ninety feet up into the air the large mass was one unrelieved, unbroken shadow, barely distinguishable from the night sky that enveloped it. Above was the skeleton of the cupola, made brilliant, fairly dazzling, in contrast, by scores of arc lamps. At that distance and in that confused tangle of light and shadow the great timbers of the frame looked spidery. The effect was that of a luminous crown upon a gigantic, sphinx-like head.

"I guess you are right," he said slowly. "But I never thought of it that way before. And I've done more or less night work, too."

A moment later Peterson came up. "Having a tea party out here?" he asked; then turning to Bannon: "Was there something special you wanted, Charlie? I've got to go over to the main house pretty soon."

"It's our friend Grady. He's come down to business at last. He wants money."

Hilda was quietly signalling Max to come away, and Bannon, observing it, broke off to speak to them. "Don't go," he said. "We'll have a brief council of war right here." So Hilda was seated on the nail keg, while Bannon, resting his elbows on the top of a spile which projected waist high through the floor of the wharf, expounded the situation.

"You understand his proposition," he said, addressing Hilda, rather than either of the men. "It's just plain blackmail. He says, 'If you don't want your laborers to strike, you'll have to pay my price.'"

"Not much," Pete broke in. "I'd let the elevator rot before I'd pay a cent of blackmail."

"Page wouldn't," said Bannon, shortly, "or MacBride, neither. They'd be glad to pay five thousand or so for protection. But they'd want protection that would protect. Grady's trying to sell us a gold brick. He hated us to begin with, and when he'd struck us for about all he thought we'd stand, he'd call the men off just the same, and leave us to waltz the timbers around all by ourselves."

"How much did he want?"

"All he could get. I think he'd have been satisfied with a thousand, but he'd come 'round next week for a thousand more."

"What did you tell him?"

"I told him that a five-cent cigar was a bigger investment than I cared to make on him and that when we paid blackmail it would be to some fellow who'd deliver the goods. I said he could begin to make trouble just as soon as he pleased."

"Seems to me you might have asked for a few days' time to decide. Then we could have got something ready to come at him with. He's liable to call our men out to-night, ain't he?"

"I don't think so. I thought of trying to stave him off for a few days, but then I thought, 'Why, he'll see through that game and he'll go on with his scheme for sewing us up just the same.' You see, there's no good saying we're afraid. So I told him that we didn't mind him a bit; said he could go out and have all the fun he liked with us. If he thinks we've got something up our sleeve he may be a little cautious. Anyway, he knows that our biggest rush is coming a little later, and he's likely to wait for it."

Then Hilda spoke for the first time. "Has he so much power as that? Will they strike just because he orders them to?"

"Why, not exactly," said Bannon. "They decide that for themselves, or at least they think they do. They vote on it."

"Well, then," she asked hesitatingly, "why can't you just tell the men what Mr. Grady wants you to do and show them that he's dishonest? They know they've been treated all right, don't they?"

Bannon shook his head. "No use," he said. "You see, these fellows don't know much. They aren't like skilled laborers who need some sense in their business. They're just common roustabouts, and most of 'em have gunpowder in place of brains. They don't want facts or reason either; what they like is Grady's oratory. They think that's the finest thing they ever heard. They might all be perfectly satisfied and anxious to work, but if Grady was to sing out to know if they wanted to be slaves, they'd all strike like a freight train rolling down grade.

"No," he went on, "there's nothing to be done with the men. Do you know what would happen if I was to go up to their lodge and tell right out that Grady was a blackmailer? Why, after they'd got through with me, personally, they'd pass a resolution vindicating Grady. They'd resolve that I was a thief and a liar and a murderer and an oppressor of the poor and a traitor, and if they could think of anything more than that, they'd put it in, too. And after vindicating Grady to their satisfaction, they'd take his word for law and the gospel more than ever. In this sort of a scrape you want to hit as high as you can, strike the biggest man who will let you in his office. It's the small fry that make the trouble. I guess that's true 'most everywhere. I know the general manager of a railroad is always an easier chap to get on with than the division superintendent."

"Well," said Pete, after waiting a moment to see if Bannon had any definite suggestion to make as to the best way to deal with Grady, "I'm glad you don't think he'll try to tie us up to-night. Maybe we'll think of something to-morrow. I've got to get back on the job."

"I'll go up with you," said Max, promptly. Then, in answer to Hilda's gesture of protest, "You don't want to climb away up there to-night. I'll be back in ten minutes," and he was gone before she could reply. "I guess I can take care of you till he comes back," said Bannon. Hilda made no answer. She seemed to think that silence would conceal her annoyance better than anything she could say. So, after waiting a moment, Bannon went on talking.

"I suppose that's the reason why I get ugly sometimes and call names; because I ain't a big enough man not to. If I was getting twenty-five thousand a year maybe I'd be as smooth as anybody. I'd like to be a general manager for a while, just to see how it would work."

"I don't see how anybody could ever know enough to run a railroad." Hilda was looking up at the C. & S. C. right of way, where red and white semaphore lights were winking.

"I was offered that job once myself, though, and turned it down," said Bannon. "I was superintendent of the electric light plant at Yawger. Yawger's quite a place, on a branch of the G. T. There was another road ran through the town, called the Bemis, Yawger and Pacific. It went from Bemis to Stiles Corners, a place about six miles west of Yawger. It didn't get any nearer the Pacific than that. Nobody in Yawger ever went to Bemis or Stiles, and there wasn't anybody in Bemis and Stiles to come to Yawger, or if they did come they never went back, so the road didn't do a great deal of business. They assessed the stock every year to pay the officers' salaries—and they had a full line of officers, too—but the rest of the road had to scrub along the best it could.

"When they elected me alderman from the first ward up at Yawger, I found out that the B. Y. & P. owed the city four hundred and thirty dollars, so I tried to find out why they wasn't made to pay. It seemed that the city had had a judgment against them for years, but they couldn't get hold of anything that was worth seizing. They all laughed at me when I said I meant to get that money out of 'em.

"The railroad had one train; there was an engine and three box cars and a couple of flats and a combination—that's baggage and passenger. It made the round trip from Bemis every day, fifty-two miles over all, and considering the roadbed and the engine, that was a good day's work.

"Well, that train was worth four hundred and thirty dollars all right enough, if they could have got their hands on it, but the engineer was such a peppery chap that nobody ever wanted to bother him. But I just bided my time, and one hot day after watering up the engine him and the conductor went off to get a drink. I had a few lengths of log chain handy, and some laborers with picks and shovels, and we made a neat, clean little job of it. Then I climbed up into the cab. When the engineer came back and wanted to know what I was doing there, I told him we'd attached his train. 'Don't you try to serve no papers on me,' he sung out, 'or I'll split your head.' 'There's no papers about this job,' said I. 'We've attached it to the track,' At that he dropped the fire shovel and pulled open the throttle. The drivers spun around all right, but the train never moved an inch.

"He calmed right down after that and said he hadn't four hundred and thirty dollars with him, but if I'd let the train go, he'd pay me in a week. I couldn't quite do that, so him and the conductor had to walk 'way to Bemis, where the general offices was. They was pretty mad. We had that train chained up there for 'most a month, and at last they paid the claim."

"Was that the railroad that offered to make you general manager?" Hilda asked.

"Yes, provided I'd let the train go. I'm glad I didn't take it up, though. You see, the farmers along the road who held the stock in it made up their minds that the train had quit running for good, so they took up the rails where it ran across their farms, and used the ties for firewood. That's all they ever got out of their investment."

A few moments later Max came back and Bannon straightened up to go. "I wish you'd tell Pete when you see him to-morrow," he said to the boy, "that I won't be on the job till noon."

"Going to take a holiday?"

"Yes. Tell him I'm taking the rest cure up at a sanitarium."

At half-past eight next morning Bannon entered the outer office of R. S. Carver, president of the Central District of the American Federation of Labor, and seated himself on one of the long row of wood-bottomed chairs that stood against the wall. Most of them were already occupied by poorly dressed men who seemed also to be waiting for the president. One man, in dilapidated, dirty finery, was leaning over the stenographer's desk, talking about the last big strike and guessing at the chance of there being any fun ahead in the immediate future. But the rest of them waited in stolid, silent patience, sitting quite still in unbroken rank along the wall, their overcoats, if they had them, buttoned tight around their chins, though the office was stifling hot. The dirty man who was talking to the stenographer filled a pipe with some very bad tobacco and ostentatiously began smoking it, but not a man followed his example.

Bannon sat in that silent company for more than an hour before the great man came. Even then there was no movement among those who sat along the wall, save as they followed him almost furtively with their eyes. The president never so much as glanced at one of them; for all he seemed to see the rank of chairs might have been empty. He marched across to his private office, and, leaving the door open behind him, sat down before his desk. Bannon sat still a moment, waiting for those who had come before him to make the first move, but not a man of them stirred, so, somewhat out of patience with this mysteriously solemn way of doing business, he arose and walked into the president's office with as much assurance as though it had been his own. He shut the door after him. The president did not look up, but went on cutting open his mail.

"I'm from MacBride & Company, of Minneapolis," said Bannon.

"Guess I don't know the parties."

"Yes, you do. We're building a grain elevator at Calumet."

The president looked up quickly. "Sit down," he said. "Are you superintending the work?"

"Yes. My name's Bannon—Charles Bannon."

"Didn't you have some sort of an accident out there? An overloaded hoist? And you hurt a man, I believe."

"Yes."

"And I think one of your foremen drew a revolver on a man."

"I did, myself."

The president let a significant pause intervene before his next question. "What do you want with me?"

"I want you to help me out. It looks as though we might get into trouble with our laborers."

"You've come to the wrong man. Mr. Grady is the man for you to talk with. He's their representative."

"We haven't got on very well with Mr. Grady. The first time he came on the job he didn't know our rule that visitors must apply at the office, and we weren't very polite to him. He's been down on us ever since. We can't make any satisfactory agreement with him."

Carver turned away impatiently. "You'll have to," he said, "if you want to avoid trouble with your men. It's no business of mine. He's acting on their instructions."

"No, he isn't," said Bannon, sharply. "What they want, I guess, is to be treated square and paid a fair price. What he wants is blackmail."

"I've heard that kind of talk before. It's the same howl that an employer always makes when he's tried to bribe an agent who's active in the interest of the men, and got left at it. What have you got to show for it? Anything but just your say so?"

Bannon drew out Grady's letter of warning and handed it to him. Carver read it through, then tossed it on his desk. "You certainly don't offer that as proof that he wants blackmail, Mr. Bannon."

"There's never any proof of blackmail. When a man can see me alone, he isn't going to talk before witnesses, and he won't commit himself in writing. Grady told me that unless we paid his price he'd tie us up. No one else was around when he said it."

"Then you haven't anything but your say so. But I know him, and I don't know you. Do you think I'd take your word against his?"

"That letter doesn't prove blackmail," said Bannon, "but it smells of it. And there's the same smell about everything Grady has done. When he came to my office a day or two after that hoist accident, I tried to find out what he wanted, and he gave me nothing but oratory. I tried to pin him down to something definite, but my stenographer was there and Grady didn't have a suggestion to make. Then by straining his neck and asking questions, he found out we were in a hurry, that the elevator was no good unless it was done by January first, and that we had all the money we needed.

"Two days after he sent me that letter. Look at it again. Why does he want to take both of us to Chicago on Sunday morning, when he can see me any time at my office on the job?" Bannon spread the letter open before Carver's face. "Why doesn't he say right here what it is he wants, if it's anything he dares to put in black and white? I didn't pay any attention to that letter; it didn't deserve any. And then will you tell me why he came to my room at night to see me instead of to my office in the daytime? I can prove that he did. Does all that look as if I tried to bribe him? Forget that we're talking about Grady, and tell me what you think it looks like."

Carver was silent for a moment. "That wouldn't do any good," he said at last. "If you had proof that I could act on, I might be able to help you. I haven't any jurisdiction in the internal affairs of that lodge; but if you could offer proof that he is what you say he is, I could tell them that if they continued to support him, the federation withdraws its support. But I don't see that I can help you as it is. I don't see any reason why I should."

"I'll tell you why you should. Because if there's any chance that what I've said is true, it will be a lot better for your credit to have the thing settled quietly. And it won't be settled quietly if we have to fight. It isn't very much you have to do; just satisfy yourself as to how things are going down there. See whether we're square, or Grady is. Then when the scrap comes on you'll know how to act. That's all. Do your investigating in advance."

"That's just what I haven't any right to do. I can't mix up in the business till it comes before me in the regular way."

"Well," said Bannon, with a smile, "if you can't do it yourself, maybe some man you have confidence in would do it for you."

Carver drummed thoughtfully on his desk for a few minutes. Then he carefully folded Grady's letter and put it in his pocket. "I'm glad to have met you, Mr. Bannon," he said, holding out his hand. "Good morning."

Next morning while Bannon was opening his mail, a man came to the timekeeper's window and asked for a job as a laborer. "Guess we've got men enough," said Max. "Haven't we, Mr. Bannon?"

The man put his head in the window. "A fellow down in Chicago told me if I'd come out here to Calumet K and ask Mr. Bannon for a job, he'd give me one."

"Are you good up high?" Bannon asked.

The man smiled ruefully, and said he was afraid not.

"Well, then," returned Bannon, "we'll have to let you in on the ground floor. What's your name?"

"James."

"Go over to the tool house and get a broom. Give him a check, Max."

CHAPTER 12

On the twenty-second of November Bannon received this telegram:—

MR. CHARLES BANNON, care of MacBride & Company, South Chicago:

We send to-day complete drawings for marine tower which you will build in the middle of spouting house. Harahan Company are building the Leg.

MACBRIDE & CO.

Bannon read it carefully, folded it, opened it and read it again, then tossed it on the desk.

"We're off now, for sure," he said to Miss Vogel. "I've known that was coming sure as Christmas."

Hilda picked it up.

"Is there an answer, Mr. Bannon?"

"No, just file it. Do you make it out?"

She read it and shook her head. Bannon ignored her cool manner.

"It means that your friends on MacBride & Company's Calumet house are going to have the time of their lives for the next few weeks. I'm going to carry compressed food in my pockets, and when meal time comes around, just take a capsule."

"I think I know," she said slowly; "a marine leg is the thing that takes grain up out of ships."

"That's right. You'd better move up head."

"And we've been building a spouting house instead to load it into ships."

"We'll have to build both now. You see, it's getting around to the time when the Pages'll be having a fit every day until the machinery's running, and every bin is full. And every time they have a fit, the people up at the office'll have another, and they'll pass it on to us."

"But why do they want the marine leg?" she asked, "any more now than they did at first?"

"They've got to get the wheat down by boat instead of rail, that's all. Or likely it'll be coming both ways. There's no telling now what's behind it. Both sides have got big men fighting. You've seen it in the papers, haven't you?"

She nodded.

"Of course, what the papers say isn't all true, but it's lively doings all right."

The next morning's mail brought the drawings and instructions; and with them came a letter from Brown to Bannon. "I suppose there's not much good in telling you to hurry," it ran; "but if there is another minute a day you can crowd in, I guess you know what to do with it. Page told me to-day that this elevator will make or break them. Mr. MacBride says that you can have all January for a vacation if you get it through. We owe you two weeks off, anyhow, that you didn't take last summer. We're running down that C. & S. C. business, though I don't believe, myself, that they'll give you any more trouble."

Bannon read it to Hilda, saying as he laid it down:—

"That's something like. I don't know where'll I go, though. Winter ain't exactly the time for a vacation, unless you go shooting, and I'm no hand for that."

"Couldn't you put it off till summer?" she asked, smiling a little.

"Not much. You don't know those people. By the time summer'd come around, they'd have forgotten I ever worked here. I'd strike for a month and Brown would grin and say: 'That's all right, Bannon, you deserve it if anybody does. It'll take a week or so to get your pass arranged, and you might just run out to San Francisco and see if things are going the way they ought to,' And then the first thing I knew I'd be working three shifts somewhere over in China, and Brown would be writing me I was putting in too much time at my meals. No, if MacBride & Company offer you a holiday, the best thing you can do is to grab it, and run, and saw off the telegraph poles behind you. And you couldn't be sure of yourself then."

He turned the letter over in his hand.

"I might go up on the St. Lawrence," he went on. "That's the only place for spending the winter that ever struck me."

"Isn't it pretty cold?"

"It ain't so bad. I was up there last winter. We put up at a house at Coteau, you know. When I got there the foundation wasn't even begun, and we had a bad time getting laborers. I put in the first day sitting on the ice sawing off spiles."

Hilda laughed.

"I shouldn't think you'd care much about going back."

"Were you ever there?" he asked.

"No, I've never been anywhere but home and here, in Chicago."

"Where is your home?"

"It was up in Michigan. That's where Max learned the lumber business. But he and I have been here for nearly two years."

"Well," said Bannon, "some folks may think it's cold up there, but there ain't anywhere else to touch it. It's high ground, you know—nothing like this"—he swept his arm about to indicate the flats outside—"and the scenery beats anything this side of the Rockies. It ain't that there's mountains there, you understand, but it's all big and open, and they've got forests there that would make your Michigan pine woods look like weeds on a sandhill. And the river's great. You haven't seen anything really fine till you've seen the rapids in winter. The people there have a good time too. They know how to enjoy life—it isn't all grime and sweat and making money."

"Well," said Hilda, looking down at her pencil and drawing aimless designs as she talked, "I suppose it is a good place to go. I've seen the pictures, of course, in the time-tables; and one of the railroad offices on Clark Street used to have some big photographs of the St. Lawrence in the window. I looked at them sometimes, but I never thought of really seeing anything like that. I've had some pretty good times on the lake and over at

St. Joe. Max used to take me over to Berrien Springs last summer, when he could get off. My aunt lives there."

Bannon was buttoning his coat, and looking at her. He felt the different tone that had got into their talk. It had been impersonal a few minutes before.

"Oh, St. Joe isn't bad," he was saying; "it's quiet and restful and all that, but it's not the same sort of thing at all. You go over there and ride up the river on the May Graham, and it makes you feel lazy and comfortable, but it doesn't stir you up inside like the St. Lawrence does."

She looked up. Her eyes were sparkling as they had sparkled that afternoon on the elevator when she first looked out into the sunset.

"Yes," she replied. "I think I know what you mean. But I never really felt that way; I've only thought about it."

Bannon turned half away, as if to go. "You'll have to go down there, that's all," he said abruptly. He looked back at her over his shoulder, and added, "That's all there is about it."

Her eyes were half startled, half mischievous, for his voice had been still less impersonal than before. Then she turned back to her work, her face sober, but an amused twinkle lingering in her eyes.

"I should like to go," she said, her pencil poised at the top of a long column. "Max would like it, too."

After supper that evening Max returned early from a visit to the injured man, and told Hilda of a new trouble.

"Do you know that little delegate that's been hanging around?" he asked.

"Grady," she said, and nodded.

"Yes, he's been working the man. I never saw such a change in my life. He just sat up there in bed and swore at me, and said I needn't think I could buy him off with this stuff"—he looked down and Hilda saw that the bowl in his hand was not empty—"and raised a row generally."

"Why?" she asked.

"Give it up. From what he said, I'm sure Grady's behind it."

"Did he give his name?"

"No, but he did a lot of talking about justice to the down-trodden and the power of the unions, and that kind of stuff. I couldn't understand all he said—he's got a funny lingo, you know; I guess it's Polack—but I got enough to know what he meant, and more, too."

"Can he do anything?"

"I don't think so. If we get after him, it'll just set him worse'n pig's bristles. A man like that'll lose his head over nothing. He may be all right in the morning."

But Hilda, after Max had given her the whole conversation as nearly as he could remember it, thought differently. She did not speak her mind out to Max, because she was not yet certain what was the best course to take. The man could easily make trouble, she saw that. But if Max were to lay the matter before Bannon, he would be likely to glide over some of the details that she had got only by close questioning. And a blunder in handling it might be fatal to the elevator, so far as getting it done in December was concerned. Perhaps she took it too seriously; for she was beginning, in spite of herself, to give a great deal of thought to the work and to Bannon. At any rate, she lay awake later than usual that night, going over the problem, and she brought it up, the next morning, the first time that Bannon came into the office after Max had gone out.

"Mr. Bannon," she said, when he had finished dictating a letter to the office, "I want to tell you about that man that was hurt."

Bannon tried not to smile at the nervous, almost breathless way in which she opened the conversation. He saw that, whatever it was, it seemed to her very important, and he settled comfortably on the table, leaning back against the wall with his legs stretched out before him. She had turned on her stool.

"You mean the hoist man?" he asked.

She nodded. "Max goes over to see him sometimes. We've been trying to help make him comfortable——"

"Oh," said Bannon; "it's you that's been sending those things around to him."

She looked at him with surprise.

"Why, how did you know?"

"I heard about it."

Hilda hesitated. She did not know exactly how to begin. It occurred to her that perhaps Bannon was smiling at her eager manner.

"Max was there last night and he said the man had changed all around. He's been friendly, you know, and grateful"—she had forgotten herself again, in thinking of her talk with Max—"and he's said all the time that he wasn't going to make trouble——" She paused.

"Yes, I know something about that," said Bannon. "The lawyers always get after a man that's hurt, you know."

"But last night he had changed all around. He said he was going to have you arrested. He thinks Max has been trying to buy him off with the things we've sent him."

Bannon whistled.

"So our Mr. Grady's got his hands on him!"

"That's what Max and I thought, but he didn't give any names. He wouldn't take the jelly."

"I'm glad you told me," said Bannon, swinging his legs around and sitting up. "It's just as well to know about these things. Grady's made him think he can make a good haul by going after me, poor fool—he isn't the man that'll get it."

"Can he really stop the work?" Hilda asked anxiously.

"Not likely. He'll probably try to make out a case of criminal carelessness against me, and get me jerked up. He ought to have more sense, though. I know how many sticks were on that hoist when it broke. I'll drop around there to-night after dinner and have a talk with him. I'd like to find Grady there—but that's too good to expect."

Hilda had stepped down from the stool, and was looking out through the half-cleaned window at a long train of freight cars that was clanking in on the Belt Line.

"That's what I wanted to see you about most," she said slowly. "Max says he's been warned that you'll come around and try to buy him off, and it won't go, because he can make more by standing out."

"Well," said Bannon, easily, amused at her unconscious drop into Max's language, "there's usually a way of getting after these fellows. We'll do anything within reason, but we won't be robbed. I'll throw Mr. Grady into the river first, and hang him up on the hoist to dry."

"But if he really means to stand out," she said, "wouldn't it hurt us for you to go around there?"

"Why?" He was openly smiling now. Then, of a sudden, he looked at her with a shrewd, close gaze, and repeated, "Why?"

"Maybe I don't understand it." she said nervously. "Max doesn't think I see things very clearly. But I thought perhaps you would be willing for me to see him this evening. I could go with Max, and——"

She faltered, when she saw how closely he was watching her, but he nodded, and said, "Go on."

"Why, I don't know that I could do much, but—no"—she tossed her head back and looked at him—"I won't say that. If you'll let me go, I'll fix it. I know I can."

Bannon was thinking partly of her—of her slight, graceful figure that leaned against the window frame, and of her eyes, usually quiet, but now snapping with determination—and partly of certain other jobs that had been imperiled by the efforts of injured workingmen to get heavy damages. One of the things his experience in railroad and engineering work had taught him was that men will take every opportunity to bleed a corporation. No matter how slight the accident, or how temporary in its effects, the stupidest workman has it in his power to make trouble. It was frankly not a matter of sentiment to Bannon. He would do all that he could, would gladly make the man's sickness actually profit him, so far as money would go; but he did not see justice in the great sums which the average jury will grant. As he sat there, he recognized what Hilda had seen at a flash, that this was a case for delicate handling.

She was looking at him, tremendously in earnest, yet all the while wondering at her own boldness. He slowly nodded.

"You're right," he said. "You're the one to do the talking. I won't ask you what you're going to say. I guess you understand it as well as anybody."

"I don't know yet, myself," she answered. "It isn't that, it isn't that there's something particular to say, but he's a poor man, and they've been telling him that the company is cheating him and stealing from him—I wouldn't like it myself, if I were in his place and didn't know any more than he does. And maybe I can show him that we'll be a good deal fairer to him before we get through than Mr. Grady will."

"Yes," said Bannon, "I think you can. And if you can keep this out of the courts I'll write Brown that there's a young lady down here that's come nearer to earning a big salary than I ever did to deserving a silk hat."

"Oh," she said, the earnest expression skipping abruptly out of her eyes; "did your hat come?"

"Not a sign of it. I'd clean forgotten. I'll give Brown one more warning—a long 'collect' telegram, about forty words—and then if he doesn't toe up, I'll get one and send him the bill.

"There was a man that looked some like Grady worked for me on the Galveston house. He was a carpenter, and thought he stood for the whole Federation of Labor. He got gay one day. I warned him once, and then I threw him off the distributing floor."

Hilda thought he was joking until she looked up and saw his face.

"Didn't it—didn't it kill him?" she asked.

"I don't remember exactly. I think there were some shavings there." He stood looking at her for a moment. "Do you know," he said, "if Grady comes up on the job again, I believe I'll tell him that story? I wonder if he'd know what I meant."

The spouting house, or "river house," was a long, narrow structure, one hundred feet by thirty-six, built on piles at the edge of the wharf. It would form, with the connecting belt gallery that was to reach out over the tracks, a T-shaped addition to the elevator. The river house was no higher than was necessary for the spouts that would drop the grain through the hatchways of the big lake steamers, twenty thousand bushels an hour—it reached between sixty and seventy feet above the water. The marine tower that was to be built, twenty-four feet square, up through the centre of the house, would be more than twice as high. A careful examination convinced Bannon that the pile foundations would prove strong enough to support this heavier structure, and that the only changes necessary would be in the frame of the spouting house. On the same day that the plans arrived, work on the tower commenced.

Peterson had about got to the point where startling developments no longer alarmed him. He had seen the telegram the day before, but his first information that a marine tower was actually under way came when Bannon called off a group of laborers late in the afternoon to rig the "trolley" for carrying timber across the track.

"What are you going to do, Charlie?" he called. "Got to slide them timbers back again?"

"Some of 'em," Bannon replied.

"Don't you think we could carry 'em over?" said Peterson. "If we was quiet about it, they needn't be any trouble?"

Bannon shook his head.

"We're not taking any more chances on this railroad. We haven't time."

Once more the heavy timbers went swinging through the air, high over the tracks, but this time back to the wharf. Before long the section boss of the C. & S. C. appeared, and though he soon went away, one of his men remained, lounging about the tracks, keeping a close eye on the sagging ropes and the timbers. Bannon, when he met Peterson a few minutes later, pointed out the man.

"What'd I tell you, Pete? They're watching us like cats. If you want to know what the C. & S. C. think about us, you just drop one timber and you'll find out."

But nothing dropped, and when Peterson, who had been on hand all the latter part of the afternoon, took hold, at seven o'clock, the first timbers of the tower had been set in place, somewhere down inside the rough shed of a spouting house, and more would go in during the night, and during other days and nights, until the narrow framework should go reaching high into the air. Another thing was recognized by the men at work on that night shift, even by the laborers who carried timbers, and grunted and swore in strange tongues; this was that the night shift men had suddenly begun to feel a most restless energy crowding them on, and they worked nearly as well as Bannon's day shifts. For Peterson's spirits had risen with a leap, once the misunderstanding that had been weighing on him had been removed, and now he was working as he had never worked before. The directions he gave showed that his head was clearer; and there was confidence in his manner.

Hilda was so serious all day after her talk with Bannon that once, in the afternoon, when he came into the office for a glance at the new pile of blue prints, he smiled, and asked if she were laying out a campaign. It was the first work of the kind that she had ever undertaken, and she was a little worried over the need for tact and delicacy. After she had closed her desk at supper time, she saw Bannon come into the circle of the electric light in front of the office, and, asking Max to wait, she went to meet him.

"Well," he said, "are you loaded up to fight the 'power of the union'?"

She smiled, and then said, with a trace of nervousness:—

"I don't believe I'm quite so sure about it as I was this morning."

"It won't bother you much. When you've made him see that we're square and Grady isn't, you've done the whole business. We won't pay fancy damages, that's all."

"Yes," she said, "I think I know. What I wanted to see you about was— was—Max and I are going over right after supper, and———"

She stopped abruptly; and Bannon, looking down at her, saw a look of embarrassment come into her face; and then she blushed, and lowering her eyes, fumbled with her glove. Bannon was a little puzzled. His eyes rested on her for a moment, and then, without understanding why, he suddenly knew that she had meant to ask him to see her after the visit, and that the new personal something in their acquaintance had flashed a warning. He spoke quickly, as if he were the first to think of it.

"If you don't mind, I'll come around to-night and hear the report of the committee of adjusters. That's you, you know. Something might come up that I ought to know right away."

"Yes," she replied rapidly, without looking up, "perhaps that would be the best thing to do."

He walked along with her toward the office, where Max was waiting, but she did not say anything, and he turned in with: "I won't say good-night, then. Good luck to you."

It was soon after eight that Bannon went to the boarding-house where Hilda and Max lived, and sat down to wait in the parlor. When a quarter of an hour had gone, and they had not returned, he buttoned up his coat and went out, walking slowly along the uneven sidewalk toward the river. The night was clear, and he could see, across the flats and over the tracks, where tiny signal lanterns were waving and circling, and freight trains were bumping and rumbling, the glow of the arc lamps on the elevator, and its square outline against the sky. Now and then, when the noise of the switching trains let down, he could hear the hoisting engines. Once he stopped and looked eastward at the clouds of illuminated smoke above the factories and at the red blast of the rolling mill. He went nearly to the river and had to turn back and walk slowly. Finally he heard Max's laugh, and then he saw them coming down a side street.

"Well," he said, "you don't sound like bad news."

"I don't believe we are very bad," replied Hilda.

"Should say not," put in Max. "It's finer'n silk."

Hilda said, "Max," in a low voice, but he went on:—

"The best thing, Mr. Bannon, was when I told him it was Hilda that had been sending things around. He thought it was you, you see, and Grady'd told him it was all a part of the game to bamboozle him out of the money that was rightfully his. It's funny to hear him sling that Grady talk around. I don't think he more'n half knows what it means. I'd promised not to tell, you know, but I just saw there wasn't no use trying to make him understand things without talking pretty plain. There ain't a thing he wouldn't do for Hilda now———"

"Max," said Hilda again, "please don't."

When they reached the house, Max at once started in. Hilda hesitated, and then said:—

"I'll come in a minute, Max."

"Oh," he replied, "all right" But he waited a moment longer, evidently puzzled.

"Well," said Bannon, "was it so hard?"

"No—not hard exactly. I didn't know he was so poor. Somehow you don't think about it that way when you see them working. I don't know that I ever thought about it at all before."

"You think he won't give us any trouble?"

"I'm sure he won't. I—I had to promise I'd go again pretty soon."

"Maybe you'll let me go along."

"Why—why, yes, of course."

She had been hesitating, looking down and picking at the splinters on the gate post. Neither was Bannon quick to speak. He did not want to question her about the visit, for he saw that it was hard for her to talk about it. Finally she straightened up and looked at him.

"I want to tell you," she said, "I haven't understood exactly until to-night—what they said about the accident and the way you've talked about it—well, some people think you don't think very much about the men, and that if anybody's hurt, or anything happens, you don't care as long as the work goes on." She was looking straight at him. "I thought so, too. And to-night I found out some things you've been doing for him—how you've been giving him tobacco, and the things he likes best that I'd never have thought of, and I knew it was you that did it, and not the Company—and I—I beg your pardon."

Bannon did not know what to reply. They stood for a moment without speaking, and then she smiled, and said "Good night," and ran up the steps without looking around.

CHAPTER 13

It was the night of the tenth of December. Three of the four stories of the cupola were building, and the upright posts were reaching toward the fourth. It still appeared to be a confused network of timbers, with only the beginnings of walls, but as the cupola walls are nothing but a shell of light boards to withstand the wind, the work was further along than might have been supposed. Down on the working story the machinery was nearly all in, and up here in the cupola the scales and garners were going into place as rapidly as the completing of the supporting framework permitted. The cupola floors were not all laid. If you had stood on the distributing floor, over the tops of the bins, you might have looked not only down through a score of openings between plank areas and piles of timbers, into black pits, sixteen feet square by seventy deep, but upward through a grill of girders and joists to the clear sky. Everywhere men swarmed over the work, and the buzz of the electric lights and the sounds of hundreds of hammers blended into a confused hum.

If you had walked to the east end of the building, here and there balancing along a plank or dodging through gangs of laborers and around moving timbers, you would have seen stretching from off a point not halfway through to the ground, the annex bins, rising so steadily that it was a matter only of a few weeks before they would be ready to receive grain. Now another walk, this time across the building to the north side, would show you the river house, out there on the wharf, and the marine tower rising up through the middle with a single arc lamp on the topmost girder throwing a mottled, checkered shadow on the wharf and the water below.

At a little after eight o'clock, Peterson, who had been looking at the stairway, now nearly completed, came out on the distributing floor. He was in good spirits, for everything was going well, and Bannon had frankly credited him, of late, with the improvement in the work of the night shifts. He stood looking up through the upper floors of the cupola, and he did not see Max until the timekeeper stood beside him.

"Hello, Max," he said. "We'll have the roof on here in another ten days."

Max followed Peterson's glance upward.

"I guess that's right. It begins to look as if things was coming 'round all right. I just come up from the office. Mr. Bannon's there. He'll be up before long, he says. I was a-wondering if maybe I hadn't ought to go back and tell him about Grady. He's around, you know."

"Who? Grady?"

"Yes. Him and another fellow was standing down by one of the cribbin' piles. I was around there on the way up."

"What was they doing?"

"Nothing. Just looking on."

Peterson turned to shout at some laborers, then he pushed back his hat and scratched his head.

"I don't know but what you'd ought to 'a' told Charlie right off. That man Grady don't mean us no good."

"I know it, but I wasn't just sure."

"Well, I'll tell you——"

Before Peterson could finish, Max broke in:—

"That's him."

"Where?"

"That fellow over there, walking along slow. He's the one that was with Grady."

"I'd like to know what he thinks he's doing here." Peterson started forward, adding, "I guess I know what to say to him."

"Hold on, Pete," said Max, catching his arm. "Maybe we'd better speak to Mr. Bannon. I'll go down and tell him, and you keep an eye on this fellow."

Peterson reluctantly assented, and Max walked slowly away, now and then pausing to look around at the men. But when he had nearly reached the stairway, where he could slip behind the scaffolding about the only scale hopper that had reached a man's height above the floor, he moved more rapidly. He met Bannon on the stairway, and told him what he had seen. Bannon leaned against the wall of the stairway bin, and looked thoughtful.

"So he's come, has he?" was his only comment. "You might speak to Pete, Max, and bring him here. I'll wait."

Max and Peterson found him looking over the work of the carpenters.

"I may not be around much to-night," he said, with a wink, "but I'd like to see both of you to-morrow afternoon some time. Can you get around about four o'clock, Pete?"

"Sure," the night boss replied.

"We've got some thinking to do about the work, if we're going to put it through. I'll look for you at four o'clock then, in the office." He started down the stairs. "I'm going home now."

"Why," said Peterson, "you only just come."

Bannon paused and looked back over his shoulder. The light came from directly overhead, and the upper part of his face was in the shadow of his hat brim, but Max, looking closely at him, thought that he winked again.

"I wanted to tell you," the foreman went on; "Grady's come around, you know—and another fellow——"

"Yes, Max told me. I guess they won't hurt you. Good night."

As he went on down he passed a group of laborers who were bringing stairway material to the carpenters.

"I don't know but what you was talking pretty loud," said Max to Peterson, in a low voice. "Here's some of 'em now."

"They didn't hear nothing," Peterson replied, and the two went back to the distributing floor. They stood in a shadow, by the scale hopper, waiting for the reappearance of Grady's companion. He had evidently gone on to the upper floors, where he could not be distinguished from the many other moving figures; but in a few minutes he came back, walking deliberately toward the stairs. He looked at Peterson and Max, but passed by without a second glance, and descended. Peterson stood looking after him.

"Now, I'd like to know what Charlie meant by going home," he said.

Max had been thinking hard. Finally he said:—

"Say, Pete, we're blind."

"Why?"

"Did you think he was going home?"

Peterson looked at him, but did not reply.

"Because he ain't."

"Well, you heard what he said."

"What does that go for? He was winking when he said it. He wasn't going to stand there and tell the laborers all about it, like we was trying to do. I'll bet he ain't very far off."

"I ain't got a word to say," said Peterson. "If he wants to leave Grady to me, I guess I can take care of him."

Max had come to the elevator for a short visit—he liked to watch the work at night—but now he settled down to stay, keeping about the hopper where he could see Grady if his head should appear at the top of the stairs. Something told him that Bannon saw deeper into Grady's man[oe]uvres than either Peterson or himself, and while he could not understand, yet he was beginning to think that Grady would appear before long, and that Bannon knew it.

Sure enough, only a few minutes had gone when Max turned back from a glance at the marine tower and saw the little delegate standing on the top step, looking about the distributing floor and up through the girders overhead, with quick, keen eyes. Then Max understood what it all meant: Grady had chosen a time when Bannon was least likely to be on the job; and had sent the other man ahead to reconnoitre. It meant mischief—Max could see that; and he felt a boy's nervousness at the prospect of excitement. He stepped farther back into the shadow.

Grady was looking about for Peterson; when he saw his burly figure outlined against a light at the farther end of the building, he walked directly toward him, not pausing this time to talk to the laborers or to look at them. Max, moving off a little to one side, followed, and reached Peterson's side just as Grady, his hat pushed back on his head and his feet apart, was beginning to talk.

"I had a little conversation with you the other day, Mr. Peterson. I called to see you in the interests of the men, the men that are working for you—working like galley slaves they are, every man of them. It's shameful to a man that's seen how they've been treated by the nigger drivers that stands over them day and night." He was speaking in a loud voice, with the fluency of a man who is carefully prepared. There was none of the bitterness or the ugliness in his manner that had slipped out in his last talk with Bannon, for he knew that a score of laborers were within hearing, and that his words would travel, as if by wire, from mouth to mouth about the building and the grounds below. "I stand here, Mr. Peterson, the man chosen by these slaves of yours, to look after their rights. I do not ask you to treat them with kindness, I do not ask that you treat them as gentlemen. What do I ask? I demand what's accorded to them by the Constitution of the United States and the Declaration of Independence, that says even a nigger has more rights than you've given to these men, the men that are putting money into your pocket, and Mr. Bannon's pocket, and the corporation's pocket, by the sweat of their brows. Look at them; will you look at them?" He waved his arm toward the nearest group, who had stopped working and were listening; and then, placing a cigar in his mouth and tilting it upward, he struck a match and sheltered it in his hands, looking over it for a moment at Peterson.

The night boss saw by this time that Grady meant business, that his speech was preliminary to something more emphatic, and he knew that he ought to stop it before the laborers should be demoralized.

"You can't do that here, Mister," said Max, over Peterson's shoulder, indicating the cigar.

Grady still held the match, and looked impudently across the tip of his cigar. Peterson took it up at once.

"You'll have to drop that," he said. "There's no smoking on this job."

The match had gone out, and Grady lighted another.

"So that's one of your rules, too?" he said, in the same loud voice. "It's a wonder you let a man eat."

Peterson was growing angry. His voice rose as he talked.

"I ain't got time to talk to you," he said. "The insurance company says there can't be no smoking here. If you want to know why, you'd better ask them."

Grady blew out the match and returned the cigar to his pocket, with an air of satisfaction that Peterson could not make out.

"That's all right, Mr. Peterson. I didn't come here to make trouble. I come here as a representative of these men"—he waved again toward the laborers—"and I say right here, that if you'd treated them right in the first place, I wouldn't be here at all. I've wanted you to have a fair show. I've put up with your mean tricks and threats and insults ever since you begun—and why? Because I wouldn't delay you and hurt the work. It's the industries of to-day, the elevators and railroads, and the work of strong men like these that's the bulwark of America's greatness. But what do I get in return, Mister Peterson? I come up here as a gentleman and talk to you. I treat you as a gentleman. I overlook what you've showed yourself to be. And how do you return it? By talking like the blackguard you are—you knock an innocent cigar——" "Your time's up!" said Pete, drawing a step nearer. "Come to business, or clear out. That's all I've got to say to you."

"All right, Mister Peterson—_all right. I'll put up with your insults. I can afford to forget myself when I look about me at the heavier burdens these men have to bear, day and night. Look at that—look at it, and then try to talk to me."

He pointed back toward the stairs where a gang of eight laborers were carrying a heavy timber across the shadowy floor.

"Well, what about it?" said Pete, with half-controlled rage.

"What about it! But never mind. I'm a busy man myself. I've got no more time to waste on the likes of you. Take a good look at that, and then listen to me. That's the last stick of timber that goes across this floor until you put a runway from the hoist to the end of the building. And every stick that leaves the runway has got to go on a dolly. Mark my words now—I'm talking plain. My men don't lift another pound of timber on this house—everything goes on rollers. I've tried to be a patient man, but you've run against the limit. You've broke the last back you'll have a chance at." He put his hand to his mouth as if to shout at the gang, but dropped it and faced around. "No, I won't stop them. I'll be fair to the last." He pulled out his watch. "I'll give you one hour from now. At ten o'clock, if your runway and the dollies ain't working, the men go out. And the next time I see you, I won't be so easy."

He turned away, waved to the laborers, with an, "All right, boys; go ahead," and walked grandly toward the stairway.

Max whistled.

"I'd like to know where Charlie is," said Peterson.

"He ain't far. I'll find him;" and Max hurried away.

Bannon was sitting in the office chair with his feet on the draughting-table, figuring on the back of a blotter. The light from the wall lamp was indistinct, and Bannon had to bend his head forward to see the figures. He did not look up when the door opened and Max came to the railing gate.

"Grady's been up on the distributing floor," said Max, breathlessly, for he had been running.

"What did he want?"

"He's going to call the men off at ten o'clock if we don't put in a runway and dollies on the distributing floor."

Bannon looked at his watch.

"Is that all he wants?" Max, in his excitement, did not catch the sarcasm in the question.

"That's all he said, but it's enough. We can't do it"

Bannon closed his watch with a snap.

"No," he said, "and we won't throw away any good time trying. You'd better round up the committee that's supposed to run this lodge and send them here. That young Murphy's one of them—he can put you straight. Bring Pete back with you, and the new man, James."

Max lingered, with a look of awe and admiration.

"Are you going to stand out, Mr. Bannon?" he asked.

Bannon dropped his feet to the floor, and turned toward the table.

"Yes," he said. "We're going to stand out."

Since Bannon's talk with President Carver a little drama had been going on in the local lodge, a drama that neither Bannon, Max, nor Peterson knew about. James had been selected by Carver for this work because of proved ability and shrewdness. He had no sooner attached himself to the lodge, and made himself known as an active member, than his personality, without any noticeable effort on his part, began to make itself felt. Up to this time Grady had had full swing, for there had been no one among the laborers with force enough to oppose him.

The first collision took place at an early meeting after Grady's last talk with Bannon. The delegate, in the course of the meeting, bitterly attacked Bannon, accusing him, at the climax of his oration, of an attempt to buy off the honest representative of the working classes for five thousand dollars. This had a tremendous effect on the excitable minds before him. He finished his speech with an impassioned tirade against the corrupt influences of the money power, and was mopping his flushed face, listening with elation to the hum of anger that resulted, confident that he had made his point, when James arose. The new man was as familiar with the tone of the meetings of laborers as Grady himself. At the beginning he had no wish further than to get at the truth. Grady had not stated his case well. It had convinced the laborers, but to James it had weak points. He asked Grady a few pointed questions, that, had the delegate felt the truth behind him, should not have been hard to answer. But Grady was still under the spell of his own oratory, and in attempting to get his feet back on the ground, he bungled. James did not carry the discussion beyond the point where Grady, in the bewilderment of recognizing this new element in the lodge, lost his temper, but when he sat down, the sentiment of the meeting had changed. Few of those men could have explained their feelings; it was simply that the new man was stronger than they were, perhaps as strong as Grady, and they were influenced accordingly.

There was no decision for a strike at that meeting. Grady, cunning at the business, immediately dropped open discussion, and, smarting under the sense of lost prestige, set about regaining his position by well-planned talk with individual laborers. This went on, largely without James' knowledge, until Grady felt sure that a majority of the men were back in his control. This time he was determined to carry through the strike without the preliminary vote of the men. It was a bold stroke, but boldness was needed to defeat Charlie Bannon; and nobody knew better than Grady that a dashing show of authority would be hard for James or any one else to resist.

And so he had come on the job this evening, at a time when he supposed Bannon safe in bed, and delivered his ultimatum. Not that he had any hope of carrying the strike through without some sort of a collision with the boss, but he well knew that an encounter after the strike had gathered momentum would be easier than one before. Bannon might be able to outwit an individual, even Grady himself, but he would find it hard to make headway against an angry mob. And now Grady was pacing stiffly about the Belt Line yards, while the minute hand of his watch crept around toward ten o'clock. Even if Bannon should be called within the hour, a few fiery words to those sweating gangs on the distributing floor should carry the day. But Grady did not think that this would be necessary.

He was still in the mistake of supposing that Peterson and the boss were at outs, and he had arrived, by a sort of reasoning that seemed the keenest strategy, at the conclusion that Peterson would take the opportunity to settle the matter himself. In fact, Grady had evolved a neat little campaign, and he was proud of himself.

Bannon did not have to wait long. Soon there was a sound of feet outside the door, and after a little hesitation, six laborers entered, five of them awkwardly and timidly, wondering what was to come. Peterson followed, with Max, and closed the door. The members of the committee stood in a straggling row at the railing, looking at each other and at the floor and ceiling—anywhere but at the boss, who was sitting on the table, sternly taking them in. James stepped to one side.

"Is this all the committee?" Bannon presently said.

The men hesitated, and Murphy, who was in the centre, answered, "Yes, sir."

"You are the governing members of your lodge?"

There was an air of cool authority about Bannon that disturbed the men. They had been led to believe that his power reached only the work on the elevator, and that an attempt on his part to interfere in any way with their organization would be an act of high-handed tyranny, "to be resisted to the death" (Grady's words). But these men standing before their boss, in his own office, were not the same men that thrilled with righteous wrath under Grady's eloquence in the meetings over Barry's saloon. So they looked at the floor and ceiling again, until Murphy at last answered:—

"Yes, sir."

Bannon waited again, knowing that every added moment of silence gave him the firmer control.

"I have nothing to say about the government of your organization," he said, speaking slowly and coldly. "I have brought you here to ask you this question, Have you voted to strike?"

The silence was deep. Peterson, leaning against the closed door, held his breath; Max, sitting on the railing with his elbow thrown over the desk, leaned slightly forward. The eyes of the laborers wandered restlessly about the room. They were disturbed, taken off their guard; they needed Grady. But the thought of Grady was followed by the consciousness of the silent figure of the new man, James, standing behind them. Murphy's first impulse was to lie. Perhaps, if James had not been there, he would have lied. As it was, he glanced up two or three times, and his lips as many times framed themselves about words that did not come. Finally he said, mumbling the words:—

"No, we ain't voted for no strike."

"There has been no such decision made by your organization?"

"No, I guess not."

Bannon turned to Peterson.

"Mr. Peterson, will you please find Mr. Grady and bring him here."

Max and Peterson hurried out together. Bannon drew up the chair, and turned his back on the committee, going on with his figuring. Not a word was said; the men hardly moved; and the minutes went slowly by. Then there was a stir outside, and the sound of low voices. The door flew open, admitting Grady, who stalked to the railing, choking with anger. Max, who immediately followed, was grinning, his eyes resting on a round spot of dust on Grady's shoulder, and on his torn collar and disarranged tie. Peterson came in last, and carefully closed the door—his eyes were blazing, and one sleeve was rolled up over his bare forearm. Neither of them spoke. If anything in the nature of an assault had seemed necessary in dragging the delegate to the office, there had been no witnesses. And he had entered the room of his own accord.

Grady was at a disadvantage, and he knew it. Breathing hard, his face red, his little eyes darting about the room, he took it all in—the members of the committee; the boss, figuring at the table, with an air of exasperating coolness about his lean back; and last of all, James, standing in the shadow. It was the sight of the new man that checked the storm of words that was pressing on Grady's tongue. But he finally gathered himself and stepped forward, pushing aside one of the committee.

Then Bannon turned. He faced about in his chair and began to talk straight at the committee, ignoring the delegate. Grady began to talk at the same time, but though his voice was the louder, no one seemed to hear him. The men were looking at Bannon. Grady hesitated, started again, and then, bound by his own rage and his sense of defeat, let his words die away, and stood casting about for an opening.

"This man Grady threatened a good while ago that I would have a strike on my hands. He finally came to me and offered to protect me if I would pay him five thousand dollars."

"That's a lie!" shouted the delegate. "He come to me——"

Bannon had hardly paused. He drew a typewritten copy of Grady's letter from his pocket, and read it aloud, then handed it over to Murphy. "That's the way he came at me. I want you to read it."

The man took it awkwardly, glanced at it, and passed it on.

"To-night he's ordered a strike. He calls himself your representative, but he has acted on his own responsibility. Now, I am going to talk plain to you. I came here to build this elevator, and I'm going to do it. I propose to treat you men fair and square. If you think you ain't treated right, you send an honest man to this office, and I'll talk with him. But I'm through with Grady. I won't have him here at all. If you send him around again, I'll throw him off the job."

The men were a little startled. They looked at one another, and the man on Murphy's left whispered something. Bannon sat still, watching them.

Then Grady came to himself. He wheeled around to face the committee, and threw out one arm in a wide gesture.

"I demand to know what this means! I demand to know if there is a law in this land! Is an honest man, the representative of the hand of labor, to be attacked by hired ruffians? Is he to be slandered by the tyrant who drives you at the point of the pistol? And you not men enough to defend your rights—the rights held by every American—the rights granted by the Constitution! But it ain't for myself I would talk. It ain't my own injuries that I suffer for. Your liberty hangs in the balance. This man has dared to interfere in the integrity of your lodge. Have you no words——"

Bannon arose, caught Grady's arm, and whirled him around.

"Grady," he said, "shut up."

The delegate tried to jerk away, but he could not shake off that grip. He looked toward the committeemen, but they were silent. He looked everywhere but up into the eyes that were blazing down at him. And finally Bannon felt the muscles within his grip relax.

"I'll tell you what I want you to do," said Bannon to the committeemen. "I want you to elect a new delegate. Don't talk about interference—I don't care how you elect him, or who he is, if he comes to me squarely."

Grady was wriggling again.

"This means a strike!" he shouted. "This means the biggest strike the West has ever seen! You won't get men for love or money——"

Bannon gave the arm a wrench, and broke in:—

"I'm sick of this. I laid this matter before President Carver. I have his word that if you hang on to this man after he's been proved a blackmailer, your lodge can be dropped from the Federation. If you try to strike, you won't hurt anybody but yourselves. That's all. You can go."

"Wait——" Grady began, but they filed out without looking at him. James, as he followed them, nodded, and said, "Good night, Mr. Bannon."

Then for the last time Bannon led Grady away. Peterson started forward, but the boss shook his head, and went out, marching the delegate between the lumber piles to the point where the path crossed the Belt Line tracks.

"Now, Mr. Grady," he said, "this is where our ground stops. The other sides are the road there, and the river, and the last piles of cribbing at the other end. I'm telling you so you will know where you don't belong. Now, get out!"

CHAPTER 14

The effect of the victory was felt everywhere. Not only were Max and Pete and Hilda jubilant over it, but the under-foremen, the timekeepers, even the laborers attacked their work with a fresher energy. It was like the first whiff of salt air to an army marching to the sea. Since the day when the cribbing came down from Ledyard, the work had gone forward with almost incredible rapidity; there had been no faltering during the weeks when Grady's threatened catastrophe was imminent, but now that the big shadow of the little delegate was dispelled, it was easier to see that the huge warehouse was almost finished. There was still much to do, and the handful of days that remained seemed absurdly inadequate; but it needed only a glance at what Charlie Bannon's tireless, driving energy had already accomplished to make the rest look easy. "We're sure of it now. She'll be full to the roof before the year is out." As Max went over the job with his time-book next morning, he said it to every man he met, and they all believed him. Peterson, the same man and not the same man either, who had once vowed that there wouldn't be any night work on Calumet K, who had bent a pair of most unwilling shoulders to the work Bannon had put upon them, who had once spent long, sulky afternoons in the barren little room of his new boarding-house; Peterson held himself down in bed exactly three hours the morning after that famous victory. Before eleven o'clock he was sledging down a tottering timber at the summit of the marine tower, a hundred and forty feet sheer above the wharf. Just before noon he came into the office and found Hilda there alone.

He had stopped outside the door to put on his coat, but had not buttoned it; his shirt, wet as though he had been in the lake, clung to him and revealed the outline of every muscle in his great trunk. He flung his hat on the draughting-table, and his yellow hair seemed crisper and curlier than ever before.

"Well, it looks as though we was all right," he said.

Hilda nodded emphatically. "You think we'll get through in time, don't you, Mr. Peterson?"

"Think!" he exclaimed. "I don't have to stop to think. Here comes Max; just ask him."

Max slammed the door behind him, brought down the timekeeper's book on Hilda's desk with a slap that made her jump, and vaulted to a seat on the railing. "Well, I guess it's a case of hurrah for us, ain't it, Pete?"

"Your sister asked me if I thought we'd get done on time. I was just saying it's a sure thing."

"I don't know," said Max, laughing. "I guess an earthquake could stop us. But why ain't you abed, Pete?"

"What do I want to be abed for? I ain't going to sleep any more this year—unless we get through a day or two ahead of time. I don't like to miss any of it. Charlie Bannon may have hustled before, but I guess this breaks his record. Where is he now, Max?"

"Down in the cellar putting in the running gear for the 'cross-the-house conveyors. He has his nerve with him. He's putting in three drives entirely different from the way they are in the plans. He told me just now that there wasn't a man in the office who could design a drive that wouldn't tie itself up in square knots in the first ten minutes. I wonder what old MacBride'll say when he sees that he's changed the plans."

"If MacBride has good sense, he'll pass anything that Charlie puts up," said Pete.

He was going to say more, but just then Bannon strode into the office and over to the draughting table. He tossed Pete's hat to one side and began studying a detail of the machinery plans.

"Max." He spoke without looking up. "I wish you'd find a water boy and send him up to the hotel to get a couple of sandwiches and a bottle of coffee."

"Well, that's a nice way to celebrate, I must say," Pete commented.

"Celebrate what?"

"Why, last night; throwing Grady down. You ought to take a day off on the strength of that."

"What's Grady got to do with it? He ain't in the specifications."

"No," said Pete, slowly; "but where would we have been if he'd got the men off?"

"Where would we have been if the house had burned up?" Bannon retorted, turning away from the table. "That's got nothing to do with it. I haven't felt less like taking a day off since I came on the job. We may get through on time and we may not. If we get tangled up in the plans like this, very often, I don't know how we'll come out. But the surest way to get left is to begin now telling ourselves that this is easy and it's a cinch. That kind of talk makes me tired."

Pete flushed, started an explanatory sentence, and another, and then, very uncomfortable, went out.

Bannon did not look up; he went on studying the blue print, measuring here and there with his three-sided ruler and jotting down incomprehensible operations in arithmetic on a scrap of paper. Max was figuring tables in his time-book, Hilda poring over the cash account. For half an hour no one spoke. Max crammed his cap down over his ears and went out, and there were ten minutes more of silence. Then Bannon began talking. He still busied his fingers with the blue print, and Hilda, after discovering that he was talking to himself rather than to her, went on with her work. But nevertheless she heard, in a fragmentary way, what he was saying.

"Take a day off—schoolboy trick—enough to make a man tired. Might as well do it, though. We ain't going to get through. The office ought to do a little work once in a while just to see what it's like. They think a man can do anything. I'd like to know why I ain't entitled to a night's sleep as well as MacBride. But he don't think so. After he'd worked me twenty-four hours a day up to Duluth, and I lost thirty-two pounds up there, he sends me down to a mess like this. With a lot of drawings that look as though they were made by a college boy. Where does he expect 'em to pile their car doors, I'd like to know."

That was the vein of it, though the monologue ran on much longer. But at last he swung impatiently around and addressed Hilda. "I'm ready to throw up my hands. I think I'll go back to Minneapolis and tell MacBride I've had enough. He can come down here and finish the house himself."

"Do you think he would get it done in time?" Hilda's eyes were laughing at him, but she kept them on her work.

"Oh, yes," he said wearily. "He'd get the grain into her somehow. You couldn't stump MacBride with anything. That's why he makes it so warm for us."

"Do you think," she asked very demurely, indeed, "that if Mr. MacBride had been here he could have built it any faster than—than we have, so far?"

"I don't believe it," said Bannon, unwarily. Her smile told him that he had been trapped. "I see," he added. "You mean that there ain't any reason why we can't do it."

He arose and tramped uneasily about the little shanty. "Oh, of course, we'll get it done—just because we have to. There ain't anything else we can do. But just the same I'm sick of the business. I want to quit."

She said nothing, and after a moment he wheeled and, facing her, demanded abruptly: "What's the matter with me, anyway?" She looked at him frankly, a smile, almost mischievous, in her face. The hard, harassed look between his eyes and about his drawn mouth melted away, and he repeated the question: "What's the matter with me? You're the doctor. I'll take whatever medicine you say."

"You didn't take Mr. Peterson's suggestion very well—about taking a holiday, I mean. I don't know whether I dare prescribe for you or not. I don't think you need a day off. I think that, next to a good, long vacation, the best thing for you is excitement." He laughed. "No, I mean it. You're tired out, of course, but if you have enough to occupy your mind, you don't know it. The trouble to-day is that everything is going too smoothly. You weren't a bit afraid yesterday that the elevator wouldn't be done on time. That was because you thought there was going to be a strike. And if just now the elevator should catch on fire or anything, you'd feel all right about it again."

He still half suspected that she was making game of him, and he looked at her steadily while he turned her words over in his mind. "Well," he said, with a short laugh, "if the only medicine I need is excitement, I'll be the healthiest man you ever saw in a little while. I guess I'll find Pete. I must have made him feel pretty sore."

"Pete," he said, coming upon him in the marine tower a little later, "I've got over my stomach-ache. Is it all right?"

"Sure," said Pete; "I didn't know you was feeling bad. I was thinking about that belt gallery, Charlie. Ain't it time we was putting it up? I'm getting sort of nervous about it."

"There ain't three days' work in it, the way we're going," said Bannon, thoughtfully, his eyes on the C. & S. C. right-of-way that lay between him and the main house, "but I guess you're right. We'll get at it now. There's no telling what sort of a surprise party those railroad fellows may have for us. The plans call for three trestles between the tracks. We'll get those up to-day."

To Pete, building the gallery was a more serious business. He had not Bannon's years of experience at bridge repairing; it had happened that he had never been called upon to put up a belt gallery before, and this idea of building a wooden box one hundred and fifty feet long and holding it up, thirty feet in air, on three trestles, was formidable. Bannon's nonchalant air of setting about it seemed almost an affectation.

Each trestle was to consist of a rank of four posts, planted in a line at right angles to the direction of the gallery; they were to be held together at the top by a corbel. No one gave rush orders any more on Calumet K, for the reason that no one ever thought of doing anything else. If Bannon sent for a man, he came on the run. So in an incredibly short time the fences were down and a swarm of men with spades, post augers, picks, and shovels had invaded the C. & S. C. right-of-way. Up and down the track a hundred yards each way from the line of the gallery Bannon had stationed men to give warning of the approach of trains. "Now," said Bannon, "we'll get this part of the job done before any one has time to kick. And they won't be very likely to try to pull 'em up by the roots once we get 'em planted."

But the section boss had received instructions that caused him to be wide-awake, day or night, to what was going on in the neighborhood of Calumet K. Half an hour after the work was begun, the picket line up the track signalled that something was coming. There was no sound of bell or whistle, but presently Bannon saw a hand car spinning down the track as fast as six big, sweating men could pump the levers. The section boss had little to say; simply that they were to get out of there and put up that fence again, and the quicker the better. Bannon tried to tell him that the railroad had consented to their putting in the gallery, that they were well within their rights, that he, the section boss, had better be careful not to exceed his instructions. But the section boss had spoken his whole mind already. He was not of the sort that talk just for the pleasure of hearing their own voices, and he had categorical instructions that made parley unnecessary. He would not even tell from whom he had the orders. So the posts were lugged out of the way and the fence was put up and the men scattered out to their former work again, grinning a little over Bannon's discomfiture.

Bannon's next move was to write to Minneapolis for information and instructions, but MacBride, who seemed to have all the information there was, happened to be in Duluth, and Brown's instructions were consequently foggy. So, after waiting a few days for something more definite, Bannon disappeared one afternoon and was gone more than an hour. When he strode into the office again, keen and springy as though his work had just begun, Hilda looked up and smiled a little. Pete was tilted back in the chair staring glumly out of the window. He did not turn until Bannon slapped him jovially on the shoulders and told him to cheer up.

"Those railroad chaps are laying for us, sure enough," he said. "I've been talking to MacBride himself—over at the telephone exchange; he ain't in town—and he said that Porter—he's the vice-president of the C. & S. C.—Porter told him, when he was in Chicago, that they wouldn't object at all to our building the gallery over their tracks. But that's all we've got to go by. Not a word on paper. Oh, they mean to give us a picnic, and no mistake!"

With that, Bannon called up the general offices of the C. & S. C. and asked for Mr. Porter. There was some little delay in getting the connection, and then three or four minutes of fencing while a young man at the other end of the line tried to satisfy himself that Bannon had the right to ask for Mr. Porter, let alone to talk with him, and Bannon, steadily ignoring his questions, continued blandly requesting him to call Mr. Porter to the telephone. Hilda was listening with interest, for Bannon's manner was different from anything she had ever seen in him before. It lacked nothing of his customary assurance, but its breeziness gave place to the most studied restraint; he might have been a railroad president himself. He hung up the receiver, however, without accomplishing anything, for the young man finally told him that Mr. Porter had gone out for the afternoon.

So next morning Bannon tried again. He learned that Porter was in, and all seemed to be going well until he mentioned MacBride & Company, after which Mr. Porter became very elusive. Three or four attempts to pin him down, or at least to learn his whereabouts, proved unsuccessful, and at last Bannon, with wrath in his heart, started down town.

It was nearly night before he came back, and as before, he found Pete sitting gloomily in the office waiting his return. "Well," exclaimed the night boss, looking at him eagerly; "I thought you was never coming back. We've most had a fit here, wondering how you'd come out. I don't have to ask you, though. I can see by your looks that we're all right."

Bannon laughed, and glanced over at Hilda, who was watching him closely. "Is that your guess, too, Miss Vogel?"

"I don't think so," she said. "I think you've had a pretty hard time."

"They're both good guesses," he said, pulling a paper out of his pocket, and handing it to Hilda. "Read that." It was a formal permit for building the gallery, signed by Porter himself, and bearing the O. K. of the general manager.

"Nice, isn't it?" Bannon commented. "Now read the postscript, Miss Vogel." It was in Porter's handwriting, and Hilda read it slowly. "MacBride & Company are not, however, allowed to erect trestles or temporary scaffolding in the C. & S. C. right-of-way, nor to remove any property of the Company, such as fences, nor to do anything which may, in the opinion of the local authorities, hinder the movement of trains."

Pete's face went blank. "A lot of good this darned permit does us then. That just means we can't build it."

Bannon nodded. "That's what it's supposed to mean," he said. "That's just the point."

"You see, it's like this," he went on. "That man Porter would make the finest material for ring-oiling, dust proof, non-inflammable bearings that I ever saw. He's just about the hardest, smoothest, shiniest, coolest little piece of metal that ever came my way. Well, he wants to delay us on this job. I took that in the moment I saw him. Well, I told him how we went ahead, just banking on his verbal consent, and how his railroad had jumped on us; and I said I was sure it was just a misunderstanding, but I wanted it cleared up because we was in a hurry. He grinned a little over that, and I went on talking. Said we'd bother 'em as little as possible; of course we had to put up the trestles in their property, because we couldn't hold the thing up with a balloon.

"He asked me, innocent as you please, if a steel bridge couldn't be made in a single span, and I said, yes, but it would take too long. We only had a few days. 'Well,' he says, 'Mr. Bannon, I'll give you a permit.' And that's what he gave me. I bet he's grinning yet. I wonder if he'll grin so much about three days from now."

"Do you mean that you can build it anyway?" Hilda demanded breathlessly.

He nodded, and, turning to Pete, plunged into a swift, technical explanation of how the trick was to be done. "Won't you please tell me, too?" Hilda asked appealingly.

"Sure," he said. He sat down beside her at the desk and began drawing on a piece of paper. Pete came and looked over his shoulder. Bannon began his explanation.

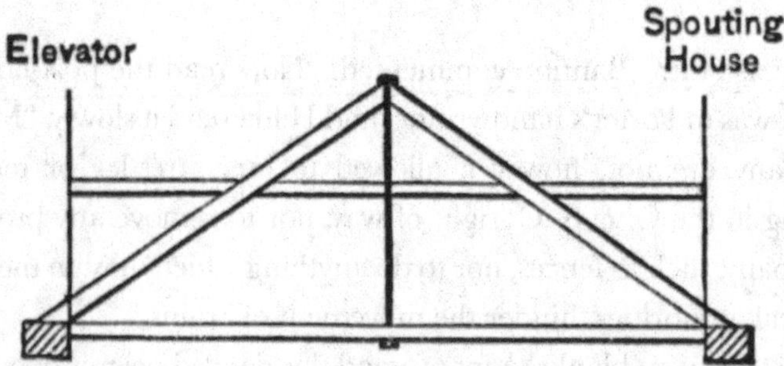

"HERE'S THE SPOUTING HOUSE"

"Here's the spouting house, and here's the elevator. Now, suppose they were only fifteen feet apart. Then if we had two ten-foot sticks and put 'em up at an angle and fastened the floor to a bolt that came down between 'em, the whole weight of the thing would be passed along to the foundation that the ends of the timbers rest on. But you see, it's got to be one hundred and fifty feet long, and to build it that way would take two one hundred-foot timbers, and we haven't got 'em that long.

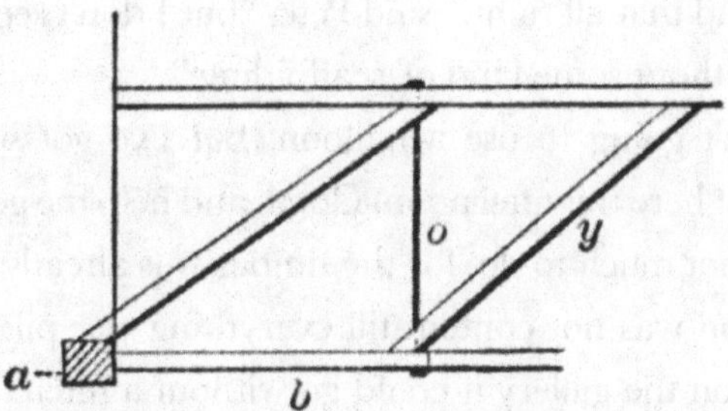

HE WAS DRAWING LINES ACROSS THE TIMBER

"But we've got plenty of sticks that are twenty feet long, and plenty of bolts, and this is the way we arrange 'em. We put up our first stick (_x_) at an angle just as before. Then we let a bolt (_o_) down through the upper end of it and through the floor of the gallery. Now the next timber (_y_) we put up at just the same angle as the first, with the foot of it bearing down on the lower end of the bolt.

"That second stick pushes two ways. A straight down push and a sideways push. The bolt resists the down push and transmits it to the first stick, and that pushes against the sill that I marked _a_. Now, the sideways push is against the butt of the first timber of the floor, and that's passed on, same way, to the sill.

"Well, that's the whole trick. You begin at both ends at once and just keep right on going. When the thing's done it looks this way. You see where the two sections meet in the middle, it's just the same as the little fifteen-foot gallery that we made a picture of up here."

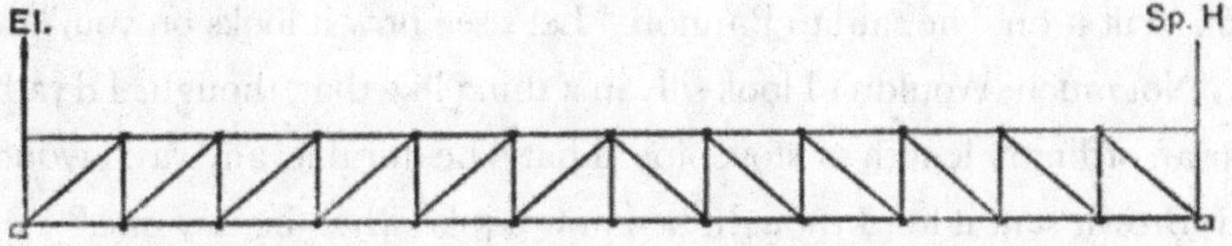

"WELL, THAT'S THE WHOLE TRICK"

"I understand that all right," said Pete, "but I don't see yet how you're going to do it without some kind of scaffolding."

"Easy. I ain't going to use a balloon, but I've got something that's better. It'll be out here this afternoon. Come and help me get things ready."

There was not much to do, for the timber was already cut to the right sizes, but Bannon was not content till everything was piled so that when work did begin on the gallery it could go without a hitch. He was already several days behind, and when one is figuring it as fine as Bannon was doing in those last days, even one day is a serious matter. He could do nothing more at the belt gallery until his substitute for a scaffold should arrive; it did not come that afternoon or evening, and next morning when he came on the job it still had not been heard from. There was enough to occupy every moment of his time and every shred of his thought without bothering about the gallery, and he did not worry about it as he would have worried if he had had nothing to do but wait for it.

But when, well along in the afternoon, a water boy found him up on the weighing floor and told him there was something for him at the office, he made astonishing time getting down. "Here's your package," said Max, as Bannon burst into the little shanty. It was a little, round, pasteboard box. If Bannon had had the office to himself, he would, in his disappointment, have cursed the thing till it took fire. As it was, he stood speechless a moment and then turned to go out again.

"Aren't you going to open it, now you're here?" asked Max.

Bannon, after hesitating, acted on the suggestion, and when he saw what it was, he laughed. No, Brown had not forgotten the hat! Max gazed at it in unfeigned awe; it was shiny as a mirror, black as a hearse, tall, in his eyes—for this was his first near view of one—as the seat of a dining-room chair. "Put it on," he said to Bannon. "Let's see how it looks on you."

"Not much. Wouldn't I look silly in a thing like that, though? I'd rather wear an ordinary length of stovepipe. That'd be durable, anyway. I wonder what Brown sent it for. I thought he knew a joke when he saw one."

Just then one of the under-foremen came in. "Oh, Mr. Bannon," he said, "I've been looking for you. There's a tug in the river with a big, steel cable aboard that they said was for us. I told 'em I thought it was a mistake——"

It was all one movement, Bannon's jamming that hat—the silk hat—down on his head, and diving through the door. He shouted orders as he ran, and a number of men, Pete among them, got to the wharf as soon as he did.

"Now, boys, this is all the false work we can have. We're going to hang it up across the tracks and hang our gallery up on it till it's strong enough to hold itself. We've got just forty-eight hours to do the whole trick. Catch hold now—lively."

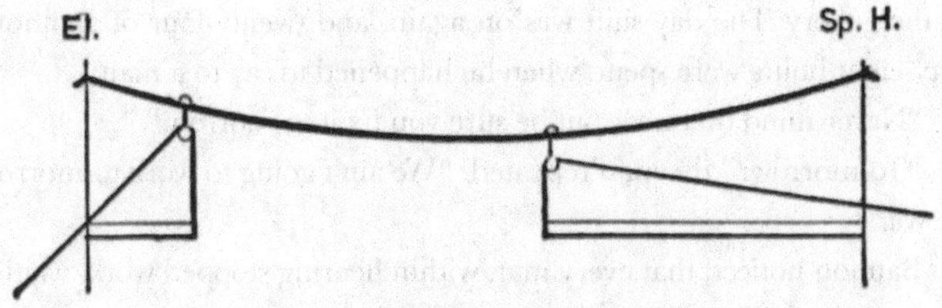

IT WAS A SIMPLE SCHEME

It was a simple scheme of Bannon's. The floor of the gallery was to be built in two sections, one in the main house, one in the spouting house. As fast as the timbers were bolted together the halves of the floor were shoved out over the tracks, each free end being supported by a rope which ran up over a pulley. The pulley was held by an iron ring fast to the cable, but perfectly free to slide along it, and thus accompany the end of the floor as it was moved outward. Bannon explained it to Pete in a few quick words while the men were hustling the big cable off the tug.

"Of course," he was concluding, "the thing'll wabble a good deal, specially if it's as windy as this, and it won't be easy to work on, but it won't fall if we make everything fast."

Pete had listened pretty closely at first, but now Bannon noticed that his attention seemed to be wandering to a point a few inches above Bannon's head. He was about to ask what was the matter when he found out. It was windier on that particular wharf than anywhere else in the Calumet flats, and the hat he had on was not built for that sort of weather. It was perfectly rigid, and not at all accommodated to the shape of Bannon's head. So, very naturally, it blew off, rolled around among their feet for a moment, and then dropped into the river between the wharf and the tug.

Bannon was up on the spouting house, helping make fast the cable end when a workman brought the hat back to him. Somebody on the tug had fished it out with a trolling line. But the hat was well past resuscitation. It had been thoroughly drowned, and it seemed to know it.

"Take that to the office," said Bannon. "Have Vogel wrap it up just as it is and ship it to Mr. Brown. I'll dictate a letter to go with it by and by."

For all Bannon's foresight, there threatened to be a hitch in the work on the gallery. The day shift was on again, and twenty-four of Bannon's forty-eight hours were spent, when he happened to say to a man:—

"Never mind that now, but be sure you fix it to-morrow."

"To-morrow?" the man repeated. "We ain't going to work to-morrow, are we?"

Bannon noticed that every man within hearing stopped work, waiting for the answer. "Sure," he said. "Why not?"

There was some dissatisfied grumbling among them which he was quite at a loss to understand until he caught the word "Christmas."

"Christmas!" he exclaimed, in perfectly honest astonishment. "Is to-morrow Christmas?" He ran his hand through his stubby hair. "Boys," he said, "I'm sorry to have to ask it of you. But can't we put it off a week? Look here. We need this day. Now, if you'll say Christmas is a week from to-morrow, I'll give every man on the job a Christmas dinner that you'll never forget; all you can eat and as much again, and you bring your friends, if we work to-morrow and we have her full of wheat a week from to-day. Does that go?"

It went, with a ripping cheer to boot; a cheer that was repeated here and there all over the place as Bannon's offer was passed along.

So for another twenty-four hours they strained and tugged and tusselled up in the big swing, for it was nothing else, above the railroad tracks. There was a northeast gale raging down off the lake, with squalls of rain and sleet mixed up in it, and it took the crazy, swaying box in its teeth and shook it and tossed it up in the air in its eagerness to strip it off the cable. But somewhere there was an unconquerable tenacity that held fast, and in the teeth of the wind the long box grew rigid, as the trusses were pounded into place by men so spent with fatigue that one might say it was sheer good will that drove the hammers.

At four o'clock Christmas afternoon the last bolt was drawn taut. The gallery was done. Bannon had been on the work since midnight—sixteen consecutive hours. He had eaten nothing except two sandwiches that he had stowed in his pockets. His only pause had been about nine o'clock that morning when he had put his head in the office door to wish Hilda a Merry Christmas.

When the evening shift came on—that was just after four—one of the under-foremen tried to get him to talking, but Bannon was too tired to talk. "Get your tracks and rollers in," he said. "Take down the cable."

"Don't you want to stay and see if she'll hold when the cable comes down?" called the foreman after him as he started away.

"She'll hold," said Bannon.

CHAPTER 15

Before December was half gone—and while the mild autumn weather serenely held, in spite of weather predictions and of storm signs about the sun and days of blue haze and motionless trees—the newspaper-reading public knew all the outside facts about the fight in wheat, and they knew it to be the biggest fight since the days of "Old Hutch" and the two-dollar-a-bushel record. Indeed, there were men who predicted that the two-dollar mark would be reached before Christmas, for the Clique of speculators who held the floor were buying, buying, buying—millions upon millions of dollars were slipping through their ready hands, and still there was no hesitation, no weakening. Until the small fry had dropped out the deal had been confused; it was too big, there were too many interests involved, to make possible a clear understanding, but now it was settling down into a grim fight between the biggest men on the Board. The Clique were buying wheat—Page & Company were selling it to them: if it should come out, on the thirty-first of December, that Page & Company had sold more than they could deliver, the Clique would be winners; but if it should have been delivered, to the last bushel, the corner would be broken, and the Clique would drop from sight as so many reckless men had dropped before. The readers of every great newspaper in the country were watching Page & Company. The general opinion was that they could not do it, that such an enormous quantity of grain could not be delivered and registered in time, even if it were to be had.

But the public overlooked, indeed it had no means of knowing, one important fact. The members of the Clique were new men in the public eye. They represented apparently unlimited capital, but they were young, eager, overstrung; flushed with the prospect of success, they were talking for publication. They believed they knew of every bushel in the country that was to be had, and they allowed themselves to say that they had already bought more than this. If this were true, Page was beaten. But it was not true. The young men of the Clique had forgotten that Page had trained agents in every part of the world; that he had alliances with great railroad and steamer lines, that he had a weather bureau and a system of crop reports that outdid those of the United States Government, that he could command more money than two such Cliques, and, most important of all, that he did not talk for publication. The young speculators were matching their wits against a great machine. Page had the wheat, he was making the effort of his career to deliver it, and he had no idea of losing.

Already millions of bushels had been rushed into Chicago. It was here that the fight took on its spectacular features, for the grain must be weighed and inspected before it could be accepted by the Board of Trade, and this could be done only in "regular" warehouses. The struggle had been to get control of these warehouses. It was here that the Clique had done their shrewdest work, and they had supposed that Page was finally outwitted, until they discovered that he had coolly set about building a million-bushel annex to his new house, Calumet K. And so it was that the newspapers learned that on the chance of completing Calumet K before the thirty-first of December hung the whole question of winning and losing; that if Bannon should fail, Page would be short two million bushels. And then came reporters and newspaper illustrators, who hung about the office and badgered Hilda, or perched on timber piles and sketched until Bannon or Peterson or Max could get at them and drive them out. Young men with snap-shot cameras way-laid Bannon on his way to luncheon, and published, with his picture, elaborate stories of his skill in averting a strike—stories that were not at all true.

Far out in Minnesota and Montana and South Dakota farmers were driving their wheat-laden wagons to the hundreds of local receiving houses that dotted the railroad lines. Box cars were waiting for the red grain, to roll it away to Minneapolis and Duluth—day and night the long trains were puffing eastward. Everywhere the order was, "Rush!" Railroad presidents and managers knew that Page was in a hurry, and they knew what Page's hurries meant, not only to the thousands of men who depended on him for their daily bread, but to the many great industries of the Northwest, whose credit and integrity were inextricably interwoven with his. Division superintendents knew that Page was in a hurry, and they snapped out orders and discharged half-competent men and sent quick words along the hot wires that were translated by despatchers and operators and yard masters into profane, driving commands. Conductors knew it, brakemen and switchmen knew it; they made flying switches in defiance of companies' orders, they ran where they used to walk, they slung their lunch pails on their arms and ate when and where they could, gazing over their cold tea at some portrait of Page, or of a member of the Clique, or of Bannon, in the morning's paper.

Elevator men at Minneapolis knew that Page was in a hurry, and they worked day and night at shovel and scale. Steamboat masters up at Duluth knew it, and mates and deck hands and stevedores and dockwallopers— more than one steamer scraped her paint in the haste to get under the long spouts that waited to pour out grain by the hundred thousand bushels. Trains came down from Minneapolis, boats came down from Duluth, warehouse after warehouse at Chicago was filled; and over-strained nerves neared the breaking point as the short December days flew by. Some said the Clique would win, some said Page would win; in the wheat pit men were fighting like tigers; every one who knew the facts was watching Charlie Bannon.

The storm came on the eighteenth of the month. It was predicted two days ahead, and ship masters were warned at all the lake ports. It was a Northwest blizzard, driven down from the Canadian Rockies at sixty miles an hour, leaving two feet of snow behind it over a belt hundreds of miles wide. But Page's steamers were not stopping for blizzards; they headed out of Duluth regardless of what was to come. And there were a bad few days, with tales of wreck on lake and railroad, days of wind and snow and bitter cold, and of risks run that supplied round-house and tug-office yarn spinners with stories that were not yet worn out. Down on the job the snow brought the work to a pause, but Bannon, within a half-hour, was out of bed and on the ground, and there was no question of changing shifts until, after twenty-four hours, the storm had passed, and elevator, annex and marine tower were cleared of snow. Men worked until they could not stagger, then snatched a few hours' sleep where they could. Word was passed that those who wished might observe the regular hours, but not a dozen men took the opportunity. For now they were in the public eye, and they felt as soldiers feel, when, after long months of drill and discipline, they are led to the charge.

Then came two days of biting weather—when ears were nipped and fingers stiffened, and carpenters who earned three dollars a day envied the laborers, whose work kept their blood moving—and after this a thaw, with sleet and rain. James, the new delegate, came to Bannon and pointed out that men who are continually drenched to the skin are not the best workmen. The boss met the delegate fairly; he ordered an oilskin coat for every man on the job, and in another day they swarmed over the building, looking, at a distance, like glistening yellow beetles.

But if Chicago was thawing, Duluth was not. The harbor at the western end of Lake Superior was ice-bound, and it finally reached a point that the tugs could not break open the channel. This was on the twenty-third and twenty-fourth. The wires were hot, but Page's agents succeeded in covering the facts until Christmas Day. It was just at dusk, after leaving the men to take down the cable, that Bannon went to the office.

A newsboy had been on the grounds with a special edition of a cheap afternoon paper. Hilda had taken one, and when Bannon entered the office he found her reading, leaning forward on the desk, her chin on her hands, the paper spread out over the ledger.

"Hello," he said, throwing off his dripping oilskin, and coming into the enclosure; "I'm pretty near ready to sit down and think about the Christmas tree that we ain't going to have."

She looked up, and he saw that she was a little excited; her eyes always told him. During this last week she had been carrying the whole responsibility of the work on her shoulders.

"Have you seen this?" she asked.

"Haven't read a paper this week." He leaned over the desk beside her and read the article. In Duluth harbor, and at St. Mary's straits, a channel through the ice had been blasted out with dynamite, and the last laden steamer was now ploughing down Lake Michigan. Already one steamer was lying at the wharf by the marine tower, waiting for the machinery to start, and others lay behind her, farther down the river. Long strings of box cars filled the Belt Line sidings, ready to roll into the elevator at the word.

Bannon seated himself on the railing, and caught his toes between the supports.

"I'll tell you one thing," he said, "those fellows have got to get up pretty early in the morning if they're going to beat old Page."

She looked at him, and then slowly folded the paper and turned toward the window. It was nearly dark outside. The rain, driving down from the northeast, tapped steadily on the glass. The arc lamp, on the pole near the tool house, was a blurred circle of light. She was thinking that they would have to get up pretty early to beat Charlie Bannon.

They were silent for a time—silences were not so hard as they had been, a few weeks before—both looking out at the storm, and both thinking that this was Christmas night. On the afternoon before he had asked her to take a holiday, and she had shaken her head. "I couldn't—I'd be here before noon," was what she had said; and she had laughed a little at her own confession, and hurried away with Max.

She turned and said, "Is it done—the belt gallery?"

He nodded. "All done."

"Well——" she smiled; and he nodded again.

"The C. & S. C. man—the fellow that was around the other day and measured to see if it was high enough—he's out there looking up with his mouth open. He hasn't got much to say."

"You didn't have to touch the tracks at all?"

"Not once. Ran her out and bolted her together, and there she was. I'm about ready for my month off. We'll have the wheat coming in to-morrow, and then it's just walking down hill."

"To-morrow?" she asked. "Can you do it?"

"Got to. Five or six days aren't any too much. If it was an old house and the machinery was working well, I'd undertake to do it in two or three, but if we get through without ripping up the gallery, or pounding the leg through the bottom of a steamer, it'll be the kind of luck I don't have." He paused and looked at the window, where the rain was streaking the glass. "I've been thinking about my vacation. I've about decided to go to the St. Lawrence. Maybe there are places I'd like better, but when a fellow hasn't had a month off in five years, he doesn't feel like experiments."

It was the personal tone again, coming into their talk in spite of the excitement of the day and the many things that might have been said. Hilda looked down at the ledger, and fingered the pages. Bannon smiled.

"If I were you," he said, "I'd shut that up and fire it under the table. This light isn't good enough to work by, anyway."

She slowly closed the book, saying:—

"I never worked before on Christmas."

"It's a mistake. I don't believe in it, but somehow it's when my hardest work always comes. One Christmas, when I was on the Grand Trunk, there was a big wreck at a junction about sixty miles down the road."

She saw the memory coming into his eyes, and she leaned back against the desk, playing with her pen, and now and then looking up.

"I was chief wrecker, and I had an old Scotch engineer that you couldn't move with a jack. We'd rubbed up together three or four times before I'd had him a month, and I was getting tired of it. We'd got about halfway to the junction that night, and I felt the brakes go on hard, and before I could get through the train and over the tender, we'd stopped dead. The Scotchman was down by the drivers fussing around with a lantern. I hollered out:—

"'What's the matter there?'

"'She's a bit 'ot,' said he.

"You'd have thought he was running a huckleberry train from the time he took. I ordered him into the cab, and he just waved his hand and said:—

"'Wait a bit, wait a bit. She'll be cool directly.'"

Bannon chuckled at the recollection.

"What did you do?" Hilda asked.

"Jumped for the lever, and hollered for him to get aboard."

"Did he come?"

"No, he couldn't think that fast. He just stood still, looking at me, while I threw her open, and you could see his lantern for a mile back—he never moved. He had a good six-mile walk back to the last station."

There was a long silence. Bannon got up and walked slowly up and down the enclosure with his hands deep in his pockets.

"I wish this would let up," he said, after a time, pausing in his walk, and looking again at the window. "It's a wonder we're getting things done at all."

Hilda's eye, roaming over the folded newspaper, fell on the weather forecast.

"Fair to-morrow," she said, "and colder."

"That doesn't stand for much. They said the same thing yesterday. It's a worse gamble than wheat."

Bannon took to walking again; and Hilda stepped down and stood by the window, spelling out the word "Calumet" with her finger on the misty glass. At each turn, Bannon paused and looked at her. Finally he stood still, not realizing that he was staring until she looked around, flushed, and dropped her eyes. Then he felt awkward, and he began turning over the blue prints on the table.

"I'll tell you what I'll have to do," he said. "I rather think now I'll start on the third for Montreal. I'm telling you a secret, you know. I'm not going to let Brown or MacBride know where I'll be. And if I can pick up some good pictures of the river, I'll send them to you. I'll get one of the Montmorency Falls, if I can. They're great in winter."

"Why—why, thank you," she said. "I'd like to have them."

"I ain't much at writing letters," he went on, "but I'll send you the pictures, and you write and tell me how things are going."

She laughed softly, and followed the zigzag course of the raindrop with her finger.

"I wouldn't have very much to say," she said, speaking with a little hesitation, and without looking around. "Max and I never do much."

"Oh, you can tell how your work goes, and what you do nights."

"We don't do much of anything. Max studies some at night—a man he used to work for gave him a book of civil engineering."

"What do you do?"

"I read some, and then I like to learn things about—oh, about business, and how things are done."

Bannon could not take his eyes from her—he was looking at her hair, and at the curved outline of one cheek, all that he could see of her face. They both stood still, listening to the patter of the rain, and to the steady drip from the other end of the office, where there was a leak in the roof. Once she cleared her throat, as if to speak, but no words came.

There was a stamping outside, and she slipped back to the ledger, as the door flew open. Bannon turned to the blue prints.

Max entered, pausing to knock his cap against the door, and wring it out.

"You ought to have stayed out, Mr. Bannon," he said. "It's the greatest thing you ever saw—doesn't sag an inch. And say—I wish you could hear the boys talk—they'd lie down and let you walk on 'em, if you wanted to."

Max's eyes were bright, and his face red with exercise and excitement. He came to the gate and stood wiping his feet and looking from one to the other for several moments before he felt the awkwardness that had come over him. His long rubber coat was thrown back, and little streams of water ran down his back and formed a pool on the floor behind him.

"You'd better come out," he said. "It's the prettiest thing I ever saw—a clean straight span from the main house to the tower."

Bannon stood watching him quizzically; then he turned to Hilda. She, too, had been looking at Max, but she turned at the same moment, and their eyes met.

"Do you want to go?" he said.

She nodded eagerly. "I'd like to ever so much."

Then Bannon thought of the rain, but she saw his thought as he glanced toward the window, and spoke quickly.

"I don't mind—really. Max will let me take his coat."

"Sure," said Max, and he grinned. She slipped into it, and it enveloped her, hanging in folds and falling on the floor.

"I'll have to hold it up," she said. "Do we have much climbing?"

"No," said Max, "it ain't high. And the stairs are done, you know."

Hilda lifted the coat a little way with both hands, and put out one small toe. Bannon looked at it, and shook his head. "You'll get your feet wet," he said.

She looked up and met Bannon's eyes again, with an expression that puzzled Max.

"I don't care. It's almost time to go home, anyway."

So they went out, and closed the door; and Max, who had been told to "stay behind and keep house," looked after them, and then at the door, and an odd expression of slow understanding came into his face. It was not in what they had said, but there was plainly a new feeling between them. For the first time in his life, Max felt that another knew Hilda better than he did. The way Bannon had looked at her, and she at him; the mutual understanding that left everything unsaid; the something—Max did not know what it was, but he saw it and felt it, and it disturbed him.

He sat on the table, and swung his feet, while one expression chased another over his face. When he finally got himself together, he went to the door, and opening it, looked out at the black, dim shape of the elevator that stood big and square, only a little way before him, shutting out whatever he might else have seen of rushing sky or dim-lighted river, or of the railroads and the steamboats and the factories and rolling mills beyond. It was as if this elevator were his fate, looming before him and shutting out the forward view. In whatever thoughts he had had of the future, in whatever plans, and they were few, which he had revolved in his head, there had always been a place for Hilda. He did not see just what he was to do, just what he was to become, without her. He stood there for a long time, leaning against the door-jamb with his hands in his pockets, and the sharper gusts of rain whirled around the end of the little building and beat on him. And then—well, it was Charlie Bannon; and Max knew that he was glad it was no one else.

The narrow windows in the belt gallery had no glass, and the rain came driving through them into the shadows, each drop catching the white shine of the electric lights outside. The floor was trampled with mud and littered with scraps of lumber, tool boxes, empty nail kegs, and shavings. The long, gloomy gallery was empty when Bannon and Hilda stepped into it, excepting a group of men at the farther end, installing the rollers for the belt conveyor—they could be seen indistinctly against a light in the river house.

The wind came roaring around the building, and the gallery trembled and shook. Hilda caught her breath and stopped short.

"It's all right," said Bannon. "She's bound to move some."

"I know—" she laughed—"I wasn't expecting it—it startled me a little."

"Watch where you step." He took her arm and guided her slowly between the heaps of rubbish.

At one of the windows she paused, and stood full in the rain, looking out at the C. & S. C. tracks, with their twinkling red and green lights, all blurred and seeming far off in the storm.

"Isn't this pretty wet?" he said, standing beside her.

"I don't care." She shook the folds of the rubber coat, and glanced down at it. "I like it."

They looked out for a long time. Two millwrights came through the gallery, and glanced at them, but they did not turn. She stepped forward and let the rain beat on her face—he stood behind, looking at her. A light showed far down the track, and they heard a faint whistle. "A train," he said; and she nodded. The headlight grew, and the car lights appeared behind it, and then the black outline of the engine. There was a rush and a roar, and it passed under them.

"Doesn't it make you want to jump down?" she said softly, when the roar had dwindled away.

He nodded with a half-smile.

"Say," he said, a little later, "I don't know about your writing—I don't believe we'd better—" he got the words out more rapidly—"I'll tell you what you do—you come along with me and we won't have to write."

"Come—where?"

"Up to the St. Lawrence. We can start on the third just the same."

She did not answer, and he stopped. Then, after a moment, she slowly turned, and looked at him.

"Why—" she said—"I don't think I——"

"I've just been thinking about it. I guess I can't do anything else—I mean I don't want to go anywhere alone. I guess that's pretty plain, isn't it—what I mean?"

She leaned back against the wall and looked at him; it was as if she could not take her eyes from his face.

"Perhaps I oughtn't to expect you to say anything now," he went on. "I just thought if you felt anything like I did, you'd know pretty well, by this time, whether it was yes or no."

She was still looking at him. He had said it all, and now he waited, his fists knotted tightly, and a peculiar expression on his face, almost as if he were smiling, but it came from a part of his nature that had never before got to the surface. Finally she said:—

"I think we'd better go back."

He did not seem to understand, and she turned away and started off alone. In a moment he was at her side. He guided her back as they had come, and neither spoke until they had reached the stairway. Then he said, in a low tone that the carpenters could not hear:—

"You don't mean that—that you can't do it?"

She shook her head and hurried to the office.

CHAPTER 16

Bannon stood looking after her until she disappeared in the shadow of an arc lamp, and after that he continued a long time staring into the blot of darkness where the office was. At last the window became faintly luminous, as some one lighted the wall lamp; then, as if it were a signal he had been waiting for, Bannon turned away.

An hour before, when he had seen the last bolt of the belt gallery drawn taut, he had become aware that he was quite exhausted. The fact was so obvious that he had not tried to evade it, but had admitted to himself, in so many words, that he was at the end of his rope. But when he turned from gazing at the dimly lighted window, it was not toward his boarding-house, where he knew he ought to be, but back into the elevator, that his feet led him. For once, his presence accomplished nothing. He went about without thinking where; he passed men without seeing who they were or what they were doing. When he walked through the belt gallery, he saw the foreman of the big gang of men at work there was handling them clumsily, so that they interfered with each other, but it did not occur to him to give the orders that would set things right. Then, as if his wire-drawn muscles had not done work enough, he climbed laboriously to the very top of the marine tower.

He was leaning against a window-casing; not looking out, for he saw nothing, but with his face turned to the fleet of barges lying in the river; when some one spoke to him.

"I guess you're thinking about that Christmas dinner, ain't you, Mr. Bannon?"

"What's that?" he demanded, wheeling about. Then rallying his scattered faculties, he recognized one of the carpenters. "Oh, yes," he said, laughing tardily. "Yes, the postponed Christmas dinner. You think I'm in for it, do you? You know it's no go unless this house is full of wheat clear to the roof."

"I know it," said the man. "But I guess we're going to stick you for it. Don't you think we are?"

"I guess that's right."

"I come up here," said the carpenter, well pleased at the chance for a talk with the boss, "to have a look at this—marine leg, do you call it? I haven't been to work on it, and I never saw one before. I wanted to find out how it works."

"Just like any other leg over in the main house. Head pulley up here; another one down in the boot; endless belt running over 'em with steel cups rivetted on it to scoop up the grain. Only difference is that instead of being stationary and set up in a tank, this one's hung up. We let the whole business right down into the boat. Pull it up and down with that steam winch."

The man shook his head. "What if it got away from you?"

"That's happened," said Bannon. "I've seen a leg most as big as this smash through two decks. Thought it was going right on through the bottom of the boat. But that wasn't a leg that MacBride had hung up. This one won't fall."

Bannon answered one or two more questions rather at random, then suddenly came back to earth. "What are you doing here, anyway?" he demanded. "Seems to me this is a pretty easy way to earn thirty cents an hour."

"I—I was just going to see if there wasn't something I could do," the man answered, a good deal embarrassed. Then before Bannon could do more than echo, "Something to do?" added: "I don't get my time check till midnight. I ain't on this shift. I just come around to see how things was going. We're going to see you through, Mr. Bannon."

Bannon never had a finer tribute than that, not even what young Page said when the race was over; and it could not have come at a moment when he needed it more. He did not think much in set terms about what it meant, but when the man had gone and he had turned back to the window, he took a long breath of the night air and he saw what lay beneath his eyes. He saw the line of ships in the river; down nearer the lake another of Page's elevators was drinking up the red wheat out of the hold of a snub-nosed barge; across the river, in the dark, they were backing another string of wheat-laden cars over the Belt Line switches. As he looked out and listened, his imagination took fire again, as it had taken fire that day in the waiting-room at Blake City, when he had learned that the little, one-track G. & M. was trying to hinder the torrent of the Northern wheat.

Well, the wheat had come down. It had beaten a blizzard, it had churned and wedged and crushed its way through floating ice and in the trough of mauling seas; belated passenger trains had waited on lonely sidings while it thundered by, and big rotary ploughs had bitten a way for it across the drifted prairies. Now it was here, and Charlie Bannon was keeping it waiting.

He stood there, looking, only a moment; then before the carpenter's footsteps were well out of hearing, he followed him down the stairway to the belt gallery. Before he had passed half its length you could have seen the difference. In the next two hours every man on the elevator saw him, learned a quicker way to splice a rope or align a shaft, and heard, before the boss went away, some word of commendation that set his hands to working the faster, and made the work seem easy. The work had gone on without interruption for weeks, and never slowly, but there were times when it went with a lilt and a laugh; when laborers heaved at a hoisting tackle with a Yo-ho, like privateersmen who have just sighted a sail; when, with all they could do, results came too slowly, and the hours flew too fast. And so it was that Christmas night; Charlie Bannon was back on the job.

About ten o'clock he encountered Pete, bearing off to the shanty a quart bottle of cold coffee and a dozen big, thick sandwiches. "Come on, Charlie," he called. "Max is coming, too; but I guess we've got enough to spare you a little."

So the three of them sat down to supper around the draughting-table, and between bites Bannon talked, a little about everything, but principally, and with much corroborative detail—for the story seemed to strain even Pete's easy credulity—of how, up at Yawger, he had been run on the independent ticket for Superintendent of the Sunday School, and had been barely defeated by two votes.

When the sandwiches were put away, and all but three drinks of the coffee, Bannon held the bottle high in the air. "Here's to the house!" he said. "We'll have wheat in her to-morrow night!"

They drank the toast standing; then, as if ashamed of such a sentimental demonstration, they filed sheepishly out of the office. They walked fifty paces in silence. Then Pete checked suddenly and turned to Bannon.

"Hold on, Charlie, where are you going?"

"Going to look over those 'cross-the-house conveyor drives down cellar."

"No, you ain't either. You're going to bed."

Bannon only laughed and started on toward the elevator.

"How long is it since you had any sleep?" Pete demanded.

"I don't know. Guess I must have slept part of the time while we was putting up that gallery. I don't remember much about it."

"Don't be in such a hurry," said Pete, and as he said it he reached out his left hand and caught him by the shoulder. It was more by way of gesture than otherwise, but Bannon had to step back a pace to keep his feet. "I mean business," Pete went on, though laughing a little. "When we begin to turn over the machinery you won't want to go away, so this is your last chance to get any sleep. I can't make things jump like you can, but I can keep 'em going to-night somehow."

"Hadn't you better wrap me up in cotton flannel and feed me warm milk with a spoon? Let go of me and quit your fooling. You delay the game."

"I ain't fooling. I'm boss here at night, and I fire you till morning. That goes if I have to carry you all the way to your boarding house and tie you down to the bed." Pete meant it. As if, again, for illustration, he picked Bannon up in his arms. The boss was ready for the move this time, and he resisted with all his strength, but he would have had as much chance against the hug of a grizzly bear; he was crumpled up. Pete started off with him across the flat.

"All right," said Bannon. "I'll go."

At seven o'clock next morning Pete began expecting his return. At eight he began inquiring of various foremen if they had seen anything of Charlie Bannon. By nine he was avowedly worried lest something had gone wrong with him, and a little after ten Max set out for the boarding house.

Encountering the landlady in the hall, he made the mistake of asking her if she had seen anything of Mr. Bannon that morning. She had some elementary notions of strategy, derived, doubtless, from experience, and before beginning her reply, she blocked the narrow stairway with her broad person. Then, beginning with a discussion of Mr. Bannon's excellent moral character and his most imprudent habits, and illustrating by anecdotes of various other boarders she had had at one time and another, she led up to the statement that she had seen nothing of him since the night before, and that she had twice knocked at his door without getting any reply.

Max, who had laughed a little at Pete's alarm, was now pretty well frightened himself, but at that instant they heard the thud of bare feet on the floor just above them. "That's him now," said the landlady, thoughtlessly turning sideways, and Max bolted past her and up the stairs.

He knocked at the door and called out to know if he could come in. The growl he heard in reply meant invitation as much as it meant anything, so he went in. Bannon, already in his shirt and trousers, stood with his back to the door, his face in the washbowl. As he scoured he sputtered. Max could make little out of it, for Bannon's face was under water half the time, but he caught such phrases as "Pete's darned foolishness," "College boy trick," "Lie abed all the morning," and "Better get an alarm clock"— which thing and the need for it Bannon greatly despised—and he reached the conclusion that the matter was nothing more serious than that Bannon had overslept.

But the boss took it seriously enough. Indeed, he seemed deeply humiliated, and he marched back to the elevator beside Max without saying a word until just as they were crossing the Belt Line tracks, when the explanation of the phenomenon came to him.

"I know where I get it from," he exclaimed, as if in some measure relieved by the discovery. "I must take after my uncle. He was the greatest fellow to sleep you ever saw."

So far as pace was concerned that day was like the others; while the men were human it could be no faster; with Bannon on the job it could not flag; but there was this difference, that to-day the stupidest sweepers knew that they had almost reached the end, and there was a rally like that which a runner makes at the beginning of the last hundred yards.

Late in the afternoon they had a broad hint of how near the end was. The sweepers dropped their brooms and began carrying fire buckets full of water. They placed one or more near every bearing all over the elevator. The men who were quickest to understand explained to the slower ones what the precaution meant, and every man had his eye on the nearest pulley to see when it would begin to turn.

But Bannon was not going to begin till he was ready. He had inspected the whole job four times since noon, but just after six he went all over it again, more carefully than before. At the end he stepped out of the door at the bottom of the stairway bin, and pulled it shut after him. It was not yet painted, and its blank surface suggested something. He drew out his blue pencil and wrote on the upper panel:

O.K.

C. H. BANNON.

Then he walked over to the power house. It was a one-story brick building, with whose construction Bannon had had no concern, as Page & Company had placed the contract for it elsewhere. Every night for the past week lights had been streaming from its windows, and day and night men had waited, ready at any time for the word to go ahead. A dozen of them were lounging about the brick-paved space in front of the battery of boilers when Bannon opened the door, and they sprang to their feet as they read his errand in his face.

"Steam up," he said. "We'll be ready as soon as you are."

There was the accumulated tension of a week of inactivity behind these men, and the effect of Bannon's words was galvanic. Already low fires were burning under the boilers, and now the coal was piled on, the draughts roared, the smoke, thick enough to cut, came billowing out of the tall chimney. Every man in the room, even the wretchedest of the dripping stokers, had his eyes on the steam gauges, but for all that the water boiled, and the indicator needles crept slowly round the dials, and at last the engineer walked over and pulled the whistle cord.

Hitherto they had marked the divisions of time on the job by the shrill note of the little whistle on the hoisting engine boiler, and there was not a man but started at the screaming crescendo of the big siren on top of the power house. Men in the streets, in the straggling boarding houses over across the flats, on the wharves along the river, men who had been forbidden to come to the elevator till they were needed lest they should be in the way, had been waiting days for that signal, and they came streaming into the elevator almost before the blast had died away.

Page's superintendent was standing beside Bannon and Pete by the foot of the main drive. "Well," he said, "we're ready. Are you?"

Bannon nodded and turned to a laborer who stood near. "Go tell the engineer to go ahead." The man, proud as though he had just been promoted, went out on the run.

"Now," said Bannon, "here's where we go slow. All the machinery in the house has got to be thrown in, one thing at a time, line shafts first and then elevators and the rest of it. Pete, you see it done up top. I'll look out for it down here. See that there's a man to look at each bearing at least once in three minutes, and let me know if it gets warm."

It took a long time to do it, but it had to be done, for Bannon was inflexible, but at last everything in elevator, annex, and spouting house that could turn was turning, and it was reported to Bannon. "Now," he said, "she's got to run light for fifteen minutes. No——" he went on in answer to the superintendent's protest; "you're lucky I didn't say two hours. It's the biggest chance I ever took as it is."

So while they stared at the second hands of their watches the minutes crept away—Pete wound his watch up tight in the vain hope of making it go a little faster—and at last Bannon turned with a nod to the superintendent.

"All right," he said. "You're the boss now."

And then in a moment the straining hawsers were hauling cars up into the house. The seals were broken, the doors rolled back, and the wheat came pouring out. The shovellers clambered into the cars and the steam power shovels helped the torrent along. It fell through the gratings, into steel tanks, and then the tireless metal cups carried it up, up, up, 'way to the top of the building. And then it came tumbling down again; down into garners, and down again into the great weighing hoppers, and recognized and registered and marketable at last, part of the load that was to bury the Clique that had braved it out of sight of all but their creditors, it went streaming down the spouts into the bins.

The first of the barges in the river was moved down beside the spouting house, her main hatch just opposite the tower. And now Pete, in charge there, gave the word, and the marine leg, gravely, deliberately descended. There is a magnificent audacity about that sort of performance. The leg was ninety feet long, steel-booted, framed of great timbers, heavy enough to have wrecked the barge like a birch bark canoe if it had got away. It went down bodily into the hold and the steel boot was buried in wheat. Then Pete threw another lever, and in a moment another endless series of cups was carrying the wheat aloft. It went over the cross-head and down a spout, then stretched out in a golden ribbon along the glistening white belt that ran the length of the gallery. Then, like the wheat from the cars, it was caught up again in the cups, and shot down through spouts, and carried along on belts to the remotest bins in the annex.

For the first few hours of it the men's nerves were hair springs, but as time went on and the stream kept pouring in without pause, the tension relaxed though the watch never slackened. Men patted the bearings affectionately, and still the same report came to Bannon, "All cool."

Late that night, as the superintendent was figuring his weighing reports, he said to Bannon; "At this rate, we'll have several hours to spare."

"We haven't had our accident yet," said Bannon, shortly.

It happened within an hour, at the marine leg, but it was not serious. They heard a splintering sound, down in the dark, somewhere, and Pete, shouting to them to throw out the clutch, climbed out and down on the sleet-clad girders that framed the leg. An agile monkey might have been glad to return alive from such a climb, but Pete came back presently with a curious specimen of marine hardware that had in some way got into the wheat, and thence into the boot and one of the cups. Part way up it had got jammed and had ripped up the sheathing of the leg. They started the leg again, but soon learned that it was leaking badly.

"You'll have to haul up for repairs, I guess," the captain called up to them.

"Haven't time," said Pete, under his breath, and with a hammer and nails, and a big piece of sacking, he went down the leg again, playing his neck against a half-hour's delay as serenely as most men would walk downstairs to dinner. "Start her up, boys," he called, when the job was done, and, with the leg jolting under his hands as he climbed, he came back into the tower.

That was their only misfortune, and all it cost them was a matter of minutes, so by noon of the thirtieth, an hour or two after MacBride and young Page arrived from Minneapolis, it became clear that they would be through in time.

At eight o'clock next morning, as Bannon and MacBride were standing in the superintendent's office, he came in and held out his hand. "She's full, Mr. Bannon. I congratulate you."

"Full, eh?" said MacBride. Then he dropped his hand on Bannon's shoulder. "Well," he said, "do you want to go to sleep, or will you come and talk business with me for a little while?"

"Sleep!" Bannon echoed. "I've been oversleeping lately."

CHAPTER 17

The elevator was the place for the dinner, if only the mild weather that had followed the Christmas storm should continue—on that Bannon, Pete, and Max were agreed. New Year's Day would be a holiday, and there was room on the distributing floor for every man who had worked an hour on the job since the first spile had been driven home in the Calumet clay. To be sure most of the laborers had been laid off before the installing of the machinery, but Bannon knew that they would all be on hand, and he meant to have seats for them. But on the night of the thirtieth the wind swung around to the northeast, and it came whistling through the cracks in the cupola walls with a sting in it that set the weighers to shivering. And as the insurance companies would have inquired curiously into any arrangement for heating that gloomy space on the tops of the bins, the plan had to be given up.

As soon as the last of the grain was in, on the thirty-first, Max took a north-bound car and scoured South Chicago for a hall that was big enough. Before the afternoon was gone he had found it, and had arranged with a restaurant keeper to supply the dinner. Early the next morning the three set to work, making long tables and benches by resting planks on boxes, and covering the tables with pink and blue and white scalloped shelf-paper.

It was nearly ten o'clock when Max, after draping a twenty-four-foot flag in a dozen different ways, let it slide down the ladder to the floor and sat down on the upper round, looking out over the gridiron of tables with a disgusted expression. Peterson, aided by a man from the restaurant, was bringing in load after load of thick white plates, stacking them waist high near the door. Max was on the point of calling to him, but he recollected that

Pete's eye, though quick with timbers, would not help much in questions of art. Just then Bannon came through the doorway with another flag rolled under his arm.

"They're here already, a couple of dozen of 'em," he said, as he dropped the flag at the foot of the ladder. "I've left James on the stairs to keep 'em out until we're ready. Better have an eye on the fire escape, too—they're feeling pretty lively."

"Say," Max said abruptly, "I can't make this thing look anyhow. I guess it's up to you."

Bannon stepped back and looked up at the wall.

"Why don't you just hang them from the ceiling and then catch them up from pretty near the bottom—so they'll drape down on both sides of the windows?"

"I know," said Max, "but there's ways of making 'em look just right—if Hilda was here, she'd know——" He paused and looked down at the red, white, and blue heap on the floor.

During the last week they had not spoken of Hilda, and Bannon did not know whether she had told Max. He glanced at him, but got no sign, for Max was gazing moodily downward.

"Do you think," Bannon said, "do you think she'd care to come around?"

He tried to speak easily, as he might have spoken of her at any time before Christmas Day, but he could not check a second glance at Max. At that moment Max looked up, and as their eyes met, with an awkward pause, Bannon knew that he understood; and for a moment the impatience that he had been fighting for a week threatened to get away with him. He had seen nothing of Hilda, except for the daily "Good morning," and a word now and then. The office had been besieged by reporters waiting for a chance at him; under-foremen had been rushing in and out; Page's representatives and the railroad and steamboat men had made it their headquarters. It may be that he would not have spoken in any case, for he had said all that he could say, and he knew that she would give him an answer when she could.

Max's eyes had dropped again.

"You mean for her to help fix things up?" he asked.

Bannon nodded; and then, as Max did not look up, he said, "Yes."

"Why—why, yes, I guess she'd just as soon." He hesitated, then began coming down the ladder, adding, "I'll go for her."

Bannon looked over his shoulder—Pete was clattering about among the dishes.

"Max," he said, "hold on a minute."

Max turned and came slowly back.

Bannon had seated himself on the end of a table, and now he waited, looking down at the two rows of plates, and slowly turning a caster that stood at his elbow. What he finally said was not what Max was awaiting.

"What are you going to do now, Max—when you're through on this job?"

"Why—I don't know——"

"Have you got anything ahead?"

"Nothing sure. I was working for a firm of contractors up on the North Side, and I've been thinking maybe they'd take me back."

"You've had some experience in building before now, haven't you?" Bannon was speaking deliberately, as if he were saying what he had thought out before.

"Yes, a good deal. It's what I've mostly done since I quit the lumber business."

"When Mr. MacBride was here," said Bannon, "he told me that we've got a contract for a new house at Indianapolis. It's going to be concrete, from the spiles up—there ain't anything like it in the country. I'm going down next week to take charge of the job, and if you'd like to go along as my assistant, I'll take you."

Max did not know what to say. At first he grinned and blushed, thinking only that Bannon had been pleased with his work; then he grew serious.

"Well," said Bannon, "what do you say?"

Max still hesitated. At last he replied:

"Can I have till to-morrow to think about it? I—you see, Hilda and I, we most always talk things over, and I don't exactly like to do anything without——"

"Sure," said Bannon; "think it over if you like. There's no hurry up to the end of the week." He paused as if he meant to go on, but changed his mind and stood up. Max, too, was waiting, as if there were more to be said.

"You two must think we've got all day to fix things." It was Pete calling from the other end of the room. "There ain't no loafing allowed here."

Bannon smiled, and Max turned away. But after he had got a third of the way down the aisle, he came back.

"Say, Mr. Bannon," he said, "I want to tell you that I—Hilda, she said—she's told me something about things—and I want to——" It had been a lame conversation; now it broke down, and they stood through a long silence without speaking. Finally Max pulled himself together, and said in a low, nervous voice: "Say, it's all right. I guess you know what I'm thinking about. And I ain't got a word to say." Then he hurried out.

When Max and Hilda came in, the restaurant man was setting up the paper napkin tents on the raised table at the end of the hall, and Pete stood by the door, looking upon his work with satisfaction. He did not see them until they were fairly in the room.

"Hello," he said; "I didn't know you was coming, Miss Vogel." He swept his arm around. "Ain't it fine? Make you hungry to look at all them plates?"

Hilda followed his gesture with a smile. Her jacket was still buttoned tightly, and her eyes were bright and her cheeks red from the brisk outer air. Bannon and James were coming toward them, and she greeted them with a nod.

"There's going to be plenty of room," she said.

"That's right," Pete replied. "There won't be no elbows getting in the way at this dinner. Come up where you can see better." He led the way to the platform, and they all followed.

"This is the speakers' table," Pete went on, "where the boss and all will be"—he winked toward Bannon—"and the guest of honor. You show her how we sit, Max; you fixed that part of it."

Max walked around the table, pointing out his own, Pete's, James', and Bannon's seats, and those of the committee. The middle seat, next to Bannon's he passed over.

"Hold on," said Pete, "you forgot something."

Max grinned and drew back the middle chair.

"This is for the guest of honor," he said, and looked at Hilda. Pete was looking at her, too, and James—all but Bannon.

The color, that had been leaving her face, began to come back.

"Do you mean me?" she asked

"I guess that's pretty near," said Pete.

She shook her head. "Oh, no—thank you very much—I can't stay."

Pete and Max looked at each other.

"The boys'll be sorry," said Pete. "It's kind of got out that maybe you'd be here, and—I don't believe they'd let you off."

Hilda was smiling, but her face was flushed. She shook her head. "Oh, no," she replied; "I only came to help."

Pete turned on Max, with a clumsy laugh that did not cover his disappointment.

"How about this, Max? You ain't been tending to business. Ain't that so, James? Wasn't he going to see that she come and sat up with us where the boys could see her?" He turned to Hilda. "You see, most of the boys know you've had a good deal to do with things on the job, and they've kind of took a shine to you——" Pete suddenly awoke to the fact that he had never talked so boldly to a girl before. He hesitated, looked around at Max and James for support and at Bannon, and then, finding no help, he grinned, and the warm color surged over his face. The only one who saw it all was Hilda, and in spite of her embarrassment the sight of big, strong, bashful Pete was too much for her. A twinkle came into her eyes, and a faint smile hovered about her mouth. Pete saw it, misunderstood it, and, feeling relieved, went on, not knowing that by bringing that twinkle to Hilda's eyes, he had saved the situation.

"It's only that they've talked about it some, and yesterday a couple of 'em spoke to me, and I said I'd ask Max, and——"

"Thank you, Mr. Peterson," Hilda replied. "Max should have told me." She turned toward Max, her face sober now except for the eyes, which would not come under control. Max had been dividing his glances between her and Bannon, feeling the situation heavily, and wondering if he ought not to come to her relief, but unable to dig up the right word. Pete spoke up again:

"Say, honest now, ain't you coming?"

"I can't really. I'm sorry. I know you'll have a good time."

Bannon had been standing aside, unwilling to speak for fear of making it harder for her. But now she turned to him and said, with a lightness that puzzled him:

"Aren't we going to do some decorating, Mr. Bannon? I'm afraid it will be dinner time before Mr. Peterson knows it."

Pete flushed again at this, but she gave him a quick smile.

"Yes," said Bannon, "there's only a little over half an hour." He paused, and looked about the group, holding his watch in his hand and fingering the stem. The lines about his mouth were settling. Hilda glanced again at him, and from the determined look in his eyes, she knew that his week of waiting was over; that he meant to speak to her before she left the hall. It was all in the moment's silence that followed his remark; then he went on, as easily as if he were talking to a gang on the marine tower—but the time was long enough for Hilda to feel her brief courage slipping away. She could not look at him now.

"Take a look at that door, James," he was saying. "I guess you'll have to tend to business if you want any dinner."

They all turned and saw the grinning heads of some of the carpenters peering into the room. There was the shuffling of many feet behind them on the stairs, and the sound of cat calls and whistling. A shove was passed on from somewhere back in the hallway, and one of the carpenters came sprawling through the door. The others yelled good-naturedly.

"I'll fix 'em," said James, with a laugh, starting toward them.

"Give him a lift, Pete," said Bannon. "He'll need it. You two'd better keep the stairs clear for a while, or they'll stampede us."

So Pete followed, and for a few moments the uproar from the stairs drowned all attempts at conversation. Only Max was left with them now. He stood back by the wall, still looking helplessly from one to the other. The restaurant men were bustling about the floor; and Hilda was glad they were there, for she knew that Bannon meant to send Max away, too. She was too nervous to stand still; and she walked around the table, resetting the knives and forks and spoons. The paper napkins on this table were the only ones in the room. She wondered at this, and when the noise of the men had died away into a few jeering cries from the street, and Max had gone to get the flags (for she had said that they should be hung at this end of the room), and the waiters were bustling about, it gave her a chance to break the silence.

"Aren't the other"—she had to stop to clear her throat—"aren't the other men going to have napkins?"

"They wouldn't know what they were for."

His easy tone gave her a momentary sense of relief.

"They'd tie them on their hats, or make balls to throw around." He paused, but added: "It wouldn't look bad, though, would it?—to stand them up this way on all the tables."

She made no reply.

"What do you say?" He was looking at her. "Shall we do it?"

She nodded, and then dropped her eyes, angry with herself that she could not overcome her nervousness. There was another silence, and she broke it.

"It would look a good deal better," she said, "if you have time to do it. Max and I will put up the flags."

She had meant to say something that would give her a better control of the situation, but it sounded very flat and disagreeable—and she had not meant it to sound disagreeable. Indeed, as soon as the words were out, and she felt his eyes on her, and she knew that she was blushing, she was not sure that she had meant it at all. Perhaps that was why, when Bannon asked, in a low voice, "Would you rather Max would help you?" she turned away and answered in a cool tone that did not come from any one of her rushing, struggling thoughts, "If you don't mind."

She did not see the change that came over his face, the weary look that meant that the strain of a week had suddenly broken, but she did not need to see it, for she knew it was there. She heard him step down from the platform, and then she watched him as he walked down the aisle to meet Max, who was bringing up the flags. She wondered impatiently why Bannon did not call to him. Then he raised his head, but before a word had left his lips she was speaking, in a clear tone that Max could plainly hear. She was surprised at herself. She had not meant to say a word, but out it came; and she was conscious of a tightening of her nerves and a defiant gladness that at last her real thoughts had found an outlet.

"Max," she said, "won't you go out and get enough napkins to put at all the places? You'll have to hurry."

Bannon was slow in turning; when he did there was a peculiar expression on his face.

"Hold on, there," called a waiter. "There ain't time to fold them."

"Yes, there is," said Bannon, shortly. "The boys can wait."

"But dinner's most ready now."

"Then I guess dinner's got to wait, too."

The waiter looked disgusted, and Max hurried out. Bannon gathered up the flags and came to the platform. Hilda could not face him. For an instant she had a wild impulse to follow Max. She finally turned her back on Bannon and leaned her elbows on a chair, looking over the wall for a good place to hang the flags. She was going to begin talking about it as soon as he should reach the platform. The words were all ready, but now he was opposite her, looking across the table with the red and white bundle in his arms, and she had not said it. Her eyes were fixed on a napkin, studying out the curious Japanese design. She could hear his breathing and her own. She let her eyes rise as high as the flags, then slowly, higher and higher, until they met his, fluttered, and dropped. But the glance was enough. She could not have resisted the look in his eyes.

"Did you mean it?" he asked, almost breathlessly. "Did you mean the whole thing?"

She could not reply. She glanced around to see if the waiters could hear.

"Can't you tell me?" he was saying. "It's been a week."

She gazed at the napkin until it grew misty and indistinct. Then she slowly nodded.

A waiter was almost within hearing. Bannon stood looking at her, heedless of everything but that she was there before him, that her eyes were trying to peep up at him through the locks of red gold hair that had strayed over her forehead.

"Please"—she whispered—"please put them up."

And so they set to work. He got the ladder and she told him what to do. Her directions were not always clear, but that mattered little, for he could not have followed them. Somehow the flags went up, and if the effect was little better than Max's attempt had been, no one spoke of it.

Pete and Max came in together soon with the napkins, and a little time slipped by before Bannon could draw Max aside and grip his hand. Then they went at the napkins, and as they sat around the table, Hilda and Bannon, Pete and the waiters, folding them with rapid fingers, Bannon found opportunity to talk to her in a low voice, during the times when Pete was whistling, or was chaffing with the waiters. He told her, a few words at a time, of the new work Mr. MacBride had assigned to him, and in his enthusiasm he gave her a little idea of what it would mean to him, this opportunity to build an elevator the like of which had never been seen in the country before, and which would be watched by engineers from New York to San Francisco. He told her, too, something about the work, how it had been discovered that piles could be made of concrete and driven into the ground with a pile driver, and that neither beams nor girders—none of the timbers, in fact—were needed in this new construction. He was nearly through with it, and still he did not notice the uncertain expression in her eyes. It was not until she asked in a faltering undertone, "When are you going to begin?" that it came to him. And then he looked at her so long that Pete began to notice, and she had to touch his foot with hers under the table to get him to turn away. He had forgotten all about the vacation and the St. Lawrence trip.

Hilda saw, in her side glances, the gloomy expression that had settled upon his face; and she recovered her spirits first.

"It's all right," she whispered; "I don't care."

Max came up then, from a talk with James out on the stairway, and for a few moments there was no chance to reply. But after Bannon had caught Max's signals to step out of hearing of the others, and before he had risen, there was a moment when Pete's attention was drawn by one of the waiters, and he said:

"Can you go with me—Monday?"

She looked frightened, and the blood rose in her cheeks so that she had to bend low over her pile of napkins.

"Will you?" He was pushing back his chair.

She did not look up, but her head nodded once with a little jerk.

"And you'll stay for the dinner, won't you—now?"

She nodded once more, and Bannon went to join Max.

Max made two false starts before he could get his words out in the proper order.

"Say," he finally said; "I thought maybe you wouldn't care if I told James. He thinks you're all right, you know. And he says, if you don't care, he'd like to say a little something about it when he makes his speech. Not much, you know—nothing you wouldn't like—he says it would tickle the boys right down to their corns."

Bannon looked around toward Hilda, and slowly shook his head.

"Max," he replied, "if anybody says a word about it at this dinner I'll break his head."

That should have been enough, but when James' turn came to speak, after nearly two hours of eating and singing and laughing and riotous good cheer, he began in a way that brought Bannon's eyes quickly upon him.

"Boys," he said, "we've worked hard together on this job, and one way and another we've come to understand what sort of a man our boss is. Ain't that right?"

A roar went up from hundreds of throats, and Hilda, sitting next to Bannon, blushed.

"We've thought we understood him pretty well, but I've just found out that we didn't know so much as we thought we did. He's been a pretty square friend to all of us, and I'm going to tell you something that'll give you a chance to show you're square friends of his, too."

He paused, and then was about to go on, leaning forward with both hands on the table, and looking straight down on the long rows of bearded faces, when he heard a slight noise behind him. A sudden laugh broke out, and before he could turn his head, a strong hand fell on each shoulder and he went back into his chair with a bump. Then he looked up, and saw Bannon standing over him. The boss was trying to speak, but he had to wait a full minute before he could make himself heard. He glanced around and saw the look of appeal in Hilda's eyes.

"Look here, boys," he said, when the room had grown quiet; "we aren't handing out any soft soap at this dinner. I won't let this man up till he promises to quit talking about me."

There was another burst of laughter, and James shouted something that nobody understood. Bannon looked down at him, and said quietly, and with a twinkle in his eye, but very firmly:—

"If you try that again, I'll throw you out of the window."

James protested, and was allowed to get up. Bannon slipped into his seat by Hilda.

"It's all right," he said in a low tone. "They won't know it now until we get out of here." His hand groped for hers under the table.

James was irrepressible. He was shouting quickly now, in order to get the words out before Bannon could reach him again.

"How about this, boys? Shall we stand it?"

"No!" was the reply in chorus.

"All right, then. Three cheers for Mr. Bannon. Now—Hip, hip——"

There was no stopping that response.

The End

MOMENT IN HISTORY:

From the **George Grantham Bain Collection** in the Library of Congress. Two Women Fencing; 1900.

3	6	8	7	4	9	2	5	1
4	5	1	6	8	2	3	7	9
9	2	7	5	3	1	4	8	6
7	1	3	8	2	6	9	4	5
5	8	2	3	9	4	6	1	7
6	9	4	1	7	5	8	2	3
8	7	5	2	6	3	1	9	4
1	3	9	4	5	8	7	6	2
2	4	6	9	1	7	5	3	8

Riddle Answer:

a candle.